RECLAIMING HONOR

RECLAIMING HONOR

MARC ALAN EDELHEIT & QUINCY J. ALLEN

Reclaiming Honor: The Way of Legend
First Edition

I wish to thank my agent, Andrea Hurst, for her invaluable support and assistance. I would also like to thank my beta readers, who suffered through several early drafts. My betas: Jon Cockes, Nicolas Weiss, Melinda Vallem, Paul Klebaur, James Doak, David Cheever, Bruce Heaven, Erin Penny, April Faas, Rodney Gigone, Brandon Purcell, Tim Adams, Paul Bersoux, Phillip Broom, David Houston, Sheldon Levy, Michael Hetts, Walker Graham, Bill Schnippert, Jan McClintock, Jonathan Parkin, Spencer Morris, Jimmy McAfee, Rusty Juban, Marshall Clowers, Joel Rainey. I would also like to take a moment to thank my loving wife, who sacrificed many an evening and weekend to allow me to work on my writing.

Editing Assistance by Hannah Streetman, Audrey Mackaman, Brandon Purcell.
Art by Piero Mng (Gianpiero Mangialardi)
Cover Design and Formatting by 100 Covers
Agented by Andrea Hurst & Associates
http://maenovels.com/

This book is dedicated to two people.
To Marc Alan Edelheit, who was generous enough
to let me play in his sandbox.
To Victoria, who was brave enough to let me play in
her life. ~Quincy

A Word on Language from Grimbok Lorekeeper

To all those readers of the common tongue of Tannis who find themselves in possession of *Reclaiming Honor*—the first Tale of Tovak—I must offer a few words on the use of language contained herein. To achieve that, of course, I must begin with an apology. My people, the Dvergr race, as a whole, do not like the other races much. Indeed, there are many who would say we are inherently and inexorably xenophobic. They would not be wrong. Our mistrust and general loathing have been hard-earned.

My apology, however, is not to provide some sort of querulous accounting for how the Dvergr feel about other races and cultures. Our feelings have been reinforced time and time again—a result of one betrayal after another, one assault after another upon my people. Humans, elves, orcs, goblins, and gnomes, to name the most common interactions, have been, as a rule, wholly unpleasant. An apology for our perfectly reasonable reaction to those events is neither offered nor warranted.

Instead, my apology is for how I decided to treat with a variety of Dvergr-specific terms utilized throughout this tome, as well as for those places in which I chose to use terms specific to the common tongue. I had guidelines, to be sure, but no hard and fast rules. All I can say is that I did the best I could.

The Dvergr are a complex people with a wide array of rich cultures spanning across our cities, societies, and even the expanse of time stretching back into the mists beyond memory. It was and has always been my intention to preserve as much of that strength and beauty as I could, whilst still conveying a reasonable and comprehensible sense of the events surrounding Tovak and his journeys, beginning with the Great March from Garand'Durbaad and culminating in events that none of us ever could have guessed would happen in our lifetimes.

It is important to note that how the Dvergr treat with numbers is somewhat different than how the other races undertake numeration. Of all the races, the Dvergr are the only thinking species with six digits on each hand and foot. This means that our counting systems, going back millennia, are based upon extrapolations of twelve rather than the more common use of ten as the base numeral utilized by the other races. Subsequently, time, distance, weight, and other measures in their gross quantities are very different for Dvergr.

For example, I could have used term *jura* as the large measure of distance undertaken by the Great March. A jura equates to roughly three-quarters of a mile, and twelve jura equal a *legiar*. However, using the Dvergr terms would have made it difficult for the reader to conceptualize the context of distance. To achieve clarity, I converted Dvergr jura to common miles. Additionally, in descriptions of shorter units of measure, I have chosen to utilize the more common terms of feet and yards. This deviation from Dvergr norms is deliberate and was chosen to give the reader an easier sense of scale for combat and the general descriptions of setting. It was a literary consideration to make it easier for the reader to quickly and easily envision those events as Tovak—and others—experienced them.

Furthermore, when treating with Dvergr-specific foods, cultural constructs, and even the beasts of Tannis, I have chosen to rely upon Dvergr terminology wherever possible. Where applicable, I have included as detailed a description as I could manage in order to make it clear that what I am relating *might* have a counterpart in the other languages or on other worlds but that the Dvergr have a term for that creature, object, or action. I do not know where you, the reader, have come from or what experiences you carry with you. Therefore, because this story is, for the most part, told from Tovak's perspective, utilizing Dvergr terminology seemed more effective.

It is my sincere hope that you do not find this mixture of both the common and Dvergr tongues confusing.

The Tales of Tovak coincide with a critical time for the Dvergr people on Tannis. Indeed, his journey from the Age of Iron and beyond the time of the Great March represents a pivotal era that held both great peril and discovery for the people of Garand'Durbaad, Garand'Tur, and Garand'Karak.

It was Tovak's hand in these events, however, that, in many respects, altered their course and, one could argue, made the Great March not only possible but successful. I bore witness to at least some of these events—the Battle of Keelbooth, for example—and while I cannot claim to have been one of his mentors, I have always looked upon him fondly. Over a span of many years, Tovak himself told me of his accounts. And I must add, with a bit of pride, he allowed me to name him a friend.

It is, therefore, with humble respect and heartfelt thanks that I present to you *Reclaiming Honor*. It is the first Tale of

Tovak. He is the one who gave hope and returned faith to my people in a time when we desperately needed both.

His was the Way of Legend.

Your humble servant,
Grimbok Lorekeeper,
Scribe to the Thane Rogar Bladebreaker

CHAPTER ONE

Tovak Stonehammer breathed in the crisp air, clenching his fists in frustration and anger as he stared out at the grasslands of the plateau rolling by. Behind, yet another conversation about him was rolling by, just as easily as the landscape.

"Thank Fortuna we're almost there. I can't wait to get off this rickety old thing....I swear, the stench of the Pariah is getting worse every day. I'm afraid it's gonna stick to me."

The voice belonged to Kutog, an arrogant Dvergr from a wealthy family who had spent their entire journey making no secret of his family's wealth, influence, and his intense dislike for Tovak's presence.

Tovak was the Pariah.

"My father says it would be better to simply put them all to death." A round of agreement from the other recruits floated up behind Tovak. "Put the honorless scruggs out of their misery...."

Tovak didn't recognize the voice and wouldn't dignify the person by looking, which was what they likely expected. Knowing who it was only made it harder for him to go about his business. He'd heard such things many times before. It never made it any easier. He had long ago learned how to ignore those who insulted and reviled him while he was within earshot. It came with who he was, a Pariah. And though words hurt, he'd suffered much worse over the years.

"The warbands shouldn't take their kind," another voice said.

"If they weren't so desperate for warriors, they wouldn't," Kutog said. "Don't worry, he'll probably piss himself at the first sight of a goblin and run."

The group laughed.

Tovak burned with shame. He closed his eyes and breathed out a heavy breath. His objective was making it to the Blood Badgers, just like the other recruits he shared the journey with. For it would only be through building his own Legend that he could finally and forever cast off the stigma of Pariah. Until then, he would endure. He had no choice.

Tovak was far from what had been his home—a place to which he would not return, at least if he could help it. He certainly never desired to see it again. The memories were just too painful. The great reinforced iron wheels of the *yuggernok*—one of the massive cargo wagons of Garand'Durbaad—ground its way across the Grimbar Plateau, carrying him one turn of the wheel at a time closer to his dreams of Legend. The yuggernok and three others of its kind traversed the rolling grass prairie in a small convoy on their way to resupply the Blood Badgers Warband.

Tovak ignored the voices behind him and whispered a prayer to Thulla as he watched the plateau pass by. He unclenched his fists and tied a prayer knot of gray cloth into a small braid hidden behind his thick auburn beard, marking the prayer's passing.

And the Way shall be opened to the faithful, so they may be tested and reclaim that which was taken from them. The passage, lifted from *Thulla's Blessed Word*, echoed in his thoughts. He knew Dvergr scripture as well as the priest who had taught him.

Like no other, that passage had sustained him through the rough times for as long as he could remember. The prayer knot was one of twelve required by scripture, and he maintained them all without fail, as one of the faithful.

He had his faith, he had his dream, and he was going to be at the forefront of the next Great March—the exodus of his people.

It was enough, enough to sustain him.

The incessant rumbling of the yuggernok, its massive wooden frame creaking and groaning with every turn of the great iron wheels, had taken some getting used to. The wagon was pulled along by a team of six *oofants*—distant cousins of elephants. They were larger, shaggy beasts of burden capable of travelling tremendous distances. Fully grown, they normally stood fifteen feet at their humps, though some occasionally reached twenty feet tall. They had long, curved tusks that reached out to lengths of eight feet and made formidable weapons against predators and raiders alike. Each of their thudding feet added its own tempo to the low, subtle thunder of the yuggernok's passage. During the long nights, Tovak had at first struggled to sleep through the racket, but in time, the sound had come to lull him to sleep as the miles passed.

Setting out from Garand'Durbaad, the small caravan of yuggernoks had traveled for two weeks, and in that time, Tovak had grown increasingly restless. His body, accustomed to the rigors of physical labor and the Academy's military training, yearned to be active once again. The only time he was able to stretch his legs was when the oofants needed rest or water.

Early on, out of boredom, Tovak had even offered to help the teamsters tend to the animals and the rig. Duroth, the lead teamster, had rejected him, saying only that they didn't want a dumb, young Pariah's bad luck. So, he had passed the days and nights by riding in the back of the covered wagon, watching the mountains in the distance slide by.

A ruddy pair of suns squatted just above the nearby ridge-line separating Grimbar Plateau from the heavily forested, orc-infested lowlands to the northwest. As the two suns set, they took with them the warmth of the day. It would turn cold again soon as daylight shifted to shadow and shadow to night, but Tovak was accustomed to cold nights spent shivering under his blanket.

He was no stranger to the cold. Under the mountain, the stone floors and cold barns where he'd worked and slept had been chilly. Hardship was something to which he had become accustomed. He shrugged his shoulders into his threadbare woolen blanket for warmth, doing his best to mind its frayed and torn edges. Unable to afford the cost of a replacement, he'd had it for years. In truth, it was almost like an old friend.

As the deepening shadows from the mountains stretched across the rolling countryside, he silently watched the tall grasses of the prairie. Almost hypnotically, they bent and swayed with the wind.

"Stand to," a harsh voice shouted, jarring Tovak out of his thoughts. He recognized Duroth's bellow and wondered if the old drunkard had been at the jug yet again. "I said, bloody stand to."

Tovak had learned to follow Duroth's orders or face the consequences, which could and often did include a cuff or, if enraged, a beating. Duroth was shorter than the average Dvergr, ill-tempered, and possessed with a genuine enthusiasm for swearing... particularly by taking Thulla's name in vain. He had long, gray hair and a braided beard tied with simple black bands.

4

At the start of the journey, Duroth had made it clear to everyone that he'd been a training instructor with the Blood Badgers once and still held the auxiliary rank of sergeant. This meant he outranked the recruits and was the ultimate authority on the oversized wagon.

Tovak and the other recruits stepped out from their berths into the central passageway that stretched from stem to stern along the interior of the yuggernok. Like Tovak, they had all recently achieved the Age of Iron and were now fit to join a warband and grow their Legend. Unlike Tovak, however, they already had secured appointments to various companies in the Blood Badgers.

It would have been easier if he'd had a clan or sponsor to arrange for his appointment. But as it was, a Pariah could only hope he would be able to join a company once he was standing before its commanding officer. As always, Tovak was on his own. No one cared a fig for a Pariah. Well, to be honest, very few did.

There were twenty recruits on board Duroth's yuggernok. They, Tovak along with them, placed their backs to the curtains of their berths and faced forward, stiffening to attention.

Tovak stood before the three-by-six-foot area of floorboards Duroth had laughingly referred to as Tovak's "berth." Without a clan, sponsor, or patron, he had been forced to pay for his own passage. Tovak had spent a week trying to arrange for a berth aboard one of the caravans, but it was always the same. One teamster after another simply turned his nose up at a Pariah.

Tovak had been losing hope when a strange impulse finally pushed him in the direction of an older yuggernok that looked to be on its last legs, barely travel-worthy. Its owner, Duroth, was its match in appearance, and he'd had a strong reek of spirits upon him. The teamster's initial reaction had been identical to the others: "Fortuna don't look kindly on Pariahs." However, when his eyes had found Tovak's purse in hand, his tune had changed. "Maybe we can work something out...."

In exchange for ten copper *suuls*, a substantial chunk of Tovak's hard-earned savings, Duroth granted enough space at the back of the yuggernok to lay out his blanket each night. It was twice the cost of a standard berth, and Duroth made no secret of having taken on a Pariah, which made Tovak's journey a lonely one.

At least he'd gotten aboard.

The corridor, such as it was, held the sleeping bunks for the other passengers and the crew. The yuggernok could sleep up to thirty Dvergr in narrow bunks shielded only by curtains and a weatherproofed canvas roof.

When unoccupied, the bunks were disassembled for additional storage space. Stacked above each bunk were crates, sacks, casks, and amphorae, all supplies destined for the Blood Badger encampment. The supplies had been strapped and tied down so they didn't shift or move during transport, and the teamsters regularly checked to make certain everything was still safely secured.

Tovak knew from speaking with them that Duroth's yuggernok was the only one in the caravan carrying passengers. The other two hauled only supplies.

"Thulla curse you young scruggs," Duroth hollered from the front as he stomped slowly down the corridor. "We're almost to the encampment. Soon enough, I'll be done with the lot of you. And I say the sooner you bugger off the better. No more nursemaiding for me, Fortuna be praised. You'll be someone else's headache after today. Bloody Thulla, I can't wait to get rid of the lot of ya."

Duroth stopped before Tovak, and his rheumy eyes narrowed.

"I said eyes forward!" he said, his breath thick with spirits. "You best get used to acting like warriors if you expect to join the Blood Badgers."

Tovak kept his face calm, impassive. Standing a head taller than Duroth, what he really wanted to do was grab the short drunkard by the collar and throw him over the edge of the platform. But that was not in the cards. The other teamsters would likely not look kindly upon such actions.

"I don't know what I was thinking," Duroth growled in a low tone so that only Tovak could hear. "I never should have let one of your kind aboard my rig," he seethed, poking his finger into Tovak's chest. "Thulla's bones, they'll probably blame me if something happens to the Blood Badgers....All you Pariahs are bad luck, boy."

Tovak shifted his gaze forward, staring over Duroth at the supplies stacked and strapped down on the other side of the corridor. He bit back the suggestion that Duroth had been too drunk at the time to see anything but the purse and more coin for another bottle of spirits.

Duroth hesitated a moment more, his jaw flexing as he considered Tovak. He let out a heavy breath that was part sigh. The stench of spirits was almost enough to make Tovak gag. Then, the old Dvergr turned and stomped back the way he'd come.

Like so many other times, Tovak wanted to say something...do something. Frustrated rage bubbled up inside him, but he kept his mouth shut. Duroth was in a position to kick him off the yuggernok and perhaps even keep him from joining a company.

All Thulla's sons and daughters have free will, and it is His domain to mete out reward and consequence as He sees fit. Tovak had always liked that passage and found a measure of comfort recalling it. He took a deep breath and pressed his lips together in silence, when something occurred to him. Duroth's drinking might have been the only thing that had allowed him to gain a berth. The great god worked in mysterious ways. Tovak sent up a silent prayer of thanks.

"The main encampment is in sight," Duroth continued, loud enough for all to hear. "Gather up your belongings and be ready to get your sorry asses off my rig the moment we come to a stop. We won't be serving no dinner for you either." He came to a halt halfway down the corridor, leaned around a recruit, and swept the curtain aside. He made a show of peering within the berth. "And clean up before you go. Don't leave nothin' behind. Your mommas didn't come along for the ride, so anything I find after your feet hit dirt is mine."

"Who does that drunken bastard think he is?" the recruit beside Tovak hissed.

Duroth swung around in a flash. The old teamster's eyes settled on Kutog, though it had not been him. Duroth stomped back down the corridor and stepped right up into Kutog's face, his nose only inches away from the recruit's chin. He slowly ran his eyes up and down Kutog's larger frame and then glared up into the recruit's eyes.

"Anything you want to say to me, rich boy?" Duroth demanded. "Or perhaps I should have a few words with your new commanding officer to let him know what a Thulla-cursed, disrespectful little cuss you are? One word from me and you'll be without an appointment, in the same boat with the Pariah there." Duroth jabbed a thumb in Tovak's direction. "What would daddy think, eh? How would you like that?"

There was a long moment of silence.

"No, sir," Kutog said. "Sorry, sir. I have nothing to say."

"That's what I thought." Duroth let out a disgusted grunt and turned on his heel. Without another word, he marched back up the corridor to the steps that led to the teamster's bench. He stopped at the first step, turned back with a disdainful sneer, and then climbed up, disappearing.

Tovak let out a breath he hadn't realized he'd been holding. It seemed that the others did the same, and then they went back into their berths. Many of the recruits traveled with armor, weapons, and even multiple packs containing their possessions. Compared to the others, Tovak had very little. All he owned fit into his small battered and patched pack.

Turning around, Tovak grabbed his blanket from where he'd discarded it, folded it carefully, and laid it aside. The other side of his berth opened up to the prairie, with only a couple of stacked crates between him and the rear deck of the yuggernok.

"At least I didn't have to walk," he said under his breath, for he had at one point, prior to securing passage with Duroth, thought he might need to. He picked his pack up from the deck and set it upon a nearby crate that had served as a table for him during the trip. The sigils stamped upon the side in black lettering indicated it was destined for someone named Struugar Ironfist, of the Baelix Guard. Tovak had spent much of his journey daydreaming about who Struugar might be and what the crate might contain. He'd had little else to do.

He untied his pack and peered inside to make sure he wouldn't be leaving anything behind for Duroth to confiscate. He found a small toiletry kit, a bone-handled comb, a book wrapped in cloth, a small wooden box, a knife, and his spare tunic. He also had another pair of socks, which had been patched numerous times by his own hand. He ran his fingers along the cloth-wrapped book, feeling the smooth fabric. It was the same type of cloth used for prayer knots, and as his fingers brushed the surface, he offered up thanks to Thulla for it coming into his possession.

Within the cloth was his copy of *Thulla's Blessed Word*, kept hidden from condescending eyes. In truth, the book was old and battered, its stitching coming loose in places, but it was one of his few treasured possessions.

A pang of sadness tinged with shame washed over him at the necessity of hiding the book from prying eyes. His people had mostly abandoned Thulla. They blamed the god for the problems they faced. Part of Tovak understood the why of it, but it still bothered him to his core that he had to hide his faith.

"'And the Way shall be opened to the faithful, so they may be tested and reclaim that which was taken from them'," he whispered. Tovak closed his eyes for a long moment. He breathed in and then out.

If only he could show his people that suffering was one of the paths to Thulla, not a reason to turn away from the great god. Was that not one of the primary lessons taught through the tale of the hero Uliand Stormhand in *Thulla's Blessed Word*?

As the first holy warrior of Thulla, his trials had been unparalleled and had only made Uliand stronger, or so the scripture taught. The loss of his family, torture, years spent fettered in chains, all of it had prepared him for divine service. The god tested his flock, and faith brought salvation. Indeed, Tovak's own faith had been his compass, his foundation, and his anchor during the worst of times.

Folded inside the book was his Warrant of Passage, proof of his graduation from the Pioneer Academy. He unwrapped the cloth and pulled the yellowed parchment out. With it, Pariah or not, he had the right to travel to a warband of his choosing and apply for a posting. The document represented years of work. It was the first step in his dream of proving that he was just as worthy as the next Dvergr and not the disgrace everyone thought him to be.

The Warrant even bore the coveted Crossed Hammers, a mark of excellence granted to top students. Not only did Tovak know his numbers and letters, but he'd also completed basic military training and gone on to complete pioneer school, a grueling twelve-week program. The Academy taught scouting skills to those deemed to have promise or the potential to become a pioneer. He hoped this achievement would allow him to sign up with one of the coveted pioneer companies. It was with the pioneers that he saw himself rebuilding Legend and breaking free of the Pariah's stigma.

He pulled a small, plain wooden box out of his pack and slid open the cover. Inside was a spirit deck, containing forty-eight placards, hand-painted by Tovak's priest, Father Danik. After *Thulla's Blessed Word*, it was his most cherished possession, and certainly his most valuable. Most Dvergr believed that spirit decks were simple folly, but among the faithful, they were believed to be a direct connection to Thulla, allowing one to divine a measure of the god's will.

The deck had been gifted to him by the cleric. Since the passing of his parents, Danik had been the one person who had offered Tovak any real measure of kindness. It was through Danik that Tovak had discovered and embraced his god. For that, he would be eternally grateful.

Stepping up to the crate he used as a table, Tovak closed his eyes and thought on Thulla.

"Of the way ahead, what must be foremost in my heart?" he asked, shuffling the deck.

He then laid out four cards, face down, before him. One by one, he flipped them over. The first card was the Traveler, depicting a lone Dvergr in white cloth, leaning upon a walking stick with a long, open road before him. The second revealed Thulla, the Taker, the deity standing with a scowl upon His face and a closed fist held against His chest. The third exposed the Road Hidden, which showed the Traveler standing before a high hedgerow, and beyond it an open, straight, cobbled path between high mountains rising on either side. And finally, he turned over Thulla, the Giver, where the god stood smiling, His hands outstretched and a bounty of fruit in one hand and a clay jug in the other.

Tovak pondered the message before him. He was obviously the Traveler. The card had come up frequently for the past few months, but the second card concerned him. What might Thulla be taking from him as his journey progressed? He had so little. What more could Thulla ask? The lesson, perhaps, lay in the next card. A new path would be made available to him, and down it would lie Thulla's bounty, but the way would not be clear. Tovak slowly nodded his head in understanding.

As always, he would keep going. Faith was the one thing that nobody could take. He would keep his faith, and with it seek out Legend with every trial. Each test that lay before him would only serve to make him stronger.

He returned the cards to the deck and slipped them carefully back into their box.

The smell of woodsmoke now filled the air. There were shouts outside, followed by a trumpeting of oofants. He glanced over the back of the yuggernok to see a formation of Dvergr warriors in full plate armor emerge into view. They were marching in the opposite direction of the wagon, passing within a handful of yards.

With an officer and a standard-bearer at the front, they looked disciplined, and dangerous. Tovak couldn't help but smile. Soon he would be one of them—a Blood Badger. The warriors carried packs and yokes. A sergeant walking alongside the formation waved. Tovak waved back but, to his embarrassment, realized the warrior had been waving to one of the teamsters driving the massive wagon. He felt his cheeks heat as the sergeant looked directly at him, and then they were past.

Tovak removed his Warrant of Passage and set it on the crate. He then put everything carefully back into his pack, including his dagger, which had been lying on the floorboards. He tied the straps tight and gave a tug to make sure the knot would not come loose.

Gazing upon the Warrant, a warm feeling washed through him. Even as a Pariah, his skill had seen him admitted to the Academy. He could scarcely still believe he had graduated and earned a Warrant, and with it, his goal now lay tantalizingly within reach. He folded it carefully along its creases and tucked it into his tunic pocket.

His field blanket came next. It took only a few moments to roll it up. He used short lengths of rope to tie the ends off and then secured it to his pack with a strap. Standing quickly, he slipped the strap over his head, settling the rolled blanket under his arm. He slipped on his pack next.

A rough bump almost knocked him over. The great wagon rattled and creaked loudly, as if in protest. Tovak looked outside again and felt a thrill of excitement. They were passing into the encampment. A deep trench and turf wall with a wooden barricade formed the outermost defensive line. Sentries slowly walked the wall, gazing out onto the prairie. To Tovak's eyes, they looked impressive in their armor and invincible. He imagined himself as one of them, guarding the encampment and helping to keep everyone secure.

The yuggernok passed through the encampment's open gate, where a detail of armored, shield-bearing infantry stood on either side, ever watchful. Full of anticipation, Tovak moved out onto the rear deck to try to get a better look at the camp, but much of it was blocked by the massive wagon and stacks of supplies. As they continued forward, the smell of smoke grew thick in his nostrils, and he quickly realized why. Dozens of campfires came into view. He picked up the stench of waste, mixed with the appetizing aroma of cooking. Tovak's stomach rumbled with hunger. As Duroth had said, there would be no evening meal for him tonight. He would have to fend for himself.

There were hundreds of tents, both large and small. He spotted an officer's pavilion, a blacksmith, a leatherworker, even a large cooking tent with a dozen long tables set off to the side with cooks and their assistants hard at work, preparing an evening meal.

Dvergr warriors were everywhere now, gathered around fires, marching in formation, and some going to or fro on whatever business they were about. Dozens sat around the nearest campfires, some in armor, others in their service tunics. Tovak saw women and children too.

He had never seen so many Dvergr gathered in one place, and he was only now coming to understand the scale of what the word "warband" really meant. The stories he'd heard as a child did not do them justice. The steady beat of hammers from a forge filled the air. Dogs barked and chased after one another, fighting over scraps.

The yuggernok passed through another defensive turf wall identical to the first. Within that were more tents, as well as an artillery park off to the left. In the fading light,

Tovak's eyes fell on a line of bolt throwers. Beyond them were several rows of catapults, massive machines with great iron wheels. Two of the machines were at least twenty feet tall, with massive beams and wooden arms for throwing stones.

In the fading light, he spotted a team of engineers working on one of the dread machines. They looked to be replacing a support beam. The yuggernok turned away and the artillery park was lost from view. Then the great wagon came to an abrupt, jerking halt. Tovak almost lost his balance. The heavy locking bolt was thrown in place with a hollow *thud* that shuddered through the floorboards.

They had arrived.

The center of the encampment was a veritable city of tents, formed around a wooden watch and signal tower. The structure rose thirty feet into the air. Tovak could just make out sentries on the tower's platform. He knew from his studies they would be equipped with a large war horn.

Tovak reveled at the sights and sounds that surrounded him. The clatter of wooden swords against shields drew his eye to what appeared to be hundreds of warriors training, sparring against one another in an enclosed area surrounded by carts. Officers and sergeants moved amongst them.

Formed into tight ranks, a company of warriors stomped by, moving in the direction the yuggernok had just come. Excitement, anticipation, and a wave of nervousness rippled through Tovak. This was where he was meant to be. He could feel it in his bones. Soon, his days of being an outcast, one barely tolerated by society, would be over. He would be a pioneer.

A growing clamor of voices rose behind him. Tovak stepped away from the railing and moved to the end of the corridor. It was full of the recruits, slinging gear over their shoulders as they got themselves ready to disembark.

"I can't wait to get to my company," a recruit said with no little amount of excitement. "My brother's been with them for two years now. It will be good to see him. Hard to believe tonight I will be part of Sixth Company."

"The Sixth are second-rate," Kutog jeered. "Everyone knows First Company is the best, and that's where I'm headed."

"Bah," the first recruit said. "What do you know?"

"My company has no equal, you dumb scrugg. Everyone knows that." Kutog struck his chest with a fist. "They only take the best, and that's me. My father told me they reject nine out of ten applicants. The Sixth takes whatever they can get, because that's all they can get."

"The best my ass," a voice replied. "You can wipe mine if you want."

Kutog spun around, but clearly could not see who had said it. His cheeks flushed with anger. Tovak almost grinned at the smug bastard's consternation.

"Make way," a voice called. "I said, make way."

It was Kyn, the youngest of the teamsters but still considerably older than Tovak. He moved down the corridor with an old, battered ladder that had seen better days. He held it over his head. His long, wild hair and heavily braided beard were the color of copper with only hints of gray. He wore a hardened leather breastplate and long hide pants tucked into knee-high boots. Two white painted slashes on his shoulder armor indicated he held the rank of an auxiliary corporal. His bare arms revealed an array of red tattoos depicting mystical patterns from shoulder to wrist. Like a captive beast, the outline of a dragon coiled around his right arm. He held the ladder easily, and as he approached, the recruits moved aside to allow him to pass.

"Get the latch, will you?" he asked Tovak as he reached the end. "Open the gate too."

"Yes, sir," Tovak replied and moved to the gate on the far side of the deck. Kyn had been the only one of the teamsters who hadn't gone out of his way to treat him badly or outright ignore his presence...although they hadn't exchanged more than a handful of words during the trip.

"Don't call me sir," he said. "I work for a living. The name's Kyn or Corporal, your choice."

"Thank you, s—" Tovak cut himself off. The habits of the Academy had become ingrained. Anyone who was serving had been a *sir*. "I mean Kyn," he corrected and then opened the gate for the teamster, swinging it wide and out into open space.

Kyn lowered the ladder over the side and then sank two rods at the top into holes bored into the deck. The bottom of the ladder almost touched the ground. Kyn gave the ladder a jerk to make sure it was secure, then stood.

Kutog stepped around Kyn and then roughly shoved Tovak aside with his shield. "Out of the way, Pariah," he growled before dropping his pack to the ground below. It landed with a heavy thud. Kutog mounted the ladder and, holding his shield to the side, climbed down one-handed.

Tovak's temper flared again. He closed his eyes and took a deep breath, forcing himself to calm down. When he opened them, he saw Kyn shake his head at Tovak.

"Boffers," the teamster grumbled under his breath. "There's always them bastards that think they are right better than the rest of us."

"It's all right," Tovak said, although he wanted to call Kutog out and beat him senseless. He dared not, though. There was too much at stake.

"You're a lot more forgiving than I would be." Kyn gave Tovak a scowl. "I'd have given him a thrashing for that. If he were on our crew, I tell you, I'd have whipped him or gotten whipped in turn. But at least I'd have stood up for myself. People like him only respect strength."

Tovak could have told Kyn that it never went well for him when he stood up to the likes of Kutog. Bastards like that always seemed to return with friends, and Tovak had none of his own. He could have said a lot of things, but none of it would matter. He knew that. "I've come a long way to get here, and he's just not worth the effort," was all he could manage. It sounded rather lame.

"If you say so," Kyn replied, sounding far from convinced, then glanced back at the other recruits, who were still getting themselves ready. "How long have you had your Age of Iron ring? You seem older than the rest."

"Four months," Tovak replied, glancing at Kyn's hand. He had noticed the ring before. "Yours is truly striking."

Kyn looked surprised by the compliment, holding up his hand to show off the incredibly detailed silver band, made in the form of a dragon with an obsidian orb set in its mouth. "My father crafted it for me."

"It's beautiful work," Tovak said, in honest admiration. "Your father has real skill." His hand involuntarily went to his own Age of Iron ring, a simple band of rough iron he kept hidden beneath his tunic on a copper chain.

Kyn paused and glanced behind him as more recruits began working their way to the ladder. "Say, I never did catch your name."

"Tovak," he said simply.

"Well then," Kyn said, clapping him on the back, "welcome to the Blood Badgers, Tovak." He glanced out at the encampment that stretched about in all directions. "And don't you worry none about that bastard." He indicated Kutog, who was heading off towards the center of the encampment with a determined stride. "He'll be getting the education of a lifetime over the next few weeks. He's full of himself now, but in a few hours, he won't be. First Company's a line formation. They're always under the eye of Karach. Lots of spit and polish and guard duty, if you know what I mean. He'll be the new guy in his company. If he shows too much cheek, they will cut him down and teach him a little humility or beat it into him if needed."

Tovak liked the thought of the latter. Kutog needed a good beating.

"Karach's warband is the best mix of small clans and clanless warriors in the whole thanedom, misfits really, all of us." Kyn pulled Tovak aside so that the recruits could begin making their way down the ladder. They began to file by. Several cast Tovak unfriendly looks before they disappeared down the ladder. Kyn seemed not to notice and instead gestured outward. There was a proud note to his voice. "I've been with the Badgers for ten years now. Let me tell you something, Tovak. All them other warbands look down on us because we're a mixed bunch. This warband knows what's what."

Tovak wondered where Kyn was going.

"Who gets all the tough jobs? Who gets all the shit assignments? So, Tovak, I ask you, who is it the Thane sends for when it matters most?" Kyn paused expectantly.

"The Blood Badgers?" Tovak offered.

"That's right, the Blood Badgers," Kyn said, with a pleased grin. "Because we always get the job done. Karach Skullsplitter is the best warchief to ever lead a warband. He's hard, but fair. We're all misfits here. Karach has taken us all in and now we're family."

"I see," Tovak said, gazing about the encampment.

"Do you?" Kyn asked. "You will not be the first Pariah the Blood Badgers have accepted. Nor likely the last."

Tovak blinked at that.

"My advice is to do your best," Kyn said. "Find a good company and build your own Legend. In time, things will change."

"Kyn," Duroth shouted from behind on the steps that led up to the driver's bench. "Quit your loafing and get that boffer's feet on the ground. We'll be unloading all night if ya keep jawing with the Pariah."

"You better get on down," Kyn said, turning to Tovak. "Old Duroth might be loud, but he's right, and despite the bark he's really not so bad once you get to know him." Kyn glanced around at the stowed cargo. "We've got a lot of work to do before we can turn in for the night."

The rest of the recruits had already debarked. Tovak stepped up to the ladder, turned, and then leaned forward as he put his foot on the first rung. His Age of Iron ring slipped out of his tunic and dangled free. He quickly tucked the cheap token back inside, but not before Kyn spotted it.

Kyn turned knowing eyes to Tovak.

"Don't you worry none," Kyn said. "You're gonna fit in just fine around here. Do you know where you're headed?" he asked, stepping up to the edge of the deck.

Tovak began to descend the ladder, then paused and looked back up. "I'm off to join the pioneers, but I don't really know where to go."

"Not everyone can make it in the pioneers," Kyn warned. "Most get turned away."

Tovak resumed climbing down the ladder. He jumped the last foot and his boots slapped down on the ground.

"I have a Warrant of Passage from the Pioneer Academy," Tovak said, patting his pocket where the document rested. "I even received a mark of excellence."

"Well done," the teamster said, sounding impressed, though his eyes took on a sad tinge. He blew out a breath and then pointed towards the center of camp. "In that case, you'll want to find Dagon Trailbreaker. He's the captain of the Second Pioneers. Everyone around here knows who he is. I've never met him, but I hear he's a real bastard"—Kyn gave a shrug of his shoulders—"but with a mark of excellence, he might just take you in, Pariah or no. Head towards the center of camp and look for a tall green and black banner with a *durvoll* on it, you know, the big dog-looking thing with six legs."

Tovak nodded. "Thank you."

"Safe journeys, young Tovak.... May your Legend never fade."

"May you always find the Way." Tovak bowed his head briefly.

Gazing down on Tovak, Kyn hesitated a moment, looked about to say more ... then turned and was lost from view.

Tovak bit his lip. Had he just read pity in the other's eyes? Tovak shook his head. Perhaps he'd just imagined it.

As he stepped away from the ladder, he found himself moving with a lighter step than he'd had in a very long time. Garand'Durbaad lay far behind him, as did his past and the pain that came with it. The mere possibility of what lay ahead filled him with a sudden excitement.

"They don't know my family," he said quietly, a smile creeping onto his face. It was why he had chosen the Blood Badgers. The warband was a mix of all the clans. "I am finally my own Dvergr." He traced a finger over his Age of Iron ring, feeling it beneath his tunic. It might be of the lowest quality, but it marked the beginning of his adulthood, where he could truly shape his own future.

It was enough.

CHAPTER TWO

Tovak felt like his future had suddenly opened before him. His past would soon be left behind, little more than a bad memory to be forgotten over time. He strode around the side of the yuggernok that had carried him, stepping past the first of the great iron wheels.

Ahead was another artillery park, much like the first he'd seen, only this one was larger. The machines were parked next to one another in neat orderly rows. The sight caused him to hesitate and stop. He stared in awe for several heartbeats, then felt an intense surge of pride. In that moment, he was proud of his people, who built mighty works and machines. The Dvergr were an old, hardy race that originated from a world far from this one. Despite being cut off from their ancestral home, they carried on, doing whatever they needed to survive amidst the Last War, a conflict of gods and ideology.

Each warband was a testament to the strength and determination of his people as a whole. And despite how he was treated, Tovak was still fiercely proud to be counted amongst them. Deep down, all he wanted to do was serve his people and prove his worth.

As his gaze roved over the machines, movement caught his eye. Three engineers carried a long iron shaft with metal fins on one end and a foot-long barbed tip on the other.

The iron glinted dully in the light of a nearby torch. They lifted the missile up to two more engineers, who struggled to set it into a deep flight groove of one of the largest bolt throwers Tovak had ever seen. They looked to be training. He couldn't imagine what such a machine might be used against. Assaulting a fortress? Punching through a gate? Perhaps even killing a beast, like a dragon? Whatever it was intended for, he knew he would not want to be on the receiving end.

Tovak tore his gaze away and glanced around. He was in a large open area, clearly set aside for yuggernoks. A half-dozen of the oversized wagons were parked near a wide enclosure, full of picketed oofants.

A team of the massive beasts were being led into the enclosure as crews worked unloading the wagons that had clearly arrived earlier in the day. Teamsters on one the yuggernoks set crates, sacks, and barrels onto a wide platform that had been raised up to the rear deck by a mobile wooden crane with iron wheels. Several smaller carts and wagons had been run up and were being loaded with the goods freshly unloaded.

An older teamster with grizzled gray hair stood nearby, looking on. He held a wax tablet and was making notes with a stylus, clearly accounting for the goods being delivered. An assistant of some kind stood next to him, holding several additional wax tablets.

The twin suns had nearly dipped behind the mountains, filling the cloudy skies above with orange and pink-laced fire. The smell of the oofants was strong, mixing heavily with smoke, sweat, and cooking that filled Tovak's nostrils with every breath. He hoped that wherever Dagon's company was camped, it lay upwind and far from the great pachyderms.

Tovak began walking again but stopped after a few feet. Movement at the front of the yuggernok caught his eye. Duroth and another teamster climbed down a rope ladder from the driver's platform. A third teamster appeared and followed after them. They stopped a moment and conferred, then strode up to the lead oofant, which they began to unharness.

Tovak watched them work, realizing a single misstep by an oofant could crush one of the teamsters. The massive animals huffed as the harnesses came off, clearly delighted to be free of the restraints. Oofants were impressive beasts. With their thick, armored hides, massive tusks, and long trunks, they were capable of crushing just about anything should they become enraged. Tovak had heard stories of such things happening.

As he watched Duroth work with them, however, the gentle, happy sounds made them seem almost harmless, like they were big puppies. Only the beasts weren't. There were warbands that trained oofants for battle.

As the first oofant was led away by one of the teamsters, Duroth turned his attention to the next oofant. He began unbuckling the straps holding the harness in place. Moving around each leg as he went, he patted and soothed the great shaggy beast, humming and clucking at it like a mother tending her child.

"That's it, Theola," Duroth said, patting her belly, "we'll have you out of that harness and eating fresh-cut grass with your sisters in no time. One of my lads will be brushing you down before you know it." Duroth was so intent, he didn't see Tovak standing there just a few feet away, watching. The teamster just kept tending to the beast of burden, like it was a well-loved child.

Kyn climbed down the ladder. Duroth spotted him and stepped back, out from under the animal. He untied the bridle, which Tovak saw had been secured to a stake in the ground.

"Get yer sorry ass over here and take Theola to the pen, you dumb scrugg," Duroth growled.

Kyn obediently jogged over.

Duroth handed over her bridle. "I ain't paying you to lollygag."

Kyn nodded and, without saying a word, grabbed the bridle, gave a strong tug to get the beast's attention, and then led Theola off towards the pen.

"See that she gets some fresh grass too," Duroth called after. "Not the stuff already in the pen."

"I will, boss," Kyn said over his shoulder. "I will."

Shaking his head, Tovak stepped away before Duroth spotted him. Tovak left the area and moved onto a street that cut through the encampment. The grassy street stretched out to his left and right. It was lined by rows of hundreds of tan communal tents. The street was thick with both warriors and civilians as they moved about on their own business. Some of the warriors were in their armor, but most wore tunics. For a moment, Tovak just stood there and looked around. The warband's camp was clearly huge, and in the growing darkness of the setting suns, he had a fleeting moment of concern about finding his way.

He turned left and began walking, looking for a side street that would take him deeper into the camp, in the direction Kyn had indicated. Tovak stepped around a pile of dung left by some animal and then had to almost jump aside to avoid being trampled by a squad marching the opposite way.

"Out of the way, scrugg," the corporal snapped.

Tovak watched them pass, then continued on. He found himself looking continually to the left and right, almost as if his head were on a swivel. There was just so much to see. He passed one company area after another. The standard for each was planted in the ground before what he took to be the commanding officer's tent. He noticed there was always an armed guard standing watch over it.

The unmistakable reek of *teska* dung was on the air. With each and every step it grew stronger. He wrinkled his nose and tried to breathe through his mouth. He'd cleaned out his fair share of stables over the years and had never become accustomed to the pungent stench. Sure enough, he came upon a penned-in area, nestled amongst the tents. The pen held a dozen teska. The shaggy, six-legged creatures chewed listlessly on feed that had been thrown down before them.

Teska, much smaller than oofants, stood about five feet at the shoulder. They were covered in thick, shaggy coats of dark fur. The heads of the males sprouted horns, but the animals were considered generally harmless, unless they became spooked and stampeded.

Tovak found a side street and took it 'til he reached another wider street that moved in what he hoped was the direction of the center of camp. The camp seemed to be a virtual maze. Like the last street, this one was of trampled grass and dirt, lined on either side by hundreds of tents.

The street was full of Dvergr, forcing Tovak to often sidestep around small details and formations of marching warriors, groups, supply carts, or mothers and their children. It was loud and noisy. He continued on, turning onto street after street.

The twin suns disappeared fully behind the mountains, taking with them the last rays of daylight and casting the entire camp in the shadow of the coming night. Torches lined both sides of the street. Each communal tent had a campfire, which meant that there were hundreds of fires around.

The entire camp was bathed in a flickering orange glow that drove back the darkness. As he moved deeper into the camp, the smells of cooking fires caused his stomach to rumble.

He reached a row of tents that had been set aside for the cooks. Animals and large insects of all sorts were roasting over open fires or were in the process of being prepared. Cooks and their assistants moved between the fires, giving the spits a turn.

Tovak stopped and stared at a multi-legged creature about ten feet long that was being roasted over a fire. He recognized it as a *murinok*, a large and deadly member of the centipede family. He'd only seen drawings of the creatures, but had heard they were exceptionally good eating, a delicacy reserved for only the wealthiest of people. The scent of its roasting flesh set his mouth to watering, and he wondered if the puffy white meat tasted as good as it smelled.

"Off with you," a cook shouted when he spied Tovak. The cook was a plump, old codger with an eyepatch, a shaved head, and a short gray beard. He wore a badly stained apron. "You should know better. There's nothing here for a camp follower. Go on, see your mommy if you want food, boy." He raised a cleaver menacingly when Tovak hesitated. "Everything here is reserved for Fifth Company. I'll have no thieving, understand me?"

Tovak was about to protest, but changed his mind and moved off towards the next tent, where more insects were being prepared. Lying on the ground were the carcasses of a dozen *heratta*, with their long antennae, giant, faceted eyes, and cylindrical bodies—basically giant grasshoppers.

A cook worked at a nearby wooden table, butchering a *krata*, one of the fearsome spiders that were known to live and hunt in the mountains. He was casually ripping the legs off, each of which gave a sickening crunch as it came free.

Tovak stood there, appalled, gazing upon the krata, which was the size of a large dog. Krata were the stuff of Tovak's nightmares. He hated spiders to begin with, and this creature was one of the worst. Even a juvenile was capable of hunting and killing a full-grown Dvergr. Worse, the creature was known to hunt in packs, which made them even more dangerous.

The cook glanced up.

"Never seen a krata before?" he asked with an amused, almost knowing grin.

Tovak shook his head. "And I didn't know people ate them."

"We don't see them very often, but you can eat 'em," the cook said enthusiastically as he pulled off another leg, giving it a hearty twist as he did so. "We'll even cook *krow*, if anyone is fool enough to try and kill one."

"Krow?" Tovak asked. He could not conceal the surprise. Krow were apex predators. He'd read in school the gigantic spiders could grow as large as twelve feet in length, and even a hatchling was reputedly dangerous.

"The warband's gotta eat," the cook said with a shrug. "As long as it's edible, we'll cook it."

"Krow? Really?" Tovak still couldn't wrap his head around it.

"I've never had the privilege of cleaning and cooking one," the cook said, "but the head cook says he has... claims it fed almost an entire company, if you can believe that. Me, I have my doubts. I think he was tryin' to pull one over on me. You see, a company eats a lot, and I mean a lot." He paused and patted the carapace of the krata with his palm. "I can't imagine a krow having that much meat, no matter how big they get."

Tovak could only shrug in disbelief. To his people, krow were the things of nightmares. Living in mountainous regions, both above and belowground, the giant spiders were frightening creatures. Though he'd never seen one, Tovak knew he'd rather face a wyrm, one of the enemy's dragons, than a krata.

"You'd best get along, lad," the cook said, glancing around, "before any of the senior cooks come along. They might think you're begging, and it could cause me some trouble for not shooing you on your way sooner. There are just too many hungry followers looking for a bite, if you know what I mean, and the warband's short on food as it is." He gave an apologetic shrug.

Tovak nodded and started to move off, then hesitated. "I've just arrived and I'm a little turned around."

"Where are you headed?"

"Center of the camp," Tovak said. "Second Pioneers."

"You'll want to keep going the way you're headed," the cook said, pointing. "Take your first right, then third left, and then follow that all the way down."

"First right then third left and go all the way, right?"

"That's it." The cook returned to the krata, pulling off the next leg.

Tovak moved on. At the next cooking tent, meat was being rotated over spits. Several piles of *durpa* carcasses that had been beheaded and skinned lay nearby. The dog-like pack hunters fed primarily on the herds of wild teska that roamed the plateau. While not considered tasty by most, their tough, gamy meat had been an occasional treat for Tovak when he'd been able to afford it.

His belly rumbled again at the sight of the cooking food. He moved on, hearing hammering of metal ahead. He passed a smith, whose hammer clanged almost painfully upon a piece of glowing steel. Tovak felt the heat from the portable forge wash over him and then he was past. In the next tent, the sides of which had been rolled up, a leather-maker was hard at work on a roughly made table. Strips of discarded leather and hide lay on the ground all around. At the same table an assistant was busy repairing the backside of a piece of chest armor.

Tovak continued on, following the directions, but came to a dead end. He was forced to ask directions again. Finally, he came upon an alley that cut between tents and led to another street that bordered the inner defensive ring of the encampment. The foot traffic on this new street was light. There was another trench, backed up by a turf wall with a barricade.

Twenty yards away, three sentries stood guard on a wooden-planked bridge. They wore plate mail and carried spears, with shields in hand. In the trench, just off to the side of the bridge, children played a game of King of the Hill. Two of the sentries watched and rooted them on. The other looked bored.

Just beyond the sentries, on the other side of the bridge, there was a slight rise with a pavilion atop, surrounded by a series of tents larger than the rest. In the pavilion and under the dull glow of lamplight, several clerks seated before long tables worked. Tovak realized this must be the warband's headquarters compound. The larger tents likely belonged to the senior officers, including Karach.

Before one of the large tents next to the headquarters pavilion and illuminated by torches stood the standard of the warband. The standard depicted a black badger head at the center of a crimson field, with bloody, bared fangs and fierce eyes. Below the badger was a black battle-axe crossed over a long-bladed sword, forming an X. The standard shifted slightly in the breeze, and as it did, Tovak felt his heart swelling with excitement. He'd made it.

Tovak could just make out the watchtower in the gloom, perhaps fifty yards away, rising into the sky, well behind the banner. It marked the center of the camp. Dagon's company was in there somewhere amongst the closely packed tents that crowded in on the headquarters compound. Tovak took a deep breath and strode forward and onto the bridge. The bored sentry turned from watching the children, stepped forward, and barred his path.

"What is your business?" He was a fierce-looking warrior with a thin scar running from his forehead down along his cheek to his chin. His heavy plate armor, black and high-lighted with the crimson of the Blood Badger Warband, was spotless and well-maintained. He leaned his spear against his shoulder as he set the bottom of his shield down on the bridge with a solid-sounding *thunk*. The guard's helm had a crimson crest of stiff bristles.

"A new recruit, sir," Tovak said uneasily. "I'm looking for the Second Pioneers."

"You want to serve under Dagon, eh?" the guard said with an almost impressed tone. "Off to be a pioneer, are you?"

"Aye, sir," Tovak said.

"Those are some pretty tough bastards. Are you sure you can cut it? They don't take just anyone."

"I have a Warrant of Passage, sir," Tovak said, feeling no small amount of pride. "From the Pioneer Academy back at Garand'Durbaad."

The sentry nodded and stretched forth his hand. "Let me see it."

Tovak reached into his tunic pocket, pulled out the thick sheet of vellum. He unfolded it and handed it over.

The guard held it up to the light of a nearby torch and gave it a once over. "Mark of excellence ...." He peered at

Tovak with an appraising eye and gave a grunt that indicated he wasn't terribly impressed. He handed it back. "Have an appointment, boy?"

"No, sir," Tovak said.

The sentry grunted again. "You'll want to head straight through here"—he motioned behind him and across the bridge—"and turn left at headquarters"—he pointed over his shoulder with his thumb to the pavilion—"to get to the Second Pioneers. Go about a quarter way around the inner ring until you see Dagon's banner. It's the—"

"—tall green banner with a black durvoll on it," Tovak finished for him as he tucked the Warrant away.

"And if old Dagon doesn't take you, don't bother going to the First Pioneers. They're not accepting new recruits. Veterans all. You need an appointment from either their captain or Karach himself to get in."

"I understand," Tovak said, nodding.

The guard stepped aside, the bottom of his shield scraping against the wooden planks at their feet. With a wave, he motioned for Tovak to be on his way. "Good luck with Dagon. You will need it."

Tovak moved past and strode across the bridge. Karach's standard seemed to glare down at him. With the sentry's words fresh to mind, he suddenly felt as if the spirit of the animal captured there somehow considered him an imposter, unworthy of joining the warband. He shook his head, glanced back at the bridge. The sentry had already turned away and had returned to watching the children play King of the Hill.

There was a fair amount of activity around Karach's headquarters. Off to one side stood a group of six warriors in plate, talking and laughing together. A short distance from them were four stern-looking officers in tunics talking amongst themselves. Tovak recognized the white marks of rank on their shoulders. They seemed to be arguing quietly over something.

A warrior emerged out through the open flap of the tent with the warband's standard. He set an urgent pace, passing between a pair of guards who were posted just outside the entrance. It was clear by his armor he too was an officer. Both guards snapped to attention and saluted, then fell back into a parade rest position as the officer stalked off into the night.

"Someday," Tovak promised himself, eyeing the tent. He had a long way to go yet before he could distinguish himself enough to be recognized by the warband's leader. "Starting today, I will begin building my own Legend."

Following the sentry's directions, he continued on. Before he knew it, he came upon Dagon's standard and tent. A guard was posted before it. The guard was extremely tall, standing a few inches taller than Tovak. He was heavily muscled, with coal-black hair and a braided beard. Beneath the shadows of a heavy brow, his black eyes seemed to catch everything and glittered in the torchlight. His face was heavily scarred, almost to the point of being a horror. Tovak resisted the urge to flinch. Unlike the other warriors Tovak had seen, this one did not wear plate mail. Nor did he carry a shield.

A pair of long knives were sheathed at his hips, and he held a large two-handed blade, point set down in the dirt, with his hands resting on the butt of the guard. Tovak recognized the weapon as a *drozjain*.

The guard's eyes followed Tovak as he approached.

"State your business," the guard ordered in a deep voice.

"I'm here to join the pioneers, sir," Tovak said, and his voice broke on the last word.

"Do you have a letter of appointment to the company?"

"No, sir," Tovak said.

"I'm not a sir."

"I'm sorry, sir." Tovak cleared his throat, embarrassed.

The guard chuckled in a half friendly manner that was laced with a confidence Tovak suddenly did not feel. "Tell me, what would the pioneers want with a young, scrawny boffer like you?"

"I've been trained," Tovak said. He reached into his tunic and pulled out the Warrant.

The guard took the document from Tovak's hands and scanned it quickly. His eyes lifted briefly before returning his attention back to the Warrant.

"Wait here," he ordered, handing it back. Pushing the tent flap aside, he turned and half-stepped into the tent. "Sorry to bother you, sir, but there is a fresh recruit to see you about joining up. He's got a Warrant from the Academy."

There was a pause from inside.

"Send him in."

Tovak felt his heart skip a beat.

"Yes, sir." The guard turned, holding the tent flap aside. "It's your lucky day. The captain will see you." He gave a nod. As Tovak moved forward, the guard put his sword out, blocking the way. Leaning forward, he lowered his voice. "The captain values honesty. Be mindful and speak true. Lie to him and he'll never forgive you." The guard raised a warning eyebrow, removed the sword, and jerked his head for Tovak to enter.

The interior of the tent was darkened and smelled of smoke from an oil lamp, weatherproofed canvas, and mold. A single lamp hung from the center support pole. A pair of moths flitted about the flame.

Tovak had expected something very different than what he was greeted with. Instead of a carpet of some kind, there was only grass beneath his boots. He spied no cot for sleeping. Dagon had a bedroll laid out against the back wall. There was a small battered wooden chest at the foot of the bedroll.

A camp table had been set up in the center of the tent. Beyond that, the tent was bare of furnishings. A set of weathered but well-maintained leather armor painted in green and black had been stacked neatly in the corner.

The captain sat on a three-legged stool before the table, with a wax tablet in one hand and a metal stylus in the other. A second lamp sat on the table. From its burning wick, a coil of black smoke twisted upward toward the ceiling.

The captain was a yellow-haired, hard-looking Dvergr, with intelligent green eyes and a thick beard that had only a few braids in it. Despite the chilly night air, he wore a light, sleeveless tunic. Tan leggings and thin, comfortable-looking boots adorned his feet.

Tovak came to a stop before the captain and snapped to attention.

"You wish to join my company, yes?" The captain's voice was hard, unfriendly. He placed the stylus down on the table, but still held the tablet.

Tovak found the captain's gaze piercing. He thought he detected a flicker of recognition but prayed that Dagon knew not who he was. If he did, it would likely see the crushing of his dreams.

"Yes, sir," Tovak replied.

"And you come bearing a Warrant of Passage?"

"Yes, sir."

"The pioneers are not for everyone, no matter what they told you at the Academy," Dagon said, with a hint of disdain at his mention of the school. "We are the eyes and ears of the warband. We fight outside the protection of the line. We move fast and strike hard. We train even harder." He took a deep breath, eying Tovak with a calculating gaze. "Consider everything you learned at the Academy nearly useless. Pioneer training only truly begins when you join your first company. It is both difficult and demanding. It changes a person…makes them harder, stronger…both inside and out. And of those we do accept in, I boot four out of every five because they can't keep up or meet my standards." He paused, an expectant look upon his face.

"I understand, sir," Tovak replied.

"I doubt that very much." Dagon placed the tablet carefully down upon the table and clasped both hands together. "And you believe you have what it takes to make it in the pioneers?"

Tovak paused, contemplating what he thought the captain might want to hear. And then the guard's words flitted through his mind. *Be mindful and speak honestly.* He decided to keep his answer simple.

"I do, sir."

A hint of a sneer crossed Dagon's lips. The captain nodded slowly, as if he'd heard the very same answer many times before, which Tovak suspected he likely had.

"You have no idea," he finally said. "We sometimes march all day and through the night. There are times where our stomachs are glued to our backbones for want of food. The First and the Second Pioneers train and fight harder than any other company in the Badgers, for with the jobs given to us, there is no room for failure. We are the elite. A pioneer in either of our companies must be the very best. Karach requires it of us, and there is nothing we would not do for our warchief." He paused. "You need to know what you're getting into, lad." He made a show of looking Tovak over. "You look fit enough. Let me see the Warrant."

Tovak handed it over, and the captain began reading through the document.

"You don't come from a wealthy family," Dagon said, his eyes moving back and forth over the Warrant. "Do you?"

"No, sir," Tovak said. "I've been on my own for ... a while now. My family is dead."

Dagon's eyes flicked up at the last part. He scowled and then returned to reading.

"Impressive Warrant," Dagon said after several moments of silence. "The master at the Academy gives you high marks."

Tovak's hope swelled. He was certain to get an appointment, wasn't he? He sent up a silent prayer of thanks to Thulla.

"I must admit, a mark of excellence is not an easy thing to achieve," Dagon said slowly. He raised his eyes to peer at Tovak, and then his forehead creased in concentration, as if he were trying to remember something. In a flash, his eyes went wide with recognition, and his features hardened. He quickly scanned the bottom of the Warrant and froze. His body stiffened, and his face became a furious mask. He looked up and locked eyes with Tovak.

"Who was your father, Tovak?" he asked in an icy tone.

Tovak's heart sank as he remembered the cards from the spirit deck. Thulla, the Taker. He knew what was coming. It was the same story, over and over again. People judged him not for who he was, but who his father had been, what he had done. He took a deep breath. He exhaled and with that breath went all the hope and happiness he'd felt since he'd stepped off the yuggernok.

"My father was Graybor Stonehammer, sir." The words came out flat, defeated. Tovak wanted to scream, cry out, curse the captain for what he knew was about to happen. But he'd grown accustomed to the role of Pariah long ago, so he stood there and said nothing more.

Dagon slowly folded the Warrant along its creases and slid it across the surface of the table to the farthest edge, toward Tovak. It was as if he somehow feared contamination.

"You don't know this, but I have two sons." Dagon's tone was harsh, cold. "I used to have three. My firstborn served under your father's command. In a snowy pass above Barasoom, he was slaughtered like a teska sold at market." The statement hung between them. Dagon's voice, like his face, was full of pain and wounded rage.

Tovak almost cringed. His shoulders slumped. He felt like the life was being sucked out of him. He knew the story all too well. He just hadn't known Dagon's eldest son had been there, a party to his father's disgrace. Would Tovak never be free?

Dagon let out a slow breath. The anger seemed to leave him. In its place was only a cold disdain. It was all coming undone. Again.

"Graybor Stonehammer failed his troops," Dagon said quietly. "He failed the village he was tasked with protecting. He failed the Dragon Fists and every Dvergr of Garand'Durbaad. And sadly, he failed *you*, too, Tovak, for you must now bear your father's disgrace, his shame. You are a Pariah, and with good reason, coward's son."

Tovak burned with a deep shame. It was as Dagon said. His father had failed in his duty and been solely responsible for a massacre by the enemy upon his people. And it was Tovak's everlasting shame to live under that cloud of disgrace and humiliation.

"There is no room in my company for you, Tovak, son of Graybor. Nor will there ever be, so long as I am its captain."

Dagon fell silent for a long moment as he glanced down at the folded Warrant. His hands shook.

"If it were up to me, you would be escorted out of the encampment and left to fend for yourself on the plateau." The captain tapped his desk with an index finger. "But there are rules we must all abide by. Karach, like the Academy, takes your kind in. Why he does that, the gods only know. He does, however, leave the decision up to the individual company commanders." Dagon fell silent for several heartbeats. He clenched and unclenched his hands and looked about to speak. He hesitated a heartbeat more. "I will not sully my Legend by exacting any sort of petty revenge against a son for the sins of the father. I will not seek to further humiliate you. Perhaps you can find a place in the warband with one of the other companies, perhaps not. There are few among us who will not remember the name Graybor Stonehammer. Your journey to the Badgers may have been for naught. Seek one of the other companies...perhaps amongst the skirmishers or even the auxiliaries...." Dagon sucked in a breath. It came out in a slow hiss. "There is a great need for labor. Somehow, someway, you might even begin to atone for the sins of your father. I will say nothing of your visit here, this day. That is the only kindness I will ever offer you. Find what position you can"—Dagon's tone hardened to cold steel—"but it will not be with the Second, ever. Understand me?"

Tovak gave a miserable nod.

"Go, now, and do not return. You are not welcome in my tent. Dismissed."

Tovak didn't say a word. He couldn't. There was nothing he could say that would change the captain's mind. He had thought his Warrant would earn him at least some scrap of respect. He had been wrong.

"I said, dismissed," Dagon repeated.

Tovak took the Warrant off the table, turned, and moved towards the tent flap.

"And Tovak," Dagon said, "if I were you, I'd lose that Warrant. Take another name, son. Granted, there is shame in that, but I think you'll find that many believe stones don't roll far from the mountain."

Tovak gave another nod. Then, without looking back, he pulled the tent flap aside and stepped out into the night.

The guard, who had wished him well only a short while before, had heard everything. Tovak could see it in his face. The friendliness was gone. There was no smile, no kindness, only cold, disdainful eyes and a grim line of tightened lips.

Tovak averted his gaze and walked out into the street of grass that stretched to his left and right. He paused, his emotions tearing at him. Rage, shame, despair—they were a maelstrom, ripping his heart to pieces. He turned his eyes towards the sky. *Why?* He sent the question up, a soul-felt plea to Thulla. He had clung to his faith, desperate for some sort of answer that didn't promise a lifetime of rejection and pain.

Will it ever change?

As he stood there, torchlight flickering faintly around him, the sounds of the camp were little more than a distant drone in his ears as memory washed over and threatened to drown him.

CHAPTER THREE

Ten years earlier....

Tovak shifted on the hard, wooden seat of his school bench, his stylus held over a wax tablet covered with names, dates, and a litany of details regarding the Battle of Farkahl Valley. He'd copied his notes from what covered the black slate board behind Master Gaelon, all of it part of a history lesson about the most recent Dvergr-Syrulian war. He was a good student and nearing graduation. He had always favored this class. He loved history, particularly learning about the great battles and heroes that had shaped the Legend of his people.

The slate blended almost perfectly with the granite walls of the school. It was the same for the desks arrayed about the room in orderly rows—twelve for the students and one for the instructor. Like every other structure in the city, the school's walls, ceiling, and even the furniture, wherever possible, had been cut, carved, or shaped from the native stone of the mountain above. A dozen mirrored lamps of silver filled the room with warm light, and a half-dozen wide windows opened up onto a shadowed stone courtyard beyond, with a splashing fountain at its center.

"As a result of her losses along the Farkahl River," Master Gaelon said, "the Empress of Syrulia was forced to withdraw with what few troops she had left. Our Thane, the mighty Rogar Bladebreaker, through speedy action, was able to cut off the human army before they could make their escape. He surrounded them with three of his best warbands: the Dragon Fist, the War Hammer, and the Blood Badgers. Bladebreaker was subsequently able to force not only a surrender but a long-term peace upon the Empress that secured our southern borders against further incursion. After many long years of bitter and bloody fighting, it was a peace on our terms."

Gaelon raised his eyes from the thick tome he held in his hands and then placed it upon the granite desk beside him. Looking almost stately in the green and black robes of the school, he was one of the youngest instructors, and yet his beard was still mostly gray, with streaks and hints of the auburn he had enjoyed as a youth. Like all instructors, his head was shaved and covered by a skullcap. It was made of plain copper, without jewel or rune, indicating he was at the bottom of the hierarchy of instructors. He was also Tovak's favorite, with a sense of humor, a delight in history, and a fondness for sidetracking lessons in favor of glorious tales of victories and heroism across the ages. "Can anyone tell me why the non-aggression pact is important today, so many years later?" There was a pause, and Gaelon's eyes shifted to the middle of the classroom. "Adelluh?"

Tovak turned at hearing the name. He had a liking for the raven-haired lass, although he'd never worked up the nerve to say more than "hello" to her in the halls of the school. He often wondered if she felt the same.

"It brought a lasting peace," she said. Tovak smiled and nodded. She was right. But there was more to it.

Hoping to impress her, Tovak raised his hand from where he sat at the front of the classroom. He felt his friend

Andol rolling his eyes—again—at Tovak's habit of knowing the answers when it came to history.

"Yes, Tovak?" Gaelon asked, the corner of his mouth turning up.

"The Horde," Tovak replied easily.

Gaelon raised an eyebrow. "Insufficient, and I think you know it. Explain your answer." It was a game the two of them often played, and Gaelon seemed to enjoy indulging Tovak's growing wealth of knowledge and reasoning.

Tovak cleared his throat. "It's my understanding that the Horde is concentrated well to the south. If they were to begin another advance, they would have to go through Syrulia to get to us, here beneath the mountain."

"True," Gaelon said. "Anything else?"

"The Horde will have a much more difficult time getting through them to us," Tovak said. "Especially now that we are no longer fighting the Syrulians. In addition to that, the Syrulians don't have to garrison the border. More importantly, the longer the empire holds, the stronger and better prepared we become."

"Precisely," Gaelon said. "And that is, in fact, how Thane Bladebreaker convinced the Empress to cease hostilities. That and the fact that we had her and the remains of her army surrounded. It was diplomacy at sword point." The instructor gave a low chuckle at his own joke.

Gaelon let his eyes move over the faces of the rest of the class.

"There was Legend to be had at continuing the conflict with Syrulia—the Thane could have taken the Empress's head—which would have removed one threat. Several of the Thane's advisors wanted to do just that. However, Bladebreaker chose to weigh the short-term risks of continuing the conflict with her successor versus the long-term threat of facing our true enemy, the Horde. It is important that you understand this point and why he did it. The Syrulians are a buffer between us and the Horde, which has already swept over much of this world our people have found refuge on. There will come a point when the Horde once again advances and we shall have to find a new home, perhaps even on another world. Do you all see the difference between a short-term gain versus the Thane's long-view strategy?"

Tovak looked to see several of the heads nodding, although Adelluh's incongruous frown seemed directed straight at him. He turned away, wondering if he'd done something wrong. Andol, sitting to his right, also gave a nod, although his understanding of history was less than rock-solid. Tovak often helped his friend study for their exams, drilling him with dates and names. Sometimes, it was for naught, but such was their friendship that Tovak helped when he could.

As Tovak turned back towards Gaelon, he saw Headmaster Grahk step into the classroom, a grim expression on his wrinkled, ancient face.

He fixed beady, piercing eyes of blue upon Master Gaelon, who had turned at the headmaster's intrusion. Grahk's thin, ash-white beard reached nearly to the floor, and the green and black robes of his station looked like they'd been draped over broom handles. A polished gold skullcap covered his head, with black runes etched along the edges. A small white crystal adorned the center of the widow's peak, and it glittered with reflected light as the headmaster moved forward with a shuffling gait.

"Excuse me, Master Gaelon," he said in a gravelly and serious tone, "but I require the presence of one of your students."

"As you wish, Headmaster," Gaelon replied, his copper skullcap glinting with lamplight as he bowed slightly for the Headmaster to proceed.

Grahk's eyes shifted to the class, passing from one face to another, until he fixed them upon Tovak. The headmaster's eyes narrowed as Tovak's widened.

Tovak couldn't imagine what sort of trouble he might be in. He'd never been called upon by the headmaster—a privilege generally reserved for those who misbehaved at school or underperformed—and he had always been an exemplary student. His father required nothing less, and he'd done his best to exceed expectations. The headmaster pointed a bony finger and then motioned for Tovak to follow him.

"Come with me, boy," Grahk said. "And bring your things."

The headmaster turned in a swirl of robes and disappeared through the doorway.

Tovak turned worried eyes to Andol, who had a questioning look upon his face. He could only shrug as he stood. There were harsh whispers and sideways glances as Tovak quickly picked up his stylus and tablet. He moved to the doorway and grabbed his cloak and pack off a hook by the door. Draping the cloak over his shoulders, he slipped his things into the pack, slung it over his shoulder, and stepped out where the headmaster stood waiting. His ancient features were a strange combination of anger and sadness, as if Tovak had done something to offend or deeply disappoint the headmaster.

"You must go home," the headmaster said. He turned on his heel and walked briskly down the hallway that led to the front entrance of the school. The hallway was softly illuminated by oil lamps set in mirrored recesses along the granite walls.

Confused, Tovak followed in the fluttering wake of the headmaster's thick robes. Fear gripped at him, and bewilderment. Never in his life had that hallway seemed so long. What was wrong?

"Headmaster," Tovak said meekly, "what's going on?"

Grahk didn't turn his head. "It is best we not speak of it, here or elsewhere. All will become clear to you once you return home." His quick footsteps echoed off the walls, broken only by the swishing of his robes as they brushed along the stone floor.

"But—"

"Enough," the headmaster hissed in irritation.

So, Tovak followed, his anxiety growing with each step as they neared the main entrance to the school. They passed a dozen doorways, some of which were open and others closed. Tovak knew they were all classrooms full of students like himself. Ahead, the wide double doors of the entrance stood open, with a pale glow from brighter lamps filling the foyer with a soft, white light.

Grahk stepped aside and motioned for Tovak to pass through. As he did, the headmaster suddenly grabbed his shoulder and spun him around. The elderly Dvergr was stronger than he appeared. His fingers upon Tovak's shoulders dug in so deep, they hurt. There was a turmoil of anger and sadness swirling within those piercing blue eyes, and for a moment, the furrowed brow of the headmaster softened. He released his hold on Tovak.

"You were a good student," Grahk said slowly. He let out a long breath that hissed out and glanced up at the school's seal set into the carved stone above the open doors. "It is a great pity. You only had half a year left before graduation. However, it would be best if you didn't come back to the school, ever." Grahk squeezed his shoulder, this time in an almost comforting manner and with fondness. "Your life is going to be very difficult from here on out. I am sorry, but we can't have the distraction and conflict your presence would bring to the school. The other parents would object. It is better this way."

"I don't understand," Tovak said. "What have I done?"

The headmaster blew out a breath. For a flashing moment, Tovak saw compassion flicker in Grahk's eyes.

"You will," Grahk said wearily. "I wish there was something I could do, but I can't change the ways of our people … nor can I change what has happened. Seek out Father Danik. He is an old friend of mine and may be able to help you find strength when it seems you can find none of your own. Remember Father Danik."

Tovak simply nodded. It surprised him to hear Grahk make such a suggestion. He had never even met one of Thulla's clerics, like most Dvergr he knew. There was little faith to be found amongst his people. Indeed, the faithful were openly ridiculed and disparaged, especially those who served the religious order, for clinging to a god who most felt had forsaken the people as a whole. Tovak's mother and father were among them. There were no symbols of Thulla in his home, and his father had gone out of his way to braid his beard without prayer knots. It was a fading tradition amongst his people, and it was widely accepted that, of the nobles who still wore them, most did so because of tradition rather than faith.

The headmaster raised his hand and pointed away from the school. "Now, go home and begone from here."

Fear clutched at Tovak's heart. He couldn't imagine what could have brought the headmaster to such a state or why he was being sent home and ordered not to return.

As he walked down the steps, the Thane's Bell rang once in the high tower above the palace, echoing across the cavern walls and stone buildings of Garand'Durbaad, marking the first hour past midday. Never before had the lantern-lit streets looked so dark and ominous or the great cavern's ceiling high above so distant and disquieting. Tiers of balconies, their windows open and radiating dim yellowed light, seemed to stare down at him with heartless scorn. The street leading from the school was relatively quiet as he worked his way towards home, barely aware of the occasional traveler that passed him by.

He felt like he'd been condemned, and he didn't even know his crime. Tovak loved school. He could not imagine never returning. What would his friends think of him for being cast out? What of Adelluh?

He moved around a teska-drawn cart full of bundles of freshly sheared wool and stepped out onto Grand Avenue, the main thoroughfare of Garand'Durbaad running straight down the middle of the city. The sounds of foot traffic washed over him, for even at midday, the avenue was full of people.

He turned left towards the back of the cavern and made his way along the avenue. Grand was nearly a hundred feet across and stretched out ahead and behind for a half-mile in either direction. A single row of twelve massive columns, each forty feet thick and covered with runes, ran down the middle of the avenue and supported the weight of the ceiling a hundred fifty feet above. A small channel of cool, clear water ran around columns flowing in the direction of the palace. The water ran down the outer surface of each column, rippling over the etched runes and causing the dark stone to glisten as it flowed into the channel. Tovak had always marveled at this engineering feat, but this time he barely noticed.

Merchants and teamsters hauled goods in small carts and wagons. A company of warriors in full plate armor marched along the far side of the avenue, a raven banner held high as they made their way towards the main gates of the city, sunlight, and the outside world. Couples and mothers with young children passed by on errands, some of them holding sacks or small wooden boxes full of goods.

He walked quickly past artisan shops, smithies, and taverns that lined the avenue on either side, with apartments above them on the second floors. Streets and alleyways opened up onto Grand Avenue from both sides, spaced unevenly along its entire length. They formed an irregular grid around the dark stone buildings that made up much of the city.

Each building was a part of the mountain, as if they had all sprung up from the floor like stalagmites. The smooth stone façades were broken only by doorways, windows, and balconies. At the center of the city, many of the buildings were two and occasionally three stories tall. The farther one went away from the center of the city, the taller the buildings grew as they approached the edges of the cavern. Along the cavern walls, affluent homes and apartments had been carved straight into the stone face, going all the way up to where the ceiling curved back inward. Cable-operated lifts rose and fell along the walls. Dotting the high ceiling were great magical lanterns that bathed the city below in brilliant white light.

Grand Avenue ran from the massive outer gates of the city all the way back to the rear of the cavern, where three sets of heavy steel doors, called the Deep Gates, stood open. When needed, they secured the city's access to a network of tunnels and underground roads crisscrossing beneath the surrounding mountains and hills to nearby towns and distant cities.

A quarter mile from the Deep Gates, Tovak crossed the Grand Avenue and turned down a narrow street. He was oblivious to everyone moving around him as his feet carried him along a path he had walked for years, towards a place of comfort and love ... towards home.

Nearing the edge of the cavern, he passed a series of simple apartment blocks that rose five stories above him. He took a right down a small dead-end street that cut between apartment blocks. Reaching the last row of apartments that butted up against the stone face of the cavern, he turned into a dim, unadorned hallway illuminated by a pair of small lanterns. There were two slab-like iron doors on either side. A pair of stone and steel spiral staircases rose up between them, one on each side. He moved to the staircase on the right and climbed the steps. He passed the first and second landings before he finally stepped off at the third into a hallway with four apartment doors. It was virtually identical to the first level save that the window was where the entrance had been on the first level.

The last door on the right stood open, weak light spilling out onto the hallway floor. He made his way toward it, dreading whatever might lie ahead. Low voices within reached his ears, speaking in hushed, angry tones as he approached.

"—least let me take her to the family crypt," a man's voice growled. "Don't let him rob her of that, too."

Her? They couldn't be talking about....

His feet froze beneath him, only a few steps short of the door. He couldn't move, dreading what lay within his home.

"She shouldn't be interred at all, Dubor," a gruff voice growled back. "You know the custom, the law. It specifically calls for the nameless to be burned, to cleanse their dishonor and sin in fire, lest it infect others."

Dubor was his mother's eldest brother. Tovak knew little of her side of the family, but he'd heard his uncle's name spoken occasionally over the years, usually in a heated discussion between his mother and father.

"Then grant a dissolution, Borol!" There was a slamming sound, as if a fist striking a table or door. "As his warchief, you have that power.... *Please*.... A dissolution would sever the tie. You owe me that."

Borol? Tovak thought with not a little dismay. Borol Ironbrand was Warchief of the Dragon Fist Warband, where his father served as a company commander.

A long pause filled the silence, and then Borol asked, "And what of the son? No dissolution will cleanse the stain upon him. Nothing short of a miracle could. What will you do? Tell me. Cast him adrift or take him in? It might be better to just cut his throat while he sleeps. Kinder I think...." All Tovak could do was stand there, wide-eyed and in shock. They were talking about him....

"You read her note," came the gruff reply. Then a hesitation. "I will do what was asked of me, because she is the one who begged. I owe her that, but nothing more. Understand me?"

There was a heavy sigh that bordered on a growl. "Very well, Dubor. For old time's sake *and* the debt I owe you, I will approve of this...." There was another hesitation, and then his tone changed from harsh to sympathetic. "My regrets for your loss. She was a good woman."

"She was that and more," Dubor said, his voice a mixture of sorrow and anger. "She was my little sister." There was a long pause. "I always knew no good would come of her union with a Stonehammer. I said as much on the day they were bonded. It mattered not. He still took her away."

"I understand," Borol said. "Do you need help moving the body?"

"No," came the simple reply. There was a catch in the throat. "I know what needs to be done. I have already made arrangements."

"Very well," Borol replied. There was a grunt. "These things now belong to the warband. They cannot be permitted to belong to him. The rest, obviously, goes to her kin."

"I'll see to all of it," Dubor replied, and there was a strange edge to his voice.

"I suspect you will," Borol said, and there was something in his voice, as if he were permitting something that, under different circumstances, he might take issue with.

Footsteps approached the doorway, and a shadow filled the space like a specter. A moment later, a tall, middle-aged Dvergr stepped out of Tovak's home. He had a heavily braided beard the color of copper reaching down to a wide, silver belt, and his auburn hair was pulled back and tied into a thick topknot.

The gleaming hilt of a fine sword sheathed at his waist stuck up from a wide belt of black leather and silver scales. He wore a blue, black, and silver cloak over his shoulders, pinned with a large silver cloak pin in the shape of a dragon fist. It was Borol Ironbrand. Tovak had seen him several times but had never met him. The warchief had a large sack hefted over his shoulder, and it was full.

Borol halted in front of Tovak and stared down, his hard, gray eyes devoid of any emotion. His lips pressed into a thin line, and then he narrowed his eyes. Tovak could not tell if it was in anger or something else.

A wave of fear and confusion washed over Tovak.

"You have your father's face," Borol said. "Now, you have his shame."

The warchief stepped around Tovak and was gone.

Tovak stood there blinking. He could hear his own breathing as Borol's heavy boots clomped down the stairs behind him.

"You." Dubor stood framed in the open doorway, glaring at Tovak. Dubor's eyes were a green that reminded Tovak of his mother. Dubor's hair, like hers, was also a pale golden color. He wore a gray tunic of soft leather and dark leggings secured in the tops of fine black leather boots.

A gold chain decorated his neck, adorned with a large, gold medallion depicting strong Dvergr hands holding a hammer and chisel. Tovak had seen a similar, albeit smaller, medallion around his mother's neck, hidden but always there.

The Stonecarvers were faceless names that, to Tovak, meant nothing but conflict between his parents. They were names that his mother would mention when she thought he was out of earshot. Her family was never openly discussed. No reason had ever been offered by either of his parents, even when he'd asked.

Tovak knew almost nothing of his mother's family, other than that they existed somewhere in the city, and he certainly didn't recognize his uncle who gazed upon him with pure loathing.

"Get in here, boy …." Dubor barked, and then he disappeared into Tovak's home, leaving Tovak just outside the doorway. His footsteps faded quickly as he moved deeper into the apartment.

At first Tovak hesitated. He didn't know what to think. It was like he was in a nightmare. He had no idea what was going on. He knew for certain something terrible had happened. He found his feet slowly carrying him towards the doorway.

"I said get in here," Dubor shouted. "There is something I want you to see." His voice was full of anger, and the very sound of it filled Tovak with fear.

As Tovak stepped into the doorway, he gasped. His uncle was nowhere to be seen.

The tapestries that covered the walls of his home were still in place, but the rest of it looked as if it had been ransacked by goblins. The Dragon Fist shield that had hung over the hearth was gone, as was his father's *zjain*, a ceremonial sword awarded to him when he had been promoted to captain. A suit of hardened leather armor in the warband's colors of blue, black, and silver was also gone from where it had been displayed with pride in the corner. The armor had belonged to his grandfather.

A long crimson couch and two large amber chairs, normally placed before the hearth, were pushed up against the walls, and the large gilded chest sitting next to the hearth had been opened. Its contents lay scattered across the thick, brightly patterned carpet that covered the floor from wall to wall. The family's clan banner, depicting a gray hammer held in a fist on a white field, lay discarded on the floor in a heap.

Tovak heard movement down the central hallway that led to the sleeping chambers. Light shone through the doorway of his parents' room, and a shadow across the hallway floor showed that Dubor stood before the lantern that hung over the bed.

For a moment, Tovak thought he heard Dubor give a sob, and the sound of it filled him with dread. Tovak slipped his shoes off and moved down the hallway slowly, fearfully. His footfalls, even on the rug, sounded like thunder in his ears. It was as if the rest of world had suddenly gone silent.

Time seemed to slow. As he reached the end of the hallway and stepped into the doorway, he saw his mother, and something inside him broke. He couldn't breathe. He couldn't move. All he could do was stand there and gaze upon her body.

She lay upon his parents' thick sleeping mat and wore her favorite dress. The dress was an emerald green, with white embroidered flowers. Her neatly braided hair lay across the side of her face and down her chest, held in place beneath her crossed arms. She looked like she was asleep, but he knew that wasn't right. Her skin, normally a rosy pink, was ashen, and her lips had turned almost black. On the floor beside her was her beloved teapot, a wedding gift from his father, and a single empty cup.

"Look closely, and never forget...." Dubor's voice came as a growl from where he stood by the window. "For it was *your* father who did this to her. Your father...."

His words were angry, biting, and they branded Tovak's heart like molten steel. Horror filled Tovak's mind, and his gut clenched in terrible pain.

"What?" he stammered. "How...? Father left almost a month ago...."

"Your father is dead," Dubor shouted. "Dead, I tell you. His failure managed to get himself and his entire company killed. The village he was tasked with protecting was razed by the enemy." Dubor pointed at the body of his mother. "Your father's failure saw the loss of over four hundred of our people, not counting the warriors of his company."

Dubor clenched and then unclenched his fists. He turned glaring eyes to Tovak, who could only stand there, stunned.

"The name Stonehammer—your name—will forever be known for the massacre at Barasoom Pass. My sister wouldn't... couldn't bear the shame of your father's failure, so she took her own life! She poisoned herself rather than live another day as a Stonehammer. Your father died a coward. When it mattered most, he abandoned his company, his duty, and his Legend. He ran from the fight and left his warriors to fend for themselves."

Tovak's world came crashing down. He couldn't breathe. The room spun around him and threatened to topple him to the floor. Tears welled in his eyes as the reality of it all pressed down upon him like a mountain. His father had disgraced himself. It could not be.

"No," Tovak gasped, having difficulty grasping that such a thing could happen.

So severe was his shock that he didn't see Dubor rushing towards him. He didn't see a fist raised. Dubor's blow, like a hammer, sent him sprawling painfully to the floor.

"You don't get to cry for her," Dubor screamed. "You are a Stonehammer, like your father before you. Child of her womb or no, your tears are an insult to her memory."

Tovak felt hot wetness on his cheek. He reached up, brushed his hand against his face, and came away with blood. He was too stunned, too shattered to speak.

"Know this," Dubor growled. "From this day forth, you will be a Pariah amongst your people." He reached into his tunic, pulled out a wrinkled piece of vellum, and held it before Tovak's eyes as if it were a death warrant. "Your mother asked me to care for you until the Age of Iron, and I am Legend-bound to grant her dying wish. You will find no kindness in my heart for you. I must now bear the embarrassment of having a Pariah in my own home. I will make you pay for that indignity."

Dubor paused, his chest heaving in great gasps. His uncle glanced over at Tovak's mother and remained there a moment. He turned back.

"Now get up!"

Tovak slowly pulled himself to his feet, his eyes cast downward. He felt intense shame. It filled his heart and threatened to consume him. He hurt for his father, who had died in shame. He hurt for his mother, who couldn't bear the shame. He hurt for himself, for he would always be his father's son, a disgrace to his people.

"Am I interrupting?" a voice said from the doorway.

Tovak and Dubor turned to see a young Dvergr, perhaps fifty years of age, standing there. His long hair was a blond color, as was a long and heavily braided beard. It was the beard that caught Tovak's attention, for it was tied off with a dozen prayer knots made from a soft, orange fabric. He also wore the tan and orange robes of a cleric of Thulla and carried a canvas litter balanced over one of his broad shoulders. His brown eyes moved from Tovak's mother to Dubor, and finally to Tovak. As their eyes met, the cleric's eyes softened, glinting in what Tovak took to be an underlying kindness and compassion.

Tovak felt shame, undeserving of any such feelings. He was a Pariah now, a nobody.

"Not at all, Father," Dubor said, his tone losing the anger and rage that had possessed him only moments before, as if it had never existed.

"I am Sen," the cleric said as he leaned the litter against the wall. "You sent for me to retrieve the remains of Amelor Stonehammer for a purification pyre," he added. "Thulla bless her passing."

Dubor glanced at Tovak, his eyes still burning with anger. "She is to be interred in the Stonecarver crypts," he said. "Borol Ironbrand has granted a dissolution of union so that she can be interred under her maiden name." He narrowed his eyes at the cleric. "She is a Stonecarver. Am I understood?"

Sen's eyes shifted cautiously from Dubor to Tovak and back again. A slight frown crossed his bearded face. "Of course," he said. "It will be as you wish, Master Stonecarver."

"And," Dubor said, gesturing toward Tovak, "I want this Pariah to help you carry her to the temple. Is that also understood?"

"It is," Sen replied, betraying no emotion but for a hardening of the eyes.

Dubor gave a satisfied nod.

Sen stepped closer to Tovak.

"Your mother?" the cleric asked.

Tovak gave a nod.

"We will take her together," he said.

Tovak said nothing, his eyes going to his mother.

"Will you be coming with us?" Sen asked Dubor.

"No," came the immediate reply. "I need to settle affairs here. I will then return home. Send me your bill, and after you have prepared the remains, give word when the Stonecarver clan should assemble for the Ceremony of Interment."

"As you wish," Sen said. "You will hear from me on the morrow."

"Tovak," Dubor said, glaring at him. "I want you to come straight to my home as soon as Father Sen is done with you."

Tovak froze. He had no idea where that was.

"Well, Pariah?" Dubor said, narrowing his eyes.

"I … I don't … know where to go," Tovak finally managed.

"Thulla's bones," Dubor growled. "Will I have to do everything with you?"

"I will take him to your home, Master Stonecarver," Father Sen said, "once we have attended to his mother."

Dubor turned his eyes to Sen and let out a frustrated breath. He nodded once and then strode past them both.

He moved into one of the other rooms, where he could be heard moving things around, as if searching for something.

Sen reached out a hand and laid it upon Tovak's shoulder.

Tovak jumped at the touch and turned to regard the cleric. Part of him wanted to cry, but the memory of Dubor's blow and his harsh words were foremost in his mind. He was a Pariah. His future was uncertain and everything he had known had just been torn down. His father had been responsible for the deaths of many people, including his mother's suicide. He felt the weight of that crushing his heart like a vice, for he had loved both his father and mother dearly. Now, he felt nothing but disgust for his father.

What have you done to me? What did you do to Mother? He wanted to cry out in both frustration and agony, but his fear of Dubor's wrath kept him silent. He felt tears prick his eyes.

"Come, my son," Sen said softly. "I will help you attend to your mother. Perhaps Thulla's words might give you some comfort. Shall we pray?"

Not quite knowing what else to do, Tovak gave a wooden nod.

"Very good, my son," Sen said and proceeded to pray for the soul of Tovak's mother.

Tovak's family, his honor, and his future had been ripped away in an instant. He had no idea where he would go from here other than his uncle's home. Beyond that, his future would be a bleak one.

Chapter Four

The present....

Tovak stood in front of Dagon's tent, clenching and unclenching his fists. A wave of sadness tore at him. As hard as he tried, he could no longer remember his mother's face. A terrible rage stole over him, replacing the sadness. He trembled slightly. He wanted to turn, storm back into Dagon's tent, and rail against the injustice of it all.

Fueled by rage, Tovak considered challenging Dagon to a fight in an Adjudication Circle. It was a tradition amongst his people. In the Circle, two could settle disagreements, grudges, and even feuds. Anyone had the right make a challenge, even a Pariah.

Tovak knew his anger at Dagon was misplaced. The captain had a right to be angry, hateful even. A hopeless breath slipped from Tovak's lips. Challenging Dagon wouldn't change a thing. He understood deep down he did not have a prayer against such a seasoned veteran. And even if by some miracle he won, it wouldn't earn him a place with the pioneers, let alone wipe away the stain of being a Pariah or the turmoil of emotions that hounded him.

Over the years, his anger had fueled his drive. It was what had kept him going. Tovak knew he was just as good as the next Dvergr, and while at the Academy, which he had fought to get into, he had proved just that.

He took a breath full of frustration and glanced toward Dagon's tent. Father Danik's voice echoed back to him.

There is a place for the fires within. Store them like food before a siege. And when the storm comes, draw upon them when and only as needed, for the storm will break and your time will come.

It was a passage from the *Tales of Uliand Stormhand*, one Father Danik was overly fond of quoting.

"The storm is still out to sea," Tovak reminded himself, feeling his anger and rage recede a little. Like a wound, the hurt was still there, a terrible ache that over the years he'd been unable to remove.

Danik had warned him. Even after joining the Great March, the stigma of his father's legacy would follow. At the time, he had not believed that possible. Now, he knew different. The shame and disgrace would follow wherever he went. It was clear he needed to earn respect. But how? How could he do that if he wasn't allowed to serve? Like Dagon, how many other company commanders would turn him away? He suspected most, if not all. It was an impossible knot.

He raised his eyes to the darkened sky above. Low-hanging clouds drifted past a cloak of midnight black and a field of stars, which twinkled back at him. The moon, just coming up over the horizon, was bright.

"I will trust in you, Thulla," he whispered. "Lead me and I will follow."

He drew in another deep breath that turned ragged and let it out slowly through pursed lips. He felt the weight of his past and the stain of his dishonor like never before. It weighed upon him.

He thought on Dagon's parting words. Could it really be as easy as leaving his family's name behind and starting fresh with one of his own making? Although he felt a certain amount of disgust at the thought of casting off the last vestiges of his family, the idea of starting over did appeal to him. What would his ancestors think when he made it to the great feasting halls? Would they shun him, just as he was being shunned in life?

Tovak kicked at the ground, dislodging a tuft of grass. He made his decision. *Yes,* he thought. *I will lose my name.* He would take on a new name and keep his Warrant hidden, along with his shame. He couldn't bring himself to discard the document, though. He had worked too hard to earn it, and one day he might be able to display it openly. That was, after reclaiming his name and honor.

He took a step in the direction Dagon had suggested, but something made him pause, pulling him the other way. It was almost palpable, and for a fleeting moment, he thought he heard his name called. He looked around and saw no one about other than the guard before Dagon's tent and a group of warriors twenty yards off and moving in the other direction.

And then he thought he heard his name called again, distantly, and the pull was even stronger. Was he imagining things? Tovak shook his head and glanced back again at Dagon's tent. The guard was looking in his direction.

"It's not fair," Tovak whispered. He started walking. His thoughts, despite his decision to take a new name, were a turbulent storm. He walked just to walk, moving from street to street, passing countless tents and ignoring everything. He wandered about the inner encampment until his legs ached.

A dog barked harshly, jarring him. Tovak stopped. He blinked and looked around. The night air was cold and he shivered. He found himself standing a few yards from the headquarters pavilion. Despite the late hour, the clerks were still hard at work under the dull glow of lamps.

Besides the sentries posted strategically about, a group of armored warriors stood just outside the headquarters pavilion, conversing quietly. Amidst them he saw something that made him pause. At the center of the group was a female. He'd heard of such warriors, but he'd never seen one before. She had long hair that had been tied into a single braid and fell down the back of her armor. Her chest plate had been painted a bright crimson, and her greaves and bracers were similarly decorated. It was clear she came from a family of some means. She held a hornbow in one hand and two zjains sheathed at her waist, one on either side. On her back were a pack and a tied leather-wrapped bundle of arrows.

She had high cheekbones, full lips, and fierce eyes that glinted in the torchlight. Gazing upon her, Tovak felt something stir within. He wasn't quite sure what it was. It was inexplicable but he felt a pull toward her. He'd never seen her before, yet he suddenly felt as if he knew her, that he'd known her since childhood. That couldn't be right. She turned her head, and their eyes met, locking for a long moment. She was clearly a stranger and yet in her gaze he thought he saw a flicker of something. Was it recognition? She blinked and Tovak suddenly felt foolish.

He turned and quickly walked away, losing himself in the traffic of the street. He came to a wagon and cart park. There he paused, breathing in and out as if he'd run a great distance. He stopped next to a torch and leaned on the side rail of a wagon. He gazed into the empty bed. The torch guttered and hissed as a light wind tugged at the flame. His thoughts were interrupted by the scent of roasted meat, causing his empty stomach to rumble.

"Great gods, boy," a voice called from just behind him. "I heard that all the way over here."

Tovak turned to see an older warrior wearing leather armor dyed a deep blue and inlaid with the gold-etched patterns of a captain. He stood nearly as tall as Tovak, with a thick mane of brown hair that filled the air around his head as if it had a will of its own. His beard also splayed out in all directions, with a half-dozen thick braids running down his chest and secured with iron beads above a belt buckle shaped like an iron fist. He was clean and tidy, like the other warriors Tovak had seen, but there was a sort of wildness to him that couldn't be entirely concealed.

The captain had a blue cloak with gold trim draped around his shoulders. He held a blue helm with a golden crest under one arm, and in his hand, he clutched a metal mess bowl that steamed in the cold air. He'd clearly just come from a cook tent.

Tovak's stomach rumbled yet again at the sight and smell of the food.

"Sorry, sir," he said.

"Never apologize for things outside of your control," the captain said and strode forward the last couple steps between them. He held out the bowl. "Have you a knife?"

"A small one … in my pack, sir," Tovak said.

"Well, don't bother getting that out. Grab mine and take some of this meat, boy." The captain twisted his body and pushed out his hip, offering the hilt of a long, simple dagger with a black leather grip. "The perks of being an officer mean I can get more whenever I want. Besides, you look like you could use some, and from the sounds of your stomach, you're famished. Make sure you take a good portion."

Tovak did as he was told, pulling the blade free. He grabbed a thick chunk of meat in his hand and sliced some off. He wiped the blade on his leggings and carefully returned it to the scabbard at the captain's hip.

"Thank you, sir," he offered, bowing his head.

"Well?" the captain said expectantly, raising an eyebrow. "What are you waiting for? Eat. That's an order."

Tovak bit in hungrily and chewed. The meat, slathered in butter, practically melted in his mouth. It was rich, tasting strongly of nuts with garlic, and was the most delicious thing he'd ever tasted.

"That's more like it," the captain said. "I always say, hunger makes the best cook."

Tovak could only agree. He took another bite and chewed, grateful for the offering.

"I'm Captain Struugar Ironfist, and by the sorry look of you, and no company cloak, I'm guessing you're in need of a home. Beghan said a recruit stopped by Dagon's tent earlier this evening. That, I am thinking, is you. Do I have that right?"

Tovak froze in mid-chew. He had no idea who Beghan was, but Struugar knew Tovak had been to see Dagon. What else did he know? Would he have offered to share his meal had he known Tovak was a Pariah? Somehow, he seriously doubted that.

"Beghan," Struugar said. "Big scarred fellow, a pioneer. He was on guard duty outside of Dagon's tent. I bumped into him at the mess. He said if I was looking for a recruit, one was wandering about. Took me a good long while to find you. That's you, right?"

Tovak swallowed the meat.

"Yes, sir. I wanted to join the pioneers, but it seems there isn't a place for me there." The words burned and filled his heart with another surge of anger at the crushing of his dreams.

Struugar cocked his head to the side. A thoughtful expression came over his face.

"Dagon's picky on who he takes," Struugar said with a half-shrug. "Me, not so much. My company is understrength, and what with the Great March about to get underway, we've not seen very many recruits come through."

Tovak took another cautious bite. Was the captain offering him a position? Hope suddenly flared, like the sparking of a fire.

"What is this?" Tovak asked, pointing at the meat in his hand. "I've never had anything quite like it."

"Some type of centipede," Struugar said. "I think the cook said murinok. Once it's coated in butter, they all taste the same to me. I prefer my murinok salted and grilled, but the cooks had already steamed it and smothered it with butter. In the army, you take what you can get and be grateful for that. I tell you, some of the cooks in this warband could ruin a hardboiled egg."

Struugar chuckled at his own joke as Tovak glanced at the meat in his hand. He had always heard of how delicious murinok was, but he never imagined it could be so tasty. He'd not been able to afford such delicacies and his uncle had only shared scraps from the family's table.

"Well, don't you worry none, son," Struugar said, clapping him on the shoulder. It was more of a blow than anything else, and Tovak nearly staggered. "We'll find a home for you yet. That is, if you are still looking to join a company?"

"I am," Tovak said.

Struugar gave Tovak a knowing nod, as if he'd fully expected the answer.

"Walk with me," Struugar said. It was not a request. The captain strode off, surprising Tovak by the suddenness of the move. He had to scramble to catch up.

Struugar glanced over at him. "What are your intentions, son?"

"To serve, sir," Tovak said eagerly, stepping in beside the captain as he bit off another mouthful of meat. "And perhaps earn a bit of Legend on my own," he added around the mouthful.

"So, what was it Dagon said to you?" Struugar raised an eyebrow. The look in his gaze was suddenly intense. Tovak had the feeling the captain already knew the answer. "What reason did he give you? Come now...you can be honest with me."

Tovak started to speak, prepared to give Struugar the whole story. He'd taken an instant liking to the captain, although it could just be the offer of food that warmed him to the other. The captain seemed relaxed, almost friendly, and he had an air about him that instilled immediate trust. However, Dagon's words echoed in Tovak's ears.

You'll find that we all believe stones don't roll far from the mountain.

"It doesn't matter, sir...beyond telling me there was no place in his company for me."

Struugar got a strange look upon his face. It passed in a flash. "Dagon can be hard as granite, that one. And unforgiving...."

They walked in silence for a few yards as Tovak ate. The butter ran over his fingers and hand. He resisted the urge to wipe it on his tunic.

"I'm captain of a skirmishing company," Struugar said. "We've spent most of our time lately on foraging and hunting duty. It's not fun work, but we serve and do what we're ordered." He motioned around them at the encampment. "In truth, the Blood Badgers would go short on supply and there'd be more than a few hungry bellies were it not for foraging. We also get dangerous jobs too, depending on what Karach needs doing. If you join us, I can promise regular food, hard work, and hazardous duty when it comes to skirmishing."

Tovak felt a pang of disappointment. Foraging and hunting. Skirmishers? That meant Struugar's command wasn't even a line company, but light troops. It was a far cry from what he'd hoped for, but it was better than a labor gang.

"I won't fool you none," Struugar continued. "My boys work hard, and when I mean hard... it's hard. We typically get up well before the rest of the warband, march many miles, then we've got work that needs doing and we get to sleep an hour or two after they do. We have to move quick wherever we go, whether it's to forage or screen the main body during a march. It isn't easy, but it's honest work." He paused, sizing up Tovak. "So, what do you think?"

"I would be grateful for any opportunity to serve, sir," Tovak said. He swallowed the last of the meat Struugar had given him. He'd been turned away by Dagon, but now he was being offered a place in the skirmishers. How could he pass it up?

It would be enough. It had to be.

"How are you with weapons? Any training?" Struugar indicated the heavy blade sheathed at his right hip by tapping its hilt with the bottom of his mess bowl. "Know how to use a zjain?"

"I do, sir," Tovak said. "I was instructed in the use of the *zjain* as well as the shield. I must confess, I was much more comfortable with the longer, two-handed *volzjain*. It just feels more natural to me, sir."

Struugar gave an appreciative nod. "Well, you are a good deal taller than average, but I'm afraid you won't find many volzjains around here. And the warband only provides a basic zjain…a shield and armor too, if you join a regular infantry company and become a striker. I have some strikers in my company as well—full plate and everything. They're veterans, of course, the best of us…but most of the rest are skirmishers and issued only leather armor." He tapped his own armor. "It's a lot more comfortable and makes us a heck of a lot more mobile, which we need to be when it comes to skirmishing outside the protection of the line." He looked over at Tovak. "How does that sound? Are you certain you want to join my company, son? Once you do, I own your ass. Other companies surely have openings. You could honestly do worse."

Tovak didn't really have to think about it. His dreams of joining the pioneers were finished. The idea of foraging and hunting for food didn't sound at all appealing. But he felt a fondness for the wild-haired captain.

"I think I'd like that, sir," Tovak said, and he found himself feeling at least a small spark of hope. The spirit cards came to mind. Thulla, through Dagon, had indeed taken from him. Struugar now presented an opportunity. He sent a quick silent prayer of thanks up to the heavens.

"Fair enough," Struugar said. "I'm gonna be a lot less friendly once you are entered into the company books. Officers are officers and you're not. Understand?"

"Yes, sir."

"Good," Struugar said. "There's hope for you yet. Do you see that banner on the left?" He pointed to a banner up ahead of them. "The one with the silver baelix on it. That's my tent, and those tents just beyond are our camp."

"Baelix?" Tovak asked. He did not know what that was. He looked where Struugar was motioning and spotted the banner rising above a medium-sized tent a dozen yards off.

Struugar was leading him towards the tent. The banner was a field of blue with a silver border. At its center was the image a silver bird of prey, talons outstretched.

A guard stood outside the tent and next to the standard. He came to a position of attention and saluted as they approached.

"They're magnificent birds…from the south…small but deadly hunters," Struugar said. "I was raised on a farm, south of Garand'Durbaad….My father kept one to hunt. He used to bring down birds for the dinner table. Beautiful creatures, baelix, covered in black feathers that gleam iridescent in sunlight." Struugar abruptly blew out a breath. "But that was a long time ago." He shook his head, stopping before the flap, and then turned to the guard. "Bex," Struugar asked. "Did you get chow yet?"

"No, sir," Bex replied, still at attention.

"Well then, off you go, while it's hot," Struugar said. "I will be fine while you are away."

"Thank you, sir," Bex said, saluted, cast a curious look at Tovak, and then stepped away.

Struugar turned back to Tovak.

"Just behind my tent is our supply tent and the rest of the company area. When we're done getting you signed in, I'll have one of my lads take you to get issued with a skirmisher kit. You will be charged for that and it will come out of your pay. Anything damaged in action will be replaced at no cost. Lose anything, break it, and it too gets deducted from your pay, which happens at the end of each week. You'll be paid two yuul, seventy-two suuls a month. There are mess deductions, of course, and the contribution to the pension fund, funeral fund, and more. There won't be much left over when it's all said and done, but it's better than no pay. Sergeant Bahr will go through that with you at the first payday."

Tovak was astonished. In all the jobs he'd ever had, he'd only received a handful of copper suuls for a month's work. For a Pariah, work had been scarce, and he'd had to take what he could get. Even after all the deductions, he guessed whatever pay came into his hands would seem like a fortune.

Struugar held aside the flap and led him into the tent. A small lantern hung from the central support pole. It provided a muted but sufficient light. The interior was almost as simple as Dagon's had been. Struugar did, however, have a cot, a desk, and medium-sized trunk. There was also a small table next to the desk, with a folded gray cloth, along with a pewter platter and a clay drinking mug. A stool and a second chest sat off to the side, and a rug had been thrown over the grass. It was old, threadbare, heavily stained, and had seen better days. Struugar stepped around the small table and set down his mess bowl on the platter. He placed his helmet on the desk, then grabbed the cloth and tossed it to Tovak.

Tovak caught it, got the meaning, and wiped his hands free of butter before handing the cloth back.

"The warband's finally got its marching orders and we'll be pulling out, early. Tonight, make sure you get what sleep you can. In the morning, Lieutenant Benthok should be back. He'll assign you to a squad. Since the warband's marching, there won't be time for the basic training we normally run all recruits through. Once you're in the field, there's work to be done." Struugar's face grew hard. "Pay attention, listen to the corporals, sergeants, and, most importantly, the officers. Learn everything you can as quickly as you can. It might just keep you alive .... Benthok will take care of the rest. Now, let's get you signed in." Struugar went to the larger of the trunks, opened it, and pulled out a thick book. He placed it upon the table with a thud and opened it. A charcoal pencil lay inside, which he picked up. "Your name? I never did get it."

CHAPTER FIVE

Tovak's heart skipped a beat, and he became still. Should he tell the truth? Should he do as Dagon suggested and make up a name? Heck, he'd already decided he would. But something caused him to hesitate. What would Struugar do if he knew the truth?

"Well?" Struugar asked, looking up. "Durpa got your tongue?"

Tovak cleared his throat.

"Tovak ...." he said. "Tovak ... Ironhammer."

He'd known an elderly beggar by that name and it sort of slipped out. Tovak had suspected the beggar had made the name up. At least there was a "hammer" in it, he thought. For so long, he'd been ashamed of his father's name, but it was the only thing that remained of his childhood, other than mostly bad memories. He had long since come to hate everything the name Stonehammer represented. But the son inside him still yearned for those earlier days of precious happiness ... before everything had been torn asunder.

Tovak sucked in a breath as he gazed upon the captain, with his pencil poised above the book. It was done, and he felt a strange sense of relief to put the family name behind him and start afresh. Why had he not done it sooner?

Struugar stiffened a fraction and then he expelled a long breath, setting the pencil back down on the book. One moment, he'd been kindly, even pleased to have Tovak join the company. He looked as if a heavy weight had settled upon his shoulders, and Tovak feared he had made a mistake. Did Struugar know? Had Dagon or Beghan told him? Was it all about to be taken away? Again?

"Tovak...Ironhammer, you say?" Struugar said slowly. He cast his eyes down to the book. "That's a strong name," he added, but his tone didn't match the words. "I don't think I'm familiar with the Ironhammers." He looked thoughtful for a moment. "You know, now that I think on it, the name reminds me of someone I once knew ...." He rubbed his jaw and turned his gaze towards the top of the tent for a moment. Then his eyes settled back upon Tovak. "This would have been long before you were born. I'd just signed up with a warband and was eager to build my Legend, very much like you," he added, glancing at Tovak. "We were at war with the Syrulians." The captain paused, his gaze becoming distant before refocusing on Tovak. "Anyway, I was a grunt and my company had been ambushed by infantry, supported by archers."

Tovak listened. As a child, he'd always enjoyed hearing about his father's war stories.

"We were in a narrow canyon," Struugar continued. "They had a few dozen archers waiting amongst the rocks, backed up by infantry. We lost half the company before we knew what was happening, including our officers and all four of the sergeants. A good number were wounded. I'd taken an arrow, myself. The damned thing punched right through my armor." He patted his chest where he'd been wounded. "We were done. There was simply no hope. I fully expected all of us to die right then and there." Struugar fell silent for a moment, as if lost in his thoughts. "And then, a voice rose above the noise of the fight. A warrior stepped forward and took charge, a grunt like me, only better than the rest of us, fearless even. To this day, I remember hearing him shout those two words as if it were yesterday. Do you know what he said?"

"No, sir," Tovak said in a near whisper.

"On me." Struugar shook his head. "I don't know. Maybe it was the way he said it, but there was confidence there. He rallied us, pulled a shattered and desperate company together. He wasn't an officer, not yet anyway. But he took charge, like he'd been born for that moment."

Tovak could imagine the warrior doing it. He wished he'd seen it, for it must have been glorious. He only wished he could be so brave in such a desperate situation.

"He ordered us to form a wedge. And as the humans closed to finish us, he raised his volzjain and pushed us forward. He started singing."

"He was singing?" Tovak was astonished by this. It was like the captain had lived through a bard's magical tale of a hero saving the day.

"A marching song…the 'Battle Hymn of Jun Rugall.' Well, I was right there with him, and as our wedge pushed forward into the enemy, we shouted that song at the tops of our lungs." Struugar raised proud, fierce eyes, looking straight at Tovak. "We drove that wedge straight into their line, tearing those bastards apart like berserkers." Struugar paused. "He was fearless, and it infected the rest of us….We fought, and we bled them. Because of that warrior, we refused to give, refused to yield, and we cut them down like wheat during the harvest. The humans broke, scrambling to get up the steep canyon walls and away from us. We killed many…many that day."

"That sounds glorious," Tovak breathed.

"Glorious?" Struugar asked in a near whisper. "No. There was nothing glorious about that day. It was kill or be killed and it was ugly business. We lost a lot of good boys."

Tovak felt slightly rebuked, but still it was a tale fit for a hero.

"The warrior?" Tovak asked. "Was it Karach?"

"No, Tovak. It wasn't the warchief, but I think you know the name as well as you know your own." Struugar moved around the table and placed his hand on Tovak's shoulder. "The warrior who rallied us, who saved all of our lives and gave us not only the direction, but the will to win, to fight back ... was Graybor Stonehammer. I owe him my life. So do a number of other lads too."

"What?" Tovak gasped, going cold. Struugar knew.

"You look just like him, you know," Struugar said. "He was your age when he joined. You sound like him too." He searched Tovak's eyes. "It's a pity you're ashamed to take his name, Pariah or not."

A wave of guilt and shame erupted inside Tovak's heart, and he struggled to force it back down, before it overwhelmed him.

"Ashamed?" Tovak said. "Of course I'm ashamed." He stared at Struugar. "He got all of those people killed and his entire company wiped out. He was a coward and a fool and I hate him for what he did to my mother and me .... Forgive me, sir, but you don't know what you're talking about."

"Is that what your uncle told you?"

"It's what everyone told me," Tovak said bitterly, "for as long as I can remember."

Struugar locked eyes with Tovak. There was a hardness in the captain's gaze. Struugar had not moved, but he suddenly appeared taller, more imposing.

"It would seem," Struugar said slowly, a deeply troubled look on his face, "that I know a good deal more about him than you do…."

Tovak said nothing.

Struugar's shoulders sagged slightly, as if some of the life had been let out of him. His face told of defeat or perhaps a failure, as if Tovak's anguish was, somehow, his fault.

"You don't know what it was like," Tovak finally said, quietly. "You couldn't possibly understand what it's like to be a Pariah." Tovak stepped back and turned away from Struugar. He fought the tears of frustration that threatened to pour down his cheeks. "After my mother… after she took her life, my uncle took me in. I was less than a slave to him, no more than a dog to be kicked and given only enough scraps to keep me alive and fit enough to do the work he loaned me out for. It felt like there wasn't a person in Garand'Durbaad who didn't know the name Stonehammer or Barasoom or that I was the one Stonehammer left alive to blame for it all. There was only one person in the whole of the city who showed me any kindness…a priest…and with his help, I managed to survive. Do you know how many times I almost gave up? If it hadn't been for the kindness of Father Danik, I would have killed myself… or one of my tormentors, which would have amounted to the same thing. The authorities would have happily ended my existence."

"You're right," Struugar said softly. "I haven't the slightest idea what you've endured all these years. I couldn't even guess, considering how our people treat with…well, with people in your circumstances."

"The word you want is 'Pariah' and it was my father who branded me with it. It's who I am."

Struugar's lips pressed down into a thin line. "The ways of our people are hard sometimes, even unfair, and far too many of us turn a cold shoulder to the suffering of others. Tovak, I won't tell you that I could possibly understand what happened after your parents were gone. It's not my place, and it would be both a lie and an insult…to you and them. What I can tell you is what I know about your father and his character."

"Don't you see?" Tovak said. "It doesn't matter what you know about him. Barasoom happened." He felt the old rage building again. He took a calming breath and asked Thulla for strength. He didn't want to lose this opportunity, but in truth, he suspected he already had. He stared at Struugar, his heart aching. "People died, and my father was blamed for it all." He shook his head, wishing he could change the past. "I'm ashamed to be his son, sir, and rightly I should be. It was all his fault."

"That may be," Struugar said. "But I will tell you, I never believed, not for one moment, that Graybor Stonehammer failed his company. I served with him for nearly ten years, and in that time, doing what we do here in the warband, you get to know someone. The Dvergr I knew was not a coward. He saved my life several times over."

"I don't understand," Tovak said. "There were survivors, warriors from his own company. They told what happened."

"Aye," Struugar said. "There were and I wasn't there. I suppose I owe you an apology…maybe a lot of us do for how you've been treated." Struugar rubbed his jaw. "There were many of us who didn't believe a word of the story that came back with the survivors."

"Then why didn't you do something?" Tovak's words were full of hurt and even a hint of accusation.

"We had no proof," Struugar said, holding up his hands.

Tovak stared down at his feet, thinking furiously. "And the eyewitnesses swore upon their Legend, didn't they?"

Struugar gave a nod, which shook his beard.

"Then it could all be true," Tovak said, "that he was a coward."

"Aye," Struugar said. "It could be. But if that were true, it wasn't the leader I knew." Struugar paused. "I should have checked in on you. I owed it to your father. I didn't even learn that your mother had taken her own life until almost a year later. I understood your uncle took you in. I thought you were in good hands."

"Why are you telling me all this?" Tovak asked. "It's not as if it's going to make any difference to me now … or tomorrow … or next year."

"Who knows what the future holds for you, Tovak? You made it this far, even graduated the Academy. I think you are the first Pariah to manage that, which is damn impressive. If you want, you can be part of my company. There will be ample time and opportunity for you to earn Legend of your own." Struugar gave Tovak's shoulder a squeeze. "I guess what I'm saying is that you should be proud of who you are and find it in yourself to be proud of who your father was. He was the bravest warrior I've ever known, and if I were you, I wouldn't let anyone say otherwise."

"Proud of being a Pariah? I wish it was that simple," Tovak said. "But you have given me a great deal to think about." His feelings were all mixed-up. Confusion? Hope? Anger? They were all there in abundance.

"Indeed, I have," Struugar said. "I know it's hard, but one way or another you'll have to come to terms with all of this … in time. For now, I'll list you with the company as just Tovak, with no clan name or with if you prefer. It is your choice. That's assuming you still want to join, after all this."

Tovak paused for a moment. It was all out in the open, at least with Struugar. Here, at last, was a fresh start, what he'd been looking for. Maybe with the Baelix Guard, he could finally put the stigma of Pariah behind him. Then something occurred to him.

"You knew I was coming," Tovak said. "You weren't just looking for a recruit and you did not run into Beghan in the mess, did you?"

Struugar's eyes narrowed. He shook his head.

"How?" Tovak asked. "How did you know?"

"Duroth sent word," Struugar said, "shortly after you arrived in camp."

"Duroth? I don't understand."

"In that pass," Struugar said, "it wasn't just me that your father saved."

Tovak suddenly felt badly for how he'd thought of Duroth and why the teamster had granted him passage. One day, if there was an opportunity, he would make a point of thanking the cantankerous teamster.

"Thank you, sir," Tovak said. "I do wish to join your company. That is, if you will still have me?"

"Good," Struugar said. "And what name should I enter into the books?"

"Ironhammer," Tovak said.

Struugar gave a nod. He made the entry in the book on the table and then moved over to return it back to the chest. He closed it with a snap. Turning back to Tovak, he said, "Don't be surprised if your real name comes out. There were others on that yuggernok."

"I understand," Tovak said. "Thank you for the opportunity, sir."

"Tomorrow is a new day, son, and knowing who your father was, I'm expecting great things from you."

"Yes, sir."

"Let me call for one of my boys, and we'll get you squared away with your kit. Once you have it, turn in for the night."

"Yes, sir," Tovak said. "And thank you again for letting me join your company, sir … and everything you've told me. I won't let you down."

"I expect not," Struugar replied with a stern eye.

"Captain?" a gruff voice called from just outside the tent.

"Enter," Struugar called out.

The flap was pulled aside, and an older Dvergr stepped in, stood to attention, and saluted. He had a bald head and iron and white streaks through his gray beard. He wore a service tunic, with a blue cloak draped around his shoulders to fend off the chilly night air. He glanced over at Tovak and then returned his attention back to Struugar.

"I'm sorry, sir, I didn't mean to interrupt."

"You didn't, Sergeant," Struugar assured him. "What is it?"

"A crate was delivered to the supply tent in your name, sir," he said. "It came by way of that scoundrel you know. Duroth sent one of his boys over with it. Said it was only to be opened by you."

"Good," Struugar said. "I will fetch it later. We were just finishing up, and you, Sergeant, have great timing."

"Yes, sir," the sergeant said, with another glance thrown to Tovak.

"Sergeant Bahr, this is Recruit Tovak, and I've just entered him into the books. Get him set up with a skirmisher's kit and show him where to bed down tonight. I'll see that Benthok collects him in the morning."

"Yes, Captain," Bahr said, with another glance over at Tovak. "Are we still pulling out in the morning, sir?"

"I stopped by headquarters. Nothing has changed," Struugar replied. "Now, I have some work to do. Both of you are dismissed."

Bahr gave a salute, then turned to Tovak. "It's customary to salute an officer."

Tovak got the hint, snapped to attention, and saluted as he'd been taught at the Academy.

Struugar waved them both away.

"Follow me," Bahr said, pulling the tent flap aside. He stepped out into the night and moved to the left with Tovak close behind.

They made their way back behind Struugar's tent, where the supply tent stood. It was twice the size of the captain's, and as they passed it, the rest of the Baelix Guard camp came into view. There were four rows of communal tents about the size of Struugar's. A wide alley ran between the tents, with several campfires. Many of the tent flaps were open, and warriors in simple tunics and leggings moved about or sat around the fires. There was the hum of conversation on the air, mixed occasionally with the harsh bark of laughter.

To the left and right of the Baelix Guard encampment were other company encampments, laid out in the same manner. The reality of it struck Tovak hard, and a thrill coursed through him. He was in the camp of the Baelix Guard...his company. For a moment, he allowed himself to revel in a genuine sense of accomplishment. Despite the pain of Dagon's rebuke, Tovak realized he had taken the first real step towards his dream. He had joined a company attached to the warband. They weren't the pioneers, but it was here he had a chance to earn Legend and leave behind his past.

Sergeant Bahr had disappeared around the corner of the supply tent. As Tovak moved forward to follow, he spotted something familiar just outside the tent that stopped him. Sitting there, in the grass beside the tent, was the crate he'd used as a table back on the yuggernok. It was unopened and marked, "Deliver to Captain Struugar Ironfist of the Baelix Guard." He couldn't believe his eyes.

The very idea that he and the crate had, somehow, been destined for the same company was a strange coincidence that left him marveling at the mysterious ways of Thulla. Was it destiny? Had the great god been trying to tell him something? He couldn't see any other answer.

"Quit gawking and get your ass over here, boffer," Bahr said from inside the supply tent. "I don't have all night."

Embarrassed, Tovak stepped around to the front of the tent, where a pair of torches illuminated the area. Inside the tent, sacks, barrels, chests, and stacks of gear were neatly arranged on all three sides. There was a small table just outside the tent, and a thick tome sat upon it, with columns and rows of information scrawled in a hasty but precise hand.

Bahr's eyes narrowed a bit. "You best get that gawking out of your system in a hurry, boy. Ain't none in the company gets time to just stand about enjoying the sights," he said in a surly tone. "Now, let's get you kitted out. It's already bloody late as it is. Just my dumb luck a recruit would come in after hours." He looked Tovak up and down once again, sizing him up slowly. His eyes came to rest on Tovak's feet, waist, shoulders, and head. "Those boots new?" Bahr finally asked.

"Yes, sir," Tovak said. "I bought them just before leaving Garand'Durbaad. They almost cleaned me out, but they were worth it."

"Well then, you won't be needing no boots," Bahr said matter-of-factly. "And don't call me sir. That's bloody annoying. You should have better sense. I work for a living. Do it again and I'll put you on report."

"Yes, Sergeant," Tovak said.

Bahr turned away and began searching through a stack of blue leather chest plates, and then grabbed one. He tossed it to Tovak, who barely caught it in time.

"Try that on," Bahr said. "It looks your size. You'll want to leave the tunic on underneath. The last thing you want is blistering, especially on a long march. That leather is boiled, hard as bone, and will rub you raw in a hurry."

Tovak did as he was told. He pulled off his bedroll and pack, making sure to put his Warrant back inside, and then he slipped the chest plate on. It settled on his shoulders. He shrugged to get a better fit, then began buckling the armor up, tightening the straps. The armor was clearly new and fit better than what he'd worn during training back at the Academy. It was also a little lighter, with a collar that left him plenty of room to move without cutting into his neck.

"Here," Bahr said and tossed a pair of bracers, strapped together. Tovak grabbed them out of the air. A set of greaves followed. He grabbed those too and set the greaves on the ground at his feet. The bracers were as hard as the chest plate, and their smooth, plain surfaces gleamed under the torchlight. As Bahr continued moving around inside the tent, Tovak put the bracers on and cinched them up so they were tight, but comfortable. The greaves went on next.

Bahr returned once again, this time holding a battered steel helm under his arm, a standard military pack in one hand, and a wide leather belt and sword in scabbard in the other. He had a blue cloak thrown over his shoulder. He handed the belt over first, and Tovak quickly put it on, setting the sheathed sword over his left hip and securing it to the belt. Then came the bowl-like helm, which he set upon his head. It was a little loose, but once the straps were tied tight, it would likely be snug.

"Don't bother putting this on," Bahr said, setting the pack at Tovak's feet. "You know how to use one?" he asked.

Dvergr backpacks were made of a light metal frame with a leather pack wrapped around it. The whole thing was secured with two long straps of metal with hooks on the upper ends that then went over the soldier's shoulders and locked into metal clips attached to the breastplate, just in front of the shoulder. The warrior's bedroll was secured underneath with leather straps. Once secured in place, the whole pack was effectively locked into position. It was bulky but allowed a warrior to carry a lot of gear over a long distance.

"I've worn one before."

"Good," Bahr replied as he stepped over to the table. "Perhaps you won't be as useless as you look. The lieutenant should be pleased."

"Benthok?" Tovak asked.

"That's Lieutenant to you," Bahr said, "and you better get used to using it or the lieutenant will have your balls for breakfast."

Bahr made several notes in the ledger and then went into the tent again. When he returned, he had a crate full of equipment. "Here's the rest of your gear. Put these things in the pack as I hand them to you … and try to remember the order. They work better if you put them in there the right way the first time. Your corporal, whoever has that sorry duty, will go over this again with you. Best learn it now, eh?"

"Yes, Sergeant."

"Fifty feet of rope, a small oil lamp, a torch head, and one flask of oil." Bahr handed them over, and Tovak slipped them into the pack, doing his best to arrange them neatly. "A cooking pot, a sewing kit, a leather cleaning kit, one whetstone, a knife for eating, two slings, two pouches of lead shot—one solid and one full of whistlers—a flask of vinegar." Bahr paused and looked up. "Don't use the vinegar for cooking. It's for treating wounds."

"Yes, Sergeant," Tovak said.

"Bandages, a metal mug, two jars of durpa fat for weatherproofing your cloak when needed, two empty waterskins, a leather haversack, and room for whatever you have in that old pack. Your entrenchment tool goes on the outside, held in place with those straps. And keep that sorry-looking blanket of yours too. It should roll up easy enough with the bedroll there and the two blankets inside. Three blankets are better than two, especially on cold nights, understand?"

"Yes, Sergeant." Tovak slipped everything inside.

"You are responsible for this gear. Anything you lose comes out of your pay. Understand?"

"Yes," Tovak said.

"Yes, what?" Bahr asked with a sharp edge.

"Yes, Sergeant," Tovak said. In less than a quarter hour, he had been given more possessions to keep track of than he'd ever had. It was a bit overwhelming, but in a strange sort of way, there was a certain comfort in all the gear. So long as he was with the warband, he wouldn't have to go without the things he needed to get by each day.

Bahr made another notation in the ledger and then pointed at the hilt of Tovak's new blade. "That zjain I've issued is used but serviceable. We'll replace it if it's broken in combat. You might want to start thinking some on getting a better one you can call your own. A good zjain will run you about seven yuul at any of the honest blacksmiths in camp. When it comes time, I recommend Jugon Foerge. He will sell you a good sword and not pauper you. Return that blade to me for the next recruit, if you get a new one, that is, and don't waste all your pay on drink. Oh, I almost forgot.

Grab one of those spears beside the tent and take it with you when you go. You're responsible for that too."

Bahr paused and looked him over. He ran a hand through his beard.

"And now for the last bit," he added, his surly manner abruptly replaced by just a hint of pride. "This here is my favorite part." He pulled the cloak off his shoulder, stepped forward, and almost reverently placed it around Tovak's. The plain, deep blue material was a soft wool that didn't scratch his skin. It was, without a doubt, the nicest cloak he'd ever owned. Bahr then pulled a silver cloak pin from his waistband and secured it in place over Tovak's right breast. The silver bird of prey glinted in the firelight, and Tovak found himself smiling at the sight of it. "Welcome to the Baelix Guard," Bahr said, the surly tone returning. "If you ever need anything, even if it's just someone to talk to, don't come find me."

"Thank you, Sergeant," Tovak said.

"I'm just doing my job," Bahr said. "You at least look presentable now."

Tovak glanced down at his new armor and the heavy cloak that was quickly warming him up. He held out his arms as he took it all in. He was a skirmisher with the Baelix Guard. A feeling of belonging he'd not felt for a long time washed over him. He had a place again.

"Now, fill up those waterskins, boy," Bahr said, the surly tone returning. "There are a couple of water barrels right around the corner there. And fill them every opportunity you get, especially while marching. You never know when you'll get another chance. Despite the added weight, it's better to have a full skin than an empty one."

"Yes, Sergeant," Tovak said. He opened his pack, pulled out the skins, and moved around where he found two tapped water barrels sitting on low stools. He filled one skin and then the other, corking them both. When he returned, he found Bahr standing there, a bored expression on his face.

"There should be room for your bedroll back there by that last fire," Bahr said. "Didn't know we'd be getting a recruit tonight, otherwise I would have had a tent pitched. We have one other without a tent. I'll have you situated the next time you come into the main camp." He glanced up towards the sky. "It may get cold, but at least it doesn't look like it's going to rain."

"Yes, Sergeant," Tovak replied.

Bahr nodded. "The latrines are that way. As long as you can smell them, you are headed in the right direction." He suddenly turned and called out to a passing warrior. "Morda."

"Yes, Sergeant?" Morda asked, stepping over to them. He was half a head shorter than Tovak, with thick brown hair that was cut shoulder-length. His beard was tied into a single tight braid. He wore only his service tunic and leather leggings dyed a dark black.

"This is Tovak. He's a new recruit. Take him back to the last fire and have him bed down next to that other recruit... you know, the one we got in one week ago. What's his name again?"

"Gorabor?" Morda offered.

"Right, Gorabor," Bahr said. "Take him back there."

"Yes, Sergeant," Morda said and turned to Tovak, sounding less than thrilled. "Come on. Follow me."

Tovak picked up his pack and slung it over his shoulder. He grabbed his spear and followed Morda down the alley past the tents and campfires. He realized that the armor, weapons, and equipment were heavier than what he'd become accustomed to at the Academy. It wasn't more than he could handle by any stretch.

As he passed by, the warriors who had not retired mostly ignored them. A few looked up with mild curiosity, but said nothing and returned to what they'd been doing. A good number were busy cleaning their kit.

Morda stopped beside the last campfire, an impatient expression on his face, where a single bedroll was already laid out. A pack, spear, and a set of armor lay on the grass beside it, but there was no sign of the warrior they belonged to.

"You bed down here," Morda said, pointing at the ground. "The latrines are back there," he added, motioning towards the rear of the last tents. "If you need anything else, I have every confidence you can figure it out on your own." And then he walked away, headed back the way he'd come.

Tovak felt a little awkward just standing there, staring at Morda's back. He caught a few of the warriors at a nearby fire looking at him, but they said nothing. When they turned their eyes away, he could see them talking to each other in hushed tones, and he thought he picked up the words "fresh meat."

He took a deep breath and let it out slowly. At least they didn't know who he was. He set his spear down in the grass and then removed his pack, laying it beside the spear.

"New recruit?" a voice called from behind him.

Tovak turned to see a smallish Dvergr with pale blond hair that had been cropped close. He had kind eyes of green and wore his beard with a half-dozen braids running down from his jawline, each one tied off with a leather cord. He appeared to be Tovak's age.

"Yes," Tovak replied. "I just joined."

"I'm Gorabor," he said and held out a hand. "Got here a few days back, myself."

"Tovak...and thanks." Tovak shook and found the other's grip firm.

"It's a lot, isn't it?" Gorabor asked as he sat down on his bedroll. He held his hands out to the fire, warming them. "When you first get here, I mean."

Tovak nodded. "It is, but I've dreamed about this for as long as I can remember."

"So did I. It's not at all what I thought it would be," Gorabor said and stifled a yawn. "It's mostly backbreaking work and lots of marching." He yawned again, this time not able to stifle it. "Look, they'll be sounding the horn soon. You better get set up and ready for sleep." Gorabor paused. "A word of warning...unless you have a good reason, they don't take kindly to excuses, especially the lieutenant."

"A hard one?" Tovak asked.

"Benthok's the hardest," Gorabor replied in a serious tone. "Like cold granite in winter. He's a real mean bastard. But he knows what he's doing—at least that's what the veterans say. I heard other companies don't have it so good. Their officers don't know one hand from the other, if you take my meaning."

Tovak said nothing as he set his pack down.

Gorabor yawned.

"It's been a really long day," Gorabor said. "We marched all the way back to the warband from our forage camp in the hills. Then Sergeant Kelloth got the brilliant idea into his head it would be a good idea to work on arms training. I'm beat. I will see you in the morning. We can talk more then." Gorabor rolled over onto his side, away from the fire, and pulled his blanket up.

Tovak undid his bedroll and laid it out near enough to the fire to stay warm without getting too hot. There were two thick blankets inside, as Bahr had said. Tovak laid them atop the bedroll. Several cut logs lay stacked next to the fire. He threw on another piece of wood for good measure.

Opening his pack, he peeked inside and looked at his skirmisher kit…it was all his. He set the pack aside, then pulled off his cloak and carefully rolled it up into a pillow, a softer one than he was accustomed to.

He set the cloak pin beside it, the silver baelix glinting at him in the firelight. Standing, he pulled off his armor one piece at a time and laid it almost reverently next to the pack. It too was his and he'd take good care of it. Gazing down at it, Tovak was suddenly reminded of his grandfather's armor. He could still see it on display in his family's home. The intricately etched breastplate had always fascinated him as a child.

Tovak pushed that memory aside as he lay down next to Gorabor, who was already snoring softly. Tovak pulled both blankets over him and rolled onto his side, staring into the fire. There was so much running through his head, he almost couldn't think straight. He took a deep breath and let it out slowly as a wave of exhaustion crashed over him. It had been both a trying and exhilarating day, and his conversation with Struugar had left him bewildered about what he should or shouldn't think about his father.

He wondered who the survivors had been. A horn sounded.

"That's ten horns," a voice shouted nearby. "Time for bed, children."

Tovak could hear other shouts across the camp as sergeants and corporals, like mother hens, set about putting their companies to bed. Tovak lifted his head to see Bahr standing by a fire, hands on his hips.

"Hit the sack and get some sleep," Bahr said. "Don't make me have to hand out any punishment charges.

Besides, we're pulling out in the morning and you all know what tomorrow's gonna bring."

"A ride with you in a supply wagon, Sarge?" a voice called out.

There was a round of laughter at that.

"That's right," Bahr replied. "I'll be thinking of you, my children, while you're marchin' off to foraging duty. Now go to bloody sleep and stop bothering old Mother Bahr."

"Will you read me a bedtime story, Mother Bahr?" someone called out from inside one of the tents Bahr gave a disgusted grunt and stomped back towards his supply tent.

Tovak rolled onto his back and stared up at the sky. He pondered the events of the day, and a sense of gratitude washed over him, a feeling he had not felt in a very long time. There was the kindness of Struugar, both for letting him join the Baelix Guard and for giving him so much to think about regarding his father. He'd been trapped for so long by his shame and anger that he wasn't sure how to move forward without it. He ran a finger over the silver baelix pin beside his head one more time, and a sense of pride flowed through him. And above it all, he had his place in the Great March. His days as a Pariah were finally over. He would be able to serve his people.

He closed his eyes and offered his heartfelt thanks to Thulla for the opportunity to build his Legend. As he drifted off to sleep, he found himself struggling with Struugar's view of his father. He felt a stab of anger. It passed as a wave of exhaustion rolled over him. He would keep moving forward, one foot in front of the other, and build his Legend. Perhaps once he had achieved that goal, he would be in a better position to seek out the mysteries of Barasoom.

With that, he faded off to sleep.

CHAPTER SIX

"On your feet, you lazy durpas," a gruff voice called out from the darkness. "Even though the sun's not up yet, I can just tell it's gonna be another wonderful day. Sunshine and roses. Come on, you layabouts, get off your asses and on your feet."

The words broke Tovak out of a deep sleep, the deepest he'd had for a long time. He had drool on his cheek. Blinking, he wiped it away with the back of his hand. Groans sounded from all around as others dragged themselves out of sleep. A bright half-moon shone down from a cloudless, starry sky. Tovak rubbed at his eyes. The sun wasn't even up yet.

He glanced over and saw no sign of Gorabor, save for a flattened area of grass where his bedroll and pack had been. Someone nearby in the darkness coughed, hawked, and spit. A few hushed voices and movement sounded from the nearest tents.

Most of the camp beyond the company area, however, seemed quiet. It was clear the rest of the warband still slumbered. He climbed to his feet, rolled up his blankets, and secured his bedroll to the pack. As he tied it off, several warriors walked by, headed towards the latrines. Tovak realized that he had to piss, so he followed them—and his nose—to a trench dug into the ground ten feet behind the last tent. He relieved himself as wordlessly as the four warriors who stood there, and then went back to where his equipment lay.

In the darkness it took him a few minutes to get his armor back on. He saw a flare of light as someone lit a torch. The night air was cold. He shivered, for the fire had died down to embers and no longer generated any heat. Satisfied that his armor was on right, he knelt in front of his pack and placed his hands on the bulge that was *Thulla's Blessed Word* within. He closed his eyes and whispered the same words he repeated every morning.

"Thank you, Thulla, for the opportunities of a new day. Blessed are those who follow your word. Blessed are they who will carry the light to your people with every breath. I am and ever will be your humble servant, 'til that solemn day when I return to your breast and stand in the glory of your magnificence."

"What was that?" the gruff voice that had awakened him asked from behind.

Startled, Tovak turned to find a short, stout officer with a salt-and-pepper beard. He stood a few feet off, peering down where Tovak knelt. There was a hardness to his squinting eyes that bespoke irritation. The officer had the appearance of a person wholly without humor, one who did not tolerate fools or perhaps even believers. Tovak found the officer's gaze unsettling.

He stood and snapped to attention.

The officer's beard had braids coming down from the ends of a bushy mustache. He wore a light leather breastplate with silver engraving, indicating he was a lieutenant, as well as bracers and greaves that looked well-used, yet maintained. His helm, tucked under his arm, was a dark metal with a pointed nose guard. The hilt of a sword poked up from a thick, silver-threaded belt at his waist, with a matching dagger sheathed on the other side.

"I asked you a question, soldier," the officer hissed, taking a step nearer. "What was that you were doing just now?"

"Nothing, sir," Tovak replied. "I was getting my kit ready."

"It did not sound like nothing."

Tovak decided to remain silent, as the officer had not asked him a direct question.

"Recruit, I'm your lieutenant. You report to me." He gave Tovak a once-over. The look on his face said that he wasn't all that pleased with what he took in. "Do you understand me?"

"I do, sir," Tovak replied, suddenly remembering what Struugar had told him last night. He realized that this must be Lieutenant Benthok.

"Think you can manage grabbing your gear and following me?" Benthok asked. "Or will you require written instructions?"

Tovak blinked. "Yes, sir. I, uh, mean no, sir?"

"Which is it, recruit? Can you follow or do I need to lay down a trail of breadcrumbs? Well, speak up."

"I can follow, sir," Tovak said.

"Right, let's go." Benthok abruptly turned his back on Tovak and started off towards the supply tent.

Tovak threw his pack over his shoulders, hooking the brackets into the metal clips of his armor. He donned his helmet, then checked that his sword was properly secured. Satisfied, he picked up the spear and then hurried after the lieutenant.

The rest of the company area was a hive of activity as warriors emerged from the communal tents. One set to work at one of the fires, which had died down to embers. He tossed several fresh pieces of wood on. It caused a spray of sparks to leap into the air. Several warriors just beyond were pulling their armor on or checking equipment. Tovak realized they'd risen early, before the lieutenant had woken the rest of the company.

No one spared Tovak any attention, but he did notice several eyes warily track the lieutenant as he passed. Despite Benthok's shorter legs, Tovak found he had to hurry to keep up, for the lieutenant set a brisk pace.

As they approached the supply tent, he saw a line of warriors had already begun forming. Sergeant Bahr was handing out small bundles wrapped in a rough-woven cloth.

Benthok moved to the head of the line and held out his hand.

"Good morning, Lieutenant," Bahr greeted cheerfully as he handed one of the bundles over. There was a sly grin to the sergeant's face. "I trust you slept well."

"Hardly," Benthok replied, apparently not noticing Bahr's expression. "I was roped into a patrol with the First. Got back into camp less than an hour ago."

"No sleep for the wicked then, eh, sir?" Bahr asked, his eyes flicking to Tovak.

"Apparently not." Benthok tossed the bundle to Tovak, who caught it. "To be eaten on the march today, not before."

"Yes, sir." Tovak looked inside and saw three small loaves of *buurl*, still warm from the cooking oven. Once they cooled, the bread would harden. The tough, tasteless gray loaves, frequently laced with bits of whatever dried meat had been on hand, would last for days before spoiling. They looked and felt very much like the river stones they were named after.

"I see you found our newest wet-behind-the-ears recruit," Bahr said.

"I did." The lieutenant was moving again, leaving the sergeant and Tovak behind.

"Better get after him, boy." Bahr jerked his head.

Tovak set off after the lieutenant, rounding the corner of the supply tent, only to find Benthok had stopped.

"Leave your pack and spear right there and put that hard bread in your haversack," Benthok ordered, pointing to the ground beside the supply tent. There was another pack and spear already on the ground. Tovak did as instructed. Benthok waited until he had finished, then started off again. Tovak rushed to catch up.

Gorabor was waiting on the back side of the tent. He stiffened to attention at the sight of the lieutenant as they rounded the corner. Gorabor saluted. Benthok did not bother to respond, other than to put his hands upon his hips and come to a stop.

"Gorabor already knows this," Benthok said, "or at least I thought he did."

"Sorry, sir," Gorabor said, his eyes flicking to Tovak in embarrassment. "I got turned around, sir."

"No excuses," Benthok hissed, with evident irritation. "No matter where the warband is, the encampment is always set up the same."

"Yes, sir," Gorabor said.

"So," Benthok said. "Since I made the mistake of assuming Gorabor knew his way to the mess and back, I will march you both down there. Between the two of you, one of you should remember the way. So, pay bloody attention."

"Yes, sir," Gorabor said.

"Ah, yes, sir," Tovak said, not quite sure what was being required of him.

"Every morning we're in the main camp," the lieutenant said, "you both will have a job. Gorabor's already had it. Like a dumb durpa, he's managed to screw it up. You both"—Benthok stressed the word both—"will go to the cooking mess assigned to our company. Follow me so far?"

"Yes, sir," Tovak said.

"Yes, sir," Gorabor said.

"Good," the lieutenant said. "You will fetch the company's breakfast, our morning rations. Then you will come right back here and distribute the rations to the company. Am I understood?"

"Yes, sir," Tovak said, wondering what breakfast would be. He hoped it was eggs and some pork. His stomach gave an eager rumble at that thought.

"When the warband marches, like today, we get issued dodders of some kind." Benthok looked over at Tovak. "You know what those are, right?"

"Pieces of fruit, vegetables, or meat in a batter that is then fried in hot animal fat," Tovak replied.

"You are not as dumb as you look. It's what I like to call 'breakfast of the victorious,'" Benthok said, then his gaze became suddenly intense, as if he had just thought of something. "The note the captain left for me says you want to be a pioneer." It was not a question.

"That's correct, sir," Tovak said.

"The skirmishers not good enough for you, recruit?" Benthok asked.

"Yes, sir…ah, I mean no, sir," Tovak said hastily, concerned he might have caused offense. It was his turn to feel embarrassed now. He felt his face flush with heat. "It's been a dream of mine for as long as I can remember."

Benthok gave a grunt.

"Half of the company dreams of being pioneers," Benthok said, glancing over at Gorabor with a sour expression. "Even this fool. Yet, incredibly he can't even seem to find his way to the mess without getting lost. Bloody idiot."

Tovak said nothing but glanced over at Gorabor, who almost quaked under the lieutenant's unforgiving gaze.

"The skirmishers are not a bad place to start," Benthok said, turning back to Tovak. "We do a lot of the same things the pioneers do and as a result they draw heavily from our ranks."

Tovak suddenly felt a surge of hope. Then he remembered his interview with Dagon. Second Pioneers was out. Dagon had made his feelings plain. Would First take him, if he proved himself? Would they accept a Pariah into their ranks?

"Regardless of what you want to be, you will learn to be a skirmisher first," Benthok said, poking a stubby index finger into Tovak's chest armor. "With the warband about to move, there will be no time for our standard basic training. You will have to learn as we go. Once we're in the field, I'll work you 'til you're ready to drop. Everybody thinks they can be a pioneer, but if you can't make it in the skirmishers, then you definitely won't cut it in the pioneers. You get me, boy?"

"I understand, sir," Tovak said quietly. "I will do my best."

"Your best likely won't be enough for me," Benthok said, and then turned and started walking again. "Follow me and pay attention so you learn the way to the mess."

Benthok said no more and led them through the darkened camp, weaving his way through the veritable maze of tents. Tovak did his best to pay attention. Few torches were still lit and even fewer fires. He could easily see how Gorabor could have gotten lost, especially at night. Tovak could smell food on the air, long before they arrived at the nearest of the cooking pavilions, where a line of warriors stood twelve deep. His stomach rumbled again.

The lieutenant stopped before the line and surveyed it for a long moment. An older cook with a severe expression handed a large cloth bag over to a warrior at the head of the line. Beside the cook stood an assistant with a tablet and stylus. Several cooks worked around a number of large pots of boiling oil, stirring with large sticks. The cook fires lit the area and the massed heat drove back the morning chill. They were clearly making dodders, for one was using a pair of tongs to pluck the sizzling balls from a pot and place them, still steaming, into a canvas sack at his feet.

"When they ask, tell them you need four bags for the Baelix Guard, and then you return. I have to go and speak with the captain. Think you can find your way back?"

Gorabor hesitated, which caused a scowl to form on the lieutenant's face.

"I believe so, sir," Tovak said.

"No dawdling, then," Benthok said. "When you get back, the company should be formed up. You issue one ration to each warrior and move on down the line until you're done. Then take one for yourself. Give whatever is left, including the sacks, to Sergeant Bahr. Don't screw this up, either of you."

"Yes, sir," Tovak said.

"No, sir," Gorabor said.

Benthok spared Gorabor a hard look that bespoke intense frustration before turning away and moving off in the direction they'd just come.

"Like I said," Gorabor said, breathing out a relieved breath. "Hard as granite in winter."

"How long have you been with the Baelix Guard?" Tovak asked.

"A week," Gorabor replied. "Been on dodder duty the whole time .... Until today, I usually came with a boffer named Dolan, but he went to help a mate to the sick tent this morning with a serious case of the shits. Dolan knew the way and, well, I didn't have to pay attention much, if you know what I mean. Watch out for him, though. He's got a mean streak."

"Dolan," Tovak said. "I'll keep that in mind."

"I sort of got lost this morning." Gorabor looked sheepish. "When I found my way back, I ran straight into the lieutenant. Fortuna must hate me. If it had been Sergeant Bahr, he would have rapped me once and then pointed me in the right direction."

"The lieutenant didn't seem too pleased," Tovak said with a grin as he and Gorabor got into line.

"I was supposed to be back with the dodders already," Gorabor said. "We aren't going to be so popular this morning."

The line moved up and they both took a couple steps forward.

"Have you seen any action yet?" Tovak asked.

Gorabor shook his head. "Since I got here, the main encampment hasn't moved, and we've been out almost every day, foraging in the foothills to the west. Mostly just bug and *dain* hunting. We haven't even run into anything more dangerous than the hoppers, and they don't bite or sting none. It's been kind of boring actually, boring and backbreaking."

"Not much Legend to be had there," Tovak said, feeling unhappy at the prospect of such menial work.

"You got that right," Gorabor replied. "What I wouldn't give to run into an orc or goblin patrol, get some excitement. Joining up sure isn't what I thought it would be. Fetch this, go get that, dig a hole. I got tired of it all real quick and I've only been here a week."

Tovak looked over at Gorabor, who nodded his sincerity as the line moved up again.

"Have you started the training Benthok mentioned yet?"

"Just a bit, like last night," Gorabor said. "It's been more work than anything else. Besides, my family saw that I knew how to use my sword, sling, and a bow. I don't know what else they can teach me, to be honest, other than pioneer hand signals. Benthok's been teaching me. I take to it like a duck to water. How about you? Any training?"

Tovak perked up at that. Benthok knew pioneer signs? He glanced back in the direction the lieutenant had gone, then returned his attention to Gorabor.

"I have had some training," Tovak said, not wanting to mention the Academy.

The line moved forward again and then they found themselves before the cook and assistant.

"What company and how many bags?" the cook asked in a bored tone.

"Four sacks for the Baelix Guard," Gorabor said.

The cook nodded, turned, and picked up two brown canvas sacks off a table behind him. He handed them to Gorabor, and then got two more for Tovak. The assistant standing next to him made a notation on a tablet.

The bags were heavy, and the dodders within, still radiating warmth, made Tovak's stomach growl. He had no doubt they'd be tastier than the buurl, which he had eaten at the Academy. It was just about his least favorite food. Still, when you were hungry, food was food. He had long since learned that lesson.

"Next."

With sacks in hand, they made their way back to the company's camp. As they passed by the side of Struugar's tent, they overheard someone say Tovak's name in a harsh tone. Gorabor looked to Tovak. Both froze in their tracks.

"That was your name, right?" Gorabor hissed quietly.

Tovak nodded. It sounded like a heated conversation was going on in the captain's tent. He could make out the glow from the lantern and two shadows within. He took a step nearer. Gorabor grabbed his arm and shook his head.

"Bad idea, Tovak."

"Go on," Tovak whispered. "I'll be right along."

"Are you sure?" Gorabor said, eyes darting towards the tent. "You could get into bucketloads of trouble eavesdropping on the captain."

"I'll take that risk," Tovak replied with an almost desperate insistence. He knew he was risking Benthok's ire and severe punishment, but he couldn't just walk past, not now.

Gorabor looked uncertain, then gave a shrug. "What do I tell Sergeant Bahr?"

"Tell him I had to hit the latrine."

"He won't like that," Gorabor said. "It's your funeral."

Shaking his head, Gorabor moved off, making his way back to the company area.

Tovak stepped closer to the side of the tent and tried to look as inconspicuous as he could in the shadows. He was grateful it was still dark out. The voices had become hushed, but no less heated.

"... honestly, I don't like the idea of having a Stonehammer in the company, sir, no matter what name we're supposed to call him by." The voice belonged to Benthok.

Tovak's heart sank. It all came back to his father again. He should have known that Struugar would tell his lieutenant.

"Will you do as I have asked?" Struugar's tone was quiet but strained.

"Of course, sir," Benthok said. "I don't have to like it, but you know I will follow your orders. I always do."

There was a long silence. "And?"

"I'll do what I can with the boffer," Benthok said, "but it still doesn't sit well with me."

"He's just another recruit, that's all." Struugar's tone was suddenly harsh. "And the gods know we're short-handed. With the mission the Badgers have just been given, we will need every sword."

"There are few of us old hands who don't remember the disaster at Barasoom," Benthok said tersely.

"And you know how I feel about that," Struugar said.

"If it becomes known that you let him in," Benthok said, "it could very well cast a shadow over our company, just when we don't need it to."

There was another long pause. Struugar said nothing.

"Are you prepared for what may come of taking him in? How do you think Dagon would react? That bastard doesn't let things like this go."

"I'll defend my actions with steel and an Adjudication Circle, should it become necessary," Struugar said.

"It may come to that," Benthok said.

"Aye, it might." Struugar gave a dark chuckle. "Besides, I already talked to Dagon."

"You did? I will of course act as your second when he challenges you to the Circle," Benthok said.

"Thank you. But it won't come to that with Dagon."

"He's good with this?" Benthok asked, sounding shocked.

"No," Struugar said. "He lives his life by the Way. He will not trouble us, nor will he speak of it."

Tovak heard Benthok blow out a long breath.

"I would dearly love to learn how you pulled that off, sir," Benthok said finally. "Truly. I may not agree with it, but

I understand the debt you owe. That said, the fate of our people rests with the success of the Great March. Finding Grata'Dagoth may save us all....Still, you know as well as I, dissension in the ranks at such a time is not good, blood debt or no."

"I'm not doing this because of the debt, Benthok," Struugar said. "And you're the only one I can trust with something as delicate as this. He just wants a chance to serve, like any one of us."

"There's more to it than just him being like any other lad. You know how superstitious the boys are."

Struugar barked out a laugh. "Don't give me that nonsense."

"It doesn't matter what you, or even I, believe," Benthok said. "Bad luck spreads, and by saddling us with him, you've planted the seed in very fertile soil." Benthok took a deep breath and let it out slowly. "Word is bound to get out who he is."

"Perhaps," Struugar said, though Tovak thought the captain sounded far from convinced.

"There is no perhaps about it," Benthok said. "And I don't know how our boys will react. I can't promise it will be good. In fact, I will bet my next pay it won't be good. Better to be open about it at the outset than hide it, especially if you truly want to give him a chance. Sir, I recommend we deal with any trouble now. Or is it something else?"

Tovak felt as if his heart were gripped by a tight fist. He heard the creaking of a stool as someone sat. The silence in the tent grew.

"I don't believe any good will come of this, but I swear on my Legend, I will follow your orders," Benthok said.

"Good," Struugar said, with a sound of finality and relief. "Now that that's settled, would you kindly go get the company formed up? We have a long day ahead of us."

Tovak heard footsteps moving towards the flap, so he slipped away before he was spotted. Anguish clutched at his heart. Yet again, he'd been given a ray of hope, while something lay in wait to darken it. His feet felt like lead as he moved into the company area.

Now that Benthok knew, how would the lieutenant's attitude change? Despite what he'd told the captain, would the lieutenant work to drive Tovak out of the company? Regardless of the lieutenant's actions, Struugar was still giving him a chance. He resolved not let his captain down. Still, what Benthok had said worried him deeply. If he was discovered for the Pariah he was, what then?

"I will just cross that bridge when I come to it," he said to himself. As he passed by the supply tent, he discovered that not only was the company formed up, but the tents had been taken down, rolled up, and stacked next to the supply tent with the supports in a pile beside them. The campfires had been extinguished and covered over with dirt. Several torches had been lit. They cast their flickering light about.

The assembled company looked impressive. Three lines of skirmishers in their dark blue leather armor stood in easy, loose lines, talking amongst themselves as they waited. Their packs, spears, and gear rested at their feet. Every third or fourth skirmisher had a hornbow secured to his pack. There was also a line of strikers in full plate, their tall shields resting bottom-edge-down in the grass.

Gorabor was already halfway down the second line of skirmishers, busy handing out the dodders. Tovak hurried his step and started down the last line. He began passing out the steaming dodders to the strikers.

"Took too long at the latrine," one warrior said when Tovak handed over the dodder. "Next time go after you've brought me my breakfast, will you?"

"Make sure you piss on his first," the next warrior said. "Tevins likes when you do that."

"Kiss my ass, Kennig," Tevins replied as he bit into the dodder and began chewing.

"His girlfriend tell you that?" another warrior asked. "To piss on it, that is?"

"You mean the one he pays?" Kennig asked. "I don't think you can call her a girlfriend."

A burst of laughter followed. Grinning at the exchange, Tovak was past. Most nodded in thanks as he handed over the dodder, but several harassed him for being late. The commentary and insults were gruff but did not seem mean-spirited, and in spite of the hazing—maybe even because of it—he truly felt like he was part of the company, part of something bigger than he had ever belonged to before. He was just the new guy and it was clear many intended to make sure he knew it.

The feeling was almost enough to overshadow Benthok's words, which were still hovering at the back of his mind. Tovak suspected Benthok was correct and he couldn't help but wonder when it all might come crashing down again. Word was bound to get out. But more importantly, what was Grata'Dagoth? It was clearly a castle of some kind, for Grata meant "Fortress of the People." He'd never heard of Grata'Dagoth and he knew of all the great fortresses. He'd had to learn them in school.

Once he'd distributed the rations and taken one for himself, he gave the bag to Bahr in the supply tent. There were only five dodders left.

"It's about Thulla-cursed time," the sergeant said, taking the bag and setting it aside. "The next time you get sent for rations, I expect you to get them before you decide to take a dump. The captain is due out any moment, and when he comes, the company will march. You could have easily kept the company waiting. That would not have gone over very well. Screw this up again, and I'll have you shoveling a mountain of teska shit. Am I clear?"

"Yes, Sergeant," Tovak replied.

"A fair word of warning, son. Better not let Lieutenant Benthok catch you dragging ass like that. There are worse punishments than spending the rest of your life knee-deep in shit. Trust me. You do not want to get on the lieutenant's bad side."

"Yes, Sergeant," Tovak said, chastened. "It won't happen again."

"That's right, it won't. Now get out of my sight before I change my mind and put you on a charge."

Tovak moved to where he'd set his gear. He slung his pack over his shoulders and grabbed his spear, ready to join the formation, although he didn't know where to fall in. He moved back towards the company.

"Tovak," Benthok said, spotting him and waving him over. The lieutenant was speaking with a sergeant. He gave a nod and handed a tablet to the sergeant, who saluted and moved off.

"Yes, sir?" Tovak stiffened to a position of attention.

"I'm attaching you to First Section so I can keep an eye on you and personally oversee your training, as well as Gorabor's. Effective immediately, you're assigned to First Squad. Thegdol is the corporal." Benthok's eyes drifted to Tovak's hand, and the trace of a scowl crossed his face. "Make sure you eat that dodder. We have a long way to go today. You will need the energy."

"Yes, sir." Tovak felt not a little concern that the lieutenant would be personally conducting his training.

Benthok looked down the line. "Corporal Thegdol."

"Sir." A stout skirmisher stepped out of the line. He had bushy orange hair and a wide nose that looked like it had been broken and squashed against his face. The effect was a hard, almost menacing look. His beard was long, with four thick braids reaching down to his waist that were tied off with green leather laces. Silver beads had been woven into his beard as well.

"The recruit's all yours."

"Yes, sir," Thegdol said, seeming not terribly pleased to have him.

Did he too know?

"Over here, boy," Thegdol said and motioned impatiently.

Tovak started to move, but Benthok held out a stiff hand and stopped him. The lieutenant lowered his voice. "We're heading out shortly. Do what Thegdol tells you. It could get dangerous out in the field in the coming days. If you listen, you might just live long enough to get the training you need to survive. Got me?"

"Yes, sir," Tovak said.

Benthok removed his hand and Tovak stepped over to where Thegdol stood.

"Tovak Ironhammer, huh?" Thegdol asked.

"Yes, Corporal," Tovak replied.

"Never heard of your family," the corporal said, then turned and pointed at his squad, who were standing behind him in formation. "This is Jodin." His finger moved down the line as he spoke. "That's Lok, Morda, Staggen, and you already know Gorabor."

Jodin nodded a greeting. Lok, Morda, and Staggen appeared as if they could care less that he was now part of the squad.

Thegdol turned and locked eyes with Tovak. "You keep up, do what you're told, when you're told, or I put you on a charge. There is always something needing doing. Punishment details help get things done. Those can come with a thrashing too. Any questions?"

"No, Corporal," Tovak replied. He suspected Thegdol was a scrapper and, judging from his muscular bearing and manner, a good one too.

"Good," Thegdol said. "Are your waterskins full?"

"Yes, Corporal," Tovak said.

"Fall in at the end of the line there and be sure to eat your ration. Marching on an empty stomach is a mistake."

"Yes, Corporal," Tovak said and moved quickly to the end of the line. He stepped in behind Gorabor, who leaned over.

"I was sure you'd get caught," Gorabor whispered.

"I didn't."

"Hear anything?"

"No," Tovak lied and then decided to change the subject. "So, what happens next? Where are we going today?"

Gorabor turned his head slightly. "We've got foraging duty again. We'll leave before the bulk of the warband marches and make camp somewhere up in the high country tonight. I have no idea how long we will stay. Only the officers know that. When we've done our bit, we will meet back up with the warband somewhere along its line of march. At least, that's what Thegdol just told us."

"All right, you lazy durpas," Benthok called, stepping up before the formation. "Packs on."

The company began hefting their packs. Tovak stuck the dodder in his mouth and secured his pack, locking the shoulder brackets down and cinching up the waist straps so that they were snug. When it felt secure, he wolfed down the dodder, almost choking in his haste. It was crispy on the outside, and slightly sweet, with the meaty bits having a nutty flavor similar to murinok, but not as potent. He guessed the meat was some sort of insect, although he couldn't tell which one.

"Company," Benthok called, stressing the word. "Attention."

At the sound of his voice, the entire company went silent, stood up straight, slapped their arms to their sides, thrust their spear butts into the grass, and came to a position of attention. Tovak did the same, like he'd been drilled to at the Academy.

Struugar strode out from beside the supply tent wearing his blue and gold armor, the cloak about his shoulders. His wild hair had been pulled back into a knot behind his head, and his beard had been brushed out. He moved to the front of the company, stepping up to his lieutenant.

Benthok, stiff at attention, offered the captain a smart salute, which was returned.

"One hundred and thirty-two present and accounted for, sir," the lieutenant reported. "Two in the sick tent. It seems like bad meat is all."

"Very good," Struugar said, then turned to regard the company. He was silent for a long moment. "Baelix Guard," he said in a strong voice. "Today, the Great March begins in earnest. Our people are finally on the move, leaving behind what we have called home for the past five hundred years. It is a sad day, but also a new beginning, a fresh chapter in our history. We will find a home, a haven where our people can prosper. But that is in the future, one I am honored to say we will have a hand in delivering."

Struugar fell silent a moment. No one said a word. It was almost as if the entire company dared not breathe. Their entire nation was on the move, and all that protected the civilians from the enemy were the warbands. There was

Legend to be had in that, Tovak decided. By just serving with the Badgers, he was doing his part to protect his people, even if they considered him barely fit to be counted amongst them.

"The Syrulian Empire has fallen. The Horde is coming," Struugar said. "You all know that. It is why each and every one of you is here with us. Well, our time has come too. The Badgers have been tasked with a mission deep into hostile and unclaimed lands. The warband will be on its own, with no support for the foreseeable future." He paused for a moment, looking over the warriors assembled before him. "I can't tell you what we have to do, at least not yet. I have my orders. When the time comes, I will tell you. If what we do succeeds, the Badgers shall be remembered for an age." Struugar paused, looking as if he wanted to say more. But then he shifted his feet. "Keep a sharp eye. Our advance patrols have encountered isolated groups of orcs and goblins, mostly in the hills and high country, exactly where we're headed. They don't seem terribly organized, but that can change fast as we march through their lands. Stay alert, work together, and protect your comrades, for we, in this company…all of us are family." Struugar paused again, sucked in a breath, and let it out. "Enough speech-making. You all know your duty. I will be going with Third Section today. Lieutenant Benthok will take First. Sergeant Kelloth will handle Second. Fourth as usual will provide protection to the forage carts. Once we're outside the encampment, the company will break up into sections. Each section will head to their assigned forage area."

The captain turned and looked over at Benthok.

"Lieutenant."

"Sir?"

"Give the order to march."

"Company," Benthok called, "right face."

The company pivoted, turning in unison. They instantly went from an assembled formation to a marching column. "For–waard, march."

The steady, rhythmic thud of boots carried the company forward, and Tovak felt a surge of pride. He'd at least made it this far. The future lay before him, even if it involved foraging.

CHAPTER SEVEN

The twin suns beat down on Tovak, heating his helm and armor to the point where it was uncomfortable. Under his feet, the tough long grass folded, one monotonous step after another. For five hours, the section had kept a grueling pace to the tempo of the stone flutes that four of the warriors had with them, Gorabor included. About the size of a fist, the flutes were made from round river rocks with holes drilled into them. Their tune helped the long miles pass.

Tovak looked up and spotted a bird of prey circling high above. He stumbled over a rock hidden in the grass, then stepped around a small boulder. Tovak was at the end of the column, marching next to Gorabor. Those to the front kicked up dust, which tickled his nose and occasionally caused him to cough or sneeze.

After setting out from the main encampment, the lieutenant had only permitted three brief breaks. Those halts in the march had been beside creeks that crisscrossed the plateau. Skins had been filled and they'd been allowed to rest for a short while, eat, and drink their fill. Then, they'd been ordered back to their feet and moved on.

Thankfully, they were not required to march in close order step but permitted to spread out a bit. There was plenty of banter, occasional laughter, and with each stride, they'd drawn closer to the western foothills that marked the boundary of the Grimbar Plateau. At the same time, with every mile they gained a little more elevation.

Tovak was worn. Sweat ran down his face and the middle of his back. The thin air had him feeling a bit light-headed too. Still, he kept on with the rest of his section, which comprised four squads. Lieutenant Benthok had remained at the front of the line of march, leading the way and chatting amiably with one of the sergeants.

The direction the company had taken led them closer and closer to the foothills that rose sharply along the western edge of the plateau. As they'd moved farther north and west, both Second and Third Sections had broken away, headed towards the narrow valleys that cut into the foothills. Somewhere amongst them, they would set up camp and forage in their assigned area.

The foothills, stretching for miles, were covered with sparse pines, the occasional boulder field, and wide swaths of mountain flowers that splashed color over the tan and green terrain.

Tovak had always thought the mountains surrounding Garand'Durbaad lovely, but he had to admit that the Grimbar Plateau, ringed by hills and mountains, had a distinct untamed beauty that appealed to him. He found he almost couldn't wait to get up in the hills and explore.

Small streams and creeks ran through many of the valleys of the foothills down to the plateau to meet up with a large river farther to the east. From his fellow squad mates, Tovak had learned the warband's line of march would likely follow that river. Or so they thought. No one knew for sure where exactly the warband was headed. Thegdol had said as much when Morda and Lok had begun arguing about it.

When they reached the foothills, Benthok led them up a relatively clear path alongside a creek that ran through a cut in a narrow valley. The hills on either side were speckled with more pines and wildflowers. Lots of game could be seen, including flocks of hoppers that fed hungrily upon the vegetation. The way ahead had plenty of room for the two-wheeled, teska-drawn carts that Tovak had learned would follow and carry not only their supplies up to camp, but also forage back to the warband.

Tovak leaned on his spear with every other step, using it like a walking stick and easing the strain of its weight on his arm, at least a little. He sucked in air as they marched up beside the wide, rocky creek bed, with a small stream of fresh water flowing freely amidst the stones.

Each breath burned in Tovak's lungs, but he was holding his own, managing to keep up. He refused to let the others see that the march was taking a toll. He would not give them the satisfaction. He called upon Thulla for strength and focused on keeping pace with Gorabor.

They marched for another hour in the hilly terrain as they followed the flowing water ever higher, towards the snowcapped mountains that rose in the distance.

"SECTION...HALT," Benthok called. The column shuffled to an abrupt halt. Tovak noted that several of the warriors leaned forward, catching their breath.

Tovak found that they had stopped in an open, flat area. They'd climbed high enough into the foothills that the hillsides were more thickly forested. The stream continued onward and disappeared around a bend about a half mile up the valley. The steep, forbidding slopes of the mountains towered over them beyond, their snowy peaks a stark contrast to the clear, blue sky.

"All right," Benthok said from the head of the column. "We make camp here. Fall out. Packs and spears down."

"You two look blown and the day's not even half over," Jodin said, eyeing Gorabor and Tovak. "My wife gives me a harder workout than this hike did."

There were a few weary chuckles at that as packs dropped to the ground. Tovak gratefully set his pack and spear down, feeling intense pleasure of having rid himself of its dead weight. He suddenly felt incredibly light on his feet and marveled at the feeling. It was like he weighed next to nothing.

"Corporals, on me," the lieutenant ordered.

The four corporals moved over to the lieutenant, Thegdol included. Tovak did not know the other three, but he watched, curious to see what was about to happen.

"I want our defenses up against those boulders there." Benthok pointed to where a row of tall, smooth granite rocks poked nearly six feet out of the hillside. They formed a line about thirty feet from one end to the other. "The trench will be dug five feet from the boulders. Move it around to that point there"—the lieutenant swung his finger about to indicate the spot—"and there and there. I will mark where I want the trench and berm so there can be no confusion. Understood?"

They confirmed their understanding with a unified, "Yes, sir."

Benthok turned and looked around the section. His eyes fell upon Tovak and Gorabor.

"You two, over here."

Gorabor shot a quick glance over to Tovak and then hurried forward. Tovak followed.

"Sir," they both said, stopping in front of the lieutenant and saluting.

"You've got marker duty," he said. "Thegdol, do you have the bag?"

"I do, sir." Thegdol held it lightly in one hand. He gave it over to the lieutenant. "I thought you might want it."

"Good thinking." Benthok tossed the bag to Tovak. The lieutenant pointed back down the way they had come. "You will mark a path to our campsite for the carts. Tovak, Gorabor's done this before, so follow his lead. The trail you mark should be made with an eye towards the carts being able to make it up here, which means the path you chose should be different than the direct route we took to hump it up here. Difficult, rocky terrain should be avoided. Think you two can manage to keep from screwing this up?"

"Yes, sir," Tovak and Gorabor said together.

Benthok ran a hand down his neatly braided beard and was silent a moment as his eyes fell upon Gorabor. "Mess it up like this morning and there will be consequences."

"We won't screw up, sir," Gorabor insisted.

"Remember, the warband's scouts have run into scattered groups of goblins in these hills. Keep an eye out and don't be heroes. If you see any of the enemy or stumble across tracks, come right back and report."

"Yes, sir," they said in unison.

Hiking down and back up the slope they'd just climbed was not something Tovak really wanted to do. His legs were still burning. All he desired was to sit down and take the load off, just for a little while, to recover. Still, he considered he was lucky to have secured a spot in the company and wasn't about to complain or show weakness before the lieutenant, who knew the truth. At least he wouldn't have to carry his pack, and he'd have Gorabor for company.

"All you need to do is mark the trail to the base of that hill over there," Benthok said and pointed. He eyed them both, and his eyes narrowed in warning. "I want you back in no more than an hour and a half."

They both nodded.

"Now, fill up your waterskins and go," Benthok said dismissively.

They both saluted.

"Oh, and Tovak?"

"Sir?"

"You can relieve yourself when you come back," Benthok said. "After the job is done, that is. Don't drag ass again, will you?"

Tovak felt himself color. The lieutenant had heard how he'd been delayed with the morning rations. Benthok's eyes were shrewd. Did he suspect Tovak had overheard the conversation in the tent? That was surely impossible. The lieutenant had no way of knowing Tovak had been listening.

"Yes, sir," Tovak said.

Benthok turned away and back to his corporals. "Give the section a short break and then get them to work. As I said, I will mark the boundary for the trench."

The corporals saluted as Benthok moved off towards the boulders.

Tovak glanced at Gorabor, who looked far from pleased at their assignment. The day was already hot and both were drenched in sweat and covered over in dust from the march.

"We're gonna need an entrenching tool," Gorabor said.

"I'll get mine." Tovak returned to where he'd dropped his pack and spear. He loosened the straps on the entrenching tool, pulled it out, and slipped the shaft through his belt, next to his sword. Grabbing one of his waterskins, he looked around at the other warriors of the section. They had sat down on the ground and were drinking from their own skins or talking. A small group huddled around a dice game. A couple more had moved over to the stream and were splashing water on their faces and arms, washing away the dust of the march.

Tovak glanced down at his own arms. He would most definitely need to wash himself, but that would come later, when there was time. A sudden pang of paranoia hit him. While he was gone, what if someone went digging through his pack and found his Warrant? They might recognize his name and then life would become very difficult. He decided the chance of that happening, though remote, was something he was not prepared to risk. He carefully and inconspicuously as he could removed the Warrant and slipped it under his armor, where it would be safe from unwanted eyes.

Gorabor had already gotten his own skin and made his way over to the stream. Tovak caught up and together they refilled their skins.

"We better get moving," Gorabor said, with a nervous glance towards the lieutenant, who was busy walking what would become the camp boundary.

"Right," Tovak said.

They headed down the slope at a quick pace.

Using his knife, Tovak whittled the end of the branch to a sharp point. Satisfied, he staked it into the ground. Then, using his entrenching tool, he hammered it down farther. Gorabor handed him a strip of red cloth from the bag. Tovak tied it to the stake. He stepped back and looked over his handiwork. A warm breeze ruffled the cloth.

He glanced around. They were back at the bottom, where the valley opened up onto the Grimbar Plateau. He could see a few hoppers in the distance, grazing on the grasses. The lieutenant's words fresh to mind, they'd kept a keen eye for the enemy. But they'd seen nothing and no other tracks but the section's on the way down. Tovak took his skin, uncorked it, and tipped it back. The water was warm but tasted good.

"Now for the climb back up," Gorabor said, his gaze fixed upward. He gave a groan. He held four other makeshift stakes under an arm and the bag. "That's gonna be one bastard of a climb."

Tovak could not help but agree. Instead of saying anything further, he started upward. They set a good pace. After they had staked the second marker, about two hundred yards from the first, Tovak paused and took a moment to stare out across the wide expanse of the plateau, admiring the distant peaks rising off in the distance. Somewhere, out on the flats, was the warband.

"Beautiful, isn't it?" Gorabor asked.

"Inspiring," Tovak said. "The open spaces take some getting used to, though. Not like home, under the mountain."

"Yeah, I know what you mean."

They stood for a few moments, admiring the view, before Gorabor shifted.

"We're not here to take in the sights," Gorabor said, handing over another cloth strip. "The lieutenant is expecting us back."

Tovak tied it around the top of the stake. The end fluttered in the breeze.

"And you're sure they'll see this?" Tovak glanced once again out onto the wide plateau. He could spot no sign of any carts or wagons.

"Yes," Gorabor said. "The lieutenant gives the teamsters a map of where he's planning on camping. They hit the foothills and then follow along until they find the right color stake. If they don't find it, well, they're reading the map wrong. It happened a week ago, when I first arrived. A teamster got lost. He was new and it was his first run, but that didn't matter. The lieutenant was hopping mad. It kept us out in the field longer than we were supposed to be." Hefting the three makeshift stakes they had left, he started up the valley. "Come on, let's move and get the next stake planted. We don't want to keep the lieutenant waiting."

"Color?" Tovak asked as he followed along. "What do you mean the right color?"

"It's why all of the cloths in the sack are red. Our section gets red, Second Section gets yellow, and Third Section gets orange," Gorabor replied. "I don't remember what the Fourth's color is, but as strikers, they rarely get foraging duty. Instead they spend their time guarding the carts and teamsters. There are two carts for each section. The teamsters assigned to us know to look for the stakes with red cloths. They park the wagons down on the plateau and run the carts up to our campsite and back to the wagons. The wagons and carts usually arrive after midday."

"I see," Tovak said.

Gorabor shrugged. "Last time we were sent out on foraging detail, Benthok had me set the markers with Dolan." He looked over at Tovak. "The bastard was almost no help at all. He complained the entire way down and then back. I wasn't happy getting stuck with the duty either, but his carping made it worse, if you know what I mean."

They walked for a short while without saying anything, keeping a good pace and sucking air as they climbed.

"Hey, did you see the all-female company?" Gorabor asked, between breaths. "They were camped next to us in the encampment."

"No," Tovak said, surprised. The change in subject caught him off guard. He remembered the female warrior he'd seen outside of the headquarters pavilion. "Why do you ask?"

"Just curious." Gorabor fell silent for several steps before turning back and flashing a grin. "There's a girl there."

"Really?" Tovak asked, having suspected as much. "I couldn't guess."

"Gulda Stonecutter. She's as beautiful as sunshine on a spring day," he said, then paused a heartbeat. "We have plans."

"Does she know?" Tovak asked, amused.

Gorabor's grin grew even broader.

"She's sweet on me. We knew each other back home, grew up together. She joined up about a year before me. If I'm honest, and let me tell you, honesty is very important to me ... I joined the Badgers to see her again."

"That's why you joined up?" Tovak stopped. He almost laughed. "Because of a girl?"

"Well," Gorabor said, stopping too. "There is the Great March after all. I'm serving our people and at the same time get to be near the girl I'm keen on. My father almost shat himself with rage when he found out I wanted to join the Badgers. He wanted me to join the Bloody Fists, his old warband."

"You joined for a girl?" Tovak was so amused, he let out a laugh.

"You wouldn't laugh if you'd seen her," Gorabor said. "She's a right looker, my Gulda is. We've even talked about marriage."

"Serious then," Tovak said.

"Yep." Gorabor turned and started climbing again. They kept moving up the valley, and the silence between them grew along with their exertions. They fashioned and planted several more markers along the way.

"I am happy for you," Tovak said and smiled. "Truly. I can't wait to meet this beauty."

"It will be my honor to introduce you to her. So, do you have a girl back home?"

Tovak's smile evaporated, and he averted his eyes, instead looking out on the plateau.

"Somebody break your heart?" Gorabor asked with a concerned look. "Left her behind, did you?"

"No," Tovak said. "Nothing like that. I just don't have anybody, is all." The last girl he'd been interested in had been Adelluh back in school, before he'd become a Pariah. None others since that time had wanted anything to do with him. For a flickering moment, he wondered what Adelluh might be doing just then. Had she found a mate? Started a family? Or was she on the Great March with her family, leaving behind their home? "I'd rather not talk about that."

"Sure, Tovak," Gorabor said. "I didn't mean to pry."

"You weren't prying," he said. "I just don't want to speak on it, is all."

Gorabor gave a nod.

They continued on, following the stream, which was on their right side, and the path of the section had taken led up to the left.

"We better put one here." Gorabor handed over one of the stakes.

Laying his spear down, Tovak pulled out his trencher once again and set the stake in the ground, hammering it down with his entrenching tool.

"Have you ever heard of Grata'Dagoth?" Tovak asked as he worked.

"No, why?" Gorabor looked back at him.

As Tovak tied off another red cloth, Gorabor clambered around a pile of large boulders and climbed on top of them to keep watch, carefully scanning the terrain in all directions.

"Nothing but scrub, trees, and grass," Gorabor said. "I think the scouts must have been wrong. There's nothing out there but unspoiled country." He let out an explosive breath, then looked over at Tovak. "Say, why do you ask about this Grata'Tatoth?"

"It's Grata'Dagoth," Tovak said, though now that he thought on it, perhaps he'd misheard the name. "I just heard the name, is all. I was wondering if you knew where it was?"

"How'd you hear of it?" Gorabor asked, mild interest in his tone.

"One of the teamsters on the yuggernok I came in on mentioned it," Tovak lied. He felt badly about that, but he'd already told Gorabor he had heard nothing at the captain's tent.

"He was probably having one over on you," Gorabor said. "Gullible recruit and all. There is no such fortress."

Tovak nodded, as if he were agreeing.

"Even if such a place did exist, I'm not sure it matters anymore," Gorabor said. "What with the Great March, we're leaving everything behind." He leaned his spear over his right shoulder and eyed Tovak. "For boffers like us, it's all the same. We march, we forage, we fight, and we die. And if we don't die, we do it all over again."

Tovak looked at Gorabor with a skeptical eye and gave a chuckle. There was more bravado there than anything else, if he was any judge.

"What we're doing is important," Tovak said seriously.

"What we're doing is foraging," Gorabor said, unhappily. "Well...setting out stakes. Soon the lieutenant will have us foraging. I'd rather fight goblins than spend my time hunting and scrounging around for mushrooms and bugs and such. I didn't join to be a scrounger."

"You joined for a girl," Tovak laughed.

"You have me there," Gorabor said. "And what a girl."

Tovak uncorked his waterskin and took a few pulls to ease the dryness in his throat. He stopped it and eyed Gorabor, who was taking several long gulps from his own skin.

"It's hot," Tovak said with a glance up at the suns. "I bet you could fry an egg on one of those boulders."

"I think the lieutenant has it out for me," Gorabor said. "He piles on extra duties every chance he gets. Rides me ragged when I mess up, too. He seems to enjoy saddling me with this job or that. 'Gorabor, you're on dodder duty, teska duty, haul some water for the company or gather firewood.' Sometimes I feel like a slave, not a warrior."

"I believe it." Tovak could sympathize, for growing up in his uncle's household, he'd often felt the same way. "I have a feeling I'll be getting every menial job he can think of too."

"Well," Gorabor said, suddenly brightening at that prospect, "now that I'm not the newest recruit anymore, I'm sure some of the jobs I've been getting will go to you."

"Thanks," Tovak said dryly, thinking about the extra jobs Lieutenant Benthok could give him for dragging ass. "Let's get the rest of these done. I don't want to get on the wrong side of the lieutenant. You can tell me more about Gulda as we go,"

"My pleasure," Gorabor said. "You know, of late she's my favorite subject."

"I have no doubt," Tovak said and resisted a groan. Though in truth, he was happy for his new friend.

While Gorabor went on and on about Gulda Stonecutter, they made their way up the valley, planting one stake after another as they climbed back towards camp.

CHAPTER EIGHT

By the time they returned to camp, Tovak's legs felt like they were on fire, and his heart pounded in his chest from the hike back up. His breathing came in ragged gasps and he was drenched in sweat. The warm summer air, combined with the two suns, had only made things worse. He glanced over at Gorabor, who looked just as fatigued. Gorabor wiped sweat from his face with a small towel he'd pulled from a pocket.

"That's some climb," Gorabor said, almost breathless. He stopped for a moment and bent over, placing his hands on his knees. "I'd not want to do it again today."

"Let's hope we don't have to," Tovak said as he wiped sweat out of his eyes. He was hot and uncomfortable in his armor. It chafed and had rubbed him raw in unexpected places. His helmet, however, was a particular torture. The unaccustomed weight on his neck was beginning to hurt something fierce. Tovak desired nothing more than to take it off, sit down, and rest his legs.

"Agreed," Gorabor said, straightening up. "We're almost there. Let's go."

They found that the campsite had been transformed. While they'd been gone, the section had dug a trench five feet deep that completely encircled the camp. Using the soil that had just been excavated, a four-foot berm had been built up along the inside of the trench and then packed down. Wooden stakes fashioned from thick branches stuck out of the berm. The ends had been sharpened to wicked-looking points. The trench and wall made the camp a formidable obstacle. At least Tovak thought so.

The nearest trees had been felled. The crack of axes sounded on the air as two sweating warriors broke up the trees for firewood just a few yards away. Tovak did not know their names, but they already had a good-sized pile of chopped and split wood.

A single fire burned in the center of camp, where Benthok stood talking to one of the corporals. Grayish smoke from the campfire drifted lazily upward into the sky. Looking for any hint of trouble and placed strategically about, three sentries with spears stood atop the berm. Their gazes were fixed outward, watchful. The one closest to them waved in greeting as he spotted them. The rest of the section, besides those working on chopping firewood, was nowhere in sight.

"Looks like they've already gotten some kills," Tovak said to Gorabor. He lifted his chin towards the hanging animals by the entrance to the camp.

"Makes me hungry, just looking at them," Gorabor said. "Always had a thing for roasted dain. My Gran liked to make dain, potato, and leek stew, which, let me tell you, was some damn good eating." Gorabor blew out a breath. "Though that wasn't too often. Dain was hard to come by back home. Have you ever had it?"

The animals hanging were small, furred plant eaters about half as tall as Tovak, with six legs, short rust-colored tails, and long ears. They had gray coats of coarse fur that were paler on their short muzzles. Tovak knew from his studies they were common in this area and usually found grazing in small herds.

Tovak shook his head. "No. Way too expensive for me."

"You missed out," Gorabor said and clapped him on the shoulder. "Well, maybe you'll get a taste while we're out here? Shame Gran won't be cooking it, though."

"You think so?" Tovak asked, brightening at that prospect.

"What? That Gran won't be cooking it?" Gorabor asked seriously, then smirked. "She was old as the rocks and died a few years back."

"No," Tovak said with a chuckle. "About getting some dain."

"It's one of the perks of foraging," Gorabor said. "We get fresh meat. Thegdol says the lieutenant always picks the best cuts for us. Besides being boring and hard work, there are advantages to being on forage duty. We tend to eat better than the rest."

"I am beginning to see that," Tovak said.

"Welcome back," the nearest sentry said as they approached. Tovak could tell he was bored and seemed eager for conversation.

The sentry stood on the berm, next to the only gap through the newly made dirt wall. A gate of sorts had been fashioned. It was more barricade than anything else and was leaning against the dirt in the gap, waiting to be put into place.

A makeshift bridge crossed the trench before the entrance to the camp. It had been constructed using four tree trunks lashed together with thick rope and set into the dirt. It was crude, but serviceable.

"Hey, Dagmar," Gorabor greeted wearily, stopping before the sentry and bridge. Struggling to control his breathing, Tovak stopped with him.

"I trust the trail is well-marked?" Dagmar asked. "Wouldn't want the lieutenant to become enraged with the teamsters again, now, would we?"

"The trail's as well-marked as we could make it," Gorabor said. "You would have to be blind to miss it."

"Shame then," Dagmar said, with a glance thrown over at Benthok, who had his back to them. The sentry turned his attention to Tovak and lowered his voice. "Our lieutenant has one of the best tempers around. When he gets stirred up, I say, it is a sight to see. Though to be honest, it's best to make sure you are not on the receiving end, if you take my meaning."

"Who got the kills?" Gorabor asked before Tovak could reply.

"Corporal Gamok nailed one, Morda got the other," the sentry said, and then glanced around, almost nervously, at the lieutenant. "I'd love to keep chatting, but you both better get a move on and report before the lieutenant notices you loitering and I get it for delayin' ya."

Tovak did not need to be told twice. He stepped onto the bridge, with Gorabor following. The two of them passed through the gap in the berm and into the camp. Benthok and the corporal turned. The lieutenant scowled at them, clearly resenting the interruption. Or perhaps, Tovak thought, it was something else, possibly to do with him?

Tovak and Gorabor saluted as they came to a halt before the lieutenant. Benthok crisply returned their salute.

An iron grate had been set over the fire, suspended over the flames by two large rocks. A kettle had been set on the grate. Tovak could smell tea and hear the kettle begin to boil.

"You could've been quicker," Benthok said. "You'll do it faster next time, or I'll have you digging latrines while the section uses them." He held out his hand expectantly. "The bag."

Tovak handed over the bag that was about half full.

Benthok glanced briefly inside and then handed it to the corporal. "Make sure this gets stowed."

"Yes, sir," the corporal said.

"You picked a good, easy trail for the cart?" Benthok asked. "It's clearly marked?"

"There should be no problems, sir," Gorabor said.

"We clearly marked the trail, sir," Tovak said, deciding to specifically answer the lieutenant's question.

"Did you see any tracks that might indicate the enemy was in the area?" Benthok asked, his eyes going from Gorabor to Tovak. The question seemed more directed at Tovak, instead of Gorabor, so he answered.

"We looked but did not see any tracks," Tovak said, "other than those the section made, sir."

Benthok gave a grunt that seemed to indicate he'd expected no different answer. After all, the section had just passed that way.

"Corporal Thegdol and the rest of your squad are up that way," Benthok said, turning his attention to Gorabor. The lieutenant pointed farther up the valley to the left, towards where the trees grew thick. "They should already be hunting. Gorabor, get on up there, report to your corporal, and make yourself useful, if that's even possible. Dismissed."

"Yes, sir," Gorabor said. He saluted, turned on his heel, and made his way out of the encampment, taking his spear with him as he went.

"As for you," Benthok said, turning his gaze to Tovak. The lieutenant's eyes tracked down to Tovak's belt and the trencher. "Since you already have your trencher handy, you just volunteered to dig the camp latrine."

"Yes, sir," Tovak said, not feeling too pleased about that. He had never much enjoyed digging. He did his best to keep his expression neutral.

"I want it over there, downhill, outside the defenses and away from the stream." Benthok pointed to where a thick log had been cut and laid on its side, about ten yards away. "They've already done half the job and have cut a log for sitting. Move it farther from the stream, say about ten yards, to that spot there by that big bush."

"Outside the camp, sir?" The question popped out before he could stop it. He clamped his mouth shut.

"There are enemy scattered about in these hills," Benthok said, not seeming to notice the impertinence of the question. "They don't seem terribly organized yet. However, if the camp falls under attack, and we must defend the walls, holding out until we can be relieved by one of the other sections... well then, when the time comes, I think we can easily dig a new latrine inside. Until then, the latrine is outside and far enough away that we don't have to smell it. Don't you agree, soldier?"

"Yes, sir," Tovak said.

The lieutenant paused and looked over at him. "Have you ever dug a latrine?"

"No, sir," Tovak admitted.

"Well," Benthok said, "there's no better time to learn than the present. Dig a trench, three feet deep, and the length of the log. There is not much to it beyond that. Understand?"

"Yes, sir," Tovak said, looking over to where the log was and then to the bush where he was to drag it.

"And when you're done with that," Benthok added, "grab one of those foraging sacks over there, take your spear, and join up with your corporal. He'll set you to work."

Tovak looked over to his left at the pile of sacks. It was shaping up to be one very long day.

"Snap to it, soldier," Benthok ordered.

"Sir," Tovak said, saluting before turning away. He stepped over to where the packs were piled. Someone had moved his pack and placed it with the others by the entrance to the camp. Tovak felt his hand go to his armor, under which was concealed his Warrant. The fact that his pack had been moved reinforced his decision to take the Warrant with him. He pulled his trencher from his belt and started towards the camp entrance, passing by Dagmar.

"Got you digging the latrine, does he?" Dagmar asked, looking amused.

Tovak gave a nod as he started over the bridge and out of the camp towards the log.

"We've all had to do it at one time or another," Dagmar said. "Better pray no one wants to use it before you're finished, eh?"

That cheery thought spurred Tovak on. He worked rapidly, first moving the log, which was fearfully heavy. Once he had dragged it in place, he began digging. It took him just half an hour to dig the latrine. Thankfully, no one came wanting to use it.

Tovak passed a bored Dagmar as he returned to camp. He grabbed a canvas foraging sack from the pile. There was no sign of the lieutenant, which was almost a relief. He glanced up in the direction Benthok had pointed and let out a weary breath. More climbing.

"Right then," Tovak said and, taking his spear, made his way out of the camp. Dagmar gave him a friendly wave as he passed by but said nothing further.

Outside of camp, Tovak paused, glancing up in the direction he had to go. The slope was steep and thick with trees. Not only did his legs ache, but now so too did his arms. He would just have to keep pushing, for he did not want to be perceived as one who gave up easily. Tovak understood such an attitude would never see him secure a spot with the pioneers or, for that matter, earn the respect of his comrades.

Thirsty, he reached over to his side and was surprised to find the skin empty. Slinging it over his shoulder, he hefted his spear in one hand, threw the foraging sack over his other shoulder, and went to the stream.

He filled the skin, then drained it, tipping it back to get at the last of the cool water. It was wonderful. He wiped his lips with the back of his forearm and then refilled the skin.

He was dirty, sweaty, and felt grimy. He splashed water on his face and arms, washing some of the dirt away. Groaning, he stood up straight and stretched out his back, which hurt. Heck, his whole body was one terrible ache. He picked his spear up off the ground. Thinking it was somehow heavier than before, he set off up the hillside, feeling the burn with each step.

Tovak climbed through the trees, setting a steady pace as he worked his way up the steep terrain. His breath once again became heavier and his body protested its exhaustion with each step. The shade from the trees was a welcome relief.

Around a hundred yards from the camp, he heard a burst of what he thought was distant laughter. It was somewhere ahead, coming from just over a small rise in the hillside. A moment later, he came across the tracks of two groups. He could tell by how the boots had been planted that they were traveling up the hill. It was clear they were from Dvergr. Tovak's training came back to him and he suddenly forgot his exhaustion. Here was a chance to practice what he'd been taught at the Academy.

Squatting, he looked more closely at the signs of passage. He picked out footprints in the pine needles that covered the forest floor, broken branches here and there, as well as freshly snapped twigs and scuff marks on a stone from a hobnailed boot.

As he moved through the trees, one group of tracks led off to the right, and another set continued in the direction the lieutenant had indicated. Tovak followed the second set of tracks. He controlled his breathing, focused on his every movement, and did his best to approach silently, as he had been taught. He moved through the undergrowth, careful with how he placed his weight, avoiding branches and twigs whenever possible.

He crested the rise, from where he'd heard the laughter, and came up to a large pine. It had wide branches covered in prickly needles. He peered around the trunk, which was large enough to conceal him. There was a clearing ahead, where a large tree had fallen and taken down several other smaller trees.

The monster of a tree trunk was half buried in the forest floor, almost as if the land were slowly swallowing it up. At its center and just before the trunk of the fallen giant were Thegdol and Gorabor bent over, their backs to him.

Gorabor was crouched and in the process of gutting a durvoll. Two more lay not far off. There were also four heratta lying in a pile—large, six-legged insects, about half as long as a person. Their wings were partially unfurled, with the translucent membranes gleaming in the sunlight that filtered down into the clearing. While he'd been digging the latrine, the others had been busy.

Tovak stepped out from behind the pine and approached. Playtime was over. He wanted to make a good impression with his corporal, for there was work that needed doing and Tovak would do his part.

"That's it," Thegdol said, motioning as if he were the one gutting the carcass. "Once you've tied off the anus, you'll want to open up the belly carefully. Make sure you don't nick the intestines or stomach as you go. That's a stench you don't want. Trust me on that one, boy."

"How high up do I make the cut?" Gorabor asked, turning his head to look at the corporal. Spotting Tovak out of the corner of his eye, Gorabor jumped with a start, almost dropping his knife.

Thegdol's hand darted to the hilt of his sword. The corporal spun, partially drawing his weapon.

"Thulla's bones," Thegdol exploded when he recognized Tovak. "You bloody idiot. Don't sneak up on people like that, especially out in the field."

"I'm sorry, sir," Tovak said, suddenly feeling foolish and embarrassed.

"I'm not a sir," Thegdol snapped angrily. "I'm a corporal. Use my rank or I will thump you something good next time you cock it up."

"Yes, Corporal," Tovak said, thoroughly embarrassed. "Sorry, Corporal."

Thegdol slid the partially drawn sword back into the sheath, the guard clicking loudly as it was rammed home. "Sneaking up on people ... that's a good way to get skewered out here. Be sure you don't do that to anyone holding a bow, or they're likely to put one in you before they realize their mistake."

"You got me good," Gorabor said, abruptly grinning. "I almost pissed myself."

"It's not funny," Thegdol said and cuffed Gorabor on the side of the head with the back of his hand. It wasn't a hard blow, but it was enough to get Gorabor's attention.

"Sorry, Corporal," Gorabor said.

Tovak felt his face heat with embarrassment. "It won't happen again, Corporal."

"It better not," Thegdol said, then turned his gaze back to Gorabor. "You're not getting paid to stand around all day." The corporal gestured at the carcass. "What are you waiting for?"

Gorabor's hands and forearms were covered in blood, as were the tips of his boots. He had wound his beard into one long braid, which he'd pushed back over his left shoulder. Dressing a kill was messy work. The evidence of that was his hands and forearms. Gorabor hastily returned to his work.

"Do you know how to dress a kill?" Thegdol asked, looking back over at Tovak, the irritation still plain in his tone.

"I do," Tovak replied. "I worked for a butcher."

The hours had been long and hard. The butcher, named Miklos, had been a real bastard of a boss. Tovak still had scars on his back from where Miklos had beat and whipped him for even the tiniest of perceived mistakes, which Tovak had done his best not to make. Still, work was work, and in truth, he had been grateful for even that job. Not much opportunity came a Pariah's way.

"Good skill to have, especially out here," Thegdol said. "I'll be sure to put you to work dressing and butchering soon enough. There's gonna be plenty of opportunity for that. The warband's lucked out with the timing of the Great March."

"How?" Tovak asked. He could not see what was lucky about their entire people having to flee their home. The Great March had always been an expected calamity, in that everyone knew it was going to happen at some point in the future. It was thought they had decades, with plenty of time to plan. No one could have guessed it would come so soon. The sudden fall and collapse of the Syrulian Empire had shocked everyone and precipitated the Great March.

"The warband's been short on supply. What's lucky is the heratta. Those hungry bugs are getting ready to migrate across the plateau to their mating grounds." Thegdol waved vaguely in the direction of the plateau. "They've been gathering in these here hills for some weeks now. Thick as fleas on a wild dog, they are."

Tovak glanced around. On the march up, he had seen a few hoppers from a distance, but none up close and not that many either. He had a hard time imagining them gathering in such numbers.

"When I was a youth," Thegdol continued, "I saw a migration. It was a damn impressive sight, millions of the hoppers. There were so many, words just can't properly describe it. They ate everything in sight, and when they moved on, the land was left barren in their wake."

Thegdol fell silent, as if reliving his youth. Tovak thought such a thing would be worth seeing but was still having trouble picturing it. The corporal blew out a long breath.

"But for now, Tovak, I need you out hunting," he said, pointing to Tovak's left. "Jodin, Lok, and Staggen are off that way." He motioned towards what looked like a shallow cut in the hillside, heading perpendicular to the valley. "With all the game in this area, they should be back soon."

As if in answer to his words, they turned at the sound of footsteps and rustling in the trees a short distance off. Moments later, Jodin, Lok, and Staggen appeared, each carrying a heratta under their arms.

"Good work," Thegdol said as the three added their kills to the pile of heratta. "A very good start to the day's catch. I think we're gonna use this clearing to gather our kills and butcher them before carrying it all down to the camp."

Lok glanced around the clearing. "It's as good as any place, I guess."

"Plenty of game in these woods," Staggen said. His voice was raspy, almost hoarse-sounding. "We'd gone no more than fifty yards before we ran into these critters in a clearing that way. Fat, dumb, and happily eating the grass."

"Aye," Lok said, pulling out his dagger with the clear intention of cleaning his kill. "We'll have an easy time of it this time out, no humping miles to find a swarm."

Thegdol eyed the three warriors for a moment. He seemed to make a decision. "No need to gut and clean your kills. Gorabor needs more work at it. Lok, Staggen, I want the two of you to keep hunting."

"Yes, Corporal." Lok sheathed his knife. "And thank you for that, Gorabor. So kind of you to volunteer."

"You're welcome," Gorabor said, with no little amount of irony, as he worked at gutting. "Happy to help a fellow squad mate."

"You can clean all of my kills, if you want," Staggen said. "Thegdol, you might want to consider that. We could make Gorabor an expert in gutting and cleaning before we next return to the warband."

Jodin chuckled at that. "He's got a point."

"I would not want to deprive you of the pleasure, Staggen," Gorabor said.

"Staggen, Lok," Thegdol said, "enough ass-dragging and jawing. Get back to work. Good hunting."

"Yes, Corporal," Lok said and jerked his head at Staggen, who shot Gorabor another amused grin before stepping away.

"Jodin," Thegdol said, "you get to take Tovak out and show him the ropes."

Jodin eyed Tovak unhappily. He was a little shorter than Tovak, with black hair spilling out beneath his helmet and a thick beard with two braids coming down from either side of his jaw. There was the trace of a black tattoo running up one side of his neck.

"I had a feeling you were going to have me do that," Jodin said.

"Is there a problem?" Thegdol asked, his voice becoming stern.

"No, Corporal," Jodin replied, "no problem at all."

"Good," Thegdol said curtly. "Find out how he is with the sling." The corporal paused and looked over at Tovak. "You did bring your sling, didn't you?"

"I have it," Tovak said and patted his hip, where the sling was rolled up neatly in a small pouch. "Shot too."

"Good," Thegdol said. "Any questions, Jodin?"

"No, Corporal," Jodin replied. He took a deep breath, and his frown turned to a weak and artificial smile. "None at all."

Thegdol looked over at Tovak. "Do what he tells you and pay attention. It may not seem like it, but it can be dangerous out here. We're hunting food for the warband, but there are things out here that will be hunting you. Don't kid yourself, boy. You have a lot you need to learn."

"Yes, Corporal."

"Get to it then."

"Come on," Jodin said wearily, pointing the way Staggen and Lok had just gone. He started moving. "We thought we saw another group of heratta off in that direction."

Tovak hefted his spear and set off after Jodin. He felt a thrill of excitement course through him. Granted, they were only hunting game, but it was a start.

Chapter Nine

Tovak and Jodin had gone about a hundred yards into the forest, leaving Thegdol and Gorabor behind. At first, nothing was said between the two of them. Then Jodin stopped and looked over at Tovak.

"It's just my luck that I got stuck with you, boy," Jodin said. "Fresh off the yuggernok and probably think you already know everything. Well, let me tell you, you don't know nothin', especially out here."

Tovak did not reply, but he noticed how Jodin's eyes returned to scanning the forest, moving from the needle-covered floor up into the trees, obviously searching for prey.

"I've been with the company for seven years. In that time, you learn a thing or two. With that learning comes trust to do a job right. The lieutenant trusts me."

"He does?" Tovak felt compelled to ask.

"Aye," Jodin said, "he does and so does Thegdol. While everyone else was making camp and you was marking the trail, I was sent to scout this area out and look for threats."

Tovak was impressed, but he said nothing.

"If you watch and listen," Jodin said, "you might learn a thing or two."

"Then I will."

"Talk is easy," Jodin said as he started moving again. "We will see."

Tovak moved with him.

"Have you ever hunted before?" Jodin asked, looking over.

"A bit," Tovak said. He had been taught to hunt as part of his training, but he'd only ever hunted birds and rabbits. There had been no opportunity for larger game. He did not tell Jodin that.

"Well, whatever you think you know, forget it. You're about to get an education, and it starts with me." Jodin glanced over at him as they continued to work their way through the trees. "Tell me, what direction is the wind blowing?"

Jodin had picked that moment to ask, precisely when the breeze had stopped.

"From ahead of us," Tovak replied immediately, pointing.

"Which means we're headed in the right direction, especially so, since we're hunting," Jodin said. "Nothing to our front will smell us coming. They might hear us if we're not careful, but they won't smell us. Understand?"

"I do." Tovak nodded his head. He was well aware of how to use the wind to his advantage, but he didn't say anything. He figured he'd let Jodin go ahead and teach, while keeping his mouth shut. Tovak knew he might even learn something from the veteran, who had much more experience than he did.

"Keep a sharp eye," Jodin said, lowering his voice a tad. "Watch for marks in the dirt, or animals in the trees. Most importantly, do your best to move as quietly as possible."

They had traveled about three hundred yards without picking up any sign of wildlife when Tovak spotted a clump of fat, black-capped mushrooms growing inside a fallen and hollowed-out tree. There were about a dozen nestled inside the rotting wood, and he recognized them immediately, as they had grown in the caverns back home. They were not only edible but considered quite tasty and used for adding flavor to food. When he'd only been able to afford leftover scraps no one wanted, he'd gone hunting the mushrooms to spice up his food.

"Hey, look," he said, pointing.

"What?" Jodin asked, turning his head in that direction. "Oh, blackheads. Good find."

Jodin stepped up to the snag. He pulled out a foraging sack he'd tucked into his belt and leaned over, looking inside the rotted-out trunk. It was clear he was checking to see if anything dangerous lurked within before he began harvesting the mushrooms. Apparently satisfied, he picked the mushrooms out one by one and dropped them into the sack. When he got to the last two, he stood up, holding them in his hand. There was a long moment where he looked at Tovak, as if deciding something, then stepped nearer.

"Here," he said, handing over the mushrooms. "Take these two. They are good for waterproofing leather and armor. It means less cleaning later."

Was Jodin kidding?

"Rub these on your bracers," Jodin said, making a rubbing motion with his hand against his forearm, "and it will keep the water from soaking in if it rains."

Tovak knew perfectly well that these mushrooms weren't used for that. He eyed Jodin, trying not to show any hint that he suspected he was being had. What was he up to?

"Waterproofing?" Tovak asked, returning his attention to Jodin, whose face was a mask of innocence. Tovak tapped the armor. "Really? I hadn't heard that one."

"Go on," Jodin said, in an encouraging manner. "Helps protect the metal from rust and keeps the leather hard. I didn't believe either, but an armorer taught me the trick.

Trust me, it works. They're also good for cooking, but since you spotted them, I am guessing you already know that."

Tovak brought one of the mushrooms up to his nose and smelled the musky flavor. "These mushrooms can add flavor to even the worst meals."

What game was Jodin playing? For a moment, he considered calling Jodin out, but then he thought he'd play along, at least for a while. It was clear Jodin was attempting to pull some sort of a prank on him. But what was the joke?

"Thanks," he finally said, having made his decision. He broke off the stem and rubbed the insides of the caps over his bracers, making sure to coat them as much as possible with the dark spores. They left a gray color on the tanned leather, which he rubbed in with his fingers until the color had mostly faded. When Tovak looked up, he saw a hint of a smile on Jodin's face. It vanished, almost immediately.

"What about you?" he asked, raising an eyebrow and offering up the other mushroom.

"Oh, I've already done mine…a few weeks ago. I did my bracers, greaves, and even my chest plate. We should bring the rest back to camp, though…you know, for the cook pot."

Jodin must have thought Tovak was a complete idiot, gullible at best. What was he up to?

"Good thinking," Tovak said.

Jodin made a show of looking around. "I saw plenty of game when I came this way before, but none now. I think we're gonna need to flush them out."

Tovak glanced around, wondering how Jodin intended to make that happen.

"This is what we are going to do," Jodin said, taking a step nearer. "You will move on up ahead a ways to the right, until you come to a small cliff face. It's not large, but you can't miss it. From there, circle back up the slope to the left and then come back towards me. Though you can't see it through the trees here, there's a boulder field up in that direction, straight in front of us." Jodin brought his hands together. "I'll meet up with you in the field. There's bound to be something up in those rocks, and if it bolts, there is a good chance it will get spooked towards one of us."

Tovak considered it and decided he did not like the suggestion or the idea of separating. Jodin was obviously figuring Tovak would come running back if he ran into anything more dangerous than a heratta. If he did, or called for help, Tovak knew he would be the butt of jokes for weeks, if not months to come. He was being set up and he did not like it, not one bit.

"What about checking me out on the sling?" Tovak asked.

"We can do that later," Jodin said with a negligent wave. "Let's take something down first, like a dain, then we can go looking for hoppers and see how you are with the sling."

"Sure," Tovak said easily, though he wanted to say no. "Off this way, to the right?" he pointed with his spear farther along the slope.

"Right," Jodin said, flashing a reassuring smile full of yellowed teeth. "Move up that way until you hit the cliff face, then swing around to the left, come back this way, and meet me at the rocks. Between the two of us, something has to get flushed out into the open."

"You got it." Tovak hefted his spear in one hand and then set off through the trees in the direction Jodin had directed.

"And don't get lost," Jodin called out after him. "I don't want to have to come find you."

"Not likely," Tovak said to himself. He moved off into the forest. Once he was out of view, he slipped back into his pioneer training, doing his best to make as little sound as possible as he moved. Tovak picked his way amongst the trees and through what little underbrush scraped out a living beneath the thick pine canopy. He moved from one tree to the next, his senses stretching to detect any sign of wildlife. He scanned the ground for tracks, listened for noise, and even sniffed at the air to pick up odd scents. Nothing, not even the birds called to one another. Something wasn't right.

He went about one hundred yards and paused, going to a knee. Tovak became still, listening to the forest around him, as he'd been trained. He heard and saw nothing out of the ordinary.

Staggen had said there was plenty of game around. The proof of that had been the easy kills they'd made. Thegdol had also said these hills were filled with heratta. So why was there no game about? Tovak could not understand it.

He went another hundred yards to where the hill turned to a tall wall of rock. It rose above him thirty feet. Tovak swung around, as Jodin had indicated. A short way from the base of the rock wall, he discovered a large field of tumbled boulders and jagged stone mixed in amongst a scattering of trees. It was what he was looking for.

He began working his way towards where Jodin had said he would be. Tovak had been so concerned about the game that Jodin was playing, he'd not stopped to consider what type of animals they would encounter. He knew from his studies these hills and the surrounding mountains were home to some pretty dangerous critters, including large spiders, like krata. Tovak had never much liked spiders.

He stopped, suddenly alarmed. The boulder field was the sort of terrain murinok preferred. They were known to use the rocks and boulders as cover in order to approach and ambush their prey. Tovak closed his eyes.

"Great, just bloody great," Tovak said to himself with a glance down at his greaves. "You are a bloody fool, is what you are."

Murinok were attracted to the mushrooms Jodin had given him. Tovak cursed himself for not remembering from his lessons at the Academy. Teams that hunted adult murinok used bunches of blackheads as bait. Now, Tovak was the bait. Jodin had seen to that.

"Just bloody great," Tovak said, for the wind was now blowing his scent over the entire boulder field. That was why there were no animals about. He was in a murinok's territory. Jodin was likely out there watching him at this very moment or waiting for him to come running or cry out for help at the first sight of a murinok.

Tovak considered his options. He could go back. If he did, he could see Jodin branding him a coward. Tovak would become a laughingstock. So, that option was out. He was also certain Jodin was not trying to kill him. No one, other than Struugar and Benthok, knew he was a Pariah. If Jodin was not trying to kill him, then the danger was not so great as it seemed, which was why he'd sent Tovak out here by himself in the first place. If there was a murinok around, it must be a juvenile.

That decided it for Tovak. He would stay and show up Jodin, turning the prank against him. Tovak resolved to see it through to the end. This was just another test and one Tovak intended to pass.

He continued forward, making his way slowly around the boulders and rocks. When that was not possible, he pulled himself over the larger boulders. He kept to the rockier portions of the slope, trying his best to make no sound as he moved deeper into the field of rocks. This was harder than it sounded, especially while wearing armor and carrying a spear. His hobnailed boots did not help either, which tended to grate on the stone when he slipped.

While he moved, he did his best to recall what he knew of the murinok and their habits. Murinok subsisted mostly on other insects that happened into their hunting grounds. They were fiercely territorial and known to fight amongst themselves over females. The killer centipedes were deadly. Adults were, anyway. Juveniles could be too. The trick was not getting bitten, for they were highly venomous. But it was the adults that presented the real threat, for they could grow as large as fifteen feet from head to tail.

Despite being territorial, a juvenile would likely run or hide from him, so all he had to do was make it through the boulder field and to the other side. That would see Jodin's prank turned back on him.

As he moved deeper into the rocky field, he kept an eye out for the telltale tracks of a multi-legged insect. He saw nothing, heard nothing, other than the occasional breeze through the nearby trees, rustling their branches.

He glanced at where he had rubbed the mushrooms on his bracers, and for a moment questioned the wisdom of continuing.

"I've come this far," Tovak said. "All I have to do is make it through the field."

He'd gone about thirty yards, moving from one boulder to the next, when the faint scent of decay caught in his nostrils. He paused and turned his head left and right, sniffing deeply. He pulled himself onto a small boulder and scanned the area. There was nothing moving. Even the nearest birds had gone silent. Then he saw tracks in the dirt around the boulder to his front.

Sliding down to the needle-covered ground, he studied the tracks and general area, letting his gaze widen to maximize the use of his peripheral vision to catch details he might not notice when looking straight on. Not far from the boulder was a streak of black, chalky goo about half a yard long. He recognized both it and the tracks from his studies. The droppings only confirmed it. Murinok.

Inspecting the area closely, he could make out the tell-tale patterns of additional tracks. They were just like the life-sized drawings of tracks his instructors had shown him back at the Academy, although these were somewhat farther apart width-wise, meaning the creature was wider and older. He suddenly went cold. He was not dealing with a juvenile, but an adult.

He moved up to the tacks and squatted down. There were two lines of indentations nearly four feet across, as if someone had poked the ground repeatedly about every six inches or so in two parallel lines.

Just ahead the number of tracks increased, forming a path of sorts through the dirt and pine needles. It was like the kind of trail deer would make through the brush, only there was no brush about. It was clearly a regular path for the creature. He moved cautiously forward. The path led to a nearby slab-like boulder. When he knelt, he could see there was a gap about a foot high and several feet wide that led down into the darkness below. Tovak held a hand up to his nose. The hole stank of decomposition. This was the creature's den. He was sure of it. He glanced around. Was it nearby? Was it watching?

The afternoon suns beat down on him, seeming to cook him in his armor, but he did not notice it. Senses heightened, Tovak drew back and away from the den. The only question now was whether to call it a day or continue. If the creature wasn't a juvenile, which Tovak now thought it wasn't, he was in real danger. He thought about retracing his steps and then disregarded that thought. He was too far into the boulder field. The forest was only thirty yards away. If he could make it down into the trees, he might be able to slip away before the murinok became aware of his presence.

Crouching low and holding the spear ready in both hands, Tovak moved forward towards the trees. The closer he got, the more tracks crisscrossed the ground around him. He also came across the remains of kills, heratta parts and bones from other animals he could not recognize. He breathed slowly, focusing on his surroundings and stretching out with his senses.

Thulla, grant me the strength to see this through.

As he moved downslope, Tovak stopped every few steps, scanning the area around him. Where was it? It was almost impossible to tell which tracks in the dirt and pine needles around the boulders were fresh and which were old. Still, he kept on, getting ever closer to the tree line and safety.

As he pulled himself up and crested a particularly large boulder at the edge of the field, he heard a faint screech and then a scuffling sound in the trees, perhaps ten yards off. Glancing in that direction, he saw a flash of pale yellow on the other side of a teska-sized slab of granite nestled in between two large trees.

Tovak froze, studying the trees and brush. For a moment, he thought he had imagined it. Then decided he hadn't. He was sure it had been the murinok. Tovak took a deep breath and let it out slowly. He was terrified, so much so his hands holding the spear shook slightly. He swallowed and steeled himself.

He slid down the boulder, making as little noise as possible, and then moved to the left of where he'd seen the flash of yellow, hoping to circle wide of the creature. He held his spear in a two-handed grip, drawing closer to the tree line, one slow and careful step at a time, until he reached the first tree and the edge of the boulder field. He paused and looked around. There was no sign of Jodin.

"Bastard," Tovak said under his breath.

His feet made almost no sound as he traversed to his left, around the far side of a tree, stepping from sunlight into shade. Tovak was sweating profusely from the heat and felt relief at finally reaching the cover of the forest. His mouth was dry as sand. As he moved around the trunk, he could just make out a faint crunching and squishing sound, over and over again, from somewhere in the brush.

Tovak circled the tree, as silently as he could, his knuckles white around the shaft of the spear. He did his best to make no sound as he took the final steps past the tree. All he needed to do was sneak off and away from the creature. Only he did not know where it was. Slowly, he made his way deeper into the trees. The brush was thick, but he knew that a few yards in it would thin considerably. He pushed aside a leaf-covered branch from a bush and stepped past it, then froze.

He found himself gazing on the tail end of a yard-long heratta. It was shifting around on the ground, and its rear legs twitched slightly. However, it was not moving of its own volition.

An icy sensation slithered down Tovak's spine.

An eight-foot-long murinok was busily chewing its way down the heratta's body; the head and part of the thorax had already been swallowed. The murinok's segmented carapace was a pale yellow-white, each hardened plate glinting under the sunlight that filtered down through the trees.

Its long, flat body was almost two feet wide but only ten inches thick. Multiple armored and segmented legs stuck out on both sides, each eighteen inches long and ending in a crimson tip that looked as sharp and deadly as any spear-point. The legs undulated along its body in a flowing pattern as it chewed. Its wide, flattened head, with four shining black eyes, gleamed like obsidian.

A cluster of small, leg-like appendages stuck out above and below its mouth, and a pair of long antennae, looking like sweeping filaments of gossamer, swayed back and forth as if tasting the air. The wide, primary fangs, each the size of spear tip, stuck out to the sides of its head.

Tovak was so close he could not only hear the creature chew, but also breathe. Tovak was horrified as he looked on as the monster consumed the heratta. He had the sudden realization that murinok looked harmless enough when rotating on a spit, but the thing before Tovak was a horror of the worst nightmares imaginable. Without a doubt, he understood he was in trouble.

The creature suddenly stopped eating and brought its head up, sniffing at the air.

Damn Jodin.

A heartbeat later, it spotted him, and its response was immediate and terrifying. It reared up into the air, lifting the front half of its body off the ground. With its head bent forward and black eyes fixed on him, it flexed its deadly fangs, from which black liquid dripped down to the ground.

"Oh shit," Tovak breathed.

Only ten feet separated them. The creature thrust its head forward in a half-striking motion that did not come close. Tovak took an involuntary step backward. The bush he'd just stepped through was at his back. The murinok screeched, the sound hurting his ears. Tovak wondered why it did not attack. Then he realized the creature must be intending to frighten him away from its kill.

It screeched and then eased back into a guttural chattering sound that pulsed from deep inside the creature's maw. For a moment, Tovak considered turning and running for his life. He took another half-step back, to gain room, wondering if he could even kill the thing if it attacked. Murinok this size were usually taken down by a team of skilled hunters.

"I am just gonna leave you with your kill," Tovak said calmly in what he hoped was a soothing tone. He took another step back, moving through the bush. "Don't mind me. Go back to feasting."

The murinok had other ideas. It moved forward over its kill and followed him through the brush to the other side. Tovak realized, with a sinking feeling, it would not let him go.

He now wished he'd turned back when he'd had the chance and climbed back up the boulder field to the cliff.

"This is Legend," he said, staring at the creature. He took a deep breath, lowered into a wide crouch, and moved to his left, towards a tree, to see if he could put it between them. The creature moved too, advancing and coiling around the tree. Tovak took several steps backward and away, giving himself room to maneuver the spear. The creature followed, letting loose another screech that was almost deafening.

Tovak took yet another step back, his fear almost getting the better of him. He wanted nothing more than to run. And yet, he knew he couldn't give in to the fear, for fear was defeat and possibly death. If he ran, the murinok would surely chase after him and Tovak had no illusion about who was faster. He had no choice but to face it and fight.

He shifted to the left and looked for the best place to stab the thing. At that moment, the murinok reared up again, showing him its armor-plated belly. The top and sides of the creature were protected by overlapping armored plates. However, the underside was less protected. He eyed the seams between plates that ran along its chest. He would need to strike there to injure it.

The murinok suddenly shrieked and dashed forward a couple of feet, its legs flailing madly as the raised portion of its body swayed back and forth. It snapped its fangs at him, still well out of range, but they clicked together like two stones. The guttural chattering increased in volume. The creature was clearly working itself up to strike.

Tovak was certain any other creature in the forest would have the good sense to let terror drive its legs into a dash for safety, but he stood his ground. To run was to die. He kept that fixed firmly in his mind. To survive he had to stand and fight. He sidestepped once again, putting the murinok between him and a tree, and waited for the opening he hoped would come.

It shrieked again, and as it did, the murinok came around the tree. Tovak made his move before it could react. He stepped forward and thrust with the spear, aiming for a gap in the segments. He put as much strength as possible into the blow. He felt the impact of the spear hammer into the armored underside, but the spearpoint slipped sideways along the armor plates. Surprised, the murinok reared back and away from the spear. Tovak stepped forward again to strike and was beginning his motion when the creature suddenly attacked, lunging down at him with lightning quickness. Abandoning his attack, he dodged to the side. Its fangs clapped together on dead air, only a hairsbreadth from his arm.

He leapt back as the murinok struck almost immediately, lunging for him again. In desperation, Tovak swung the spear as a club and whacked the creature in the head. It wasn't a hard blow, but the murinok drew back, its legs waggling as it hissed at him.

"Focus," he shouted, berating himself, for he knew he might not get another chance.

The murinok screeched again in reply.

Tovak yelled incoherently back at it, finishing with, "Come on, you bastard!"

He took a deep breath and prepared himself as it undulated before him. He tried to get a sense of the rhythm... keeping pace with the motion and anticipating where his target would strike. Its motions were almost hypnotizing, and he realized that his own body was shifting side to side slightly in pace with the swaying body of the creature. It was like the two of them were dancing, only this was the dance of death. One of them would be leaving this boulder field alive and Tovak intended that to be him.

He flowed with the murinok as it moved, shifting left and right. The creature seemed confused by his will to stand his ground.

"Not used to someone staying to fight, are you, now?" Tovak asked it. The murinok hissed in reply.

He made a few furtive thrusts with the spear, trying to provoke it into hasty action. On his fourth thrust, the murinok shrieked again. Tovak was already moving forward as it charged him. He thrust with the spear, aiming for a seam between plates. The tip struck the creature dead center and right along the seam he had been aiming for. His arms shuddered with the impact as the two of them came together in a crash. He felt the spear tip sink into its body, but the creature was practically on top of him and its fangs clamped shut on his shoulder armor with incredible force. Tovak screamed in pain from the powerful impact, and for a single instant he feared the murinok had bitten clean through the armor.

The monster let out a shriek and danced backward and away from him, almost ripping the spear shaft from his hands as it flailed violently to get free. Unwilling to part with the weapon, Tovak pulled back hard on the spear. It popped free, and with it, a stream of white fluid spurted from the wound.

The murinok dropped to the ground and flopped about for several moments, then in a flash, spun its body around. It began moving away, and Tovak realized it was trying to flee. He had hurt it, and bad, for some of the creature's legs had stopped working. His instincts took over. In desperation, he darted forward, and then jumped onto its back, trying to pin it to the ground. The creature stumbled under his weight. Tovak raised the spear over his head and then, putting all his strength into it, drove the spear down into the neck joint, just behind the head, where there was a small gap in the armored plates.

There was a mere moment of resistance, then the spear went deep, the point exploding out the other side to the ground below. Thick, milky liquid sprayed from the wound over his arms and face. The murinok let out a horrendous, pain-wracked screech. It began to buck, and a heartbeat later, Tovak was thrown and sent flying through the air. He hit a tree, hard, and everything went white.

Coming to, he blinked and found himself lying on the ground. He tried to sit up, but dizziness washed over him. Where was he? What had happened? He shook his head, trying to clear the fog from his mind. After a moment, it passed, and with a rush he remembered the monster.

Tovak rolled onto all fours and almost retched as the dizziness came again. Taking a deep breath, he rose unsteadily to his feet. His head hurt something fierce where it had connected with the tree trunk.

It took a moment for him to gain his balance and steady himself. He looked around, searching for the creature. He spotted the murinok a few feet away. It was alive and thrashing about, which meant it was still dangerous. His spear was nowhere to be seen, so he drew his sword.

The murinok spotted him and gave a screech that seemed filled with pain, suffering, and sudden panic. He cautiously approached the wounded monster. It was clearly thrashing about in its death throes, which were becoming weaker by the moment. He spotted the remnants of his spear. The creature's flailing had shattered the shaft, leaving only the tip embedded in the neck joint.

For some reason, Tovak felt suddenly sad for the murinok. Gazing upon it, he realized what a truly a magnificent creature it was. It had been the master of this area for some time, at least until Tovak had trespassed into its domain. The sadness came from the suffering. Tovak advanced, intending to end it. Eyeing him, the creature gave a half-hearted shriek, attempted to draw away, then spasmed, collapsing to the ground. A gust of air was exhaled from its breathing slits and the murinok fell still. It was clearly dead.

Tovak puffed out his cheeks and stood there, staring at the murinok. Completely worn out, he allowed the sword point to fall and rest on the ground. His heart pounded in his chest. He was still dizzy from the blow he had taken. The fear that was only now fading from his thoughts, left his nerves tingling.

"Thulla's bones," a familiar voice called out from behind him.

MARC ALAN EDELHEIT & QUINCY J. ALLEN

Tovak turned to see Jodin standing there, a few yards away. His spear was held at the ready. He was breathing heavily, as if he'd been sprinting.

"I—" Tovak started and then stopped, his head still ringing. "You weren't in the boulder field. I killed it," he said, disbelief filling his voice.

"I don't believe it," Jodin breathed, stepping up to him and staring down at the creature. "You killed a damn near fully grown murinok."

"It was either that or...."

"You should be dead," Jodin said, going pale, his eyes moving from Tovak to the dead murinok. "I thought it was only a—"

"Jodin," a voice called out. "Tovak."

"Shit," Jodin said, looking around. "Shit, shit, shit." Then, he raised his voice. "Over here."

Thegdol and Gorabor emerged from the trees. They both had their swords drawn. They were sweaty and red-faced. It was clear they had run.

Jodin shot Tovak a nervous glance, and he looked like he was about to say something, but he clamped his mouth shut and waited for the other two to join them.

Thegdol and Gorabor ran up and came to a sudden stop when they saw the murinok.

"Great gods," Thegdol said, looking from the murinok to Tovak. "Are you all right, son?"

"I killed it," Tovak said, still feeling dazed at what had occurred and more than a little woozy. His head ached something fierce. This day had gone nothing like he had imagined it would when the company had set out before first light. He felt like sitting down. His legs trembled with fatigue.

"Are you injured?" Thegdol asked.

158

"I...." Tovak paused and looked down at himself. He was covered over in the murinok's white blood. There was some red there too, his own. A quick examination showed that he had a shallow cut on his arm and he felt hotness on his cheek. He reached up and came away with blood. The cut seemed minor.

"It doesn't look that bad, no more than a scrape," Thegdol said, looking him over carefully and probing the wound on his cheek with a finger. Tovak winced at the touch.

"I killed it," Tovak said again. His voice seemed to come from a long way away.

The corporal paused and looked into Tovak's eyes. "What do you mean, you killed it? That's a good sized-adult there."

"I killed it," Tovak said woodenly. He felt incredibly tired. All he wanted was to sit down and have a drink of water and then fall asleep. Gods, he was terribly thirsty. He pulled his skin out, unstopped it, and began drinking. The warm water felt like mana from the heavens.

Thegdol's gaze shifted over to Jodin.

"Where were you?" Thegdol asked, his eyes narrowing dangerously. "Care to explain what happened here?"

"Ah," Jodin said. "I, ah ... it was supposed to be a joke."

Thegdol's expression hardened. He turned to look at the monster for a long moment. He sheathed his sword and then rounded on Jodin.

"This wouldn't be the murinok hunting ground you reported finding, would it?" Thegdol asked. "I believe you said it was a juvenile? I heard you telling the lieutenant."

"I, ah ...." Jodin stammered, clearly at a loss for words. "It was only a prank, Thegdol, honest."

"Thulla's bones, Tovak," Gorabor said. He sheathed his sword and moved closer to the murinok, nudging it with a boot. "Killing that thing must have been something to see."

"Shut up, you," Thegdol barked at Gorabor. He turned a genuinely angry glare on Tovak before swinging back around to face Jodin. "I told you to show him the ropes and see how he was on the sling. Perhaps I was mistaken? I don't recall asking you to take him murinok hunting."

"Thegdol," Jodin said. "I…."

"Shut up, you great bloody idiot," Thegdol shouted, then looked up toward the heavens. "I am truly saddled with idiots. The gods must hate me." He turned to look at Tovak. "You took on an adult murinok by yourself. That was a damn fool thing to do. All three of you are idiots, idiots."

"What did I do?" Gorabor asked. "I was with you."

Thegdol let out a long breath that hissed through his teeth.

Tovak's legs went weak. He sat down on the ground and began undoing the straps to his helmet. His hands shook and it took a moment, but he gratefully lifted the heavy helmet off his head and set it on the ground. It felt wonderful to have it off. His hair was drenched in sweat.

Staggen and Lok appeared and made their way over. They too had clearly heard the creature and come running to help.

"Wow," Lok said, gazing down at the carcass. "That is one big critter."

"We're gonna eat good tonight," Staggen said.

Thegdol closed his eyes and pinched the bridge of his nose.

"Corporal," Tovak said. "I—"

Thegdol held up a hand, stopping Tovak. "I don't want to hear it."

"But—" Tovak said.

"No buts. You can explain later," Thegdol said, and shot an angry look at Jodin. "I am sure the lieutenant will love to hear both of your excuses. For now, let's get this monster gutted and cleaned."

Tovak made to stand, but Thegdol pushed him back down with a firm hand.

"Not you. Take a moment and rest. That's an order."

"Yes, Corporal," Tovak said and then laid down on the ground. He looked up at the blue sky above through the pine canopy. The two suns were working their way towards the horizon as evening was fast approaching. The sky was incredibly blue, with a slight tinge of red. He thought he'd never seen such a wonderful color. A moment later, he closed his eyes and sleep took him.

CHAPTER TEN

"Good gods," Staggen said, wearily, "I'm tired."
Staggen was half a head shorter than Tovak and broader through the shoulders. He looked to be several decades older, with auburn hair kept in a single, long braid. He had piercing green eyes and a red beard. Lok, on the other hand, was only a few years older than Tovak, with dark eyes and a thick mane of brown hair. His beard reached his belt. He was the same height as Staggen, but of a much leaner build.

"Come on," Lok said, sounding just as exhausted. He knelt before the makeshift litter they were building. "Let's finish this. Slide the stakes underneath the poles, about two feet apart, there and there."

Jodin and Staggen did as instructed. Tovak stood ready and handed over another pair of crude stakes that he'd fashioned from pine limbs, first one to Staggen and the other to Jodin. Once the stakes were in place, Lok and Staggen began securing them with leather straps to the crossbeam. Both worked quickly and with an efficiency that told Tovak they'd done this very thing many times before. They had already constructed one litter and now were finishing the second.

Thegdol had permitted Tovak an hour's sleep, then kicked him awake. Tovak felt more exhausted, if that was possible, than before. He was still a little dazed from the blow to his head and had a persistent headache. His body felt battered and bruised. Nearly every part of him ached.

Worse, he was dirty, grimy, and covered almost from head to toe in the murinok's dried blood. It left him feeling sticky and itchy. He felt a desperate need to clean up, but in truth was so tired he almost did not care—almost.

A few feet away, Thegdol and Gorabor had finished butchering the murinok. It had taken them some time, because they had had to first crack the shell and peel back the armored plates to get at the meat inside. That had taken serious effort. They had already loaded the first litter, securing the meat tightly in place with rope, leather straps, and the forage sacks they'd brought with them.

"Is it ready?" Thegdol asked, looking over as he stood. He wiped his hands clean on a rag. "We're finished here."

"It is," Lok said, standing up.

"Let's get the rest of the meat loaded and secured," Thegdol said, glancing up at the sky. The last of the suns' light was shining on the tops of the trees. "I'd like to be back to camp before it's wholly dark."

"Agreed," Staggen said. "No telling what might come out at night to hunt, be it orc, goblin, or wild creature."

Tovak did not like the sound of that. He shared a glance with Gorabor. The other gave a half-shrug of his shoulders, then reached for the first hunk of meat. They set to work, with Gorabor and Tovak carrying the butchered meat over to the newly made litter. Staggen, Jodin, and Lok busied themselves tying it down. When the job was done, Tovak stood back and stifled a yawn as he surveyed the section's handiwork.

"Don't start that now." Lok slapped Tovak on the shoulder in a playful manner. "You already had your nap. The rest of us weren't so lucky."

"I could use another," Tovak said.

"If you think you're tired now," Staggen said, "this ain't nothin'. Once, I went three days without sleep. You remember the siege at Carin'Holg, don't you, Thegdol? That was one bastard of a time."

"Enough talk," Thegdol said. "Lok and Staggen will take the first litter. Jodin and Gorabor have the second."

"What about me?" Tovak asked.

"We will take turns," Thegdol said as he took a drink from his waterskin. He wiped his lips with the back of his arm before continuing. "When someone tires, they will let us know. Until then, we follow along. Understand?"

"Yes, Corporal," Tovak said.

"All right, children," Thegdol said, addressing the entire squad. "The terrain ahead is difficult and rough. We set a steady pace and go slow. Watch where you place your feet. I want no turned ankles and I certainly don't want the litters dropped and the meat ruined. You get tired, you speak up and the next person up will take your place. Questions?" Thegdol paused, glancing around. "No? Let's go then."

They set out, with Tovak and Thegdol following. They traveled in silence for a bit. Then, Thegdol reached out an arm and slowed Tovak so they fell a few paces behind the litters.

"Tovak, you are the luckiest son of a bitch I've ever known," Thegdol said quietly. "I don't know how you managed to take down a nearly full-grown murinok by yourself... I really don't. It was a daft thing to do. You should be dead. You realize that, right?"

"Yes, Corporal," Tovak said, not quite knowing what else to say.

"Jodin was an idiot for playing such a prank," Thegdol said, "and you were stupid for deciding to take on a murinok by yourself. If you'd been killed, it would have been on me. The lieutenant would have held me to account. Got that?"

"I'm sorry, Corporal," Tovak said. "By the time I realized it wasn't a juvenile, it was too late to back out. I tried skirting around it, but ended up walking right on top of it with a fresh kill."

"I don't want excuses," Thegdol said. "What I want is for it or something like it not to happen again." Thegdol tapped the side of Tovak's helmet. "Use your bloody head next time."

Tovak wanted to say that it had not been his fault, but he knew that was not quite true. Yes, Jodin had played a prank on him, but he'd been somewhat wise to it and had gone along anyway. He had done it to prove himself to the others. He should have been smarter and because of his lapse in judgement had almost died for it.

"You got lucky today," Thegdol said. "Don't get comfortable being lucky, because that luck might one day fail you. When that happens, you will end up stone-dead. And you are no good to the company dead."

"In the future"—Tovak sucked in a long breath—"I will use my head."

"Let's hope you do," Thegdol said. "As it is, the lieutenant will not be too happy with us and there will likely be consequences for you and Jodin." Thegdol fell silent for several heartbeats. "Do something stupid like this again and I promise you will regret it something fierce. Do we understand one another?"

Tovak's eyes locked for a moment with Thegdol. The corporal seemed deadly serious. He gave a simple nod. With that, Thegdol increased his pace to catch up with the others. Tovak silently resolved to not let his corporal down again. He would live up to Thegdol's expectations, even if it killed him doing it.

The sun had set by the time they made it back to the camp. Coming down the hill and emerging from the tree line, Tovak saw that the entire section was back. The smell of roasting meat was on the air and it set his mouth to watering.

"Looks like we have company," Staggen said and pointed ahead of them towards the camp, thirty yards off.

"I think I see Gulda," Gorabor blurted excitedly. He and Tovak were carrying the same litter. It was hard work. "That's her," Gorabor said.

Tovak looked up and, sure enough, there were four warriors standing before the camp entrance. They were clearly female, wore brown leather armor with green cloaks, and carried bows. He could see more of them inside the camp.

"What are the archers doing here?" Gorabor asked, looking over at the corporal.

"A squad of them were sent up with the carts," Thegdol said. "The lieutenant mentioned it to me before we began foraging. They've been temporarily attached to our section. In fact, each section is getting a squad of archers. Apparently, there is some concern for our safety, what with the warband moving into hostile lands and all. As a result, orders came down from the captain to fold the archers in while we're out in the field. The lieutenant wasn't too excited about it."

Tovak wondered why Benthok wasn't happy about being reinforced. It seemed to make good sense, but he was too weary and short on breath to ask. Besides, he'd already made a fool out of himself once today with Jodin's prank. He was unwilling to do so again.

Both sentries on their side of the encampment waved at them. Thegdol held a hand up in reply as they neared.

Two carts were parked by the entrance to the camp. The teska were still hitched, though one of the teamsters was busy unhooking their harnesses for the night.

"Looks like that's Corporal Hilla, if I'm not mistaken." Thegdol gestured at one of the archers by the entrance. She was speaking with two of her archers. A moment later, she finished whatever she'd been saying and the three of them walked into the camp. Thegdol glanced around at his section as they drew nearer. "I don't think I need to mention to anyone not to fool with her or her girls."

"Aye," Staggen said, "she'll gut you and use your balls as sling shot." Staggen let out a heavy breath. "Though she's such a beauty, I think I'm inclined to let her try."

"Friend of yours?" Gorabor asked, half-jokingly.

"She used to be ... a long time ago."

"She's trouble, Staggen," Thegdol said. "Best leave that in the past, where it belongs."

"Aye," Staggen said, "you're probably right. But sometimes I wonder."

"Don't," Thegdol said. "You know I am right."

"Playing with fire, Staggen," Lok said. "But then again, you like to play with fire, don't you?"

Staggen was silent for a heartbeat. "Sometimes, getting burned is part of the fun."

"Your funeral then," Lok said.

"Leave the litters here," Thegdol said.

They set the litters down next to the carts. Tovak massaged his hands, for they ached from carrying the damn thing. He noticed that Jodin and Gorabor were doing the same.

"Wow," Dagmar said, coming up. "Your squad took down a murinok? Judging from the amount of meat, it must have been a good-sized one. I thought what Logath's squad did was impressive, but this ...."

Dagmar's eyes went from the meat to Tovak, his eyes running over the white blood that had long since dried and then back to the meat packed on to the litters.

"Did you use this one as bait, Corporal?" Dagmar asked with a grin.

"Don't you have something that needs doing?" Thegdol asked Dagmar in a sour tone. "Or do you want me to speak with your corporal and have him find you some work?"

"No, Corporal," Dagmar said hastily, "that won't be necessary."

Dagmar moved off quickly, heading in the direction of the latrine, but not before sparing Tovak another glance. Tovak took a moment to look around. With everyone from the section about, the camp was a hive of activity.

"Smells like krata," Staggen said. "I could do with some of that."

"Yeah," Lok answered and gestured towards the central fire. "One of the other squads must have caught a trapdoor spider. We're gonna have to watch out for those nasty buggars, then, when we're out and about."

"Well," Staggen said, "at least we'll be eating good tonight."

Tovak looked towards the center of camp. Several fires were going. An older Dvergr in simple clothes and a long apron stood there, rotating the handle of a spit by the central fire. Tovak had not seen him before, but he was dressed like the other teamster. Upon the spit was a charred and hairless krata. The teamster was slowly turning the spit, giving it a quarter-turn at a time. Tovak shivered at the sight of the large spider, which was about the size of a big dog.

"Unload the meat, then stack it in the cart. When that's done, get whatever you require from your packs and go to the stream to wash up," Thegdol said. "We're late and I need to report to the lieutenant. He'll be wanting to know why. Dismissed."

Jodin glanced sharply at Thegdol, but the corporal did not seem to notice. Thegdol set off into the camp and towards the lieutenant, who was standing on the other side of the central fire, talking to two of the section's warriors who were standing to attention. Tovak thought it did not appear as if it were a pleasant conversation, for the lieutenant seemed agitated and was leaning forward as he spoke. He jabbed a finger into one of the warrior's chests. The conversation also seemed very one-sided.

Jodin glanced over at Tovak and his face hardened. Feeling a sudden stab of anger, Tovak met the other's gaze and held it. The prank had almost cost him his life. Jodin turned away as they began untying the straps and rope from the litters. They worked in silence and it took only a short while to unload and then load the meat into the cart bed with the rest of the section's bounty. When the job was done, Jodin spared Tovak another sour look before stalking off towards the camp.

"Don't worry about him," Gorabor said as Staggen and Lok followed after Jodin. "Thegdol's not too happy with him and I'm sure the lieutenant will have something to say about it too, after he hears what happened."

Tovak could only nod. What sort of punishment would the lieutenant mete out for being stupid? And, Tovak knew without a doubt, regardless of the prank, he had acted foolishly. There would be consequences for him as well. Thegdol had confirmed as much.

"Come on," Gorabor said, his eyes on Gulda. She had clearly been posted to duty on the wall and was standing a few paces away from the sentry, by the bridge. She looked to be around Tovak and Gorabor's age, with green eyes and a long braid of reddish-blonde hair. Her features were strong, and though she was pretty, Gulda's gaze, which was fixed upon Gorabor, reminded him of a hawk in search of prey.

"Hi, Gulda," Gorabor said, almost shyly as they stepped up to the edge of the berm and just below her.

"Gorabor." She stepped nearer and gave him a veiled smile. There was a glint in her eye, and Tovak realized immediately that Gorabor had not been exaggerating. She was happy to see him, just as he was her. They looked at each other for a long moment and Tovak suddenly felt uncomfortable, as if he were intruding upon something intimate. He started to move away, when Gorabor caught his arm. "Tovak," Gorabor said. "I'd like to introduce you to Gulda."

Her gaze flicked to him, going rapidly from foot to helm. Covered in the murinok's blood, Tovak knew he looked quite the sight. She cocked an amused eyebrow and it was clear she was wondering what had happened to see him in such a state.

"It is my pleasure to make your acquaintance," Tovak said, offering a slight bow.

"Mine as well," Gulda said. "Any friend of Gorabor is a friend of mine."

"Friend?" Tovak asked, looking over at Gorabor. It had been years since he'd had a true friend.

"We're squad mates," Gorabor said, "why not friends too?"

Tovak became very still at that. He cleared his throat as Gorabor turned back to Gulda.

"Tovak killed an adult murinok today." Gorabor thumped Tovak on the back proudly. "All by himself too."

"A feat worthy of a toast," Gulda said and seemed genuinely impressed, though there was something mocking about her tone.

Tovak did not feel like toasting his success. In truth, after speaking with Thegdol on the march back, it now felt like he'd failed. "I'd settle for a bath."

She laughed at that and he found it was a pleasant sound. It had been a long while since a girl laughed at something he said, rather than at his expense.

"You certainly need one." Her gaze went to Gorabor's arms, which were coated in dried blood from butchering. She wrinkled her nose. "I think you both could use some bathing."

"Go on without me, Tovak," Gorabor said. "She's gonna have to put up with my stench a little longer. I will catch up with you in a bit."

Tovak nodded and moved past Gorabor and into the camp. He headed towards where his pack lay, apparently undisturbed. He opened his pack, dug through it, and pulled out a spare tunic, the leather cleaning kit, a small towel, and the whetstone for his sword. He also grabbed his other waterskin, which was full, and drank heavily from it. He took both waterskins and walked out of the camp, past Gorabor, who was still talking with Gulda. So intent were they on each other that neither seemed to notice him as he passed.

Tovak made his way down to the stream. There were several others already there, though no one he knew. They were either bathing or busily working on their kit. Conversation was in the air, but it was muted and confined to a handful of individuals. The sense he got was that everyone was tired and worn out. It had been a long day.

He took his helmet off and then his armor. Relief was immediate. Tovak stood there for a long moment, enjoying the feeling of not carrying the extra dead weight he'd humped around all day. He took a tentative step and felt light as a feather, though his feet hurt. He was certain he had blisters from the march. Still, it was marvelous, and he savored it for several moments. Then the feeling passed, and the weariness returned. He had work to do before he could relax.

Tovak sat down on a large rock next to the stream. The water gurgled by, making a pleasant, almost relaxing sound as it flowed around the rocks. His armor stank of sweat and worse, smelling quite sour. *Heck*, Tovak thought, *I stink too.* He considered cleaning his armor first and then decided against that idea. He knelt at the edge of the stream. The first thing he did was wash his hands, arms, and face. Then, he stripped. Setting his boots aside, he put his abused feet into the stream and almost let out a sigh of relief. Then he began washing the rest of himself clean. It took longer than it should have, for Tovak spent extra time scrubbing. He wanted the blood, dirt, and grime gone, all of it.

The water was cold, frigid even, but the air was warm and it felt good. Once he was clean, he slipped on the fresh tunic and made sure to tuck his Warrant securely into its pocket and out of sight. The clean tunic was a relief in and of itself. Tovak examined his blisters and popped two before turning to his tunic and washing it. He did not have any soap. He would have to ask Sergeant Bahr for some when the section returned to the encampment.

He did his best at cleaning the tunic, scrubbing it against a large rock. Some of the murinok blood would not come out, no matter how hard he scrubbed. The tunic appeared to be permanently stained. After giving it some more attention, he reluctantly concluded there was nothing he could do about it. The tunic was as clean as he was going to get it. He wrung the tunic, squeezing tightly, then shook it, trying to get as much of the water out of the wool as possible.

Next, he began working on his kit, starting with his helm. There was a small dent in the left side where his head had connected with the tree during the fight with the murinok. He would need to find an armorer in the main encampment to repair it. Tovak wondered how much that would cost and whether he could afford it.

The plates on his left shoulder armor were also damaged. There were two clear indentations where the murinok had tried to bite him. He touched the indentations and shivered as he realized how close he'd come to death.

"Stupid, Tovak," he said to himself, in a whisper only he could hear. "Real smart."

He put such thoughts aside and worked on cleaning the armor, as he'd been taught at the Academy, first brushing it free of dirt and grime, hunting through all the grooves and nooks for even a speck of dirt. In the dying light, this was more difficult than it sounded. He knew he would have to check over his work in the morning. When he was satisfied he'd done a decent job, he made sure to wipe it down with a wet towel. His instructors had been quite fastidious in their inspection of his work. Tovak had no reason to assume Thegdol and Benthok would be any less thorough.

It was completely dark when he was done with his armor. The moon was rising, though it was hidden behind a cloud. A torch that one of the others brought to the stream illuminated those working on their kit. Under the poor light, Tovak checked over his work once again and found himself pleased with what he saw.

He filled his waterskins, topping them off, and then started cleaning and sharpening his sword. He ran the stone across the blade several times. He heard footsteps behind him. Turning, he saw Thegdol approaching with a cleaning kit and a pair of waterskins in his hands. Jodin,

Lok, and Staggen were following along behind. They broke off from the corporal and moved upstream to a free spot where there was some room.

"Corporal," Tovak greeted.

Thegdol's eyes shifted over to Tovak's armor, but he did not say anything about whether he approved or not. Tovak got the sense his corporal was unhappy and deeply displeased. There was just something about Thegdol's manner that said as much.

Thegdol settled down by the stream, a few feet away. The corporal began unfastening his armor before removing it with a soft groan. He set it by his side, then sat down on a large rock at the edge of the water and took off his boots.

Tovak returned his attention to the edge of his blade. He ran the stone down it several more times, then carefully scraped his fingernail with the edge, watching a thin layer of the nail curl away. Satisfied that it was sharp enough, he rose to his feet. His legs were so done in, they trembled slightly from the effort. He sheathed his blade and then gathered up his armor as Thegdol leaned forward and began washing his hands.

Tovak turned and took a few paces towards the camp. He stopped, looking back. He hesitated a moment more. Then he spoke.

"I'm sorry if I caused you any trouble with the lieutenant."

Thegdol froze for a heartbeat, then he went back to his washing. "Apology accepted. Now, leave me in peace, boy."

"Yes, Corporal," Tovak replied.

He walked back to camp, passing Gorabor, who was headed towards the stream with his own kit and waterskins. His new friend seemed in excellent spirits.

"How'd it go?" Tovak asked, stopping.

Gorabor grinned and slapped Tovak on the shoulder. "She's still keen on me."

"Glad to hear it."

"I'll see you in a bit," Gorabor said, continuing on his way to the stream.

Tovak watched Gorabor for a moment, then walked into camp. He nodded to Gulda, who was still standing by the entrance, where she'd been posted. He returned to where he'd left his pack and opened it. He took a moment to pause and placed his hand upon *Thulla's Blessed Word*, which was still wrapped up inside his pack.

"Thank you, Thulla," Tovak whispered. "Thank you for seeing me through."

Tovak took a deep breath. Word must have gotten around about his fight with the murinok, for there were plenty of eyes on him, but nobody said anything. Laying aside his armor, he packed away his brush, small towel, and cleaning kit. He laid his freshly cleaned tunic over the back of his pack, but not before wringing it out again. With any luck, it would be dry by morning, and if it wasn't, well then, the sun would dry it out soon enough.

He stood and his legs protested with the movement. He looked around and realized he had no idea where his squad would be bedding down for the night. His squad mates were all at the stream cleaning up. Well, when they returned, he would find out soon enough where he could lay his bedroll. Tovak made his way over to the fire, where the teamster was slowly rotating the spit, to take a closer look at the spider. The scent of the roasting krata was incredible.

"Care to give this beastie a few turns for me?" the teamster asked, spotting Tovak. "My arm's getting tired. Damn thing's heavier than a pregnant teska, but it's gonna be good eating."

"Sure," Tovak said, stepping up to the fire. A light gust of wind blew smoke into his face. He held his breath until it passed.

"Here." The teamster tossed Tovak a towel. "So you don't burn yourself, laddie." He gestured at the spit. "The metal's hot."

Tovak nodded and, using the towel, took over, giving the spit a slow turn. He could feel the warmth of the metal through the towel. The heat of the fire beat against him too, to the point of it being uncomfortable. "I'm Tovak."

"You can call me Shrike."

"Shrike?" Tovak asked, for it was an odd name.

"Aye," Shrike said, "my nickname. It was given to me by my mates, back when I was able to march with the best of you boys." Shrike blew out a breath and tapped his right knee. "Bum knee ended my soldiering career something quick. Instead of mustering out, I joined the teamsters. It was either that or go home, and I didn't want to go home."

Tovak did not say anything to that, for he knew it must have been a blow to Shrike's sense of self-worth. There was not much Legend to be had amongst the teamsters. All they did was drive the wagons and carts. Tovak suddenly felt such thoughts were ungenerous. He supposed in a way there was honor in what Shrike did, for without the teamsters, the warband would quickly go hungry.

Shrike stepped back up to him, eyes on Tovak as he rotated the spit.

"Keep it steady, a nice slow turn, yes, just like that." He stepped around Tovak and, using a towel, grabbed a ladle that had been hanging on the other side of the spit. Sitting under the roasting krata and amidst the flames was a small iron pot. Its contents bubbled. Shrike dipped the ladle in and then poured the liquid over the shell of the krata. It was bacon fat mixed with water.

As he gave the spit another turn, Tovak examined the monstrosity of the spider that was roasting away before him. Its fangs and venom sacks had been removed. The hairs had burned off, leaving only a smoke-charred, smooth surface. He stared into its now-blackened face and shook his head in dismay. He could not imagine coming upon such a monster out in the wild, but someone from one of the other squads had. Heck, a few hours back he'd not thought he could face down an adult murinok and live to tell the tale.

"I don't believe I've seen you before," Shrike said, looking at him closely and squinting slightly. He dropped the ladle back into the pot. "You're new to the company."

"Yes," Tovak said.

"Well," Shrike said, "you joined a right solid bunch. Some good boys in this company. Let me tell you, you could have done worse than join the Baelix Guard."

Tovak said nothing, just gave a nod and the spit another turn.

"Proud of what you did today?" Shrike asked. "It was you, right? What all of them have been jawing about? The new guy killing a murinok?"

Tovak froze.

"Aye," Shrike said, "I heard about you and the murinok. So, I'll ask you again. Are you proud, boy?"

"Proud?" Tovak turned his gaze away from Shrike's and back to the krata.

"Proud," Shrike said. "It's not every day you take out an adult murinok by yourself. That's quite a feat. So, are you proud of yourself, boy?"

Tovak fell silent. He ran his gaze about and found more than one pair of eyes upon him. They quickly looked away.

He felt himself scowl and gave the spit another half-turn as he considered his response. Then, after a moment more, he looked back at Shrike. "No, not really. It almost killed me, and to be honest, I'd not want to take one on again by myself. If I never see another murinok, unless it's on the dinner table, I will count myself fortunate."

Shrike gave a low chuckle that was part cackle. "You're not a daft bugger, then. I guess there is some hope for you."

"Thanks," Tovak replied and gave the spit another turn. He did feel some pride in the deed, but it was overshadowed by the thought of what could have happened. That and whatever Benthok had in store for him and Jodin. He was not looking forward to that encounter, when it came. Thoughts of the lieutenant caused him to look over to where Benthok sat on his bedroll. He had a sheet of vellum out and was writing something with a charcoal pencil. Tovak wondered if it had anything to do with him and Jodin. He hoped not.

"It should be soon," Shrike said, interrupting his thoughts.

"'Til it's done?" Tovak asked, looking back at the teamster. He had to admit, the smell of the roasting krata was driving him crazy with hunger.

"Yep. Once we hear the pop, we can serve this monster up and fill our bellies."

"Pop?"

"Top of the shell," Shrike said. "That's how we know these things are ready to eat."

The teamster poured another ladle of bacon juice over the carapace. "You see, the heat from the fire pressurizes and cooks the insides, and at just the right moment, the shell along the back ruptures and cracks open with a burst of tender, succulent, white meat just begging to be eaten.

The legs are also full of goodness. This one's kinda small, but it should be enough to feed the section."

"Small?" Tovak asked, thinking the thing was enormous.

The krata sizzled and hissed as it cooked. Steam escaped from the leg joints. Tovak gave the spider another full turn, righting it. The moment it was righted, with a sizzling *POP*, the back of the krata broke open. Tovak jumped and almost dropped the towel. A thick line of white, puffy meat had pushed its way out, as the shell of the carapace had cracked open. A cheer went up from some the nearest warriors. They began rising to their feet and started to make a line, mess bowls in hand.

"Give me a hand with this, son," Shrike said, moving to the other end of the spit and taking a second towel from where it had been tucked into his belt. "When I say, 'Lift,' we lift together, okay?"

"Right," Tovak said.

"Now, lift."

Tovak did as instructed, grunting with the effort. They lifted the spit away from the fire and placed the steaming carcass, legs down, on the ground.

"That's one heavy beast." Shrike held out his hand towards Tovak. "Lend me your dagger, boy, will you?"

Tovak pulled his dagger out and handed it over.

Shrike stuck Tovak's dagger into the white meat and then carved out a healthy portion. He stabbed the meat he'd cut away and then handed the dagger back to Tovak with the point up, and the meat glistening in the firelight. Juice ran down the hilt and onto the teamster's hand.

"There you go, son," Shrike said, "for your help. You can come back with your mess bowl and line up with the rest for more. Now, step aside. I need to feed the rest of this hungry bunch." Shrike looked over the line that had formed and raised his voice. "You're all animals, don't you know that? You don't care about the effort and time that goes into cooking something right. It's an art. All you want to do is eat... no matter who cooks it. Savages the lot of you, no better than animals."

"You're the only animal I know, Shrike," a voice from the line called.

"Aye," Shrike answered, "that I am. It's probably why I like you bloody skirmishers."

"Thank you, Shrike," Tovak said, and stepped aside.

Shrike gave an absent nod, then turned back towards the line.

"Corporal Logath," Shrike said to the first in line. "Since it was your squad that brought down the krata, as squad leader, you get the largest portion."

"I expected nothing less," Logath replied with a wide grin. "Serve me up, Shrike."

Shrike carved off a chunk of meat as Logath held out his mess bowl. Logath had bushy orange hair and a wide nose. Logath's cheeks were pockmarked. His beard was long, with four thick braids reaching down to his waist that were tied off with green leather laces. Silver beads had been woven into his beard.

"Not a bad first day out, eh, Shrike?" Logath asked as the teamster put the meat into the bowl.

"It's why I volunteer to haul for foraging duty," Shrike said. "Despite the risks, I'm always fed well and, more importantly, I get to do what I love, to cook. It is one of the few joys left to me. Can you believe they won't let me cook back in the main encampment? The cooks are afraid an old teamster like me will show them up." Shrike shook his head sadly.

"Nah, Shrike, it's because you're an animal," a voice from the line said. "They'd rather cook the animals than work with them."

Shrike laughed and so did a few of those in line.

"Their loss and our gain," Logath said.

"Exactly," Shrike said, sounding pleased. "Next."

Amused by the exchange, Tovak stepped away to where he'd left his pack. As he sat down, he took a bite, and found the krata meat not only hot, but quite tasty. He wholeheartedly agreed with Corporal Logath. Shrike was wasted as a teamster.

Chapter Eleven

Tovak set his mess bowl down on his thigh. It was his second helping. His stomach was satisfyingly full and he felt slightly groggy, lazy even. His head still hurt from the blow it had taken during the murinok fight, and his body ached something fierce. He took a pull from his waterskin and then rubbed at his tired eyes while yawning. The wine ration had been distributed. An untouched skin lay next to his pack, where he'd left it.

Tovak had never been much of a drinker. This was primarily because he'd rarely had enough surplus money to spend on wine and spirits. But that wasn't why he'd not started in on the skin, like everyone else. As exhausted as he was, Tovak feared the wine would put him right to sleep. So, he'd made the decision to save it. He would enjoy it on the morrow.

Tovak would have liked to consult his spirit deck. For as long as he could remember, he had done so on a daily basis. It had given him comfort, but also guidance. He dared not pull it out, for fear of ridicule. The same went for *Thulla's Blessed Word*.

He yawned again and then looked up. The lieutenant was looking in his direction. Their gazes locked. Benthok's expression was grim, cold even. Tovak knew without a doubt the lieutenant was unhappy with him. Benthok held his gaze a moment more and then turned his attention away when one of the corporals asked a question of him.

Free of the lieutenant's scrutiny, Tovak puffed out a breath, then glanced around. The section was seated about the camp. Most were reclining against their packs, drinking or eating the last of the food. A few were gaming, rolling dice, or throwing bones. Several of the section were even asleep. Across from the cook fire, Logath was regaling a small group of rapt listeners with some sort of a tale. Tovak only caught the occasional word. The group roared with laughter every so often. After a hard, long day, it was a pleasant and relaxed atmosphere. But for the lieutenant's ire towards him, Tovak liked it.

Then the lieutenant abruptly stood and moved towards the central fire. The mood instantly changed. All conversation stilled and even Logath ceased his storytelling. Tovak felt suddenly ill, for he knew the moment of reckoning was at hand.

"Shrike," Benthok asked. "Did you save some food for the sentries?"

"Aye, sir," Shrike said. "That I did, that I did."

"Good." The lieutenant looked around and spotted Gorabor. He had just returned from the stream and cleaning up. Gorabor was heartily digging into his food. "After we're done here, you will take food to the sentries."

"Yes, sir," Gorabor said, setting his bowl aside and standing to attention.

"Sit down," Benthok said, glancing towards the mess bowl, "and finish your meal first."

Gorabor sat down, as ordered, but he did not resume eating. His eyes were on Benthok. It was at that moment Tovak noticed that all eyes were on the lieutenant. It was so quiet that Tovak could clearly hear the pop and hiss of the main fire from ten feet away.

"Listen up," Benthok said, though that was hardly necessary. "There is a matter we need to deal with before tonight's lesson on hand signals."

Here it comes, Tovak thought, and closed his eyes. A moment later, he opened them. Whatever the punishment was, he'd earned it. He might not like it, but he resolved to take whatever the lieutenant dished out. It was the honorable thing to do. The worst that could be done to him would be kicking him out of the company, and Tovak thought that an unlikely prospect.

Benthok moved around the fire and looked at Jodin, who had been sitting with Lok and Staggen. Jodin froze and hastily swallowed the mouthful of food he'd been chewing.

"Jodin, Tovak, front and center," Benthok said, in an almost deathly quiet tone.

"Sir," Jodin said, jumping to his feet and moving towards the lieutenant.

Tovak rose as well and stepped up next to Jodin. They both stiffened their backs, standing to attention.

"You're a fool," Benthok hissed at Jodin. "You could've gotten Tovak killed today."

Jodin said nothing, just stared fixedly ahead.

The lieutenant took a step away and swung his gaze around the section. "What is my one rule out here?"

No one answered.

"Could the corporals help me with this one? For it seems Jodin isn't the only one to have forgotten."

"To not separate," Thegdol said. "While foraging, we stick together."

"Why is that rule in place?"

"Because if you go out on your own, it's a good way to get dead, especially if you run into more than you can handle," Thegdol offered.

"We are stronger as a group," Logath said, speaking up, while staring directly at Tovak. "The individual is easily overcome, as should have been the case today."

"Exactly." Benthok snapped his fingers. "While hunting and foraging, you are never to separate. This is ground we do not know. Not only is it easy to become turned around and lost in the woods of these hills, but there are dangers." Benthok gestured out into the darkness.

The lieutenant turned back to Jodin. "Now that the corporals have helped refresh memories, what is my one rule out here, Jodin? I do hope you were listening."

"Not to separate, while foraging," Jodin said.

"Perhaps earlier today you forgot that order?"

"No, sir," Jodin said. "I did not."

"Care to explain yourself, then?"

"It was supposed to be just a prank, sir, a joke, nothing more."

"Did I ask for an excuse?" Benthok pointed over to Tovak. "You didn't just let one of our own go out alone. You sent the newest, greenest, most inexperienced member of our company out there by himself, to what you knew was murinok ground. If I'm wrong, please correct me."

Tovak felt his cheeks burn as Jodin said nothing.

"It was ill-thought-out at best and dangerous, and you should have known better. Not only are we moving into hostile, untamed lands, but the wildlife in these hills are as deadly as they come."

Benthok fell silent. He was staring directly at Jodin. Tovak could feel the intensity of that gaze. The anger almost radiated outward from the lieutenant, like heat from a fire. Jodin, for his part, said nothing. The silence stretched for several heartbeats, then Benthok broke it.

"Well, what do you have to say for yourself? I want to understand your thinking. Why would you send a fresh recruit into a murinok's hunting ground? Help me understand, will you?"

Jodin's mouth opened and closed, then opened again.

Benthok took a half-step nearer, invading Jodin's personal space. "I asked you a question, soldier. I expect an answer."

"I thought it was just a baby, sir," Jodin said, "a juvenile. I did not know it was an adult."

"Juveniles are still dangerous," Benthok hissed. "Do you desire Tovak dead?"

"Dead? No, sir. I—I, uh, I was watching," Jodin blurted. "I was watching him the entire time. He wasn't alone, sir, not for one moment. I was there to help, if needed."

Tovak felt astonishment, and he looked over as a dull whisper started amongst the camp. Jodin had watched the entire fight? Then Tovak remembered he was supposed to be at attention. He faced front again, looking straight ahead. The lieutenant seemed not to have noticed. Benthok had gone very still.

Jodin had gone completely white in the face as he realized what he'd just admitted. Sweat beaded his brow and his hands began to shake slightly. The lieutenant turned to look first at Tovak and then Thegdol behind him, who appeared just as stunned.

"Corporal, didn't you tell me Tovak brought the murinok down by himself?" Benthok asked. "Without any help, do I have that correct?"

Thegdol's expression hardened as he gazed first at Jodin and then the lieutenant. "I did, sir."

RECLAIMING HONOR

Benthok turned back to Jodin. Tovak could feel the tension hang in the air.

"You watched, but did nothing to help? Tell me that is not what occurred?"

"It happened so fast," Jodin said, in a tone that was far from convincing.

"That is not the answer I was looking for," Benthok said. The lieutenant clenched his right fist, as if he were going to strike, then after a heartbeat relaxed and unclenched it.

"Sir, I, uh," Jodin stammered, "I was there to help."

"And yet, you didn't," Benthok said. "Did you freeze?"

"Sir, I didn't mean ...."

"Shut it," Benthok snapped, then leaned forward and whispered something in Jodin's ear, so that only the two of them could hear. Jodin began to tremble violently, his eyes locked with Benthok. There was true unadulterated fear there.

The lieutenant took a step back and rubbed his jaw as he considered Jodin.

"We are the company," Benthok said in a voice that was almost a whisper and had Tovak and everyone else straining to hear. He raised his voice and it became firm as iron. "We are the company. Each one of you is its beating heart. We rely upon each other and in that reliance comes a sacred trust, a brotherhood in arms. Without trust, we are nothing. Without each of us, working together, relying upon one another... the company is nothing." Benthok fell silent and ran his gaze around the section. The eyes that stared back at him were grim and hard. "It all comes down to trust, the foundation upon which our company is built." Benthok hammered a fist into his palm. "We must trust each other. Pranks like the one that Jodin pulled erode that trust and hurt all of us. When everything goes balls up and we are in

187

the shit...trust in the comrade next to you is all we have. Take that sacred trust away and we are nothing, there is no company, just a bunch of individuals."

The lieutenant let that hang in the air a moment, then sucked in a breath and blew it out slowly as he turned back to Jodin and Tovak.

"For your actions, Jodin—perhaps I should say lack of action to aid one of our own—you're on buurl rations for five days. No meat, no dodders, just hard bread and water. I'm revoking your spirit and wine ration as well. You will be fined half of your next pay, which will go to the funeral fund. For the foreseeable future, you will be assigned to latrine duty." Benthok paused. "Corporal Thegdol?"

"Sir?"

"As Jodin's corporal, you will inspect the latrines daily," Benthok said.

"Yes, sir," Thegdol said. "It will be my pleasure, sir."

"It is my hope, Jodin," Benthok said, "that each morning, as you muck out the latrines, you will reflect upon your failure to the company. In short, I expect you to learn. Do we understand one another?"

"Yes, sir," Jodin said, and his shoulders sagged a fraction with evident relief.

"As an experienced member of our company," Benthok said, and there was real disappointment in the lieutenant's tone, "I expected better of you. You are lucky I am not having you lashed."

"It won't happen again, sir," Jodin said.

"By Thulla, if it does," Benthok said, in a quiet tone that was filled with menace, "I will do as I said I would, and I do not mean the lashing."

"No, sir," Jodin said, with a slight tremor in his voice. "It won't come to that."

Benthok gave a curt nod and then abruptly turned to Tovak.

"Even though you were the butt of the intended prank, when you realized what you faced, you continued on. What were you thinking? Going after an adult murinok, and by yourself too? I really want to know."

The lieutenant's eyes were piercing and seemed to capture Tovak's gaze. It was as if Benthok were looking right into his soul. Tovak wanted to avert his gaze but could not.

"Well?"

"I have no excuse, sir," Tovak said. "It was bad judgement and I will not make the same mistake twice. On my Legend, I swear it so."

"That's right," the lieutenant said in the same cold, hard tone he'd just used with Jodin. "There is no excuse for your behavior. In fact, I know for certain you weren't thinking. No sane individual would ever take on an adult murinok by himself. Are you crazy, perhaps not quite right in the head?"

"No, sir," Tovak said. "Just lucky, I guess, sir."

"Luck? Some put their stock in luck. I don't. By rights, all we should have found of you, assuming we found you at all, was a patch of blood on the ground. Lucky or no, you're a fool." Benthok looked to Jodin, who was still standing to attention by Tovak's side. "Fools, both of you, without a lick of common sense." Benthok pointed a finger at Tovak, tapping him on the chest. "If it was luck, you best make Fortuna an offering, and soon. Thank her for your good fortune." He shook his head slightly and then raised his voice so the entire section could hear him clearly. "Out here, we reward good thinking and good hunting. In my opinion you exhibited neither of those qualities. Fortuna got that kill, not you."

Tovak said nothing, for he'd not been asked a direct question. Benthok eyed Tovak for a long moment, as if he had something more to say, then turned to the rest of the section and placed his hands on his hips.

"With all the hopper swarms gathering in these hills for the migration, we're going to be running into bigger and more dangerous predators, not to mention goblins and orcs. What you're filling your bellies with is a perfect example of what we're likely to see more of. The fact that we ran into our first trapdoor spider, as tasty as it is, means you must be on guard and cautious. Stay on your toes. More importantly, use your head. Nobody, and I mean nobody, goes traipsing around alone. You go in pairs. And"—he stared daggers over at Jodin—"if you want to pull a prank, make sure it doesn't put anyone's life at risk." He fell silent for a long moment. The lieutenant raised his voice, looking around at the section. "Am I understood?"

"Yes, sir," came the massed reply.

"Tovak," Benthok said. "You'll have to prove to me that your judgement is sound, because as it is, I believe it to be suspect. Is that understood?"

"Yes, sir," Tovak said, feeling his cheeks flush with shame. Still, he knew he'd earned this and he had to sleep in the bed he'd made.

"You've got teska duty tonight and tomorrow morning," Benthok said. The lieutenant spared one more look around at the assembled section. "Finish your meal in peace. Before we turn in there will be a lesson. That is all."

Tovak blinked in surprise. His punishment was nothing compared to Jodin's. He was keenly aware it could have been so much worse. The lieutenant spared him one last unhappy look and turned away, moving towards the cook fire. Tovak puffed out his cheeks and returned to his seat.

"Gorabor," Benthok said, "have you finished?"

"I can finish after, sir," Gorabor said. "I don't mind running grub to the sentries first."

"Right, then," Benthok said. "Off you go."

Gorabor got to his feet and made his way over to Shrike. The teamster was already reaching for the bowls he had sitting close to the fire.

Tovak gazed down into his mess bowl, at the last bites of krata meat. He no longer felt hungry. Still, he knew he had to eat, for tomorrow was likely to be another demanding day. He finished his food and washed it down with some water from his skin.

He rose to his feet, prepared to go to the stream and clean his mess bowl. As he did, he caught Jodin glaring at him. There was no comradeship in that gaze, only heated anger. He'd made an enemy this day, and in a very short amount of time too. The rub of it was, none of it had been his fault. He turned away from Jodin and made his way out of the camp for the stream, where he found one other washing his mess bowl.

"Crazy or not, it took guts facing down a murinok," the warrior said.

Tovak looked up from rinsing his bowl. He did not know the warrior.

"I'm Dran, from Corporal Gamok's squad."

"Nice to meet you," Tovak said.

"A word of warning," Dran said, "if you will take it?"

Tovak gave a nod, wondering what was coming.

"You showed up Logath and his squad today," Dran said. "He won't like that."

"What?" Tovak asked surprised. "Logath? How did I do that?"

"His squad took down the krata," Dran said. "Normally that's quite an achievement, something to be celebrated."

"And I killed the murinok," Tovak concluded.

"That's right. You showed him up." Dran dipped his bowl into the stream.

"He's gonna take offense over who took down the bigger animal?" Tovak asked, finding the proposition of such a grudge almost preposterous. "And hold that against me? What happened to us being one big family?"

"It's got nothing to do with that," Dran said. "Logath is very competitive. He aims to win at everything, even dice, and when he doesn't, well, he tends to hold a grudge."

Dran shook the water from his mess bowl and stood. "Nice talking with you, Tovak." He walked off, back towards the camp.

Tovak watched Dran walk off and then turned his gaze towards the heavens. It seemed he was making more enemies than friends. He finished washing his bowl and headed back to camp.

"Drop what you're doing," Thegdol called out, just as Tovak made his way over the bridge and past the berm. "Time for sign instruction."

Tovak perked up at those words. Benthok and Thegdol were by the fire, which had been freshly fed. Its light pushed back against the darkness. Tovak had been taught some of the sign language at the Academy. He'd enjoyed it and had even excelled at using the finger speak. It was how the pioneers communicated without talking and was something he could see being useful to the skirmishers as well, which was likely why the lieutenant was teaching it.

"None of you are even close to being proficient in advanced signing," Benthok said. "Lots to learn, and if you're looking to be recommended to a pioneer company, you must master not just the basics, but the advanced signs too."

Tovak started over, moving with the rest of the section and gathering around the lieutenant. Thegdol spotted him, pushed through the press, and stepped up to Tovak. The corporal pulled him aside.

"You'll need to water both teska and gather whatever manure they've left for the camp forges," Thegdol said. "There'll be a bucket for the water, a sack and shovel for the manure hooked on the back of each cart. See that the animals are watered, the manure gathered up. I will be checking on your work. Oh, and don't forget to brush the beasts down too. There should be a brush in one the buckets, and if there isn't, speak to one of the teamsters. They will tell you where it is."

Tovak glanced over at the lieutenant, and then Thegdol, confused.

"What about the sign language class?" Tovak asked, not wanting to give up on it.

"The lieutenant assigned you punishment duty," Thegdol said. "That supersedes tonight's instruction. Now get going."

"Yes, Corporal," Tovak replied, crestfallen.

He turned and started walking to the bridge. Just beyond the camp and at the edge of the firelight, he could see the picketed teska grazing on the hill grass beyond the trench. Behind him, he heard Benthok's voice as the lieutenant began his instruction.

Tovak shook his head, feeling miserable. He was tired and worn out from his first full day with the company. While he got punishment duty, the others were being taught what they needed to become pioneers. It seemed unfair, though he knew it wasn't. He'd earned his punishment. Then, Tovak came to an abrupt halt. He half-turned and glanced back, recalling what Benthok had said. *Recommended for the pioneers.* Could the lieutenant do that? Could Struugar?

A moment of hope flashed through Tovak, before being dashed. A heavy fist clutched tightly at his heart. No, he thought, recalling what he'd overheard outside of the captain's tent. Benthok didn't even want him in the company. He thought, as a Pariah, Tovak was bad luck. There would never come a time when Benthok would recommend him for anything, other than menial duty. Tovak blew out a breath and continued walking.

"Hey, boffer."

Tovak had been lost in his thoughts. Gulda, still on watch, walked along the top of the berm back towards the bridge and over to him. As she gazed down, from the edge of the berm, he could see what Gorabor saw in her. She really was a pretty girl.

"Gulda," he greeted.

"You lived to tell the tale of taking down a murinok," Gulda said. "You did good today, even if your lieutenant didn't think so. Well, I have to admit it was pretty boneheaded, but you lived and that's what counts."

"Thanks," Tovak said. Her words had been meant to help, but they still did not make him feel better. He had messed up.

"No matter what others think, luck is an advantage." With that, she turned and walked back the way she'd come. Over her shoulder she said, "Enjoy teska duty."

Tovak made his way over to the first cart. Outside of the firelight of the camp, he took several moments to allow his eyes to slowly adjust to the moonlit darkness. He grabbed the bucket off the hook on the rear support. The brush was inside, large and heavily bristled. He placed it in the bed of the wagon and then retrieved the second cart's bucket.

Holding both bucket handles in one hand, he went to the stream, patting the neck of the closest teska as he went by. Teska were docile animals and quite affectionate, almost pet-like. He'd worked with them before, when he'd been employed as a stable hand.

Tovak knelt next to the stream. He filled the buckets to the brim. When he stood, he groaned as his legs protested mightily. He paused, transfixed by the vast expanse of the plateau. The moon hung low over the horizon, casting the land in a soft, silvery glow, almost looking otherworldly.

An owl hooted in a nearby tree. The light chill of the mountain air felt good. It was a serious improvement over the day's heat. He could smell the campfire and the roasted krata. There was even the nasty stench of teska droppings mixed in, but he didn't mind so much.

For a moment, despite his troubles, it felt good just to be alive, to have survived. He was in a beautiful place, serving his people. Granted, he'd damaged his reputation with the section, but it didn't seem so bad when put in perspective. Here was an opportunity, finally, to make something of himself, and Tovak intended to do so.

"Thank you, Thulla," Tovak breathed and returned to the teska. "Hey, boy," he said to the first teska, and set the bucket within easy reach. "If you are a boy." In the darkness, he could not tell.

The creature sniffed at the bucket, making a heavy chuffing sound, then began loudly lapping the water with a thick pink tongue, splashing some as it drank. He could hear Benthok going over the signs, but the class was too far away for him to hear what was being said clearly. He placed the second bucket before the other teska. It immediately began drinking.

"At least you don't care what I am," he said and fell silent for a few heartbeats. He leaned in close to the teska's furry ear and whispered, "I'm a Pariah."

He leaned back and watched the animal for a few moments.

"See?" he said. "No reaction. You don't care. Animals never do, not like people."

Tovak returned to the stream, filled the buckets once more, and let the teska drink their fill. When they stopped drinking, he hung the buckets where he'd found them. Tovak grabbed one of the heavy-duty canvas sacks. It stank terribly and was already partially full. He found a small shovel in the cart's bed and went about his next task—a most unpleasant one—of collecting the animals' droppings.

Shovel firmly in hand, Tovak took a deep breath and held it as he scooped the rank manure into the sack. When he had to, he tried to breathe through his mouth, but that didn't help much. He could literally taste the powerful-smelling manure. There was nothing fouler than teska dung.

When he finished, he hung the now half-full sack on the cart and returned to the stream. He cleaned the shovel first, then his hands, making sure they were stink-free, even picking under his nails. When he was done, his fingers were nearly numb from the cold water. He returned the shovel to where he'd found it. His next and final task was to brush both animals down.

Tovak had done this before and knew what to do. He started work on them, making sure his strokes were straight and firm, working to get any dirt and knots out of the fur. He was so fatigued from the day's exertions, not only did his legs shake, but so too did his arms. The brushing down of the animals took a good deal of time, especially if done right. And Tovak intended to do the job right. He did not want either of the teamsters complaining. He would not let Thegdol down again.

As he worked in the moonlit darkness, he found himself growing wearier by the moment. He caught himself yawning repeatedly. It was becoming a struggle. All he wanted was to lie down and go to sleep.

"You do good work."

Tovak jumped, startled, and spun around. Shrike was standing a few feet off. "Shrike, you scared me stiff."

"Been watching you," Shrike said. "Normally, I am the one that cares for Missa."

"His name is Missa?" Tovak glanced at the teska he'd been working on. The shaggy beast uprooted a clump of grass and began munching away.

"Her," Shrike said, stepping nearer. "She and me have been together a good long time. Like me, she's reliable and good-natured."

Tovak almost laughed. "I thought you were an animal?"

"We're all animals inside," Shrike said. "It's when the animal comes out that we should be worried."

Tovak gave a half-chuckle. He wasn't quite sure if Shrike was jesting or, for that matter, what he meant by the comment.

"You go on back to camp," Shrike said. "I'll finish the brushing of Missa. She likes it better when I do it, anyhow."

"Are you sure? I've been assigned to this duty." Tovak did not want to give the lieutenant grounds for disciplining him further.

"I am," Shrike said, taking the brush from Tovak's hand. "Your lieutenant can speak to me if he has an issue with it. Besides, you had a tough day, tangling with a murinok and all. I think you've done more than enough."

"Thank you," Tovak said, feeling relieved that his work for the day was at an end.

"No thanks needed," Shrike said. "Just keep the game coming and I'll happily cook it."

"That's a deal."

"Oh," Shrike said. "Best try and keep from doing daft things for a while, eh? I think you might live longer."

Amused, Tovak started for the camp. Gulda still stood atop the berm as he passed by, about ten paces away. He gave her a wave as he crossed the bridge into the camp. She did not see it, as her gaze was elsewhere.

Tovak found that the class was finished. The section had been dismissed and bedrolls were being laid out. He spotted Thegdol, Lok, and Staggen off to his right, laying out their bedrolls and preparing to bed down for the night. He retrieved his own pack and joined them.

Kneeling, Thegdol looked up at Tovak. The corporal had just laid out his bedroll and was digging through his pack. "Done already?"

Placing a hand on the ground, Thegdol started to get up.

"Shrike said I'd done enough," Tovak said.

"Then you have," Thegdol said, and abandoned the attempt at standing. He pointed to a pack four feet away. "Set your bedroll next to Gorabor's, there."

"Corporal Thegdol"—Benthok's voice carried over the camp from where he sat by his own fire—"has the sentry rotation for tonight been addressed?"

"It has, sir," Thegdol said. "The rotation's set. Corporal Gamok has the watch tonight."

"Excellent," Benthok replied, then raised his voice. "Time to turn in. We have a long day waiting for us in the morning. Hit the sack."

Tovak set his pack down and undid his bedroll. He quickly laid it out, just as Gorabor walked up.

"Hand me my spear, Tovak, would you?" Gorabor asked, pointing at it, where it lay next to his pack.

"Sure," Tovak replied. He grabbed the weapon and handed it over. He was surprised to see Gorabor in his armor. "Sentry duty?"

Gorabor nodded. "Me and Jodin have first watch. It's my first time standing watch."

"Well, at least one of us will be getting a good night's sleep," Tovak said.

"Ha ha. No napping for me," Gorabor said.

"If either of you ever get caught napping while on sentry duty," Lok said in a deadly serious tone, "it's punishable by the lash or worse if it happens in the field."

"Worse?" Tovak asked, looking over.

"Death." Staggen drew a finger across his neck, then lay down and pulled his blanket about him. "If you're caught napping, the lieutenant would probably kill you with his own bare hands and take pleasure in it too."

"Out here," Thegdol said, sounding incredibly weary but just as serious, "a sentry who shirks his duty puts all of our lives at risk. As such, the penalty is quite harsh. When I first joined up, I saw a sentry from another company put to death for sleeping during his watch. The punishment was administered by his own squad. They were ordered to beat him to death with clubs."

An uncomfortable silence filled the air about them.

"Well, that settles it then," Gorabor said, with a nervous chuckle. "No napping for me."

"You report to Corporal Gamok," Thegdol said to Gorabor. "He's in charge of the watch tonight. Get going before you're late."

Gorabor nodded his understanding and moved off.

With that, Tovak went to work on his bedroll. He laid it out and rolled up his cloak for a pillow. Most of the section were already down. Tovak could hear the first of the snores.

He glanced around at the camp once more. The central campfire burned brightly, casting flickering shadows against the berm. He sucked in a breath of the cool mountain air and once again found himself enjoying his surroundings. The moon had risen about halfway above the horizon, and there was a slight halo around it.

"When will I get sentry duty?" Tovak asked Thegdol as the thought popped into his head.

"When the lieutenant feels you can be trusted with it," Thegdol said. "Until then, your nights should be uninterrupted bliss. Enjoy it, while it lasts. Now, get some sleep and stop bothering me. It's been one bitch of a day."

Tovak could not disagree. It had been one bitch of a day. He laid down, pulled his blanket up about him, closed his eyes, and let the exhaustion take hold. He was asleep in moments.

CHAPTER TWELVE

The section had been awoken well before dawn. The sky had not even lightened when Thegdol, already wearing his armor, nudged and kicked his squad awake. Tovak felt far from rested, but he dragged himself to his feet, visited the latrine, and packed away his bedroll and blanket before wearily donning his armor. The air was cool, almost crisp, and the star-speckled sky above clear. A breakfast of warm porridge, which Thegdol called mush, waited for them. To his surprise, Tovak found he enjoyed it. The wine he'd saved from the night before helped to wash it down and dull his aches and pains.

When the first of the two suns came up, they discovered a swarm of hoppers had, during the night, settled into the valley. There were thousands of them all around. Some of the heratta munched on grasses, while others chewed at the newer growth of the pines that covered the hillsides. With every passing moment, more of the hoppers, wings buzzing madly, flew in, landing amongst their fellows, with one thought...to feed. The sight of them had sent not only a shock of excitement but amazement through the entire section. Tovak had never seen anything like it.

Benthok ordered the squads out with their slings. The day's focus would be on taking down as many of the big insects as possible. The lieutenant had also ordered the teamsters, as soon as was reasonably practical, back down the hill, with a request for additional carts and wagons to be sent to his location.

As Tovak had teska duty, he helped the other teamster load the last of the kills onto the carts. Both were filled with the previous day's bounty, including Tovak's murinok.

The teamster's name was Reng, and Tovak found him disagreeable and surly. He was also unkempt, smelled foul, and looked not to have bathed on a regular basis. His hair and beard were a greasy, wild tangle. Together, they ran rope over the bundles of dressed carcasses and butchered meat and then covered it all over in a canvas tarp.

When they were done, Tovak eyed the back of Shrike's cart, where the remains of the murinok were loaded. In a way, he was glad the creature had not been cooked and served to the section. He would not have felt right eating it.

Then it came time to hitch the animals up to the carts. As they worked, the rest of the section departed, filing by one squad at a time. Assisting the teamsters, Tovak watched them go with not a little regret. He wished he'd not had punishment duty and felt once again like he'd let Thegdol down.

The hitching of the first teska had gone well enough. The animal was easily led by the bridle and seemed cooperative. Once Reng had the teska in position, they began securing him to the cart.

When it came time to hitch Missa, she refused to budge from her grazing. She ignored all tugs on the bridle and even Shrike having a talk with her.

"By Thulla's great big ass, I don't think she's inclined to be hitched." Reng spat on the ground by Tovak's feet.

"She'll move," Shrike said, rubbing Missa's neck, "when she's ready."

"Bah." Reng climbed up onto the driver's bench of his cart. "You need to beat her, like the rest of us do. Then she'd be willingly led. I'm tired of wasting time. I'll see you down at the wagons, if you ever make it."

Shrike gave a negligent wave of his hand, as if to convey he did not care what the other teamster did. And with that, Reng cracked his whip harshly and started off slowly, moving downhill and following the cart tracks they'd made the previous day on the way up to camp.

In the end, it had taken a lot of cajoling and patience on Shrike's part to get Missa to the cart and hitched. He even went so far as to bribe the shaggy teska with several carrots. Shrike pulled himself up onto the driver's bench then, with a grunt, disengaged the cart's brake. Taking the reins and whip in hand, he sat down and looked down on Tovak.

"I'd hazard I'll be seeing you later," Shrike said. The teamster slapped on an old wide-brimmed hat against the heat of the suns, which were now both climbing over the horizon. The hat, once dyed a dark brown, was now a fast-fading tan. It, like the cart Shrike drove, had seen better days. "Thanks for the help hitching the old girl up. It's much appreciated."

"See ya later, Shrike," Tovak said as the teamster gave a flick of the whip, cracking it in the air. Missa made a deep, startled chuff and began lumbering forward, all six legs going. The oversized wheels of the cart, in need of an oiling, creaked loudly with each turn. The other cart was still in view, bouncing down the hill and already more than two hundred yards ahead. Shrike gave another crack of the whip and Missa picked up the pace.

Tovak watched for a moment, then turned and walked back to camp. He was terribly sore from the previous day's exertions, though his head no longer hurt. Besides sore muscles, his blisters made walking uncomfortable. Tovak did his best to put the discomfort from his mind, for it would surely be another demanding day. The life of a skirmisher certainly did not seem to be an easy one.

Only two sentries had been left behind at camp. Dagmar had been posted near the entrance. Tovak did not know the other sentry, who stood watch from the opposite end of camp. The rest of the section was out hunting.

"A fine day," Dagmar commented, leaning on his spear. "A terribly fine day, if I don't say so."

"Is that because you're on sentry duty and not out working, like the rest of the section?" Tovak asked. "Or is it because it looks to be a cooler day than the last?"

"You wound me, sir." Dagmar straightened and placed a hand to his chest armor. "But, in truth, if I'm being honest, you might be right."

"About which part?" Tovak asked.

"Both," Dagmar said with a grin and then leaned forward. "Do you want to know the secret to making one's life easier as a soldier?"

"Sure," Tovak said.

"To do as little work as possible," Dagmar said, "and avoid any extra details the officers, sergeants, and corporals want to find for you. Though to be honest, sometimes it is harder figuring out how to make that happen than doing the work like everyone else."

"Right," Tovak said, shaking his head with amusement, and continued into the camp. Thegdol had left him instructions. Once he was done with the teamsters, he was to grab his haversack, two skins of water, and join the squad just down the hill. He was also to bring his sling and all the shot he had. Tovak did not want to dally. He gathered up his gear and set out. Without another word to Dagmar, who was walking away from him along the berm and gazing outward, Tovak left the camp. He headed downhill in the direction the squad had gone.

He found them less than five hundred yards away in an open area free of trees. They had already brought down more than two dozen hoppers. The kills had been collected, dragged over, and tossed onto a pile. Thegdol had the squad spread out in a short line, twenty feet to the front of the heap of carcasses.

The air was full of the insects' buzzing wings and chittering as sunshine warmed the entire valley. The good weather seemed to bring in even more hoppers, who flew in over the ridge in search of food. As Tovak drew closer, he watched two that buzzed overhead land forty yards away in the long grass.

Morda was back with the squad, after having been sent to the captain with a message from the lieutenant. Tovak was so new to the company, he'd not even missed his fellow squad mate nor noticed his absence until he had returned, shortly after dawn. It brought the squad's number back up to seven.

Thegdol had formed them up into what only could be described as a loose skirmish line, with five feet of space between each member. The grass was waist-high and swished as Tovak moved through it. Jodin looked 'round, spotted Tovak, and shot him a sour look. Thegdol caught the look and turned, tucking his own sling into his belt. The corporal began walking over to meet him. The wind gusted, and for a moment, it almost looked like the corporal was wading through a swaying sea of green.

"What took you so long?" Thegdol asked him.

"One of the teska did not feel like being hitched."

"They can be stubborn," Thegdol said absently and glanced toward his line, then back to Tovak. "Let's see how you use that sling."

Tovak removed his sling.

"Best have him sit this one out, Thegdol," Jodin said. "We don't want an amateur scaring the bugs away, now, do we?"

Tovak felt a stab of anger at the words. He was no amateur with the sling.

Thegdol turned an annoyed look on Jodin before returning his attention to Tovak. "If you had seen fit to test him with the sling as I had instructed yesterday, Jodin, then I wouldn't need to check his skill with it now, would I?"

"You're right, Corporal. Why take the chance though?" Jodin pressed, as shame and anger seemed to war for a moment on his face before settling on just plain anger. "The hoppers are within easy reach and packed so tightly, one miss could see them all chased off. Let him prove himself later, back at camp. He can fetch and carry for us."

Tovak did not like that idea.

"I can use the sling, Corporal," Tovak said, as confidently as he could. "I was considered quite good at casting."

Thegdol rubbed his jaw, then glanced out in the field. "Okay, Tovak. I'm inclined to give you a shot at it."

"You're making a mistake," Jodin said.

"It's my mistake to make," Thegdol said, looking directly into Jodin's eyes. "Quit your grousing and focus on doing your job before I put you on a charge."

Jodin closed his mouth with a snap, turned away, and immediately let his sling fly. Fifteen feet away, he dropped a hopper. Tovak was impressed, for the shot had been rapidly made.

"Ever hunt heratta before?" Thegdol asked.

"No," Tovak said.

"The hoppers are preparing for their annual migration across the plateau. They are mindlessly focused on feeding, almost to the point where they ignore everything else. The trick is nailing them in the head. You do that, they generally drop stone-dead and don't spook the others. Hit them anywhere else and…."

"The rest fly off, right?" Tovak asked.

"Yeah. It's okay to miss, as long as your shot doesn't hit one of them. Wing one of them, and the wounded beast will give the alarm. Best not to do that, eh?" Thegdol gestured out to the field before them, which was scattered over with hoppers. "The critters are making it easy on us. We take a few down, gather them up, then advance several yards and kill some more. If we're careful, and don't scare them off, well, we don't have to chase after them. That means less humping and the distance for lugging the carcasses back to camp is shorter. Understand?"

Tovak did and glanced down at the short sling in his hand. He was very good with it. When hungry and without the means to buy food, he'd used it to bring down rodents and bugs in the caverns. Before the Academy, Tovak had been good with the short sling. His instructors had tirelessly drilled him in its use, making him cast thousands of stones and lead shot until he'd been what one instructor called "exceptional."

"Come with me," Thegdol said, and started over to the pile of carcasses. Thegdol partially picked up a hopper on top of the heap. The heratta was about three feet long, with large wings that fell open limply to the side. The corporal touched the back of the insect's head with a finger, where there was a neat round hole. "You want to hit it in this area, here. Do so, and it will drop stone-dead and not spook its buddies into flight. Think you can manage that?"

Tovak looked up at the nearest of the hoppers before replying. He studied them for a long moment.

"I do."

"All right," Thegdol said. "Let's move up to the line and you can make your first cast."

Thegdol led him up to the squad and the loose line they'd formed.

"Did you see that shot?" Staggen said to Lok, who was next to him. "That must have been sixty feet."

"More like fifty feet," Lok said.

"Liar," Morda laughed. "It was thirty."

"You both need to learn to estimate range better," Staggen said. "Perhaps then you will hit more of what you're aiming at."

Lok glanced over at Staggen and grinned as he placed a shot into the sling pouch. "A child could have made that shot."

"Not likely," Staggen said with a good-natured chuckle. "I'd like to see you try the same."

"Focus, children," Thegdol chided. "Don't get distracted with banter. Make your shots count."

"This is great fun," Gorabor said, looking over to Tovak as he came up next to him with Thegdol. "If you miss, well … as long as the shot doesn't hit any of them, they don't spook. Stupid bugs, but good fun."

"Right," Thegdol said to Tovak. "Time to cast. Pick out a target and let's see what you can do."

Tovak stepped forward, two paces. He scanned the field before him. There were six heratta within easy range. He picked one out, about forty feet away. His body was still sore and tight from the previous day. He cracked his neck and rolled his head around to loosen up a little. It helped. Then, he stretched out his throwing arm.

The rest of the squad had stopped what they were doing to watch. Jodin gave a nasty chuckle. Tovak ignored him and put the lead shot into the sling pouch, which was made of two coarse strips of leather. He focused on his target, staring at it with both eyes open. He cleared his mind, so that there was only him and the animal he wanted to take down. He fixated upon a small point at the back of its head as the hopper tore at the long grass and munched away.

Tovak took a breath and let it slowly out, then in a smooth motion, he cast, using an underhand swing. He made sure not to swing too hard, for if you did, the sling would make a cracking sound and he did not wish to scare off the other hoppers. He felt the satisfying release as the shot flew free. A moment later, there was a soft thud. The hopper had been hit, right where Tovak intended. It stiffened before twitching once, then fell over on its side, disappearing in the grass.

"Well," Thegdol said, coming up and clapping him on the shoulder armor. "Looks like you will not be needing instruction in how to use a sling. That was a mighty fine shot, a mighty fine shot, indeed. You might even give Jodin a run for his money when it comes to slinging."

Tovak glanced over at Jodin, whose face had hardened at the corporal's words. The other turned away to make another cast.

"Heck of a shot," Gorabor said, drawing Tovak's attention.

"Thanks."

Lok gave Tovak a nod of approval and then went back to casting himself.

"Tovak," Thegdol said, "I want you on the left there, next to Gorabor. Stay with the squad. We move forward together, when I say and not before. I've brought extra shot. So, if you run out, speak up. We're gonna hunt for the next half hour, then break. After, we'll spend some time hauling our kills back to the camp and the carts. Then we will do some more hunting."

"Yes, Corporal."

"Make sure with this grass you remember where your kills are," Thegdol said. "With the warband being short on food, I don't want to leave anything behind."

"Understood," Tovak said.

"Good, now get to work." Thegdol stepped away.

Tovak set to work with the squad. They brought down at least two dozen more hoppers before Thegdol called a halt to their work. Then, they began the laborious and tiring job of humping the kills back up to camp and the waiting carts. The air grew warmer as the day progressed, and the work saw the squad leaving their cloaks behind after they'd broken for lunch.

The lieutenant divided the section into two groups for the afternoon's hunt. First and Third Squads were to spend the afternoon together. Second Squad, which Tovak had learned was led by Corporal Drall, as well as Fourth Squad, were ordered farther up the valley, supported by four archers. Lieutenant Benthok had gone with them.

The two squads did not actually work together but near one another, separated by three hundred yards of space. Thegdol and Logath had thought this made better sense. By covering more ground, they might be able to harvest more hoppers as they advanced.

During the hopper slaughter that followed, Tovak and the others even started to have fun, turning it into a competition of sorts to see who could get the most kills. The only part Tovak did not like was hauling their kills back to camp. It was hard under the suns, hot work. As the suns approached the halfway point between noon and the horizon, Benthok's voice called down to them.

"Thegdol, Logath," he shouted through cupped hands, looking directly down on them from the vantage point on a small hill. "Bring both your squads up here."

"You heard the lieutenant," Thegdol called. "Let's get moving."

It didn't take long for the two corporals to move their squads and climb the hill to where Benthok waited. Tovak wondered what the lieutenant had in store for them.

"We're bringing in so many kills, the carts are having trouble keeping up. So, we're going to slow it down a little and have a contest between squads," the lieutenant announced. "A little fun and healthy competition, if you will."

"A contest sounds like a grand idea, sir," Logath said. "Anytime Third gets to show up First, we will."

"What do you have in mind, sir?" Thegdol asked.

"Take a look." The lieutenant led them to the other side of the hill and pointed to a small field. It sloped gently down and away, to rise again into a forested ridgeline. An unbelievably large swarm of heratta had gathered in the field. There were thousands of them. The nearest were about ten yards away.

The lieutenant pulled a sling from his belt and placed a single shot in the leather pad. He raised the sling over his head and in a quick, well-practiced motion, let fly at a heratta about fifteen yards away. The shot hammered into its head, making a soft *cracking* sound. The insect flinched once and rolled over onto its side, its large hind legs and wings quivering. The heratta nearby shuffled a few steps, but did not cease their feast upon the grass, apparently too engrossed in filling their bellies to acknowledge the death of a comrade.

"That's how it's done," Benthok said with a satisfied nod.

"Nice shot, sir," Logath said. "Very nice, indeed, sir."

"Right, then, alternating by squad," Benthok said, "each of you are going to aim to kill one of those hungry bugs. If you don't score a headshot and take it right down, the injured hopper will spread the alarm, and the whole swarm will go with it. At that point, the game is over. The squad with the fewest kills gets to haul those kills and the ones you previously made back on the other side of the hill up to the carts. The winners get to take a break and review signs with me. How does that sound?"

Tovak felt a surge of excitement.

"First Squad will be honored to show up Third, sir," Thegdol said with confidence.

"Unlikely," Logath replied. "All my boys are veterans and damn fine with the sling. I've seen to that. Besides, old boy, you've got two fresh recruits. I think this contest is already in the bag."

"Big talk," Thegdol replied. "Let's see if you can back it up"—Thegdol paused for a heartbeat and stressed the next part—"old boy."

"There isn't any backing up anything," Logath said. "Perhaps your new recruit's luck will carry you, because I won't."

Bane and Dolan from Logath's squad, along with two others that Tovak didn't know yet, turned sour looks upon Tovak. It seemed the anger at being shown up was not confined to just Logath.

"Corporals, form your lines," Benthok ordered. "I want Third on the left and First on my right. The squad leaders will go last. The more senior of the squads go first, so we'll at least bag a few of these things before we spook them. Regular shot only. Questions?"

"No, sir," Logath said.

"I'm good, sir," Thegdol said.

"Right," Benthok said. "Let's get to it."

Each squad formed up in their own line, slings at the ready.

"Hold on," Benthok said. "First Squad has seven and Third five, with Dagmar on sentry duty. To be fair, we will keep this an even contest. Tovak, since you're the newest member of our company, step on out of line. You too, Morda."

Tovak felt a pang of regret wash through him. He wanted an opportunity to prove himself, but he did as was ordered and took two steps back. Morda stepped out of the line too.

"Begging your pardon, sir," Logath said, "but I think I should get to decide who gets left out."

Benthok's gaze shifted to Logath. He lifted an eyebrow. "What makes you say that?"

"This, I want to hear," Thegdol said.

"Well, sir," he said, "since Thegdol thinks First Squad is the best, it only stands to reason if we pick the two to step out, it'll even the odds. Don't you agree, sir?"

Benthok appeared amused by the suggestion. He turned to Thegdol. "Any objections?"

Thegdol cocked his head to the side, a thoughtful look on his face. He eyes flicked briefly to Tovak before turning a smile on Logath. "None at all, sir, none at all."

"All right, Corporal Logath," Benthok said. "You may pick two members of First Squad to sit the contest out, except Corporal Thegdol."

"Yes, sir," Logath said. "I wouldn't dream of asking him to sit. It would be no fun without his participation."

"Uh huh," Thegdol said. "Since when do you care about fun when it comes to games of skill? So, who do you want to sit out?"

"Jodin," Logath said without hesitation, "and Morda."

Thegdol scowled. "You would take Jodin, my best shooter, from me, wouldn't you?"

"You wouldn't want him going against one of his oldest friends, would you? It might leave hard feelings. On the other hand, we wouldn't want anyone accusing him of playing favorites in the event he missed, now, would we?"

"Old friend," Jodin said, shooting Logath a distinctly unhappy look, "there would have been no missing and you know that, friends or no."

"Jodin and Morda it is," Benthok said, now thoroughly amused at the banter. He clapped his hands together. "Tovak, you're back in."

A surge of excitement and a good bit of nervousness coursed through Tovak. After yesterday's screw-up, he would have another opportunity to prove himself and show his value to Thegdol. He quickly stepped into the last position as Jodin moved over to stand by the lieutenant.

"Mirok, move forward five paces and pick your target," Benthok ordered, looking at one of Logath's boys. "You may cast when ready."

The contest had begun.

CHAPTER THIRTEEN

Mirok moved forward towards the nearest of the hoppers about ten yards off. He slipped a shot into his sling, took a deep breath, and then eyed his target. Raising the sling, he swung and then let fly. A heartbeat later, there was a crunch as the shot hammered home. The hopper quivered once as it was hit, and then its legs gave out. The bug sank down onto the ground, as if it were lying down to sleep.

"That's the way to do it," Logath said. "Good shot."

"Third Squad has one point," Benthok announced as Mirok moved over to stand with Jodin and watch the next cast.

"Lok, you're up," Benthok said.

Lok moved forward, to roughly where Mirok had been standing.

"You've got this," Thegdol encouraged.

"Of course I do." Lok glanced at Logath, winked, and then took a deep breath, focusing on a hopper a half-dozen yards ahead of where the first one had fallen. He loaded his sling, raised it above his head, swung, and released in a fluid motion. The shot was spot-on. The hopper tipped over on its side and lay still.

"First Squad gets one," Benthok said. "All tied up.... Dolan, you're next."

Lok stepped away from the firing line and joined the others by Benthok.

Dolan moved up, his sling already loaded and held lightly in a hand. He sighted a hopper off to the right, about ten or so yards off. Without any preamble, he raised the sling, swung it, and sent the shot hissing downrange. There was an audible crunch. The hopper's back legs tensed for a moment, as if it wanted to leap, and then it too fell over onto its side, one leg kicking lightly up in the air.

"Third Squad gets one," Benthok said. "They're on top again."

Tovak chewed his lip. The nearest of the heratta had been killed, making the coming shots more difficult, as the closest living ones were five yards farther out.

"We're gonna move the shot line forward six paces," Benthok said, "to keep the contest fair."

Tovak said a silent prayer of thanks as they shifted forward. He looked on the mass of insects before them and thought it an astonishing sight. The long grass in the field was literally disappearing before their eyes as the bugs ripped and tore at it, eating hungrily away with single-minded purpose.

"I'd like to go next, sir," Gorabor said, speaking up, which seemed to surprise everyone, Tovak included.

The lieutenant looked over at Thegdol with a raised eyebrow.

"It's fine with me, sir," Thegdol said. "Logath, do you have any problems with a change in the order?"

Logath was silent for several heartbeats as he considered Gorabor.

"I am getting old just standing here," Benthok said. "Well, Corporal? Do you have an objection?"

"No, sir," Logath said, "I have no problem letting one of Thegdol's pups go before their turn."

"You're up then," Benthok said to Gorabor and held out a hand towards the imaginary shot line. "I like the initiative."

"Thank you, sir." Gorabor eagerly stepped up to the line and loaded his sling. He stared at the field of hoppers for what seemed like a long time, taking long, slow breaths, and then raised his sling.

"Think your pup will make his shot?" Logath asked abruptly.

Gorabor lowered his sling and glanced over at Logath meaningfully.

"Sorry, boy," Logath said. "I did not mean to interrupt your concentration. By all means, please continue."

"Gorabor, take your shot," Benthok said.

"Yes, sir," Gorabor said and raised his sling for an overhead cast. He threw, and as he did, Logath gave an explosive sneeze. The shot seemed to curve slightly after Gorabor released it, flying wide of its mark. It bounced off into the grass. Gorabor sucked in a breath as it nearly clipped the back end of a hopper behind his target. A graze would have startled the creature enough to give the alarm and could have sent them all flying into the air.

"First Squad misses," Benthok announced. "Third Squad is up one."

"Thulla curse me," Gorabor said, throwing his sling down into the dirt and looking back on Logath with a heated expression.

"Was that really necessary?" Thegdol asked Logath.

"It's the grass," Logath said, wiping his nose with a soiled rag. "It tickles my nose something fierce."

"I bet it does," Staggen said.

"Still, boy," Logath said, turning to Gorabor, "this should be a lesson. You should be able to cast accurately, no matter the distractions."

"Logath is right," Benthok said. "In battle, there will be plenty to distract you. Best to stay focused."

"Yes, sir," Gorabor said, his unhappy gaze fixed on Logath.

"Still," Benthok said, turning to Logath, "if there are any more unwanted distractions, Corporal, I will begin deducting points. Is that understood?"

"Yes, sir," Logath said, then turned away slightly and blew his nose mightily into the rag.

Gorabor picked up his sling and moved off to stand with the others, who had already cast.

"It's not over yet. We'll still get 'em," Thegdol said, patting Gorabor on the shoulder as he went by.

"Barrol," Benthok said. "You're up, with a chance to make it a serious lead."

"Nothing to it," Barrol said, stepping up to the line. He loaded his sling, took a short breath, and then swung. His shot went wide, missing the hopper's head by a near foot.

"Thulla's bones, curse it," Barrol hissed.

Though he was relieved Barrol had missed his cast, Tovak felt himself frown with distaste at the mild curse. He'd heard worse in his time, but too many people these days felt free to take Thulla's name in vain. There should be more reverence for the great god.

"I thought you said your boys, veterans all, were good," Thegdol said. "That you trained them yourself."

"It must be the wind," Logath said.

"The wind my ass," Thegdol said.

"A miss from Third, but they're still up one," Benthok said. "Staggen, I believe it is your turn."

Staggen stepped up to the line, sighted his target, and, without hesitation, swung and let fly with an easy motion. His shot hissed out and drilled the head of the nearest hopper, dropping it where it stood.

"And we're tied again," Benthok said.

"Nice shot," Barrol said from the side.

"That was a good cast," Lok said.

"Very good," Barrol agreed.

"Why thank you. I've been doing this since almost before I was walkin'," he drawled. "My father used to have contests like this with me and my brothers. The loser had to muck out the barn stalls, so there was motivation to win, and besides, I don't like to lose."

"Bane," Benthok said. "You're up."

Bane stepped up as Staggen moved away. He sighted a hopper near to the one Staggen had killed. He paused for a moment, staring at it, and then, in a smooth motion, he lifted the sling overhead with both hands and swung. There was a loud crunching sound. The force of the blow knocked the hopper right over. It lay on its side, legs twitching feebly.

"Third gets a kill and is back up one," Benthok said.

"Thulla's bones," Staggen said. "Nice shot...ya bastard."

Once again, Tovak felt a slight distaste with his squad mate's choice of words, but it wasn't the time or even his place to speak up. Not many held a high regard of their ancestral god. No matter what he thought or how much he believed, there was simply nothing he could do to change things.

Bane gave Staggen a slight bow and then stepped aside.

"Tovak," Benthok said, "it's your turn."

"You should just give up now," Logath said to Thegdol.

"Why's that?" Thegdol asked. "Gonna sneeze again?"

"The boffer's new, with no training," Logath said, sparing Tovak a huge grin. "We've already won."

"Is that so?" Thegdol turned his gaze to Tovak, a thoughtful expression on his face. "Show him how it's done, kid."

Tovak felt a sudden surge of pride. His squad leader had faith in him. He was nervous down to his boots, but he knew he could do this. He stepped up to the invisible line, closed his eyes, and took a deep breath, trying to control his pounding heart. He felt everyone's eyes upon him.

Tovak understood he had to put that out of his mind. He heard Jodin and Dolan whispering behind him. It sounded like they were making a wager. He shut it and everything out, clearing his mind as he'd been taught. He had a sudden recollection of something an instructor had said during his training: *When you have a target to kill, there is only the target. The rest of the world must cease to exist. Remember to focus.*

He hefted his sling and slipped a shot into the pouch. Searching the field before him, he singled out a heratta slightly larger than the others. It was about twelve yards away. The creature had the whole of its left side facing him and it made an excellent target. He let its faceted eye fill his vision. His mark was just behind the eye, beneath the wide, waving antennae that twitched at the air with slow, swooshing motions as it ate grass.

Time slowed. Tovak breathed in and held it. *There is only the target....*

He raised the sling and let fly in a smooth motion.

Crunch.

His shot had drilled into the heratta's head, right where he'd aimed. The insect's legs stiffened, as if it were about to leap, then it sagged and, a heartbeat later, rolled over onto its side.

"I don't bloody believe it," Logath hissed through his teeth, looking over at Tovak in astonishment and barely concealed anger.

"Dead on," Tovak said under his breath, with a look thrown to Thegdol. The squad leader shot him a wink of approval. Tovak turned to see his whole squad looking pleased. It was a good feeling and one he wanted to savor, for there had been few of those. He walked over to join them.

"Nice shot," Gorabor said, slapping him on the back. "You nailed it."

"Lucky shot is more like it," Logath said.

"Oh, I don't know, Logath," Staggen said, raising a dubious eyebrow. "Looks to me like he hit exactly what he was aiming at. Wouldn't you agree, Bane?"

Bane returned only half a nod, punctuating it with an annoyed grunt.

"That's what I thought," Staggen said, with more than a bit of satisfaction. "Nice job, Tovak."

"Enough," Benthok said. "There is too much jawing going on. It's tied. Logath is up."

"I hope you sacrificed something to Fortuna today," Thegdol said. "I have a feeling you are going to need it."

Logath gave him a funny look and then stepped up to the line, drawing out his sling with a flourish. He placed a single shot into the leather pad and then scanned the heratta, making a show of picking his target. He took a deep breath, raised his hand, and let fly.

The shot flew out, and for a moment it looked dead on, but at the last instant, the heratta shifted in the grass, taking a hop forward. The shot missed by a hair's breadth. The projectile hit the grass and bounced up in a low arc, careening into the thick leg of another hopper just a few feet beyond.

The startled insect let out a chattering cry and leapt into the air, its translucent wings buzzing out a fierce drone. In the blink of an eye, the entire swarm took flight, and a deep, thrumming buzz filled the air. Most of the hoppers moved as one, clumping together in midair. For a moment their massed bodies blocked one of the suns as they sailed farther up the valley, only to disappear into a stand of trees about quarter mile away. When they were all gone, there were only three hoppers left, about thirty-five yards off and still gorging themselves on the grass.

There was a moment of awed silence at what they had just witnessed. It had been like a massive flock of birds taking flight, only more impressive.

"First Squad wins—" Benthok started, but Thegdol held up a hand and spoke.

"Begging your pardon, sir," Thegdol said. "That just doesn't seem right to me. Since we're tied, I don't believe the game is over yet, sir. There still be hoppers out there, sir."

"Not according to the rules I set out," Benthok said.

"I'd like my turn, sir," Thegdol pressed. "To put First Squad up proper-like, if you don't mind, sir."

"Very well," Benthok said. "You may take your cast, Corporal."

"And there's no need for the line to move up either, sir," Thegdol said.

This seemed to surprise the lieutenant.

"Are you certain?" Benthok asked, looking out on the last of the hoppers. "That's a difficult shot for a short sling."

"I am sure, sir," Thegdol said, taking up position on the invisible line.

"Thegdol's opportunity to win it all, then," Benthok said. "You may cast when ready."

Thegdol stood up straight, eying the nearest hopper. He held his sling loosely in his right hand, while the other stroked his beard.

"You've got this, Thegdol," Staggen said.

"Easy as mead," Morda added.

"You're gonna miss," Logath said and gave a nasty chuckle.

"Like you did?" Thegdol asked, without turning his head.

Logath's cheeks colored, but he clamped his mouth shut.

Tovak held his breath.

Thegdol took in a deep breath and let it out slowly. His finger dipped into the pouch at his waist and drew forth a lead shot, which he placed in the sling. In a single, fluid motion, he raised the weapon, swung it over his head, and let fly as hard as he could. It was a powerful throw and the sling cracked in the air as the shot flew outward and slammed into the target's head with a loud *smack*.

First Squad, Tovak included, erupted in a riotous cheer that frightened the last two hoppers, who had not gotten the message yet. They leapt into the air and went sailing away after their fellows.

"I declare First Squad the victors," Benthok said. "Excellent shot, Thegdol, well played."

"Thank you, sir," Thegdol said and then walked over to Logath. He held out his hand. "No hard feelings?"

"I'd say that hopper moving at the last moment was just a little bad luck for you, wouldn't you?" Benthok looked meaningfully at Logath.

"Yes, sir," Logath said, though he did not sound convinced. "It was bad luck with my shot, is all."

Logath turned his gaze back to Thegdol, and despite his words, it was clear he was simmering with barely contained rage. The corporal of Third Squad looked down at the extended hand, forced a smile, and then shook. "No hard feelings."

"We're one big happy family again," Benthok said, clapping his hands together. "Corporal Logath, take your squad and gather up the carcasses here and on the other side of the hill. We'll be breaking camp as soon as we have everything in and the last of the kills loaded onto the carts."

"We're heading back tonight?" Logath seemed surprised by that. "With all these hoppers about?"

"Yes," Benthok said. "I received orders from the captain. The warband is making good time, and from what I understand, Karach wants to pick up the pace even more. We can't linger here another night or we will be playing a game of catch-up with them, and that we do not want to do. No, we're heading back to the warband tonight. Now, Corporal, kindly get your squad moving."

"Yes, sir," Logath replied, snapped to attention, and offered a salute.

Benthok returned the salute.

"Third Squad," Logath called, "we'll start work at our original position. Let's go."

Third moved out, quickly cresting the small hill and disappearing down the other side.

"First Squad," Benthok said, "take a seat. Time for class."

They sat down around the lieutenant.

"As skirmishers," Benthok said, once everyone was settled, "operating outside of the safety of the main line, you might one day have need of the finger speak, and when it matters too. So pay attention."

Tovak was grateful to be off his feet. His legs still ached badly. He took a pull off his waterskin, then stopped it closed.

"Let's review the signals I've been teaching you these past few weeks, to see what, if anything, has stuck," Benthok said. "Thegdol, you already know all this, so no helping."

"I wouldn't dream of it, sir," Thegdol said in a weary tone. "I need a nap anyway, sir."

With that, Thegdol removed his helmet, leaned back on his hands, and turned his face towards the suns. The corporal closed his eyes.

Benthok held up a hand and made a quick gesture. The signs were small, almost jerky motions of the fingers that Tovak knew only a keen and trained eye could clearly interpret.

"Gorabor, what did I just say?" Benthok asked.

"Move forward silently," Gorabor replied.

"That's right," Benthok snapped his fingers. "Good memory. Now, I am going to sign it again. Repeat the motions for me, all of you. Good," Benthok said, waiting and watching. "Very good. And this?" He made another sign and then touched his ear. "Lok? What did I just say?"

"Move to the left?"

"Close," Benthok said. "The distinction is that I touched my left ear. I didn't say I wanted anyone to move to the left. If I had given the sign to 'move' in that direction, like this"—Benthok used an open palm to point—"then you would be correct. If I had pointed to my eyes, it would have meant 'look.' Motioning to the ear, with this sign here"— he repeated the finger speak—"indicates that I've heard something to the left and that those with me need to listen." He looked at them expectantly. "Do you understand the difference?"

"I do, sir," Lok said.

"Good," Benthok said. "Then show me."

Lok made the same sign.

"Now everyone else," Benthok said.

They repeated the sign, including Tovak. Benthok stepped forward, correcting Jodin. What Benthok was teaching were the basics. Tovak felt a wave of disappointment as the eagerness for the lesson fled. He'd already learned this and more. He was starting to realize that what he'd been taught at the Academy put him well ahead of the rest of his squad. If this material was new and Thegdol's squad was just learning it, then, at least for a while, there wouldn't be much Benthok would be teaching him.

Over the next hour, the lieutenant went through quite a few different signals, with Tovak's squad mates calling out the answers. It was clear the squad had a lot to learn. Not once did Tovak raise his hand. He just watched and remained silent, as he did not want to call attention to himself. Between the others and the lieutenant's patient prompting, they mostly managed to get what had been signed, but there was no telling who would give the correct answer. At points it was almost painful for Tovak not to point something out.

Gorabor seemed to know far more than the others. However, none of them had a complete understanding of what Tovak considered the fundamentals of finger speak. He was the expert amongst them and they did not even know it. It galled him that he had to keep it hidden.

"You're picking this up quick," Gorabor hissed, leaning close after Benthok made them repeat a complicated sign and then practice amongst themselves. "He flashes the sign and you repeat it almost exactly. You might be a natural at this, like me."

Tovak looked over at Gorabor, suddenly alarmed that his friend might begin asking uncomfortable questions.

"Okay," Benthok said, looking over their heads in the direction of the camp, "the carts are back and we're just about done with today's class."

The lieutenant eyed the squad, and, with his right hand, he pulled at his beard, tugging on it twice, before scratching.

"I have one last sign I want to see if you can figure out. It is a combination of some of the signs we covered today."

The lieutenant ran through a series of signs, all eyes save Thegdol following. The corporal appeared to be asleep.

"Lie down on the ground," Lok blurted.

"What?" Gorabor exclaimed. He choked back laughter at the other's sudden hard look and discomfiture. Lok's answer was far from correct.

Morda and Staggen shared a glance filled with amusement. Of all of them, Lok was struggling the most.

"But I thought—" Lok started.

"No," Jodin interrupted, speaking up. "I think the lieutenant signed the order to retreat."

Gorabor raised his hand and when Benthok nodded, said, "Stop fighting, fall back, and fade."

"Not quite." Benthok ran through the signs one more time.

Tovak knew the answer. He looked at Benthok, whose eyes were shifting from one face to another, although he never even glanced in Tovak's direction.

"Anyone?" Benthok asked. The lieutenant had been sneaky and obviously expected everyone to fail.

Heartbeats ticked by. Tovak could no longer hold back, because it was so simple and so terribly obvious. Sure, it was a trick, but he had no idea why they were having trouble with it.

"Gorabor is the closest, but they're all wrong," Tovak said quietly, then instantly regretted speaking up. *Oh, shit,* he thought.

"You think you know the answer?" Benthok asked.

"I do, sir," Tovak said, realizing there was no backing out now. He held up his left hand and repeated what Benthok had done. "That does mean 'stop fighting, fall back, and fade,'" he said. "Before you made that sign, you tugged on your beard twice with your right hand. I believe that indicates whatever sign comes next should be reversed, which would suggest you are calling for a full frontal attack and that you think someone may be watching."

"That can't be right," Lok said.

Thegdol opened his eyes and sat up, looking straight at Tovak. The corporal's brow was furrowed.

"How could you know that?" Jodin exclaimed.

Gorabor looked confused.

"Yeah," Thegdol chimed in. "How could you possibly know that? I wasn't even watching and I know the lieutenant gave an advanced sign."

"Enough," Benthok said. "Tovak is right. Remember, finger speak is just as much a language as what comes out of your mouth. Whatever I speak, I can say almost as quickly with my hands. That's why it is so important to learn. When it comes to a need for silence, finger speak is the best way to communicate. What I signed was supposed to be a trick question. Tovak even got the underlying meaning. When signs are given, you need to pay close attention. Observation is one of the hallmarks of being a pioneer. You must try to see everything and miss nothing. Understand?"

"Yes, sir," the squad chorused.

"Tovak," Thegdol asked, with an edge in his voice, "how did you learn sign?"

Tovak cursed himself for the slip. He didn't want to tell everyone he'd been trained at the Academy and had been rejected by the pioneers. It would bring up uncomfortable questions he was not prepared to answer. "I just know about signs."

"I think you're playing games with us," Jodin accused. "You've been trained, you lying bastard. I knew there was something shifty about you."

"Keep your mouth shut, Jodin." Benthok shot him a severe glare. "You're in the shithouse with me as it is. You are a veteran who has proved himself repeatedly in battle. Had you not done so, what you did out there with the murinok and Tovak might be construed the actions of a coward, if you get my meaning."

Jodin said nothing, but his eyes never left Tovak. They were filled with hate and loathing. Tovak wondered how much of that Jodin turned on himself.

"I'd like to know how he knows the signs, myself, sir," Thegdol said. "It doesn't figure, now, does it? How does a wandering recruit, fresh off the yuggernok, know advanced sign?"

Benthok let out a breath, closed his eyes for a long moment. When he opened them, they were clear and focused on Tovak.

"Give Thegdol your Warrant," Benthok said quietly.

"What?" Tovak asked, sitting up straight. "No."

"I figure you have it on your person," Benthok said. "If I were in your boots, I would keep it close. Now, give it to him."

"Sir?" Tovak replied, his guts churning.

"I said"—Benthok filled his voice with iron—"give him your Warrant of Passage. Your corporal has a right to know what he's working with. That is an order."

"Warrant of Passage?" Thegdol asked, with eyebrows raised. "You went to the Academy?"

"I did," Tovak said in a quiet tone. He'd never felt so cornered in his entire life. He was stuck. There was no way out. He was terrified of what he knew was about to happen next. But he also felt an intense wash of anger that he was being forced to expose his past, especially after Captain Struugar had allowed him to start afresh. He glanced at his friend,

Gorabor, and felt sick. It wouldn't take long for the entire company to learn the truth.

Feeling a sudden intense hatred for the lieutenant, Tovak locked eyes with Benthok, reached inside his chest plate, and carefully pulled out the folded document. Without turning away, he handed it over to Thegdol.

"So, it's true?" Thegdol asked, staring at Tovak. He unfolded the document and began reading. As his eyes scanned down the Warrant, he said, "You should be in the pioneers, not with us, son."

Benthok's eyes never left Tovak as Thegdol continued to slowly read. Then the corporal's shoulders stiffened.

"Tovak Stonehammer," he whispered and raised angry, knowing eyes to Tovak.

Feeling despair and a terrible hopelessness, Tovak almost cringed under his corporal's gaze. He wished that the ground would open under him and swallow him up. He let out a single, self-pitying chuckle, and then shook his head in disbelief. It seemed that Thegdol was very familiar with his name, and in all the wrong ways.

"As in Graybor Stonehammer and Barasoom?" Thegdol asked, lowering the Warrant. "I had an aunt and uncle who were killed in the village at Barasoom, their children too."

The rest of his squad mates appeared confused. Thegdol seemed to be the only one who had heard of his father's disgrace. Tovak thought he might vomit.

He turned his gaze to Benthok, who was looking upon him with a cold, calculating expression. Was there anyone in his life who wasn't going to somehow have a connection to Barasoom? He had a sinking suspicion he would never be free of it.

Tovak stood.

"I have a Pariah in my squad," Thegdol whispered, looking from the Warrant to Tovak and back again. "A bloody Pariah."

"What?" Gorabor asked, blinking. It was clear he was not quite understanding, then it dawned upon him and his face clouded over with anger and disgust.

Tovak knew that, without a doubt, he'd just lost a friend.

Jodin stood and spat on the ground by Tovak's feet. "Pariah."

"It's done," Benthok said.

Tovak looked at the lieutenant. The coldness had gone. In its place he saw a strange expression. It wasn't anger. It was perhaps frustration coupled with something bordering on sorrow, and he couldn't figure out why Benthok, of all people, would have that reaction. Benthok had forced the issue. Why?

The lieutenant had come into this hating Tovak, or at least believing Tovak was bad luck. He would have expected Benthok to look pleased, or at least satisfied. But sorrow?

It didn't matter, though. Soon enough, everyone would know he was a Pariah. His life in the company would become just as difficult and uncomfortable as it had been back home, perhaps even worse.

"I'll take that," Benthok said, taking the Warrant from Thegdol's trembling hands. "I think we're just about done here," he added. "Corporal, break time's over. Go help Logath finish up with hauling and loading carcasses."

"Yes, sir," Thegdol said, clambering to his feet. "First Squad, on your feet. With me."

The corporal started off, with the others following, Tovak included.

"Hold up, Tovak," Benthok said, a firm edge to his voice.

Thegdol gave Tovak one last parting look before he walked off with the others over the crest. They disappeared down the other side of the hill. Benthok opened the Warrant and read, slowly. His eyes moved from one line to the next, and when he got to the end, he simply folded it up again.

"You may hate me for what I did," Benthok said. "But in truth, I freed you from a lie. Lies bring no Legend, and any Legend built on a lie is no Legend at all. There is no doubt you will suffer from what I've done." His tone was neutral. There was no anger, no condescension ... just a simple statement of fact. He handed the Warrant back to Tovak, who took it and absently slipped it behind his breastplate. "But suffering brings strength."

Tovak had barely heard him. The weight of what he was about to endure pressed down on him, like a mountain upon the bedrock. He was utterly crushed by it.

"Tovak," Benthok barked suddenly. "Do you understand me?"

"Yes—yes, sir," Tovak replied, blinking.

"You have skill and potential. One day, you may thank me ... or maybe you will forever curse me ... but this *had* to be done, and it was better sooner than later, boy, or it would have been worse for you."

Without another word, Benthok turned and strode off.

Tovak watched the lieutenant walk away, then turned his gaze towards the heavens. He stared at the blue sky as turmoil and dread raged in his heart. Tovak felt tears of intense frustration prick his eyes. He angrily wiped them away.

"Why?" he asked. "Why do I suffer so?"

There was no answer. There never was. Faith was like that. He felt his shoulders sag and glanced around. He could not stand on this hilltop forever. He knew that. Doing so would change nothing. He needed to continue onward, as he always had. Tovak took a deep, shuddering breath. He'd lived through tough times before. He could do it again and for as long as Thulla required it of him.

"This changes nothing," he told himself, anger trembling his tone. He balled his fists. "I came here to pursue my own Legend and that is what I will do, no matter how difficult that will be. I will soldier on. By Thulla, I swear it so."

Tovak took another deep breath, steadying himself, and let it out slowly. He set off after his squad and whatever the future held.

CHAPTER FOURTEEN

The march back to the main encampment seemed to take an eternity. Benthok pushed the section hard, keeping up a grueling pace, with only a handful of brief breaks for water when they happened across a stream or small brook cutting its way across the plateau.

No one talked with or walked next to him. Most didn't even look in his direction or turned away when he caught their gazes. Gorabor had said nothing to him. Gorabor had even refrained from playing his flute, although several of the others had broken out theirs and played a lively tune to keep to the pace. Tovak found he unconsciously stepped to the tune, as did the rest of the section.

His isolation as an outcast had begun. It had also given Tovak plenty of time to think. He knew Gorabor felt betrayed and rightly so. In essence, Tovak had lied to him. He'd lied to all of them. He felt bad about that.

He had experienced loneliness before. The sting of being ostracized was nothing new, but never had it pressed in on him so completely, nor felt so thoroughly oppressive. For a brief but blessedly short time, he'd truly been part of something. Now, that was gone, snatched away by Benthok, and he was once again just another Pariah forced to make his way in the world amongst those who reviled and resented his very presence. The pain of it burned, fueling not only his misery, but also his anger.

As they marched, the suns descended beneath the western hills. By the time the camp came in sight, it was dark. The moon was hidden behind a thin layer of clouds. The encampment was a bright swath of light on an otherwise darkened horizon. It was impossible to miss, even at a great distance. The glow of campfires illuminated the clouds above. Tovak wondered what the goblins and orcs thought, for surely in the nearby hills they could see the thousands of campfires on the plateau—perhaps even from as far away as the mountains.

The lieutenant led the section around to the main gate that had been erected on the northeast corner of the encampment and faced the direction the warband was headed. Other companies and sections were arriving, along with a supply train numbering over thirty wagons. They were forced to wait their turn to enter. The column finally moved forward and through the gate, which rose above the camp, nearly thirty feet in height. The sound of shouting drew Tovak's eyes to the upper walkway, and he saw a warrior high above him who he recognized, which was a surprise. It almost made him miss a step.

An officer with some sort of a baton in hand stood atop the walkway, shouting at Kutog, the wealthy recruit who had been so rude and condescending back on the yuggernok. The officer was tearing into Kutog for some infraction or failing. Tovak heard the words "idiot" and "moron." He watched the officer raise the baton. It fell, hitting Kutog's helm with a loud *CRACK* of wood on metal.

The sight of it lifted Tovak's spirits a bit. He wasn't the only one having a rough time of it, and he had no doubt that

Kutog had earned what was coming to him. *Besides,* Tovak thought, *misery loves company.* Then something else occurred to Tovak. Kutog would have marched all day in full plate armor and spent the afternoon and evening digging the massive trench or constructing the wall that now surrounded the encampment, only to get stuck on sentry duty. Even with all the hardships Tovak knew he was to endure, he realized he'd rather be out foraging and away from the encampment than being stuck where Kutog was. He was a skirmisher and there was some freedom in that, even for a Pariah.

They passed through the gate, leaving Kutog and the irate officer behind. The encampment was laid out almost identically to the way it had been his first night with the warband, only on different ground. The banners and tents, those he could recall, were in roughly the same place. What at first had seemed like a confusing jumble of disorder clearly had some sort of order to it.

There was a good deal more activity than he remembered, with the streets and avenues between the tents full of armored and unarmored warriors alike. The only appreciable difference was that there were no inner berms and trenches. Benthok led the section through the camp to the very center, where the watchtower rose into the air. As they neared, Tovak saw it was still being assembled. He thought it incredible that when the warband moved it was disassembled and then put back together again.

The lieutenant led the section on an unerring course that ultimately brought them directly to Struugar's tent and the company area. Benthok brought the small column up to the tent. The captain was nowhere to be seen.

"SECTION... HALT," Benthok shouted. "Left face."

The column halted and turned to face where Benthok stood in front of Struugar's tent. Every one of them was tired and worn, except, it seemed, for Benthok himself. There was a tirelessness about the lieutenant that, despite Tovak's new loathing for him, he could not help but respect.

"Good job out there," Benthok said, addressing the section. "I am extremely pleased with our haul this time. I am confident the captain will be satisfied as well." Benthok paused. "Corporals, I sent word ahead. There should be a hot meal waiting for us. Get some grub in your squads. We're not done for the day. Training after mealtime."

There were several groans at that.

Benthok's face hardened in the torchlight.

"For that," Benthok said, "we will go for a run around the camp, after we finish weapons drill." Benthok gave the section a grim smile. "I do so love a good run. Don't you, Corporal Thegdol?"

"Aye, sir," Thegdol sounded off enthusiastically. "A run sounds grand, just grand."

This time, there were no more groans, though Tovak sure felt like he wanted to. His legs burned from the exertion of the march. He'd been looking forward to removing his armor and taking the load off his feet.

"Dis-missed," Benthok said, then turned and made for Struugar's tent. A moment later, he disappeared inside. The section broke up and walked wearily back towards their camp behind Struugar's tent.

Tovak followed the others past Struugar's tent. As he moved by the supply tent, he saw the company area had been set up just as it had two nights prior. There were four rows of tents, with a wide alley going down the middle. Several campfires had been set and the light from them pushed back on the night.

The members of his own section were moving to their assigned tents. Sergeant Bahr stood outside the supply tent and next to a table with a large iron pot. The contents steamed and Tovak smelled stew. A line had formed before the table and a cook's assistant ladled the stew into wooden bowls.

As he walked down the middle of camp, there were greetings from those sitting around the campfires directed at members of First Section and a good deal of friendly ribbing about losing the race back to the encampment and being late for dinner. There were friends and comrades all about him, and he knew with utter certainty that none of that goodwill would be shared with him. Whatever chance he might have had at developing any friendships had evaporated the second Benthok asked him for the Warrant.

He recognized some of the faces from handing out the dodders. If he was not mistaken, they were members of Third Section, but he wasn't quite sure. Tovak was still too new to the company. As he looked around, he decided half of the company must still be out in the field.

When he reached the rear of the camp, he found no one around the fire that had been set there. He removed his pack. A smaller tent had been pitched next to the last communal tent. Laying his pack down on the ground by the fire, he breathed a sigh of relief as he stretched some of the soreness out of his shoulders. He removed his helm and set that on his pack as well, twisting his neck a few times to loosen the muscles.

He pulled out the Warrant, opened the top of his pack, and slid it inside. There was no point in keeping it on him anymore. It no longer mattered if anyone saw it. For good or ill, the secret was out. Tovak turned and faced the flames of the fire, staring into their depths as if he might find some answer, some balm that would soothe what his life was about to become. The fire burned brightly, and in those flames, he found only a promise of more pain and suffering.

His stomach rumbled, breaking him out of his self-pity. He went back up through the middle of camp towards the food. He spotted Logath and Jodin standing outside a nearby tent, talking with several warriors from Second Section. As he passed by, Jodin pointed. The others just stared as if in disbelief.

Tovak shook his head and moved on. There was nothing he could do about it now. The news would take its course, just as it had so many times before. He found a half-dozen members of First Section in line. He joined them and waited patiently for his turn.

Morda, in line ahead of him, turned and glanced back. He faced back to the front without a word. Staggen stepped up behind him, followed by several members of Fourth Squad from his section. Tovak glanced back. Staggen said nothing. His face was devoid of any emotion at all. He was simply waiting his turn and looked bored.

The line moved, and before Tovak realized it, he was standing before the table with the stew.

"I will be needing a new spear," he said to the sergeant as the cook's assistant ladled Tovak some stew.

"Good gods," Bahr said, sounding suddenly exasperated. "Broke your spear already? Don't you know you are expected to care for your equipment? Tell me, you weren't fool enough to use it for digging? That's what your trencher is for. Bloody fool idiot."

"No, Sergeant," he said, "it broke while I was fighting for my life."

"Against what?" Bahr asked.

"A murinok," Tovak said and even to his ears it seemed unbelievable. "I killed it and, well, the murinok in its death throes sort of broke it."

"You?" Bahr asked, his face full of disbelief. "I've heard some shit in my time, but you expect me to believe that? It's coming out of your pay, boy."

"But—" Tovak started.

"Don't 'but' me, boy," Bahr cut him off. "I ought to give you a thump for lying to me."

Tovak stood there, stunned. He didn't know what to say.

"He's not lying, Sergeant," Staggen said.

Tovak turned. Staggen locked eyes with Tovak only for a moment, but there was something there Tovak didn't recognize. Was it sympathy? Honesty? Or something else? Staggen then looked at Sergeant Bahr.

"Tovak got an adult murinok, and all by himself too," Staggen said, flatly. "He may be a lot of things, but he sure as heck got that murinok, and broke his spear in the doing of it."

"Thank you," Tovak said to Staggen.

"No thanks are needed," he said tersely. "My Legend required I speak up."

Tovak felt gut-punched as he turned back to Sergeant Bahr. It hadn't been friendship or even camaraderie that had driven Staggen. It was the obligation of Legend. In Staggen's actions, Tovak keenly felt his squad mate's rebuke. Shame filled his heart.

Bahr glanced between Staggen and Tovak, then shook his head.

"Stop by in the morning and pick up a new one before the company marches," Bahr said. "I'll make the entries in my ledger and list it destroyed in action. You will not be charged."

"Thank you, Sergeant," Tovak said.

The cook's assistant handed Tovak his bowl of stew and began ladling the next bowl.

"My apologies for doubting you. Oh, I had a tent set up for you and Gorabor." Bahr nodded towards the back of the camp. "Last tent on the left-hand side. It's small, but it should do. After we get a few more fresh recruits, I'll break out a communal tent and take that one back."

"Yes, Sergeant." Tovak made to turn away and came to an abrupt halt. He couldn't spend the night in a tent with Gorabor. It would be awkward... too hard. "Am I required to sleep in the tent, Sergeant?" Tovak asked, looking back.

"No," Bahr said slowly, a look of confusion on his face, "I—"

"Then if it's all the same to you, I'll just sleep by the campfire," Tovak said. "Gorabor can have the tent to himself."

Bahr stared at Tovak for a prolonged moment, and then his eyes slid to Staggen and back again. Tovak's squad mate said nothing. A flickering look of concern crossed the sergeant's face, and then he simply gave a shrug, as if he had more important things to worry about.

"Suit yourself, boy," Bahr said. "Sleep under the stars or even in the rain if you like. Just don't come bitching to me if you want another blanket. You've been issued all you're gonna get. Now get moving. Staggen there looks hungry enough to eat a teska by himself."

"Yes, Sergeant," Tovak said. Without another word, he walked back to where his backpack lay. As he walked, he felt eyes upon him. He ignored it. No one had come to sit by his fire. That did not surprise Tovak. He sat down and started eating with mechanical efficiency, for he did not know how long he had before the lieutenant called them out for drill.

He barely tasted the thick, savory stew. He didn't feel the cool night air. And despite the sounds of the warband all around him, he heard nothing. The silence that pressed in on him, however, was as palpable and familiar as an old friend. Before he knew it, he was picking at the remains of the stew. He tried not to feel sorry for himself, but it was incredibly difficult not to.

Second Section returned from the field. They marched up to the captain's tent and were dismissed, whereupon they dispersed into the company area. Tovak chuckled grimly. By morning, he had no doubt the entire company would know the name Tovak Stonehammer … and his shame. A day after that, perhaps even the entirety of the warband would know.

Benthok appeared, emerging from the captain's tent.

"First Section," the lieutenant called, "time for some combat training. Fall in."

Setting his nearly empty bowl on the ground beside him, Tovak rose to his feet and put on his helm. He made his way over to the assembly area and took his place with his section. Gorabor came up behind him, stepped past without a word, and then took his place in line next to Tovak.

The corporals began doing a head count. Thegdol stepped up, looked them over, and then, as the senior corporal present, took reports from the other corporals. He marched up to the lieutenant.

Thegdol exchanged a salute. "All present and accounted for, sir."

"Take your place, Corporal." Benthok looked over the section. "SECTION … right face. Forward, march."

The section stepped off, marching in close order. There was less foot traffic moving between the rows of tents, but not by much. The lieutenant marched the section through the encampment, turning right along the main avenue formed by company tents. They came to and entered a large, open area about thirty yards across, with rows of medium-sized wagons parked in a square. Torches around the perimeter and throughout the open area shed plenty of light about and smoke too. A supply tent sat just outside the square, with wooden training weapons and shields neatly stacked out front.

Two squads of heavily armored strikers faced off inside, occupying one side of the area. They battered at each other, slamming wooden shields and fighting to get the upper hand. Their battle shouts and war cries seemed real enough. Tovak was impressed by their ferocity as they went at it. It was almost as if a real battle were being waged.

"Section, halt. Right face."

Tovak turned with the rest of the section. The lieutenant stood looking upon them.

"When I say, grab a training sword and then form up by squads. First and Second will face Fourth and Third over there." Benthok pointed just behind him.

A sergeant with only one arm emerged from the supply tent to watch.

"To warm up, we will begin with individual sparring, using the zjain," Benthok called. "After the day's hard work, it should be good fun. This will be followed by formation drill. While you are sparring, attempt to score points only. That is a touch of the sword against your opponent. Keep everything somewhat civil and try not to get overenthusiastic. I expect to see bruises, the occasional laceration, but no broken bones. If there are, you will find yourself on punishment detail."

"Shields too, sir?" Thegdol asked.

"No shields," Benthok said. "This will be a one-on-one exercise and is more suited to the type of action we will see in the field, where you might have to fight alone against the enemy's skirmishers and without the protection of a shield. Now"—Benthok paused—"grab a weapon."

The entire section broke formation and moved towards the supply tent. Each took a wooden training sword as the supply sergeant handed them out. The lieutenant moved over to watch as he waited.

Tovak stepped up when it was his turn. He spotted a stack of larger wooden swords, volzjain, piled in a corner of the supply tent. He looked over at the lieutenant. "I'm better with a longer, two-handed weapon, sir."

"I know you've been trained by the Academy weapons masters. I want to see what you can do with a zjain," Benthok said. "Master it, and then we can talk about how good you think you are with a longer blade. Now take your weapon and get in line with the rest your squad."

"Yes, sir." Tovak grabbed a battered training sword. It was heavier than the real thing. Training swords usually were. The cord grip was also rougher, coarse. He walked back to where his squad had formed up.

"Tovak," Thegdol said. "Take your place next to Gorabor and Jodin."

He stepped into place and found himself facing Bane from Third Squad.

"Bane," Logath said, coming up from behind. "I will take your position. You can have mine."

"Yes, Corporal," Bane said, moving over.

Logath stepped into Bane's spot. The corporal had a distinctly malicious look on his face as he gazed at Tovak across from him. Jodin now faced Bane and Gorabor faced Dolan.

"I'm gonna teach you some manners and show you your place, Pariah." Logath slapped the wooden blade in his hand a few times. "You should never have come to the warband."

"Ready positions," Benthok called.

Tovak knew without a doubt he was in store for a beating. Logath was a veteran with years of experience and arms training behind him. If only Benthok had been willing to let him take a volzjain, he might stand a chance here. It was at times like this where he'd come to understand that Thulla was giving him a lesson. He looked over at Thegdol, but his corporal simply returned his gaze and said nothing.

"I'm listening," Tovak said to Thulla.

"What was that, boy?" Logath asked.

"Nothing," Tovak said. He had not realized he had spoken aloud.

He set his stance, as he'd been taught, raised the wooden training sword into the ready position, elbow bent, blade tip held at eye level, and body turned. He raised his back arm up and slightly behind him for balance and in position for blocking, grabbing, and punching. The only thing Tovak figured he had going for him was his reach over Logath, who was shorter by several inches, and he planned on using that to his advantage as much as possible.

The rest of the section assumed the same stance, and then they waited for Benthok's signal.

Logath's eyes were intense as he stared down Tovak.

"Too bad about that shot you missed, eh, Corporal?" Tovak said, deciding he had nothing to lose. Perhaps he could anger Logath into a rash mistake.

Out of the corner of his eye, Tovak saw Gorabor glance at him with a look of shock.

Logath's eyes narrowed dangerously.

"I'm gonna enjoy giving you a beating, Pariah," Logath growled. "Bastards like you always need to be taught a lesson."

"Begin," Benthok shouted from down the line.

Logath's weapon dipped, circled, and slapped Tovak's blade down and to the side in the blink of an eye. The corporal moved lightning fast. Tovak tried to recover, raising his arm to block the blow he knew was coming, but he was late and slow. Logath's weapon smashed into his helmet.

If it hadn't been for the helm, the blow probably would have knocked him out cold. Still, Tovak staggered back a step, stunned. Another lightning fast blow knocked his weapon from his hand, and then a fist came out of the haze and crashed into his jaw, hard.

Blinking, Tovak shook his head and realized he was sitting on his butt. He wasn't entirely certain how he'd gotten there, but there was no doubt he was on his ass. He shook his head again, struggling to clear his mind.

"Haa," Logath shouted and stepped back. "How'd you like that?"

Tovak groaned to himself. Looking up, he saw that Jodin, Dolan, Gorabor, and Bane were all barely going at each other. They were making a good show of it, but Jodin and Dolan's eyes kept flicking his way to watch. Tovak looked down the line to where Benthok stood, staring at him, while the rest of the section continued to trade blows.

"Hold and reset!" Benthok shouted. "I said hold."

The clacking of wooden practice swords petered off. Although the lines had shifted, as opponents had pressed each other forward and back, Tovak had been the only one knocked down. He pulled himself to his feet as the section quickly stepped back to their starting points.

He dusted himself off and then bent down to pick up his weapon from where it had been knocked into the dirt. He faced Logath once again, and as he did, a sense of anger surged through him. Logath had set out to humiliate him, hurt him, and it was clear he intended to do it again. He was a bully and Tovak had over the years developed a pure hatred for bullies.

"I can take whatever you can dish out," Tovak said to the corporal. He moved forward, stepping back up to his starting position, and raised his weapon into the ready position.

"We'll see about that," Logath said.

Tovak took a deep breath and searched the corporal's face, trying to discern where the attack would come from. He'd been taught that you had to be mindful of the whole of your opponent. Logath was wound up, a single, tense muscle, seeming ready to spring.

"Begin," Benthok called out.

Logath's blade snapped out, moving under Tovak's, but Tovak was already stepping back, allowing his opponent to come forward. Logath's blade found only empty air. Without missing a beat, Logath thrust forward, the blade tip aimed at Tovak's sternum. Tovak blocked the weapon with a clatter of wood on wood, pushing it out and away from his body, towards the corporal's off hand. Logath reacted instantly and lifted his elbow, danced to the side, and raised the weapon up over Tovak's blade, bringing it around and down in a flash.

Tovak stepped back again, raised his weapon across his body, turned his shoulder towards Logath, and managed to just barely catch the attack with his blade. *CLACK.* Then Logath stepped in and landed a heavy punch into Tovak's ribs. If he hadn't been wearing his leather breastplate, it probably would have cracked bone, but all it did was push him off balance. Logath didn't wait for him to recover. His blade whipped around, coming down towards Tovak's head from the other side.

Tovak raised his blade to block again and then saw Logath adjust the direction of the strike at the last moment. Instead of coming at Tovak's head, Logath swung straight down between their bodies. There was a meaty *THWACK* and sharp pain flared across Tovak's thigh, like it was on fire.

He cried out, staggering in his tracks, and then out of nowhere, Logath's blade smacked into the side of his helmet, filling his vision with blinding light. A moment later, he found himself once again on his ass, blinking.

"Hold and reset," Benthok called and then began moving through the two lines, giving pointers and speaking words of encouragement or passing along his critical insights. When he got to Tovak, he looked briefly down with a frown and then passed without a word. Tovak painfully pulled himself to his feet.

The lines started to reform again as Tovak tried to clear his head from the fog. He looked to his right and saw Thegdol standing there, with what he took to be a disappointed look. Tovak's corporal shook his head once and then turned to face his own opponent.

Logath, Bane, and Dolan were sharing amused looks. The sight of it fueled his anger. He glanced at Jodin to see that his squad mate wasn't laughing, but he too appeared amused. Gorabor, on the other hand, looked uncomfortable, perhaps even ashamed. That hurt more than the blows Logath had given him.

Tovak glanced to his left and spotted Benthok. The lieutenant had stopped at the end of the line and then faced back to watch the next round. His face was impassive, as cold as stone. He locked eyes with Tovak, and his lips moved in one silent word.

Fight.

Tovak blinked again, wondering if the blow to his head had him seeing things. He climbed painfully to his feet, wincing. His thigh burned with pain, and he knew a nasty bruise was forming. His head hurt too. He dusted himself off and then stepped over to where his training sword had fallen. It was ten inches shorter than the longer volzjain, which he was more comfortable using. The grip was also too short, with the wooden guard placed precisely where he wanted to put his forward hand in a two-handed grip.

He made a decision...and curse the consequences. If Benthok wanted him to fight, well, then he would fight—only his way.

He picked up the training weapon, turned it over, and stuck the point down in the ground. With both hands, he slammed down on the cross guard, dislodging it from where it had been wedged, leaving him with what was now a short but two-handed weapon. He would meet Logath's quickness with strength. He glanced at Benthok, who merely looked on as if he'd not seen what Tovak had done.

"Positions," the lieutenant called.

Tovak stepped up to the line and found Logath grinning broadly at him, clearly eager.

"Ready for some more, boy?" he sneered.

"I was ready long before I ever met the likes of you," Tovak said, shifting his body to face Logath. He took a deep breath and let it out slowly, pushing away all thought save that of the fight ahead.

Logath guffawed and looked over to Bane, who grinned back at the corporal. With a roll of his eyes, Logath then returned his gaze to Tovak. "As long as you're back for more, I couldn't be happier."

Tovak said nothing. His jaw ached from where Logath had struck him. He felt a hot wetness running down his neck.

He reached up and touched his cheek, coming away with blood. Tovak took up the two-handed grip on the makeshift volzjain he'd just created. He settled into the familiar stance he had been taught, the one that was so much more natural to him, and faced Logath fully. Immediately, Tovak felt more confident, more comfortable. His right foot was ahead of the other half a pace, and he held the weapon firmly in both hands, slightly away from his body and angled forward from the waist.

Tovak knew he was taking a risk by deviating from the instructed form, but he didn't really care at this point. If Benthok wanted to punish him for not playing by the rules, he'd take it like a warrior, but he wasn't going to just stand there and let Logath continue to beat on him.

He'd had enough and he intended to tell Logath that in a way that the corporal could not misunderstand.

Tovak stiffened his arms and gripped his weapon tightly. Logath was skilled with the zjain. That much was clear. Tovak stared at the corporal. He drew in his breath slowly, letting his gaze run down Logath's body and up again. He exhaled, allowing his pain and embarrassment and even his anger to flow out with it. As he locked eyes with his opponent, he saw the same arrogance and malice there, coupled with a profound confidence that Tovak was about to put to the test.

"Begin," Benthok called.

Logath's weapon tip dipped and came around, once again lightning fast. It smacked into Tovak's blade, but this time, the weapon wasn't merely slapped out of the way. Tovak's double-handed grip and rigid stance held firm. He pushed back, leveraging the blade with both hands and shoving Logath's weapon aside and down with a good deal of force. Logath was surprised but not caught unaware. He immediately recovered and stepped back to avoid Tovak's counter-thrust. Then Logath moved back in, swinging his weapon around in a downward slash.

Tovak's weapon rose and caught the attack easily. There was a loud *CLACK*.

Logath drew back and swung again, this time from the other direction, driving Tovak back a step. Tovak blocked again, and again, each time their weapons meeting with a *CRACK* that seemed louder than the last. Tovak's hands were going numb from the repeated and painful blows to the blade, but he stuck at it, pulling Logath forward into a rhythm: attack-parry, attack-parry, attack-parry.

Then Logath saw an opening and brought his blade around, a victorious look on his face, but Tovak had been waiting for it and there was no opening. It had been a ruse. He stepped forward in a flash, drawing his weapon back a few inches, and then slashed forward and down with blinding speed and force. He hammered his blade straight down the middle of Logath's face. Splinters flying, the blade caught the corporal on the crown of his helmet with a loud *CRACK*. Logath's head snapped back from the blow and stopped him dead in his tracks. Tovak stepped forward to strike again. Logath recovered quickly and just barely managed to block Tovak's strike. For a moment, they strained against each other, grunting.

Logath forced Tovak's blade back. Then, releasing the weapon with his right hand, Tovak heaved with an uppercut, putting everything he had into the blow. He caught Logath on the chin, connecting squarely. The squad leader's head snapped to the side, and he tumbled backward onto his ass.

Tovak felt a fierce sense of exultation and moved in, his anger suddenly returning in a rush and fueling him forward. Logath struggled to sit up, his weapon still in hand.

MARC ALAN EDELHEIT & QUINCY J. ALLEN

He raised it in a clumsy warding gesture. He was clearly still dazed, but he saw Tovak coming at him and tried to scoot back out of the way, desperately holding his blade in a blocking position to protect himself.

"Bastard," Tovak roared and slammed the weapon down as hard as he could. Their two blades connected with a loud *CRACK*. Both training weapons broke with the impact, and the upper half of Tovak's slammed down onto Logath's helmet.

"Tovak," Benthok barked. "That's enough."

Tovak froze, breathing hard, and then stepped backward. He stared down at what remained of his weapon and realized he had gone too far. He let the grip slip from his fingers, which had gone numb from the repeated blows. The stump of the training weapon fell to the ground before Logath. He turned, expecting to see Benthok angry, but instead, the officer's eyes were fixed squarely upon Logath, as was the rest of the section. Everyone had stopped what they were doing to watch the fight play out between him and Logath. Silence reigned across the training ground.

Slowly, the lieutenant walked over to them. He blew out a frustrated breath, then fixed his gaze upon Tovak.

"This was supposed to be a zjain exercise," he said. "Every skirmisher must master the zjain and practice with it until they know it better than themselves. Could you have misunderstood my instructions? Because the stance you chose was not for the zjain."

"No, sir," Tovak said, struggling to catch his breath. "I did not misunderstand."

For a moment, Benthok appeared as if he was going to say something else, but then glanced down at Logath, who was still somewhat dazed and bleeding from a cut on his lip. The corporal held his head in both hands.

"Logath," Benthok asked, "are you all right?"

"I've been better, sir," Logath said, dragging himself, almost painfully, to his feet. He looked a little unsteady and held a hand to the side his head. "I'm a tad dizzy is all."

"That was a pretty nasty blow. Head back to camp and have Sergeant Bahr check you out," Benthok said. "He will decide if you need to be sent to the doctors."

"But, sir," Logath protested, with a glance thrown to Tovak. "I'll be fine in a moment. I've had worse."

"No doubt, but that's an order," the lieutenant said.

"Yes, sir," Logath said.

"I'll come find you later to talk about what just happened."

Logath blinked and then looked sharply at his lieutenant. He swallowed. "Yes, sir."

Logath offered a salute, which Benthok returned. Without looking back, Logath pushed through the line, brushing by Tovak. Staggering slightly, he made his way out of the training area. The entire section's eyes were upon his back.

"For the rest of you," Benthok said, raising his voice with an edge in it, and took several steps away from Tovak. "This is zjain training, not a bloody spectator sport. Eyes front."

Thegdol stepped over to Tovak. "You're bleeding."

Tovak was surprised to see concern in the corporal's eyes.

"It's just a cut, Corporal," Tovak said, feeling it.

"Are you injured anywhere else?"

"My thigh hurts something fierce and I have a headache"—Tovak tapped his helmet—"but I think I will live."

"I believe so, too." Benthok turned back to them. "Tovak, go grab two more training weapons."

"Two, sir?" Tovak asked.

"Yes," Benthok said. "You will need a new sparring partner. I will step in for Logath."

Great, Tovak thought. Now Benthok wanted to beat on him too.

Tovak wasn't sure he could take much more, but as ordered, he started off to the supply tent for two training swords. Behind him, Benthok barked out an order to the rest of the section. The sparring resumed.

"That was some fight," the one-armed supply sergeant said as he handed over the weapons. Tovak took them and returned to Benthok.

"Corporal Thegdol," Benthok called.

"Sir?"

"Oversee the section's drill while I work with Tovak."

"Yes, sir."

Benthok took Tovak aside, well behind the drill line.

"Every night, after your duty for the day is done, you will seek me out for extra training," Benthok said. "If I am unavailable, Corporal Thegdol will fill in. Is that understood?"

Tovak blinked, surprised. Was this a punishment?

"I asked if you understood me, soldier."

"Yes, sir," Tovak said. "I do."

"You must become as proficient with the zjain as you claim to be with the volzjain. Judging from what you did to Corporal Logath, I'd say you are good with a two-handed weapon. However, in this warband, every skirmisher must master the zjain. Had you been proficient at it, Corporal Logath would not have been able to handle you so roughly." Benthok held up the training blade. "This is the weapon of the skirmisher and a fine one at that. It's deadly in the right hands, lightweight, and easily carried all day. Heavier weapons and gear tend to not just slow us down, but add to fatigue. That's why we're not issued plate armor and heavier gear, like shields. You can move quickly with this weapon over rough ground and through the forest, without worrying about it becoming a hindrance. As a skirmisher, it is well-suited to our needs and skirmishing with the enemy out beyond the protection of the main line. If you don't master it, you will end up dead and might just get someone else killed in the process. If you are dead, you are no good to me. So, you will master it, before some orc on the battlefield cuts you down for lack of skill."

"Yes, sir," Tovak said.

"I will work with you to improve your skill with this weapon," Benthok said. "Only then we will go on to other weapons."

"Yes, sir," Tovak said.

"Now, assume the fighting stance for the zjain."

Tovak did as ordered.

Benthok stepped forward, walking around him, eyes on his stance.

"Elbow in towards your body more," Benthok said. Tovak made the adjustment. "Back hand lowered slightly, and keep it loose. Don't make a fist." Tovak did that too, and then Benthok stepped in and adjusted his back arm a little more. "There," the lieutenant said firmly. "That's right. Do it that way every time."

"Yes, sir," Tovak said as Benthok took a position opposite of him.

"When I say 'begin,' I want you to attack me."

Tovak nodded.

"Begin," Benthok ordered.

Despite being spent, Tovak attacked, lunging forward. With lightning fast reflexes, Benthok parried the strike easily, raised his elbow, and thrust forward, jamming the point of his blade into the center of Tovak's chest. He moved quicker than Logath and the force of the blow had not been particularly hard, just enough to stop his forward momentum. The lieutenant was not seeking to hurt him, but instead instruct. Why?

"Use of the zjain requires that your wrist, elbow, and shoulder become fluid, like a snake," Benthok said, stepping back and lowering the training weapon, "and for every attack, there is a parry and a counter. If you master weapons you are not comfortable with, when you face an opponent using one, you will find yourself better armed."

"Yes, sir," Tovak said.

"Over time, you will learn to become proficient," the lieutenant said. "I do not like to waste my time, so make sure you listen and learn."

"Yes, sir," Tovak said. "I will."

"Let's begin again."

CHAPTER FIFTEEN

A hobnailed boot nudged Tovak firmly out of a deep sleep. Groaning, he rolled over from his side onto his back and opened his eyes to pre-dawn darkness, accented by the pale light of the moon. The fires and torches had gone out. Above him stood Benthok. An insect chirped somewhere nearby, and the smell of woodsmoke lay heavy on the air. Tovak felt stiff from sleeping on the hard ground. He was also cold.

"It's almost four horns." In the near darkness, the lieutenant's face was like shadowed granite. "Wake Gorabor and get yourself organized for the day. Then go and fetch the company's dodder rations. The captain wants to be well into our march before the first of the suns comes up."

Tovak tried to blink the sleep out of his eyes and failed. He yawned deeply as he sat up and wondered how long he had slept. It clearly had not been enough.

"You do remember the way?"

"Yes, sir," he said. "I do."

Tovak yawned again, hoping he did indeed remember the way to the cook tents. His entire body ached something fierce, especially his thigh where Logath had landed a particularly hard blow. Raising his arms to stretch, he winced at the burn that shot down from his shoulders to his fingers, a result of his training with Benthok. It had proved not only instructional, but also demanding. He climbed to his feet. There wasn't a part of him that didn't hurt in some fashion.

"Don't worry," Benthok said, seeming to understand how he felt. "Once the march begins, you will loosen up and it won't feel so bad."

"I hope so, sir," Tovak said, "because I ache something fierce."

"Stretching helps. You might want to try it." With that, Benthok turned on his heel and walked away towards the supply tent. Tovak watched him go, disappearing back into the night a few yards off.

The rest of the company slumbered away, as did much of the encampment. Tovak envied them. In the distance, he could hear some activity and the occasional shout. A dog barked and then another one answered. He glanced down at his bedroll with longing. He needed more sleep but he knew he would not get it.

As was his custom, he knelt down and placed his hand upon his pack, feeling for the lump that was *Thulla's Blessed Word*.

He whispered, "Thank you, Thulla, for the opportunities of a new day. Blessed are those who follow Your word. Blessed are they who will carry the light to Your people with every breath. I am and ever will be Your humble servant, 'til that solemn day when I return to Your breast and stand in the glory of Your magnificence."

His morning prayer complete, he stood again, groaning softly as he did it. He stretched out his arms, back, and legs as the lieutenant had suggested. It hurt, but at the same time, when he was done, Tovak felt a little looser.

He grabbed one of his waterskins and took a swig to wash the foul taste from his mouth. A gust blew by, ruffling the fabric of the tents and causing him to shiver. Tovak grabbed his cloak, which he had used as a pillow, and shook it out before wrapping it around his shoulders.

He turned towards the tent, suddenly feeling uncomfortable, and found himself hesitating. Tovak let out a long breath and then slapped the tent flap.

"Gorabor?" he called out quietly, not wanting to wake the rest of the company. "Gorabor, time to get moving."

He heard a rustling inside, but there was no reply.

"Gorabor?" he said again, raising his voice. He slapped his palm against the tent three times. "Wake up."

"Hmmph?" Gorabor mumbled, and Tovak heard him shifting about inside.

Tovak pulled the tent flap back and poked his head in. The interior of the tent was dark. He could just barely make out Gorabor wrapped up in his blanket.

"Get up," Tovak said. "The lieutenant wants us to get the dodders."

"Right," Gorabor replied, a bit sleepily. "I'll be out shortly."

Tovak let the flap fall back into place. He felt the sudden intense need to empty his bladder. He had drunk his entire ration of wine the night before and now it demanded to be released. The cold air did not help either. He made his way to the latrine, which stank terribly. He relieved himself and then returned. The fire next to where he'd bedded down had long since gone out. He held his hands out and could still feel some heat radiating from the ashes, but it wasn't enough to warm him much. He settled for rubbing his hands together.

He rolled up his bedroll, secured it to his pack, and began putting his armor on. Gorabor emerged from the tent and stretched, yawning powerfully. He spared a quick, but unhappy look at Tovak and then without a word headed off to the latrines.

Tovak let out a melancholic breath. He filled his water-skins from the tapped water barrel by the supply tent. The barrel had been placed on top of an old crate. Inside the supply tent, a single lamp burned, the glow of which filtered out through the flap. Tovak could hear someone, likely Sergeant Bahr, moving about inside. He returned to his pack to find Gorabor putting his armor on just outside the tent. Gorabor's pack and spear lay by his feet. Tovak secured the waterskins to his pack.

"Bloody armor," Gorabor groused.

Tovak looked up to see Gorabor struggling with a strap on his left side. He was trying to tie it one-handed, and the darkness made the effort more difficult.

"Let me help you with that." Tovak moved to assist.

"I can manage, thank you," Gorabor said brusquely, turning away from him. "I don't need help from you."

"Okay," Tovak said and backed off.

"All right, ladies," Thegdol called out from behind them.

The corporal walked down the middle of the encampment, slapping the sides of several tents roughly with a stick as he went. "Beauty sleep isn't going to help a single one of ya. You're all beauties in my eyes. Get up and get ready. It's gonna be a fine day, my beauties, I can just tell. We've got another fine day ahead of us."

"How is he always so cheerful in the morning?" Gorabor asked. "I swear I don't think Thegdol ever sleeps."

Warriors emerged from their tents, stretching and rubbing the sleep out of their eyes. There were several more calls from the other corporals as they rousted the company. Tovak heard the clatter of gear, armor, and weapons as the company readied themselves for the day. Thegdol spotted Tovak. For a moment, the corporal's expression hardened, then he turned away and walked back the way he'd come, stopping to speak briefly with Jodin, who had just emerged from one of the tents.

"You ready?" Gorabor asked from behind him.

Gorabor had his armor on and had managed to secure it. His spear rested on the ground, next to his pack. The sight of the spear reminded Tovak he needed to speak with Sergeant Bahr to get issued a new one. He met Gorabor's eyes for a moment and hesitated, wanting to say something, but he knew it would not matter. He was a Pariah. There was nothing he could do to change that.

"Well?" Gorabor looked impatient.

"Yeah," Tovak said. "I'm ready."

"Let's get this done, then," Gorabor said.

Grabbing their packs, they made their way towards the supply tent. Before they'd gone ten feet, Logath stepped out from a tent, saw Tovak, and blocked his path, forcing him to stop short. Gorabor came to a halt as well.

"You got lucky last night," Logath said, leaning in close enough for Tovak to smell his foul breath. "I assure you, that won't be happening again."

"We have to get the dodders," Tovak said, not wanting any trouble with the corporal. "You are holding us up."

"Fetching our breakfast, like a good dog, eh? When you're done with that, you can fill my squad's waterskins. Perhaps then, I'll pat your head, like a good dog. Would you like that, boy?"

"Did you just call him a dog?" Dolan asked, stepping out of the same tent.

"I think he did," Bane said, coming over and joining them.

"Logath," Bane said, "I think you're on the right path. We should put him to work. Save us the trouble of some grunt work."

"I think I might just do that," Logath said. "Well, boy, how would you like me to put you to work?"

"If Corporal Thegdol instructs me to assist you, then I will," Tovak said. "He's my squad leader. You are not. Now, get out of my way. I have a job to do."

Gorabor looked over sharply at Tovak, clearly shocked.

"Got brass balls, do you?" Logath said, eyes narrowing dangerously.

"He's got balls, that's for sure," Bane said with a nasty chuckle. "I think it will be fun snipping them."

"What was Struugar thinking?" Dolan asked, looking over to Logath. "Pariahs are just plain, old-fashioned bad luck. Everyone knows that. Why would he accept him into the company?"

"The captain likely felt sorry for this little piece of teska shit." Logath glanced at Bane, then turned his gaze back to Tovak, fingering the hilt of the dagger at his belt. "You better watch yourself, boy. There was a Pariah over in Third Company a few years back. He was uppity too, just like you…didn't know his place. He didn't last long. His squad let the orcs have their way with him. The same can happen to you, if you're not careful with your betters."

Tovak's anger surged and he balled his fists, taking a step forward. He'd had enough of bullies.

"What's going on over there?" a sharp voice barked out. Benthok was standing a few feet away, a stern look upon his face. "I told you to get the dodders, Tovak. Stop wasting time and snap to it."

"Yes, sir," Tovak said. He looked at Logath one last time and shot him a wink. Then, without saying a word, stepped around him and continued on for the supply tent, with Gorabor following. Benthok's unhappy gaze flicked to him for a moment, then turned to Logath and the others.

"There's plenty to do," Benthok said. "Don't make me find work for you, Corporal."

"Wouldn't dream of it, sir," Logath said. The three quickly dispersed, going their separate ways.

Tovak's anger simmered as he set his pack on the ground by the supply tent. Gorabor did the same, then met his gaze, and for a moment, it appeared as if he was going to say something. Whatever it was, Tovak wasn't sure he could bear any pity from his former friend.

"Let's get moving," Tovak said, speaking first. "Hopefully we can find our way there and back without the lieutenant's help."

"That would be nice," Gorabor said with a glance in the lieutenant's direction.

Despite the darkness, Tovak had little trouble finding their way. He was generally good at remembering directions, once he'd eyeballed how to get somewhere. He led Gorabor unerringly through the camp. When they reached the cooking tents, the dodder ration line was even longer than it had been the last time.

Tovak and Gorabor joined the end of the line. Neither saying a word to the other, they patiently waited their turn to collect the sacks. The silence between them was palpable. Every now and again, Tovak caught Gorabor casting side-long glances in his direction. Then, after what seemed like an interminable wait, it was finally their turn.

"What company and how many sacks?" the cook asked.

Tovak held up four fingers and said, "Baelix Guard."

The cook nodded, handed over the four requested sacks, and waved for the two of them to step aside. An assistant standing next to the table made a notation on a tablet.

"What are they this time?" Gorabor asked, holding one of the sacks up to his nose. He inhaled deeply, clearly enjoying the smell of the freshly cooked dodders.

"Heratta," the cook replied with disinterest.

"They smell great," Gorabor said.

Tovak had to agree, but he remained silent.

"There's something not quite right with you, mate," the cook said, sourly. "No one likes army food. Now, off with both of you. You're holding up the line."

They hefted the sacks, which were radiating warmth, and made their way back to the company, again, without exchanging a word. By the time they returned, the tents had been broken down, rolled up, and stacked.

All four sections had formed up into three ranks. The company stood at ease, with their packs and spears resting on the ground before them. Benthok waited off to the side of the formation, speaking in low tones with Thegdol and a sergeant Tovak had learned was named Kelloth.

Tovak and Gorabor set about distributing the dodders.

"Just open the bag," a corporal from Third Section said quietly when Tovak approached. "I'll get it myself. I don't want you touching my food."

The corporal's disgust was plain. Tovak kept his face blank. Inside, however, he was seething. Bottled up rage, shame, and embarrassment tore at him.

"You tell him, Karn," the warrior behind the corporal said. "And the same goes for me. I don't want no dirty Pariah fingering my food."

"Aye, filthy Pariah. You should do the honorable thing and just kill yourself," Corporal Karn said, "but then again, you have no honor, no Legend. It's too much to expect one of your kind to do the right thing."

There was a mutter of general agreement at that from Karn's squad.

Despite his anger earlier at Logath, Tovak found himself falling into an old and familiar practice of ignoring the hatred. He did his job. He moved on, trying not to let it bother him. But the truth was it tore at him terribly.

And when he'd finished with distributing the dodders, he took one for himself, bit into it, and walked over to the supply tent, where Bahr stood waiting for him. Tovak held out the near-empty bags to the sergeant. Bahr accepted them and set them on a small camp table that was set up before his tent. A three-legged stool sat underneath the table and a thick ledger lay atop. It was clear that the camp table served as the sergeant's desk.

"Sergeant, I'll need that new spear," Tovak said.

The sergeant stepped close. "Don't worry about them dumb boffers. You're not the first Pariah I've seen go through this warband, boy, and you won't be the last. Some have proven themselves, some not. You, if I am any judge, will."

Tovak looked at the sergeant, surprised. He had not expected any support from Bahr, just the same treatment he'd received from everyone else. Bahr's words were more than welcome.

"Time, patience, and strength will get you through this," Bahr said. "Do your job, stay out of trouble, and keep your chin up. Show them your worth, earn their respect, and change a few minds. They'll come to terms with you. I promise, in time it will get easier. And if you're the spiritual sort, then a few prayers to Thulla won't hurt none either, now, will it?"

Tovak became still at the mention of his god. Few these days bothered to speak openly about faith, that was, if they kept it. Most didn't, and in some circles, such talk was dangerous. Did Sergeant Bahr keep the faith?

"Thank you, Sergeant," Tovak said and meant it.

"Don't thank me," Bahr said, turning away to grab a spear he had clearly set aside for Tovak. It was leaning against a large crate and close at hand. "I don't like Pariahs either, but I've taken a shine to you."

Wondering why, Tovak took the spear.

"The lieutenant and your corporal told me more about how you took down that murinok," Bahr said. "That takes guts."

"I was so scared," Tovak admitted, "I almost shat myself."

"Admitting that takes guts too," Bahr said and then pointed at the spear. "Try not to break this one, will you?"

"No promises, Sergeant," Tovak said with a sudden grin. He then picked up his pack from where he'd set it on the other side of the supply tent and slipped it on. Hefting the spear, he took another bite of the dodder and strode, somewhat stiffly, down the middle of the formation.

He could have walked around, behind the company, to his position with First Squad. However, Bahr's words were fresh to mind. He wanted to show them all that nothing they said would wound him. It was a show of defiance and one he decided necessary. Tovak fully intended to claim his place here. He sensed their eyes upon him, felt the disgust and the animosity, as if it were a tangible thing that poured forth. He ignored it all. He would show them what true Legend was about, even if it killed him in the end.

Tovak reached the end of the formation and fell in, next to Gorabor. He set his pack and spear on the ground and, like the rest of the company, waited for Benthok to call them to attention. Thegdol broke off from the lieutenant. The corporal approached and then slowly walked down the line of his squad, looking at their armor and equipment. It wasn't a formal inspection, but it was clear he was checking to see that his boys were presentable. Apparently satisfied, Thegdol took his place at the head of First Section, where his own pack and spear lay.

Sergeant Kelloth, who had remained speaking with the lieutenant, abruptly snapped to attention, offered a salute, and then he too took his position to the right of the formation. Benthok waited several moments, glanced back towards the captain's tent, and then moved out to stand before the company.

"Right then, you lazy durpas," Benthok called. "Packs on."

The company began hefting their packs. Tovak picked his own up and put it on. The lieutenant waited until the entire company had their packs on and spears in hand.

"Company," Benthok called, stressing the word and dragging it out. "Stand to attention."

The whole company pulled themselves to attention, spears immobile at their sides and backs straight, gazes fixed forward. Moments later, Captain Struugar strode around the corner of his tent and up to the lieutenant. Benthok, standing to attention, snapped off a crisp salute. The captain was wearing his armor, like the rest of them. Struugar returned the salute.

"One hundred thirty-four present and accounted for, sir," the lieutenant reported. "None in the sick tent."

"Small miracles, then," the captain said, then lowered his voice and said something to the lieutenant. Benthok gave a curt nod and moved over to Struugar's side as the captain turned to face his company. Tovak thought Struugar looked tired and perhaps even a little worn.

"The Great March continues," Struugar said. "Our mission has not changed. That means more foraging for us. We're moving back up into the hills again. The scouts report they are thick with heratta, so that'll be our focus. I hope you like hoppers, because it's all you're likely to get from the cooks for some time."

"At least it's not durpa, sir," Corporal Thegdol said, and that brought a chuckle from several who were standing to attention.

"Too true," Struugar said and then sobered. "A word of warning, though. The pioneers ran into a large band of orcs yesterday, not far from where we will be operating." He waited a moment to let that sink in. "It was a sharp fight and we took some losses, but our boys gave more than they got and forced the orcs off. It is expected that encounters like these will increase in frequency. You need to be on your toes from here on out. The easy days are over. We're moving into territory that's far from friendly, so nobody goes out alone. Out in the field, if you feel the need for a piss, be sure to take a friend."

Struugar paused a moment.

"As you forage, keep your eyes open for signs of the enemy, and if you notice anything, drop what you're doing and report immediately to your squad or section leaders." Struugar glanced over at his lieutenant. "I'll be working with Second Section today. Lieutenant Benthok will remain with First and Sergeant Kelloth will take Third. Fourth Section will be on wagon escort duty again. More on where the warband is headed in the coming days. Stay safe, stay alert. That is all." The captain turned to Benthok. "Let's get the company moving."

"Yes, sir," Benthok said, and then turned to face the formation. "Company, left face, forward march," he called, and with armor chinking, the company stepped off.

CHAPTER SIXTEEN

With Corporal Hilla's squad of archers following at the rear of the small column, First Section left the wide-open expanse of the plateau and, once again, marched up into the hills. The going was difficult, seeing the section climbing up and down a series of steep hills before entering a valley. The valley, several miles wide, was thick with grass and littered with the occasional patch of trees and scrub brush. A stream cut its way in a meandering path down the middle of the valley. It was a peaceful setting and Tovak found himself enjoying the view as they trudged along, one mile after another.

Once they left the main encampment, the line of march had spread out and become more relaxed. Tovak walked by himself. No one wanted to share the miles with him. A few feet behind, Gorabor was speaking with Staggen. After them came Lok and Thegdol. Morda and Jodin were to Tovak's front. Staggen was lecturing on the advantages of having a good pipe at the end of each day.

"It strengthens the constitution," Staggen said, thumping his chest armor. "Look at me, I never get sick or catch a cold."

"All from having a pipe?" Gorabor said. "I've never been one for the pipe. My mum wouldn't let me try it, said smoking was a nasty habit. She wouldn't even let Da smoke."

"That's cause she never tried it," Staggen said. "If she had, she'd know, like my ma did. Who do you think taught me the benefits of a good pipe, eh?"

"It really keeps you from getting sick?" Gorabor asked.

"Aye, it does," Staggen said, "laddie."

"You are full of teska dung," Lok said, with a laugh from behind them. "Don't listen to him, Gorabor. He is a right awful liar. Shameless bastard, he is. Staggen gets sick, just like the rest of us, smoking a pipe or not. He's just fond of the taste, is all. Probably wants to get you hooked, so he can borrow a smoke when he's out."

"I would never dream of lying to you, lad," Staggen said in an exaggerated tone of hurt. "Honestly, Lok…stretching the truth, maybe, but lying to young Gorabor here? Never."

Tovak listened with half a mind as the banter continued. It had been like this for the last few hours. His gaze strayed out into the valley and then to the slopes that surrounded it. This was truly a beautiful, unspoiled place. Heratta were scattered throughout the valley, nothing like the numbers they had seen on their last excursion to the hills but still a good many. More hoppers could be seen gathered along the slopes to the hills.

The lieutenant angled the column of march to the right and they began climbing back up into the hills and out of the valley. The slope was steep, craggy, and boulder-strewn. Tovak decided that, when the time came to mark the trail to camp, it would not be the easiest of jobs.

"Why can't we camp down in the valley?" Gorabor asked between labored breaths. "There is plenty of game out there. All this climbing is killing my legs."

"Welcome to the army, son," Staggen said. "Nothing is ever done the easy way."

"Don't listen to him," Lok said. "It's got nothing to do with easy or not or where there is or isn't game. The lieutenant is moving us up into the hills for safety. He will pick us a campsite that not only has some elevation to it but is also somewhat secluded."

"Why elevation?" Gorabor asked, glancing back.

"If we camp in the valley," Lok answered, "anyone in these hills around us can look right down on our camp and see where we are, especially at night when we've got fires going. It makes us an inviting target for orc and goblin raiders with balls enough to take us on."

Tovak looked at the hills with fresh eyes, wondering if any of the enemy had seen the column enter the valley. He hoped not.

Cresting the hill, yet another greeted them. The slope was steep. Without hesitation, the lieutenant led the section into the trees and upward, following a small stream. This brought them to a wide, flat, grassy area that was flanked on either side by sloping ridgelines.

The collapsed ruins of an old farmhouse lay in the center of the field. The roof had long ago fallen in and was now a pile of overgrown debris. Only two of the stone walls remained standing and they rose a few feet above the grass and brush that had grown up over much of the ruin.

Tovak wondered why someone had taken the trouble to settle so far away from any hint of civilization. What had happened to the people who had lived here? Who were they?

Beyond the ridges that hemmed in the field, the landscape seemed to grow rockier and steeper as the mountain slopes reached towards the sky. They had entered the high country, and Tovak could feel a slight chill in the breeze blowing down from the snowcapped mountains.

"Section...halt," Benthok called out. The column ground to a stop.

Tovak was breathing heavily and, like everyone else, sweating profusely. He pulled out his waterskin, unstopped it, and took a heavy swig. If the lieutenant selected this spot for a camp, it was certainly secluded, and it had the elevation Lok spoke of. His gaze traveled up the mountain slopes. Though if anyone was up there, they would easily be able to look down upon the camp. There was not much one could do about that, which was why they fortified the camp.

"Logath, Bane, and Dolan, you three have marker duty," Benthok ordered as he turned to face the section. "Corporal Thegdol, do you have the bag?"

"I do, sir." Thegdol stepped forward and handed it to Logath.

"Wouldn't this be better suited to the Pariah, sir?" Logath asked and pointed at Tovak.

Benthok had looked away and was staring up at the nearest mountain. He turned a hard gaze back to Logath. Tovak could sense the lieutenant's anger at being questioned.

"Did you ask me a question, Corporal?" The lieutenant's tone was filled with irritation. "I might have missed it, as I was not paying attention."

"No, sir," Logath replied, hastily.

"Good," Benthok said. "The path we took up here is unsuitable for the carts. You've got your work cut out for you marking a route the teamsters can traverse."

"Yes, sir," Logath said and then offered a salute. "We'll get the job done, sir. Bane, Dolan, you two are with me. Let's get moving."

They stepped out of line, dropped their packs, and moved past, heading in the direction they had just come. Tovak stood there, pleasantly surprised. He was wondering why he and Gorabor had been spared. As the newest member of the company, he'd fully expected to be saddled with the duty again. From the looks of the rest of the section, it seemed they were thinking the same thing.

Benthok looked down to the end of the line.

"Corporal Hilla," he called, eying the archers who had met up with them just outside of the encampment. "Select one of your girls to go with the marker crew, in the event there's any trouble. An archer may come in handy. The rest will have sentry duty while the section constructs our camp for the night."

"Yes, sir," Corporal Hilla said. She stepped out of the line and pointed to a tall, dark-haired archer behind Gulda. "Cena, you're assigned to Corporal Logath."

"Yes, Corporal." She fell out of line, dropped her pack, and followed after the three skirmishers as they moved past her.

"Corporal Thegdol," Benthok said, "I want our camp set up over there." He pointed to a wide, flat area, not far from the stream, which disappeared into the trees a few hundred yards away. The stream appeared to climb up the slope of the ridgeline. "I will mark out the boundaries for the trench and wall. Get us some firewood too. Once Shrike gets up here, he will want to begin cooking."

"Yes, sir," Thegdol said, stepping out of line. "Corporal Gamok, take Fourth Squad up into those trees over there"— he pointed to their left—"and start working on a supply of firewood. We'll also require stakes for the trench."

"Fourth Squad," Gamok called, "drop your packs, refill your skins at the stream, and then grab your axes. We've got a job to do, boys."

"Packs off," Thegdol called to the rest of the section. "Take advantage of the stream while you have the chance. For those who did not get my subtle hint, fill your water-skins. Fall out."

Without another word, the section fell out, moving towards the stream.

The suns were straight overhead, and it seemed the clouds had gone out of their way to avoid providing any hint of shade to those laboring away. Tovak wiped the sweat out of his eyes. The trench was almost completely dug. The excavated dirt was used to build the defensive berm, which was in the process of being packed down.

Tovak had been assigned to help dig the trench. It was backbreaking work that saw him perspiring heavily. As the burning ache in his arms, shoulders, and back increased, he found himself wondering if it would have been better to have been assigned marker duty. But then, he disregarded such thoughts. His people were of the mountains, rock, and soil. This was good, honest work and, truth be told, Tovak did not mind doing it.

From the trees came the steady staccato crack of axes as Corporal Gamok's squad worked. Shortly after the work on the trench started, Fourth Squad had begun hauling in a steady stream of not only firewood, but defensive stakes for the trench and berm.

Even Thegdol joined in, laboring alongside Tovak, so close that they almost at times bumped shoulders. What really surprised Tovak was that the lieutenant was also working. After he'd finished marking out the camp, Benthok had produced a trencher from his pack and set to work digging, breaking ground alongside his soldiers. Tovak still felt angered with Benthok, but at the same time, he felt a growing respect towards the lieutenant.

Tovak wiped sweat from his face and glanced over at Thegdol. The other warriors kept their distance from him, including Gorabor, but none of them hazarded any open abuse with the corporal or lieutenant within easy earshot. All Tovak received was the occasional hostile glance.

Since they'd left the encampment, his corporal had been close at hand, never straying more than a few yards. He glanced over at Benthok and felt his brows furrow. The captain had selected a different section to accompany today. Why had Benthok remained with First Section? Was it because of Tovak? He glanced over at Thegdol, wondering.... Whether it was coincidence or not, he was grateful for the peace and freedom from abuse the corporal's presence granted. He returned to the task at hand and kept on digging.

"Corporal Thegdol." Lieutenant Benthok had appeared and was looking down on the corporal from outside the trench. "Care to inspect the work?"

"Aye, sir." Thegdol reached up a hand to the lieutenant and was hauled out of the trench. "I believe we are nearly done, sir."

"My thoughts too," Benthok said. They set off, walking slowly around the camp as they inspected the defensive works.

"All right," Thegdol called, a short time later. "That's enough. Take a break."

Tovak felt a vast relief at those words.

"Squad leaders on me," the lieutenant said as he strode across the bridge and into camp. He paused and looked back. "Corporal Thegdol, has a latrine been dug yet?"

"No, sir," Thegdol replied.

"Since I sent Jodin out to scout, assign someone the job," Benthok said.

"Aye, sir." Thegdol turned and scanned about. His gaze passed right over Tovak to Gorabor. "Gorabor, you're on the latrine. Dig it over there." He pointed. "Downstream please, if you don't mind."

"Yes, Corporal," Gorabor replied. He pulled himself out of the trench and began moving to where Gamok's squad had set a log not far outside the gap in the berm.

Tovak was surprised he'd not been picked for the extra duty. He gave a tired shrug of his shoulders and then climbed out of the trench. Along with several others, Tovak made his way into camp, where his pack waited.

"Incoming," Gulda, posted on sentry duty near the bridge, called out.

Tovak looked and saw Logath, Dolan, Bane, and Cena returning. They were sweaty and out of breath.

"Corporal Logath," Benthok called as soon as they entered the camp, "your timing is impeccable. Kindly join us."

"Yes, sir," Logath said, then turned to Bane and Dolan as Cena stepped away towards Corporal Hilla. "Get some water and eat something. I imagine the lieutenant will want to send hunting parties out before long."

The corporal made his way over to the lieutenant and the other three corporals, leaving Bane and Dolan behind. Bane shot Tovak an unfriendly glance but said nothing as he passed by.

Tovak ignored him, grabbed his pack and spear, and found a spot well away from the campfire that Gamok's squad had just started. Placing his back against the newly constructed berm, he opened his haversack and peered inside.

The night before, they'd been issued with precooked rations for the next day. It wasn't much. Each soldier had been issued with a half-pound of an unknown salted jerky, which had come out of a dusty crate packed with salt, and three rolls of buurl. When the rations had been issued, Sergeant Bahr had called it "meat surprise" and then cautioned the company not to eat any of it until the following day as marching rations.

Tovak was hungry. He pulled out the small bundle wrapped in a rough woven cloth. Unfolding the cloth, he exposed the three hard loaves of buurl, their gray, rock-hard surface about as unappealing as the river rocks they were named after. He dropped one of the rolls into his mess bowl. The hard bread made a solid-sounding *clunk*. Tovak hated buurl. He poured water over the roll and filled the bowl about halfway, hoping the bread wasn't too hard and the water would quickly soften it so it was edible. Setting the bowl aside to sit for a time, he waited and enjoyed the feeling of doing nothing.

Eventually, Tovak stirred himself. Pulling out his dagger, he poked at the roll, testing. The hard outer shell gave a little. He cut a piece and chewed the bland, earthy-tasting bread. It was as if it had been made with sawdust. Swallowing hard, he repeated the process, until he'd managed to down the entire roll. Tovak could not bring himself to eat the other two rolls. Instead, he carved off a bite of the dried mystery jerky and found it just as unappealing. It was so salty, it made him thirsty to the point where he drained the rest of his waterskin.

Tovak yawned and glanced around. Several of the section had taken advantage of the break and gone to sleep. Tovak realized he was dead tired too. Leaning back against the berm, he shut his eyes and was almost instantly asleep.

"Right, you lazy bastards," Thegdol called loudly. "On your feet. Break time's over. It's time to earn your pay."

Tovak opened his eyes. He felt groggy, but surprisingly rested. He glanced up at the sky. The two suns had not moved much, so he'd not slept that long. He pulled himself slowly to his feet and cracked his neck. Gorabor was standing with Gulda, who had been posted on the berm for sentry duty. They had been talking, but with Thegdol's words, that was done. Gorabor moved over to his pack.

"If you haven't already done so, fill your waterskins," Thegdol said. "Squads are to form on their corporals outside camp. Bring your slings and shot. Leave your spears."

With that, Thegdol himself turned and walked over the bridge and out of the camp.

Tovak made his way to the stream, where Staggen and two warriors from Fourth Squad were already filling their own skins.

"Hey, look, Balor," a warrior by the name of Fallon said, "it's our resident Pariah."

Balor, blond with thick arms and virtually no neck, raised his eyes. He spotted Tovak and spat in the dirt next to the stream. "Make sure you fill those things downstream of us," he snapped. "I want none of your filth in my drinking water."

Staggen rose stiffly to his feet and walked past Tovak, back towards Thegdol.

Tovak ignored them and moved downstream a few yards. Untying his helmet and setting it aside, he dunked his head into the stream. The cold water brought instant relief from the heat and felt wonderful.

"Son of a coward," Fallon said, "you're a disgrace."

"You got that right," Balor replied. "I used to be proud to be in the Baelix Guard ... but now ... I don't know anymore."

Tovak continued to ignore them as he washed the sweat and dirt off his hands and arms, then set about filling his waterskin.

"Balor, Fallon," Corporal Gamok called out from behind Tovak. "Stop dragging ass."

Tovak turned to see Gamok with the rest of his squad, waiting impatiently a few yards away.

"Yes, Corporal," Fallon said. They finished filling their waterskins and then walked off to join their squad.

"Tovak," Thegdol called. "You're keeping me waiting. I don't like to be kept waiting. Get a move on."

First Squad had gathered around Thegdol. Tovak joined them, wringing out his beard as he came.

"The lieutenant wants us to head up that way." Thegdol pointed uphill to the northwest. "Jodin was sent out earlier to have a look around and he spotted heratta up there in the trees."

"A lot of them," Jodin said, "just up that way, about three hundred yards. We should have an easy time of it."

"Any murinok?" Tovak asked. The words slipped out before his mind could catch up.

Jodin's gaze hardened.

"None of that now," Thegdol said. "We've got work to do and don't need to be fighting amongst ourselves. We work as a team. It is that simple. You both got that?"

"Yes, Corporal," Tovak said.

"Jodin?" Thegdol asked when the other did not reply.

Jodin gave a curt nod.

Thegdol patted his sling, which was secured to his sword belt. "Everyone have their sling?"

There were nods all around.

"I have extra shot." Thegdol patted a bag hanging from his belt. "If you need more, come see me. Remember to stay together and keep a sharp eye. Any questions?"

There were none.

"Let's go then."

They began moving uphill, and before long entered the tree line, which was boulder-strewn. The temperature under the shade of the trees was cooler. The ground was rough and the going was difficult, so any relief at being out of the suns was short-lived. They came to a small clearing, where several trees had fallen.

"If there is any trouble, and we get separated, this will be our rally point." Thegdol stopped and made a point to look at both Gorabor and Tovak. "Remember this spot."

"Yes, Corporal," Tovak said.

Gorabor gave a nod.

"Let's head up that way and see what we find." Thegdol pointed farther up the hill and started off, the squad following.

After a short hike up the slope, they found themselves on an open, rocky ledge of sorts covered with pines, mountain grasses, and an occasional rock outcropping. Four hundred yards to their front, the slope climbed again, but this time into thick forest. There were several dozen heratta scattered about to their front, with more beyond those.

"Looks like we've come to the right place," Morda said.

"Grab your slings," Thegdol ordered. "Drag your kills to this spot here. We will dress them later. Now, spread out a bit and make your shots count. I will not remind you to stay in sight."

They set to work, spreading out. Tovak brought down two hoppers in rapid succession. He dragged them back to the collection point and met Staggen, who had just dropped off a hopper.

"That's a big one," Tovak said, admiring the kill. It was the largest heratta he'd seen so far.

"He's a big buggar, isn't he? The mother of all daddies, I guess," Staggen said, with a pleased grin. Then he seemed to remember himself. He turned his back on Tovak and walked off the way he'd come.

Tovak blew out an unhappy breath and returned to where he'd gotten his last kill. He was about to continue forward when he spotted a denser clump of trees off to the right, just at the edge of the hill. The ground below was covered in a patchwork of shadows. It looked like animals had bedded down in the area with some frequency, as the grass was flattened and there were tracks all about. He had no idea what kind of animal had made the tracks. And then he saw something that made him smile. There was a ring of small, dark purple mushrooms surrounding the entire area.

He glanced around and saw Thegdol a few feet off. Just beyond him was Gorabor, dragging a dead hopper to the collection point.

"Corporal, look what I found," he said, pointing. "Dain caps."

The mushrooms, like the blackheads he'd found before, were perfect for adding flavor to meals.

Thegdol glanced in the direction Tovak was pointing, then stepped over.

"Good eye," Thegdol said. "These will make Shrike very happy." Thegdol pulled a small foraging sack from his belt. He tossed it to Tovak. "You found them, you get to pick 'em."

Thegdol turned and stepped away.

Tovak got down on his hands and knees and began to gather the mushrooms. He'd harvested about three-quarters of the patch and nearly filled the bag when he heard movement, the crunching of a boot on dirt. He looked up and saw Jodin. He and Morda stood, just a few feet away, where the hill ended and dropped off, down a steep, grassy slope.

"Rooting around like a little piggy, are you? Thegdol's got you doing proper work now." Jodin laughed and Morda joined in. Tovak felt a stab of anger snap at him.

Still laughing, Jodin kicked dirt in Tovak's direction. Chunks of small stones peppered him in the face.

Rage bubbled up inside Tovak, and he lost his hold on the fury that burned within his breast. He slowly rose to his feet and stepped up to Jodin.

"Say it again," Tovak barked, shoving Jodin hard in the chest. "Say it again."

Jodin staggered back a step and nearly went over the lip of the hill.

"I don't need to," Jodin said and grabbed Tovak's arm. Before Tovak could react, he was pulled forward. Caught off balance, he stumbled by, teetering on the edge of the hill. Jodin stuck out his foot and shoved Tovak in the back, sending him careening down the grassy slope.

Tovak yelped, rolling over several times before regaining control and sliding the last few yards, until a boulder brought him painfully to a complete stop. He lay there a moment, stunned, then sat up. He was covered over in dirt and grass. It would take a lot of work to get his armor clean. He pulled himself to his feet and looked up the hill. Jodin and Morda stood there, laughing at him. Fury filled his heart. Before he knew what he was doing, he was scrambling on all fours back up the hill.

"You filthy coward," Tovak shouted as he scrabbled his way up towards his tormentor. "Watched me while I fought the murinok and did nothing. Is this your way of making yourself feel better? Are you going to stab me in the back next?"

The laughter ceased.

"You dare call me a coward?" Jodin raged back at him.

"Best own it, because that's what you are." Tovak moved up the hill and stood before Jodin. "Throwing me down a hill? Kicking dirt on me? What would you call that? A deed worthy of Legend? I am not your enemy."

"No," Jodin said. "You are worse, Pariah."

Tovak poked Jodin in the chest plate. "Say what you will. Call me whatever name makes you feel better and helps you to sleep at night. It was I who killed the murinok, not you. No, you just looked on like a scared little girl and watched. I would rather be named a Pariah and son of a coward, than be a coward like you."

Jodin's face went crimson, and he cocked his fist. Tovak raised his arm to block it.

"Enough," Thegdol's voice boomed, and they turned to see the corporal and Gorabor approaching at a run. Staggen and Lok were running over too.

Jodin lowered his fist and turned to face the corporal.

"Thegdol, I demand an Adjudication Circle," Jodin said, seething mad.

"Don't be a fool, Jodin." A concerned look came over the corporal. "With the Great March, aren't there more important things to concern ourselves with?"

"He called me a coward to my face," Jodin shot back.

Thegdol sucked in a breath, his eyes going to Tovak.

"I'm within my rights," Jodin said.

"Aye," Thegdol said, "you are within your rights."

"Then I demand satisfaction."

"You seriously want a Circle?" Thegdol asked and shook his head in disbelief. "I ask you to reconsider. I saw you throw him down the hill. You provoked this, Jodin."

"I will not change my mind, for I am no coward."

"The lieutenant will have to grant your request for a Circle," Thegdol said. "Be certain you want to take this little spat to him."

"Spat?" Jodin glared over at Tovak. "There is nothing little about it. Either we have an Adjudication Circle or I'll find another way to settle this, one you will not like."

"I don't take kindly to threats," Thegdol said and it came out almost as a growl.

Jodin was apparently undeterred. "I want a Circle. My Legend demands it."

Thegdol took a long breath and let it out slowly. He stared at Jodin for several heartbeats and then shifted his gaze to Tovak. He ran his fingers across his chin and through his beard thoughtfully. He was clearly trying to think of a way to defuse the situation.

"Do you accept the challenge?" Thegdol asked Tovak in a weary tone.

Now that things had come to a head, Tovak's rage was starting to fade. He'd never been in a Circle before and knew they frequently ended in death. He took a deep breath and looked at Jodin. Suddenly, the rational part of him felt like an Adjudication Circle was the last thing he wanted. But the other part, the one still fueled by rage, wanted nothing more than to pound the coward into a broken heap of blood and bone.

So be it. The die had been cast. Jodin had started it. Tovak would finish it. If nothing else, his Legend demanded that he accept the challenge.

"I do," Tovak said.

"All right, you dumb bastards," Thegdol said, his voice a mixture of resignation and disappointment, "let's go see the lieutenant."

They found Benthok back at camp, speaking with Shrike and Corporal Hilla. The three of them turned when they saw the squad approaching without any kills. Benthok met them at the bridge.

Thegdol stepped forward and saluted the lieutenant.

"What's wrong?" the lieutenant asked.

"Sir," Thegdol said, "I regret to inform you that Jodin has challenged Tovak to an Adjudication Circle, demanded it even."

"Has Tovak accepted?" Benthok's gaze locked onto Tovak.

"He has."

Benthok's eyes shifted between Jodin and Tovak. "You know Karach frowns upon Circles, yes?" he asked Jodin.

"I do, sir," Jodin said, "but they are not forbidden."

"This is hardly the time for such contests," Benthok said, "hardly the time. The company is understrength as it is. We can't afford to lose anyone."

"I demand satisfaction, sir," Jodin said.

"Why?"

"He called me a coward, sir," Jodin said.

"Did you?" Benthok asked.

"I did, sir," Tovak said.

"Why?"

"It was in the heat of the moment, sir," Tovak said.

"Jodin threw Tovak down a hill," Thegdol said. "Words were exchanged after that. I was able to intercede before it became more, but not soon enough to stop the challenge, sir."

Benthok turned an unhappy gaze to Jodin. His jaw flexed for a moment. "Jodin, you are on track for promotion to corporal. To this point, your service has been nothing if not exemplary. There is a chance that going through with a Circle could see all your hard work thrown away. You may lose your opportunity for promotion. Do you understand me on this?"

"I understand, sir," Jodin said, "but I will not be called a coward, especially by the likes of him."

Benthok blew out a long breath.

"Would you care to withdraw your challenge, should Tovak apologize?"

"Sir?" Tovak exclaimed. Would the lieutenant humiliate him even more, by forcing him to apologize to Jodin? The thought of such a possibility was maddening.

"Quiet, you," Benthok snapped.

"I will not withdraw my challenge to the Pariah, even if he apologizes. I want satisfaction. I intend to put him in his place, sir."

"Very well," Benthok said, suddenly sounding resigned. "Jodin has made a legitimate challenge. We will see that he gets his opportunity for satisfaction, as Legend demands." Benthok paused a moment and then recited the words of the Circle's official arbiter. "The Circle shall be forged. As is our way, the two combatants shall face each other. The gods will judge this test of strength, skill, pain, and blood, as is their right, and choose the rightful winner. And in the choosing, this matter will be resolved, for the truth shall rest with he who stands victorious."

Benthok glanced again at Tovak, a strange look upon his face. "You have been openly challenged and have accepted. It is your honor and right to choose the method of combat. That said, I would prefer to keep this contest nonlethal, and without weapons that might easily see one of you dead."

"Then, sir, no armor. No weapons. I choose bare fists," Tovak said.

Benthok raised an eyebrow, and for a moment his features seemed to hold a glimmer of approval.

"Bare fists are acceptable," Jodin said. "I am going to pound you to pulp, boy."

"So, shall it be," Benthok said. "A Circle has been called and will be joined."

CHAPTER SEVENTEEN

The suns were just disappearing behind the mountains, and deep shadows filled the field. A short distance from camp, near the collapsed farmhouse, the entire section stood in a circle ten yards across, facing inward. The archers had been placed on sentry duty to watch over the camp during the fight, and Shrike was once again busy cooking before the main fire. The smell of roasting heratta drifted over to them.

The Circle had been formed. With the exception of Tovak and Jodin, everyone wore full armor and held spears, butts set on the ground and tips pointing straight up to the heavens. Benthok stood in the middle of the Circle, and he carried a stout club he had fashioned from the branch of a nearby tree. Its purpose was to discipline any combatant who didn't adhere to the rules of the Circle, specifically his rules, since he was the arbiter. If weapons had been involved, Benthok would have been armed with his sword and a shield.

Tovak stood on one side of the ring, stripped down to his boots and leggings. He'd removed everything else, so that Jodin would not have anything to grab hold of. Curiously enough, Gorabor had chosen to stand in the Circle, directly behind Tovak, as his second. It was a place of honor and his job was to morally support Tovak, should he have need.

Since Tovak did not have any supporters in the company, Gorabor's placement in that position of honor was likely Thegdol's doing to see that Legend was satisfied.

Across the Circle, Jodin stood with his fists on his hips, looking deadly serious and confident. He had removed his armor and wore heavy leather leggings and a thick, woolen shirt that clung to his muscular body. His boots were laced up tight, all the way to his knees. Logath stood behind him as his second and was whispering something in Jodin's ear, to which the other gave a vigorous nod.

Benthok raised the club, holding it out flat between the two combatants. "The Circle has been formed," he said loudly, so those gathered could hear him clearly. "These two will now meet in single combat to determine who is just and who is not, who has been wronged and who did the wronging."

Benthok paused and looked between Jodin and Tovak. "There are to be no killing blows. There will also be no crippling injuries, no breaking of limbs, no biting, no eye-gouging, and no strikes to the groin. When this is over, I expect you both to get back to work, regardless of who is victorious. And make no mistake," he added, seeming to speak to everyone gathered, "when the gods have chosen the victor and this Circle is broken, I expect you to put aside any differences and accept the decision." He looked at Jodin. "Agreed?"

"Yes, I agree," Jodin said, eyes fixed upon Tovak.

Benthok looked to Tovak.

"Agreed," Tovak said. He'd let the gods decide who was right. He had his faith, and he'd been wronged. He sent a prayer up to Thulla for strength.

Thulla, grant me—

He stopped himself. No. He wouldn't ask Thulla for strength, not for this. The Circle was sacred, and all the gods would bear witness and decide. It would be inappropriate for him to ask for special favor from one and not all. Within the Circle, the will of all the gods mattered. It would be what it would be.

Tovak felt a tickle of nervousness. Over the years, he'd been involved in plenty of fights. The manual labor he had been forced to perform just to survive had made him strong, and more often than not he'd been able to hold his own when it came to bare-knuckles fighting. But this was different. He had never before entered an Adjudication Circle, and the thought that he was about to gave him pause.

"Let the combatants approach," Benthok said, keeping the club held before him.

Tovak and Jodin moved forward slowly.

"Good luck," a quiet voice said from directly behind Tovak. Tovak stopped and glanced back, surprised. Gorabor gave him an encouraging nod. Tovak answered the nod with one of his own and then continued forward towards Jodin.

They stopped a few paces apart, Benthok's club suspended between them. They both raised their fists, preparing to do battle.

"You know the rules, and I expect you to follow them," Benthok said in a low, warning tone. "Break them and you will have me to answer to. Are you both ready?"

Jodin and Tovak nodded at the same time.

The skirmishers around the Circle raised their spears together and began pounding them into the ground. They beat out a rhythm, and the sound of it fueled Tovak's ire. Before him was a tormentor. Before Jodin, a long line of tormenters over the years had done their very best to make his life an unending ordeal of suffering. That was at an end. Tovak resolved to no longer stand by and take what was dished out. He would stand up for himself, and it started here, in this Circle, with Jodin.

"Begin," Benthok commanded, raising the club and leaping backward out of the way.

Jodin rushed forward in a flash, cocking a fist. Tovak prepared to block it, but then Jodin's foot came up in a quick kick to Tovak's midsection, catching him by surprise. The air whuffed out of Tovak's lungs and he staggered back as Jodin pressed forward. He shot a punch at Tovak's head. Tovak blocked, but just a hair too late. It caught him on the cheek. A flash of pain stunned him, and the glancing blow spun his head sideways. Jodin sent his other fist low and under Tovak's guard, catching him in the ribs with a dull thud that knocked the air from his lungs. Tovak grunted and leapt backward, raising his guard as he tried vainly to suck air back into his lungs.

A cheer rose from around the Circle. It only served to infuriate Tovak, for he knew that many saw Jodin's challenge as a means to put him, the Pariah, in his place.

Still struggling to breathe, he stepped backward several steps, an attempt to buy time. Jodin followed, a confidence in his bearing that spoke of someone who knew they had already won the fight. Tovak reached up to his cheek, which stung terribly, and pulled away a bloody hand. The blow had reopened the cut to his cheek that Logath had given him, and he could feel the blood running down his face to his chest.

"I'm going to enjoy this," Jodin growled.

The spears kept pounding as Tovak stepped backward and out of reach, his vision beginning to gray.

Then, he could breathe again. He sucked in a gulp of sweet air, relishing it like never before. Tovak took another deep breath and let it out slowly. With each breath, his ribs and side hurt. Pain was a teacher he knew all too well. Pain didn't cow him; it spurred him on, fed his anger.

Tovak stopped his backpedaling and Jodin closed in on him. As he did, Tovak stepped forward, sending a quick jab at Jodin's face. Jodin shifted sideways and countered with a hook aimed at Tovak's head. Tovak leaned back, let it slide by, and ducked under, coming up into Jodin's stomach hard with a right-handed uppercut. Jodin grunted with the blow and moved back, but Tovak stepped forward and shot a left cross that caught Jodin squarely in the face. The force of it hurt Tovak's fist.

Jodin staggered back, blinking. He recovered quickly and let loose a flurry of hooks, almost haymakers, that forced Tovak to step back.

"It stings, doesn't it?" Tovak said.

Jodin shook his head and then settled back into a fighting stance. A trickle of blood flowed from his nose. Jodin reached up and wiped at the blood that was soaking into his mustache. His eyes narrowed and he started forward, this time warily and with grim determination.

They squared off again, exchanging a few jabs here and there to see who would leave an opening first. They circled each other slowly, the spears pounding out a rhythm that seemed to carry itself into the punches being thrown. The rhythm took him. Punch, block, jab, dodge. And with every punch, Tovak let his right hand lower, opening an avenue to his jaw. It was a calculated risk, one he hoped Jodin would fall for.

Suddenly, Jodin twisted his shoulders and stepped in, aiming a left cross at Tovak's head, just as Tovak had hoped. Tovak ducked, preparing to let it slide by and come up again into the left side of Jodin's exposed ribs, but the attack was a feint.

Jodin reversed and sent a right hook up into Tovak's jaw that connected with a meaty *THWACK*, sending lights flashing around inside his head. Tovak staggered. His knees went wobbly, and he tasted blood. Jodin came around with a haymaker that slammed into the side of Tovak's head, sending him stumbling sideways. More flashes filled Tovak's vision, and he could no longer hear the pounding spears. All he could hear was a ringing in his head.

He tried to regain his balance, but Jodin followed and kicked Tovak in the side. Tovak grunted and dropped to his knees, blinking furiously, but he never took his eyes off his opponent.

Another cheer went around the Circle, the sound of it a distant thrum in Tovak's ears. Pain lanced across his head and chest, carrying with it fuel for the rage that was building within him.

Jodin stepped up and shot out a kick, this time aimed at Tovak's head. It was a finishing strike and seemed to be coming for him in slow motion. Tovak leaned to the side, letting the boot slide by, a hairsbreadth from his head. He let his anger flow and rose, surging forward. His shoulder caught Jodin between the legs, and Tovak lifted him up off the ground, roaring in rage as he wrapped his arms around Jodin's midsection and slammed him down onto the ground with a heavy *THUD*.

Tovak staggered to the side, almost tripping over Jodin's legs, and as he did, a collective gasp went around the Circle. He turned back to face his opponent, who had rolled away, coming up to one knee in a defensive position. Jodin was clearly dazed, but not enough to leave an opening for Tovak to finish him. He rose to his feet. The confidence that Jodin had started the fight with was gone. He narrowed his eyes and raised his fists again as the spears continued to beat out their rhythm.

Tovak raised his fists as well and moved forward. Each step matched the beat of the spears, and he let that momentum carry him forward. He let a right jab fly. Jodin blocked it and loosed a right cross. Tovak was expecting it. He sidestepped the powerful blow, grabbed Jodin's forearm as close to the wrist as he could, and stepped in, twisting with his whole body as he bent forward, a maneuver he had been taught back at the Academy by the hand-to-hand instructors.

He heaved with his arms and, using Jodin's momentum, sent him flying to slam down onto the ground once again. The breath whooshed out of Jodin's chest. Tovak was unwilling to let Jodin get back to his feet. It was time to finish this contest. He leapt on top of his stunned opponent, straddling his chest, and sent his right fist down like a hammer across Jodin's jaw. Jodin's head snapped sideways, sending bloody spittle flying. Tovak reversed and hammered down with a left, and more blood sprayed sideways.

Tovak raised his right fist again, staring down at his opponent with hate-filled eyes, and as he was about to strike, a firm hand clamped a vice-like grip upon his wrist.

"It's over, son. You've won."

Tovak blinked and tugged to try to break free and found he could not. He looked up, staring into the face of the lieutenant. Why was he being stopped? Then, he glanced back down at Jodin and realization hit home. Jodin's eyes had rolled back in his head. Blood flowed thickly from his nose, and his right cheek was cut deeply, with a stream of blood running down the side of his face onto the grass.

Tovak wanted to continue pounding until his fists were drenched in Jodin's blood. The savage fury beating within his chest demanded it, but the lieutenant's grip was firm. Then something checked him, and a semblance of rationality returned. He sucked in a deep breath. It came out ragged and with it went his rage, hate, and fury. Tovak's shoulders sagged a fraction.

He had bested his enemy. There was no need to punish him further. The Way taught the path to Legend. Punishing a defeated opponent was not honorable and there was no Legend to be had in that.

The lieutenant seemed to sense that Tovak understood the fight was over and he released his wrist. Tovak lowered his fist, climbed off Jodin, and sat down in the grass. His heart was pounding in his chest. He took another deep breath and puffed out his cheeks. His hands began to tremble.

"The decision has been made," Benthok said. "The gods have spoken and chosen the victor."

The spears had stopped pounding, and there was nothing but silence around the Circle.

Tovak rose unsteadily to his feet and stared down at Jodin. His vision swam a moment as a dizzy spell took him. He shook his head and it passed. Jodin's eyes fluttered and then focused on Tovak and the lieutenant standing above him.

"You have lost," Benthok said.

Jodin shook his head in disbelief and tried to stand. He fell almost immediately and lay on his side, dry retching. He spat up some blood, then looked wildly up. "No. It's not over."

"It's over," Benthok said firmly. "Time to accept it and move on."

"Never," Jodin said, and tried to stand again. He staggered drunkenly before falling backward to a sitting up position. He was clearly shaken up. "No. I will never accept this. I can't have lost."

Tovak felt his anger return. He advanced, reached down, and grabbed Jodin's collar, gripping it tightly. The shirt was stained with blood. He lifted Jodin partway off the ground until they were almost nose to nose.

Benthok took a step closer, raising his club, but Tovak ignored him.

"I've been treated like dirt by people like you for longer than I care to remember," Tovak said, loud enough for the whole Circle to hear his words, for this wasn't meant just for Jodin, "and all for something I had nothing to do with other than an accident of birth." He tightened his grip on Jodin's shirt, drawing him closer. The other's eyes widened in sudden fear. "Nobody gets to treat me like dirt, ever again. Not you"— Tovak shook Jodin, and then pointed with his free hand at those gathered around the Circle—"not them, not anybody."

He dropped Jodin back to the ground and stepped away, casting his gaze around at those gathered.

"I am here to serve," Tovak said, his voice trembling with emotion and exhaustion, "to be part of this company. Is that too much to ask, to serve?" Tovak fell silent a moment. He wiped blood off his cheek and in the dying light of the day glanced at his blood-covered hand. All eyes were on him. "Pariah or no, I follow the Way. Anyone who disputes that, a challenge and the Circle waits. Beat me you might, but I will never back down, never stop, for I claim a place amongst you ... even if, in the end, it kills me."

He turned and stared at Logath for a long, hard moment. Logath's face was expressionless. Tovak shifted his gaze to Benthok. He locked eyes with the lieutenant, and the look on Benthok's face was a surprise. The lieutenant appeared pleased.

"You gain Legend this day," Benthok said quietly, so only the two of them could hear. "Your place is most assuredly with the company. I am proud to have you serve under my command."

Tovak was silent for a long moment, thoroughly astonished. Then his legs wobbled as the world swam. Gorabor stepped forward and gripped his shoulder, helping him remain on his feet.

"May I go, sir?" The dizziness passed.

"Dismissed, soldier."

Tovak gently pushed Gorabor away and steadied himself. He brought himself to a position of attention and saluted. The lieutenant returned his salute. Tovak turned, passed Gorabor, and staggered out of the Circle, headed straight back into camp.

He looked up to see Gulda standing guard atop the berm. Her eyes followed him, and as he passed by, she nodded to him once and then turned her eyes back to the perimeter. The other sentries standing watch had turned their gazes to him as he entered. Their faces were stony. But something made Tovak feel as if the world had turned for him, if even just a little. He was done allowing others to walk over him.

Shrike, working by the fire, glanced in his direction briefly as Tovak passed. "You win?"

"Yes," Tovak said over his shoulder as he made his way over to his pack. His hands had started to shake violently.

"I was hoping you would."

Tovak sat down hard and leaned on his pack. He felt drained, exhausted, more so than he'd ever felt in his entire life. He ached and hurt something fierce. He placed a hand on his pack and felt where *Thulla's Blessed Word* lay, tucked away. The feel of it brought him some comfort.

Grabbing his waterskin, he took a few gulps and then poured the rest over his face. He fingered the cut on his cheek. It had just been reopened, was all.

"That was a heck of a fight," Thegdol said.

Tovak looked up to see his corporal standing before him. Behind him, the rest of the section was streaming back into camp.

"You did well," Thegdol said.

"Thank you, Corporal," Tovak replied. He wasn't sure what Thegdol intended.

"Let me see that cut on your cheek."

Tovak saw Thegdol was carrying a stopped jar and rag. He opened the jar and soaked the cloth with vinegar. Tovak could smell the pungent scent.

"That's an order, son," Thegdol said as he knelt before Tovak. Thegdol inspected the cut, probing it gently with his fingers, prompting a wince out of Tovak.

"Was that your first Circle?"

"It was."

Thegdol probed the wound again.

"Hurts," Tovak said.

"It should, though it's not too bad," he said. "You don't need any stitches." He dabbed at the wound with the rag. The vinegar burned like fire, but Tovak held still, taking the pain. Thegdol wiped the blood from Tovak's face and then handed him the rag. "It should stop bleeding soon. Make sure you keep that wound clean. I don't want it spoiling. You may end up with a bit of scar from this. If you do, consider it a badge of honor."

"Yes, Corporal," Tovak replied.

"Are you injured anywhere else?" Thegdol asked. "How are your ribs?"

Tovak felt his ribs. "I hurt, but I seem to be whole."

"If the pain gets worse," Thegdol said, "you let me know straightaway."

"Yes, Corporal."

"I want you to swear on your Legend you will tell me if the pain worsens," Thegdol said.

"I swear," Tovak said.

That seemed to satisfy the corporal, for he gave a nod.

"Clean yourself up, attend to your kit, and then get some rest, all right?" Thegdol stood, patting him on the shoulder. "It was a good fight, honestly won."

"I will, and thank you."

Thegdol was about to turn away and then stopped. "Eat something before you turn in, even if you're not hungry. After today and that fight, you need food."

Tovak nodded.

"Corporal?" Tovak asked, his thoughts shifting to Jodin. "Did I injure Jodin badly?"

"Corporal Logath is seeing to him," Thegdol said. "You might have broken his nose, but I believe that is the worst of his injuries."

With that, Thegdol walked off, leaving him alone. Tovak lay back on his bedroll and closed his eyes.

He blinked as someone nudged his leg. Tovak realized that he'd fallen asleep. He sat up and pain lanced through his side, snapping him fully awake. He groaned. Then looked around. The section was lined up and receiving their dinner from Shrike. Then memory returned in a rush. He'd won the Circle. Had that really happened?

"Tovak?"

He looked up and over to his left to see Gorabor holding out a steaming bowl. He held another one in his other hand. "I brought you some food. Shrike gave you a double portion. He said you'd need it."

Tovak was moved by the gesture, not only from Shrike but from Gorabor getting him food. He accepted the bowl and was surprised to find it was his own mess bowl.

"I hope you don't mind," Gorabor said. "I did not want to wake you. I went in your pack and got your bowl."

"I don't mind," Tovak said and then cleared his throat. He no longer had anything to hide. He looked down at the steaming meat, which smelled delicious, then back at Gorabor, who sat down next to him.

"I wanted you to win...and...." Gorabor bit at his lip, almost embarrassed by his own words. "And I'm sorry for...well, for my part in all this, turning my back on you. You did not deserve that. I never imagined what it must be like as a...." He hesitated, a shameful look on his face. "As a Pariah."

Tovak did not know what to say. He had not expected this, so he remained silent.

"For what it's worth," Gorabor rushed on, "I don't care who your father was. From here on out, you're just another member of my squad, my section, and my company. I swear on my Legend, I will treat you as you deserve."

Part of him wanted to think this was just some trick. There had been so many over the years. But then, he recalled Gorabor's words before the fight—*good luck*—and he realized that Gorabor meant it. There was no deception on his face. An unexpected warm feeling washed over him, a feeling he hadn't felt for a very long time.

Tovak cleared his throat. "Thanks." It sounded rather lame to him.

"I would consider you a friend," Gorabor said, "that is, if you will have me."

"A friend?" Tovak asked. "Are you sure about this? Befriending a Pariah won't make you very popular. There's no need for it. It'll be easier on you, if you leave me alone."

"I don't care what they think, any of them," he said. "You showed true Legend today. I would consider it an honor if you'd name me friend again."

"I—" He couldn't continue. He swallowed as he became choked up.

Gorabor seemed to understand. He gave a nod.

"Rest and eat," Gorabor said. "I think you need it. You took a beating out there."

Tovak could not disagree. Jodin had hammered him something fierce.

"I have to hurry and eat," Gorabor said. "I'm on first watch, so we can talk later, all right?"

Tovak nodded and realized just how much he was starting to hurt.

Gorabor rose to his feet and moved to his pack a few yards away, sitting down to eat.

Tovak pulled out his knife, speared some of the hopper meat, and took a bite. He immediately winced. His jaw hurt something terrible.

CHAPTER EIGHTEEN

Tovak dropped the heratta onto the growing pile and straightened up stiffly. A gust of wind worked its way through the trees, causing the leaves and pine needles to rustle. As if they were old men freshly risen from bed, the tree limbs creaked and complained as they swayed overhead. He glanced up at the sky, watching the canopy above shift with the wind.

The first of the two suns was almost directly overhead, the brightness causing him to squint. The sky was a perfect blue, without even the wisp of a cloud. Under the shade of the canopy and with the wind, the temperature was quite comfortable. Tovak thought it almost the perfect day, as it was not too hot and not too cold.

"How much longer do you think we will be hunting?" Gorabor asked as he dropped a hopper next to the one Tovak had just dragged over.

"Do you have somewhere else to be?" Tovak asked, amused by his friend's impatience. He grinned at his joke and almost instantly regretted it, as his jaw and cheek hurt terribly from his fight with Jodin the previous evening.

"Funny," Gorabor said, then kicked his kill lightly with his boot. "Seriously, I've had my fill of hunting bugs. So, when do you think we will pack up and head back to the warband?"

Tovak glanced over at Thegdol as he considered Gorabor's question. The corporal was several yards away and had just brought down a hopper with his sling. He decided there was no telling when they would head back. He turned his gaze back to Gorabor. "I'm the new guy here, remember? You tell me."

"Whenever the lieutenant says, I guess," Gorabor said, answering his own question. "I suppose I could ask Thegdol. He might tell me."

"You could." Tovak ran a hand through his beard and glanced back towards the corporal. The rest of the squad, Lok, Staggen, and Morda, were just beyond. Benthok had assigned Jodin some special duty, which had kept him from joining the day's hunt. Tovak suspected the lieutenant's motivation was more to keep the two of them apart for a time, to allow for tempers to cool. Not for the first time, Tovak wondered how Jodin would take the loss in the Circle.

Besides Gorabor, there had been almost no conversation amongst his squad mates as they left the camp and marched up to the where they would spend the day hunting. It was as if they were uncomfortable around him, not quite sure how to deal with his victory in the Circle. Even Thegdol had seemed standoffish, almost cold.

Tovak cracked his neck. His entire body was one big hurt. Not only had the fight left him in serious discomfort, but he'd woken up incredibly stiff. It had taken more than a little effort to drag himself out of his bedroll. At first, he wasn't quite sure how he was going to make it through the day. But with each passing hour, it got a little easier and he felt less stiff, though he still hurt.

He glanced down at the knuckles on his left hand. They were red and bruised. He clenched his hurt hand and flexed it a few times, trying not to wince at the pain.

"With that cut on your cheek and those two shiners," Gorabor said, "you look a right mess."

"I feel a right mess," Tovak said and then stretched out his back. His side was terribly sore but stretching seemed to help a bit.

"If I ran into you in a back alley," Gorabor said, "I might fear for my life. Heck, after what you did to Jodin, who needs a back alley? I'd just run at the sight of you."

Tovak laughed and then winced as pain flared not only in his jaw, but his side too. He held out a hand, palm outward. "Don't make me laugh, please, I beg you."

Gorabor grinned and wagged a finger at him. "That's what you get for accepting a challenge."

"I think I might have learned my lesson," Tovak said.

"Only time will tell if that's true," Gorabor said, thoroughly amused.

A horn blared from the direction of the camp, two short blasts. Tovak's head came up, his pain and discomfort forgotten.

"That's the recall," Gorabor said as the horn blew a second time.

"The recall?" Tovak asked. "They want us back?"

"Something must be wrong," Gorabor said. "They're not supposed to use the horn while out in the field, unless it is important. At least, that's what Jodin told me."

"Gather 'round," Thegdol called from behind them.

Tovak and Gorabor jogged over, as did Staggen, Morda, and Lok.

"What do you think is wrong?" Staggen asked.

Tovak saw the worry in the veteran's eyes and that concerned him more than a little bit.

"We'll find out when we get there," Thegdol said in an even tone that betrayed no emotion whatsoever. "The camp is only a short distance off. Until we know what's going on, we leave the kills here. We can always come back for them." The corporal turned his gaze to Gorabor, who had rested his hand on his sword hilt. He looked ready to draw the weapon. "There's no need for swords. Keep it sheathed, lad, until I say."

Gorabor colored and removed his hand from the hilt.

"We go quietly, but with eyes open and in teams of two. I want five feet of spacing between each team. Staggen and Lok will go first, then Gorabor and Tovak. Me and Morda will bring up the rear. Staggen, you're on point. No need to rush, keep it a slow and steady pace. Understand?"

"Got it," Staggen said.

Tovak felt there was something calming in being given direction. The corporal's manner was full of confidence too, and that helped.

"Listen, if the camp had fallen under attack," Thegdol said, "the horn call would have been different. They would have sounded the call to arms. We don't know why we've been recalled. It could just be the section's been ordered to break camp early, or it could be something more serious. Stay calm but keep your eyes open. Any questions?"

Thegdol looked around. There were none.

The corporal clapped his hands softly together. "Right then, let's get moving."

Splitting up into teams, they made their way through the trees, moving in the direction of camp. Staggen led, with Lok a couple steps behind. No one spoke, but with each step, heads swiveled and eyes scanned the forest. Tovak kept expecting orcs or goblins to rush them. With every gust of wind, the forest made noise and Tovak found his hand often straying to his sword hilt.

Then, as they neared the edge for the tree line, Staggen came to an abrupt halt. He looked back around and

motioned for the rest of them to come up. As they gazed outward across the field, Tovak saw the section's camp was full
of skirmishers. It appeared as if they had been reinforced.

"That can't be good," Staggen said, glancing over at the
corporal.

"No, it's not," Thegdol agreed. "The nearest section is
Third, and their camp is two miles to the south. No one else
is supposed to be out this way but us." The corporal heaved
a sigh. "So I'm guessing that's them."

"You're probably right," Staggen said.

"No sense wasting daylight," Thegdol said.

Grass whispering about their feet, the corporal led them
across the field. As they neared the camp, they saw a line of
bodies on the ground by the entrance. There were eight
of them upon makeshift litters; their faces were covered in
blankets.

"Gods," Lok breathed, in evident horror.

Staggen approached the nearest body, knelt, and lifted
the blanket to look at the warrior underneath. He let out a
long hissing breath through his teeth and set the blanket
carefully back, then patted the chest of the deceased. He
looked up at Thegdol, sorrow in his gaze.

"Angor from Third Section," Staggen said.

"Aye," Thegdol said, glancing towards the camp. "All of
Third's in camp, though I don't see Sergeant Kelloth."

Tovak looked towards camp. The sentries on watch
had been doubled. They gazed outward and seemed more
vigilant than before. Then his gaze traveled back to the
bodies. It wasn't the first time he'd seen the dead. These
were Dvergr who, the previous day, he'd handed dodders
to. They had treated him poorly. Still, gazing upon their
remains, Tovak felt nothing but a deep sadness wash over
him for their passing. He said a silent prayer, asking Thulla

to help them cross over to the ancestral feasting halls in the great beyond.

Thegdol spat on the ground, turned away, and started for the bridge. The squad followed after him. At the bridge, the corporal motioned Dagmar over. "What happened?"

"Third was ambushed this morning by a band of goblins," Dagmar said. "They managed to fight them off and kill most of 'em. Third took some casualties in the process." Dagmar paused and glanced towards the lieutenant. "Your squad is the last one in. The lieutenant's been waiting for you."

Thegdol took the hint and made his way over the bridge, once again closely followed by his squad. The lieutenant spotted him almost immediately.

"Corporal Thegdol, join us, if you would."

The lieutenant, looking grim, was standing with the other corporals from First Section and one from Third, Corporal Karn. Most of the section, clearly having just come in, were gathered in a loose group around them. Benthok held a dispatch in his hand.

Third Section sat scattered around the inside of the camp, leaning against their packs or the dirt of the berm. The sight of the Third was alarming. They appeared exhausted and thoroughly worn out. The shock was evident in their vacant and hollow expressions. To Tovak's horror, some were covered head to toe in blood, both goblin green and Dvergr red. A number were asleep, having clearly just laid down and passed out. One, sitting on the ground, was rocking back and forth as he wept into his hands. Another crouched down next to him and patted him gently on the back, while saying something into his ear.

"A bad business, this," Benthok said, glancing around before fixing his attention on Corporal Thegdol.

"Yes, sir," Thegdol said. "A terrible loss."

"Thegdol, you're being promoted."

"Promoted?" Thegdol asked. "To sergeant?"

"Sergeant Kelloth's been killed," Benthok said. "You are now the senior sergeant for the company."

"Bloody gods," Thegdol breathed in dismay, his eyes moving in the direction of the bodies. "Kelloth's dead? I don't believe it, sir."

"He's gone," Benthok said in a gruff tone that almost suggested he was having difficulty believing it too. "He died as a warrior should, sword in hand and leading from the front."

"What of Bahr?" Thegdol said. "He's senior to me, sir."

"Sergeant Bahr is not here," Benthok said and then shook the dispatch. "You are. The captain has made you Sergeant Thegdol."

There was some shifting of feet from the other corporals. Tovak noticed that Logath looked distinctly unhappy. Whether that was because of what had happened or Thegdol's promotion was unclear.

"Yes, sir," Thegdol said, then softened his tone. "I'm sorry for Kelloth's loss, sir."

"He was a good warrior." The lieutenant cleared his throat, clearly moved by Kelloth's loss. Then his tone became firm. "You have big boots to fill, Sergeant."

"Yes, sir," Thegdol said. "I know I do."

"The captain…." Benthok said, becoming all business. He ran his gaze around the gathered corporals and skirmishers from First Section. "The captain sent Third Section to us and the wounded back to the encampment. He's taken Second Section to pursue the goblins."

"By themselves?" Logath asked, seeming surprised by that. "Is that wise, sir?"

"Before his death, Sergeant Kelloth was able to rally Third Section and counter-attack. They killed most of the attackers," Benthok said. "The captain believes the goblins to be from an isolated tribe and is following them back to their den to be certain. You all know Struugar. They won't even know he's coming." Benthok paused to suck in a breath. "The captain, with Second Section, will join us come morning."

"After this," Logath said, "shouldn't we be headed back to the warband?"

"Agreed," Gamok said and glanced over at some of those from Third Section. "They look done in, sir."

"They will recover," Benthok said, with a glance to the nearest members of Third Section.

"And if the goblins are not from an isolated tribe?" Logath asked. "They could be advance scouts for an enemy force."

"Then the captain will soon learn the truth and send us word," Benthok said. "Until that eventuality, we have a job to do. We stay. Those are the captain's orders."

"Yes, sir," Logath said.

"The warband did not march today and is right where we left them." Benthok held up a hand. "Before you ask, I don't know why. With the wounded, the captain sent a report of what occurred to headquarters. His orders are to scavenge as much as we can, and then, as a company, we will head back tomorrow afternoon. He expects the warband to resume marching at dawn."

Tovak, like everyone else, just listened. The lieutenant did not seem to mind. Tovak realized Benthok was telling them what they needed to know so that there was no confusion or misunderstanding.

"Who gets my squad?" Thegdol asked.

Benthok paused for just a moment as he glanced down at the dispatch in his hand, then looked up.

"Jodin," Benthok said, "front and center."

Jodin detached himself from the crowd. He stepped up to the lieutenant, coming to a position of attention.

"The captain has promoted you to corporal of First Squad."

Tovak's stomach clenched at the news.

"Thank you, sir," Jodin said, with no hint of pleasure at his promotion. Then again, Jodin's face was badly bruised and he was sporting two black eyes. His nose was also swollen. He looked frightful, and for a heartbeat, Tovak had difficulty believing he'd done all that damage himself.

"The captain does not yet know about the Circle. If he did, I seriously doubt he would have promoted you. That aside, I expect you to comport yourself professionally," Benthok said, "and make sure there are no more challenges. Violate the faith the captain has placed in you and I promise I will personally break you back to the ranks."

"Yes, sir," Jodin said. "There will be no issues and no more challenges. You and the captain will have no cause to regret my promotion, sir. On my Legend, I swear it."

Benthok gave a reluctant nod, then looked over at Logath. "You are now senior corporal."

Could it get any worse? Tovak felt his heart sinking into his chest.

"Yes, sir," Logath said.

Jodin his squad leader and Logath senior corporal. All Tovak could do was stand there and stare at Benthok, utterly dumbstruck. The lieutenant did not seem to notice. Instead, Benthok swung his gaze around First Section. His face hardened.

"Those eight," Benthok said and pointed in the direction of the bodies, "are why we need to stay vigilant, alert, and on our toes. There are scattered tribes of goblins and orcs living in these hills. We are trespassing on their land and they don't bloody like it. You stay alert and on guard when out beyond the perimeter or you could end up like them." The lieutenant paused and glanced up at the sky. "There is a good deal of light left. We will continue the hunt. Third Section, along with the archers, will remain guarding the camp. Grab some grub from your haversacks and make sure your waterskins are full. Just as soon as I am done with the corporals, you will be heading back out to hunt. Now, get going."

Tovak, not feeling hungry, made his way with most of the rest of the section towards the stream. Only a few went for their packs.

"Logath's right," Morda said as he filed his skin. "We should be heading back to camp. It's a risk, us just being out here now, especially if the goblins are from an enemy force somewhere in these hills."

"Right or not," Staggen said, "we have our orders. We stay. There's no changing that and no sense in debating it."

"What do you think, Lok?" Morda asked, ignoring Staggen.

Lok grunted, filled his waterskin, and then stopped it shut. He glanced back towards the bodies. "I think we lost mates, and whenever that happens, it's a bad day."

Their eyes shifted to the dead of Third Section.

"Poor bastards," Staggen said.

"It doesn't seem quite real," Gorabor breathed.

"It is," Lok said. "Out here, it's either kill or be killed. This is our profession and it ain't always roses."

At that, Lok left them. Staggen followed, with Morda a few moments later.

Tovak took the opportunity to splash water on his face and arms.

Gorabor waited a moment for the others to get out of earshot. He let out a worried breath, which caused Tovak to look over.

"What about Jodin?" Gorabor asked in a whisper. "Do you think he's gonna hold a grudge?"

"It is what it is, I guess," Tovak said. "There is nothing I can do about it, is there?"

"It's not quite fair," Gorabor said. "You just beat him in the Circle. He acted with dishonor and still gets promoted. It's not fair, I tell you."

"Life's not fair," Tovak said, feeling intense frustration. He stood and saw Jodin emerging from camp, along with the other squad leaders from First Section. "That's been the story of my life."

"First Squad," Jodin called, "form on me."

Gorabor and Tovak moved over. Logath was forming up his squad a few feet away. He knelt down before them and began speaking intently. Tovak could not hear what was being said.

Jodin motioned for his squad to close around him.

"All right." Jodin locked eyes with Tovak for only a moment, a curious expression on his face, and then he looked at the other members of his squad. "Logath's squad and a pair of Corporal Hilla's archers are going to be joining us momentarily. Thegdol will be coming too. We are heading up that way"—he pointed to the north, up towards rugged terrain in a vague sort of way—"to see if we can track down something big."

"Big?" Morda asked, eyes narrowing. "What's up there? What have they found?"

"Logath thinks a murinok has staked out its territory about a mile from here." He paused and glanced over at Tovak. "From the tracks they saw, it may be full-grown."

"Thulla's bones...." Morda said, turning his gaze to Tovak. A good-natured grin split his face a heartbeat later. "Can we leave Tovak behind? People say Pariahs are bad luck."

Tovak stiffened, but then realized Morda was jesting when his grin grew wider.

"Shut it, Morda," Jodin snapped, sounding genuinely irritated. Staggen threw a shocked look to Jodin. Lok stood up straight. Tovak almost didn't believe what had just happened. Jodin kept his eyes fixed on Morda. "You heard Benthok. Playtime is over. Tovak is a member of this squad and that's the end of it. No more harassment or jokes about him being a Pariah. If there is, you and I will have words. Am I understood?"

Morda blinked a few times and then finally got his mouth to work. "Yeah...yeah, we're clear, Corporal."

"Good," Jodin said, and there was no mistaking a tone that wouldn't tolerate misunderstanding. "Thegdol has put First Squad on lead for this hunt." He turned to Tovak. "You tracked that murinok down, right?"

"Uhhh...." Tovak started, surprised by the question, but then decided honesty was in order. He would mislead no more. As the lieutenant had said, there was no Legend in that. "Not exactly. Once I realized it was an adult, I tried to avoid it. That did not work out so well."

"From where I was watching, it looked like you were hunting it." Jodin scowled for a moment. "But you learned to track at the Academy, right? Like a pioneer?"

"Yes," Tovak said. "I received high marks."

"Good," Jodin said. "The lieutenant said you have skills and I should use you. So, I am going to use you."

Tovak was once again surprised, but he did not reply. He remained silent and waited for Jodin to continue.

"You will have point for this hunt," Jodin said.

Tovak gave a nod. This he had not expected, nor the lieutenant's faith. Then, he realized what they were going after, a fully grown murinok. He went cold at that thought.

"I want you all to know something," Jodin said, locking his eyes with Tovak. His gaze then passed over the entire squad. "I am putting my personal feelings aside, and if you are harboring any, you will too. Is that understood?"

There was a slight hesitation as the four of them glanced at each other.

"Yes, Corporal," Morda, Staggen, Lok, and Gorabor said in unison.

Jodin was silent for a long moment before turning to Tovak.

"I expect you to show me those skills you learned at the Academy."

"I'll do my best, Corporal," Tovak said.

"Losers do their best," Jodin said curtly. "Winners get the job done."

"Corporal Jodin, is your squad ready?" Thegdol asked as he walked up.

"Yes, Cor—I mean Sergeant," Jodin replied. "We're good to go."

"Excellent," Thegdol said. "Then let's get moving."

CHAPTER NINETEEN

They traveled more than a mile up and over a series of hills, into a thoroughly forested landscape that climbed steadily towards the mountain slopes. The canopy overhead was so thick, it kept the forest floor in a sort of perpetual dusk. There was very little undergrowth, which made the climb fairly easy. The ground was covered over in thick carpets of moss and the previous season's leaves, which rustled as they were trod over. Between the hardwood trunks, lichen-covered boulders seemed to haphazardly sprout up from the ground.

Tovak thought the forest ominous and primeval. The chill temperature reminded him of the underground back home. The forest was also silent as a tomb. It was as if it had never known the tread of a boot.

Tovak glanced back. Spread out behind him in loose lines that angled away were both squads. They were at the area Logath had identified as murinok ground. Tovak returned his attention to his front and continued moving forward. He kept an eye out for tracks, droppings, and the remains of kills. The forest floor was thick with leaves and pine needles.

As they gained in elevation, Tovak found himself moving from one large outcropping of boulders to the next. Snaking his way along the forest floor as quietly as possible, he checked carefully behind each boulder for the murinok and every time felt an intense relief at not finding it lying in wait.

Tovak came to a break in the trees. A boulder field stretched out before him, at least two hundred yards long. He judged it to be at least three hundred yards wide. He paused and discovered a familiar scent on the air. It was dank, slightly foul, and smelled strongly of decay. His eyes raked the boulder field and saw nothing.

He turned slightly and signed to Thegdol that he'd smelled something. The sergeant gave him a nod and then stepped near Jodin and informed him before doing the same to Logath. The news was quickly passed through the two squads.

Gripping his spear tightly, Tovak stepped out into the field of stone and felt the light of the two suns warm his face. He moved around the first of the boulders. On the far side, he saw what he'd been looking for—really, in a way, what he'd been dreading to find. Murinok droppings. Tovak knelt and ran a finger through it, rubbing it between his fingers.

It was old and dry, crusty even.

Tovak stepped away from the outcropping and held up his fist so that those following a few feet behind could see. He glanced back. Both squads dropped to a knee.

He pointed to Thegdol, Jodin, and Logath, then made the sign for them to come to him.

Both Logath and Jodin motioned for their squads to hold position and then, with Thegdol, moved forward.

"What did you find, lad?" Thegdol asked in a low whisper.

Tovak pointed to the long, thick black streak that marred the side of the boulder. The sight of it made him a bit uneasy, because the animal that produced it had to be twice the size of the one he'd killed. Thegdol looked at the streak and became very still. Logath sucked in a hissing breath and then let it out slowly.

Tovak scanned the ground for tracks. At first, he didn't see them, but as his eyes moved farther out from the droppings, he found a pattern of tracks more than twice the width of the one he'd faced. The scale of it caught him off guard.

"We may have a problem," he whispered and pointed at the tracks. "This is a very large beast."

He read genuine concern in Thegdol as comprehension dawned.

"Based on the size of those tracks, that's bigger than any murinok I've ever even heard of," Jodin said.

"Maybe too big," Logath said.

Thegdol gave a grunt, eyes scanning the boulder field. "Perhaps."

"The question, as I see it," Jodin said, "is do we continue with the hunt or pull back and look for easier game?"

"Something this big will be difficult to kill," Tovak warned. "We're talking about a real monster, much larger than the one I faced."

"That was a big bug," Logath said.

"We have two squads and a pair of archers," Jodin said. "It's not like we're dealing with a dragon. So, the question remains...do we continue or pull back and look for easier game? Me, I am leaning towards going after it."

"Have you ever fought a dragon?" Logath hissed back.

"No," Jodin admitted, becoming heated. "Have you?"

"I've never faced a dragon either," Thegdol spoke before Logath could answer, "but this isn't likely to be what I would call an easy undertaking, Jodin."

"The sergeant is right," Tovak agreed. "Even for fourteen of us, I have a feeling this will be difficult."

"What do you know about difficult, boy?" Logath said. "Your opinion should not even matter here. You shouldn't even have a place with us. Keep quiet and let your betters hash this out."

Tovak stiffened, feeling a sudden return of his anger.

"You may have forgotten," Thegdol said to Logath, "he killed a murinok by himself. Have you ever taken down a murinok?"

Cheeks coloring, Logath shook his head.

"Ha! would consider him our resident expert," Thegdol said, "since there is no one else that I know of in the company with any murinok experience."

"It's not experience. It was all luck," Logath said. "The lieutenant said so himself."

"Do you think we should turn back?" Thegdol asked Tovak, ignoring Logath. There was a seriousness in his voice. Tovak paused for a moment and licked his lips as he considered his answer.

"Yeah," Jodin said, with an expectant look. "What do you think?"

"You are going to listen to him now?" Logath said. "Between the three of us we've got years of experience behind us."

"Yes," Thegdol said, shooting Logath a meaningful look. "I want to hear his opinion before I make my decision as to whether we proceed or not."

Logath's lips drew together into a thin line.

Thegdol turned his attention back to Tovak and he arched an eyebrow.

Tovak's guts churned as he mulled over his response. He thought about his fight with an eight-foot murinok. While it hadn't been easy, he had done it single-handedly. He'd been able to find a soft spot, get his spear in, and in the end kill the thing. That was all they would have to do here. The only difference was scale, and there was plenty of help.

"As I see it," Tovak said slowly, "we have one of three choices. We can go back to camp and forget about this venture, we can go back to camp and get more help, or we can just go after it."

"I say we go for it," Jodin said.

"I say we go back," Logath said. "When I suggested we come out here, I had no idea the thing was such a monster. There is no sense in taking the risk."

"Come on, Thegdol, we can do this," Jodin said.

"I still did not hear your opinion," Thegdol said to Tovak. "I should like to hear it."

Tovak glanced to Jodin, who gave him an encouraging nod.

"Let's go find it," Tovak said, not quite believing his own voice.

"Ha." Jodin slapped his thigh lightly. "What do you say, Thegdol?"

"All right," Thegdol replied. "But if this thing is too much for us, we pull back."

Jodin patted Tovak on the shoulder, while Logath shot him an unhappy scowl.

"Tovak will continue to lead," Thegdol said.

Tovak let out a slow breath. "I want Gorabor to watch my back as I move forward. Murinok are ambush predators. I need someone to watch my back."

"Done," Thegdol said, turned slightly, and beckoned to Gorabor.

Gorabor came forward, a curious look on his face. He was clearly wondering why he'd been called.

"Congratulations," Jodin said. "Tovak just volunteered you for an important duty."

"What duty?" Gorabor asked, looking to Tovak with suspicion.

"I am so pleased you asked," Jodin said. "You will watch his back as we move forward and hunt the murinok. You got that?"

Gorabor paled slightly. "Yes, Corporal."

"So, since you are on point and will be taking most of the risk, how do we want to do this?" Jodin asked, turning to Tovak.

"You both are gonna end up a nice snack for the beast," Logath said. "Thegdol, this venture is madness."

"I've made my decision, Corporal," Thegdol snapped quietly. "That is the end of it."

Logath gave a nod.

Thegdol turned his attention to Tovak. "I normally tell people how to do their job, but Jodin asked the correct question. Since it is your ass hanging out in the open, how would you like to proceed?"

Tovak glanced down at the ground. He took a deep breath, recalling his fight with the murinok. He ran through the options in his head, thinking about what they had to work with.

"We're growing old just standing here, boy," Logath said.

"Okay," Tovak said, "this is what I think we should do. The underside will be the creature's weak point."

"The underside?" Logath interrupted. "Are you kidding me? How are we going to get at its belly? Ask it to roll over so we can rub its tummy?"

"Logath," Thegdol said in a warning tone.

"When the murinok attacked me, it reared up and showed me its underside," Tovak explained. "I was able to stab it between the plates when it lunged. On its back and sides, the armored plates overlap one another, making it nearly impossible to injure it. Spears just won't penetrate the armored plates. So, the weak points are the head and belly."

Tovak paused to suck in a breath. He glanced behind at the two squads and then motioned with his hands to help describe what he wanted. "We need to spread both squads out in one long line behind me, as we move forward." He drew a line in the dirt at his feet, with two dots just ahead of the midpoint. "That way, as we advance into the boulder field, if the creature is off to the left or right of me, someone will hopefully spot it and give the warning. Either way, we will cover more of the field this way." Tovak paused a moment to see if there were any objections or questions.

"Go on," Thegdol said.

"When we find the murinok, we need to come at it from all sides, surround it, so that it can't focus on one individual. Our initial goal should be to distract it while looking for openings to attack. I'd also think the best slingers should focus on the murinok's eyes. It's gonna be a hard shot, but if we're lucky, we might blind it or at least hurt it."

"What about the archers?" Jodin asked. "Should they shoot its head too?"

"I doubt arrows can get through its armor," Tovak said. "They should be waiting for the murinok to rear up. When it does, they should aim for the weak point between the plates. If arrows don't work, then we will have to get in close and use spears. That's when it will really get dangerous."

Gorabor stared at his friend in growing horror and let out a long, worried breath. "You are crazy."

"That's what I think," Logath said.

"I'm good with the plan so far," Jodin said, sounding almost eager for what was to come.

Tovak wondered if Jodin felt the need to prove himself.

"Aye," Thegdol said. "It's as solid a plan as any." The sergeant turned to Jodin and Logath. "Go back and explain to your squads what we're going to do."

"I can't get you to reconsider this, can I?" Logath asked Thegdol.

"No."

With that, the two squad leaders moved back to their squads, gathered them up, and started explaining the plan.

"Thanks a lot," Gorabor said, sarcasm thick in his voice. "You could have picked someone else, you know... to be murinok bait with you."

"Someone had to get the duty," Tovak said, "and I'd rather share it with a friend."

"I'm already beginning to regret naming you friend," Gorabor said, then grew serious, eyes roving the boulder field. "We're really going to do this, aren't we?"

"Yes," Thegdol said, "we are."

"Then," Gorabor said to Tovak, his voice hardening with resolve, "I've got your back."

"I knew you would," Tovak said. "It's why I chose you."

Tovak turned his gaze forward and began scanning the rock field to their front. Nothing moved. Where was it?

"They're ready," Thegdol said. "I'll be with Jodin. Don't take any unnecessary risks. Neither of you have anything to prove. Understand me?"

"Yes, Sergeant," Tovak said.

"And you?" Thegdol said when Gorabor did not immediately reply.

Gorabor was staring out into the boulder field, his gaze distant. Thegdol nudged him.

"No unnecessary risks," Gorabor said. "Got it."

"Good luck." With that, Thegdol moved back. Tovak watched him go for a moment and suddenly felt terribly alone. Then he turned to Gorabor.

"You ready?"

"Did you seriously just ask me that?" Gorabor asked. "No, of course I'm not ready. We're hunting a fully grown murinok. Who's ready for that kind of thing? Me? No, sir, no how."

"Well, neither am I," Tovak said. "Stay back about five feet and keep an eye out. You see it, you tell me immediately."

"You'll be the second to know," Gorabor said. "That is, unless I'm running for my life. Then you are on your own."

"Very funny," Tovak said.

"Who's joking?" Gorabor said, then grinned.

Tovak cast a sidelong glance at Gorabor, and a feeling of friendship—no, kinship—filled him. The danger he was about to face didn't seem as daunting, nor did he feel alone anymore. Gorabor had his back, and it was enough.

Without another word, he turned and started forward, deeper into the boulder field.

Tovak moved slowly, taking two or three steps before pausing to scan their surroundings. He was sure the murinok would be lurking in wait, somewhere out in the boulder field. He saw nothing. So, he kept going, one slow and careful step after another. Halfway through the field, he came to a complete stop. He searched the rocks, scanning about them while straining with his ears. Still nothing. Where was it?

He kept going. Slowly, steadily, they worked their way to the far side of the field, where the forest continued up the hill before them. He glanced back at Thegdol, who, with the two squads, was less than five yards behind. The sergeant gave him an encouraging nod.

Tovak stepped back into the forest. It was thick with evidence of the creature. Tree trunks were scratched free of bark, while others had been snapped in two like a twig. There were tracks nearly everywhere, but still no creature.

Tovak paused and went to a knee. He pulled out his waterskin and took a drink, then passed it over to Gorabor, who drank and then handed it back. Despite the day not being overly hot, he was perspiring heavily from the climb.

"How large a range do these things have?" Gorabor asked.

Tovak looked over at his friend and then turned his gaze back to the terrain about them with new eyes. "I don't know. I'd not considered that."

"Since this one is larger than the murinok you took down," Gorabor said, "it must need to eat more."

"To eat more," Tovak said, finishing the thought, "it must have a larger hunting ground, range farther afield."

"Makes sense to me," Gorabor said.

"What's the holdup?" Thegdol had come forward.

"We were thinking," Gorabor said, "that since it's a larger creature, it must range farther afield for game."

Thegdol scowled at that. He pointed ahead. "How do we know, if we continue forward, we are heading towards its lair or den or whatever you want to call it?"

"We don't," Tovak said.

"Can you track it?" Thegdol asked.

"There are tracks all over," Tovak said, pointing down to the ground. "I can't tell what's new and old. What I can tell you is that the creature's been all over this ground, so we're in the right place."

"I see," Thegdol said, considering the problem. "So, the direction we're headed is as good as any at this point?"

Tovak thought about that for a moment. He felt they were heading in the right direction. He was sure of it. He had had such feelings in the past, and when he'd followed them, they had panned out right. Something was tugging him onward, urging him forward, almost like a sixth sense. "I…." Tovak paused, unsure about continuing.

"What?" Thegdol asked.

"I think we're headed in the right direction," Tovak said, thoughts racing and trying to come up with a plausible explanation that did not make him sound crazy. He had earned some respect and did not want to lose it. "The farther up the slope we climb, the more tracks there are."

Thegdol considered that a moment. "Very well, we will continue."

Tovak stood and started again, slowly climbing the forested slope, with Gorabor following a few steps behind. A half mile up found them emerging from the forest into a rocky canyon, with sparse vegetation and towering walls. Marks of the creature's passage were everywhere, including reddish scrape marks against the stones and conical dents from its legs pressed into the loose ground. There was also an increased number of the black, chalky droppings left by the thing. Tovak glanced back at Thegdol, who motioned for him to continue.

The canyon was about two hundred yards across and still there was no sign of the creature. The ground became loose with scree and there were more tracks now than before. After another quarter mile, they came to a narrower area in the canyon, about seventy-five yards across, where the boulders had been dug up, pushed outward, and piled along the sides of what were now vertical cliff walls rising at least three hundred feet on either side. Had the creature pushed the rocks to the side? If so, it must have incredible strength.

The whole area smelled of decay. Tovak wiped sweat from his brow. There were long dirt mounds ahead. They came across a deep trench. From the looks of it, the creature had dug it out. Tovak wondered to what purpose.

He climbed down into the trench and then out the other side, stopping to offer Gorabor a hand up after him. They went another ten feet and came to an abrupt halt. The scene before them, as ominous as it might have otherwise been, was not at all what he had expected. At first, Tovak did not fully understand what he was seeing. Then, it dawned on him. A tremendous fight had taken place here and the evidence was all around.

Great swaths of the grass had been trampled or gouged up. Boulders had been shattered. Dozens of juvenile murinoks, less than two feet in length, littered the area. Some had been crushed into the dirt, others seemingly torn apart. And at the center of it all, on its side, lay the armored shell of a mighty murinok. It was ten feet wide and at least thirty feet long.

Tovak puffed out his cheeks and allowed his hands holding his spear to relax. He moved slowly forward, with Gorabor at his back. The murinok had been gutted, and the meat inside removed. From the glistening nature of the entrails, which had been left in a large heaps off to the side, he judged that the kill was relatively fresh. Flies buzzed madly about in a frenzy.

Someone had beaten them to the prize.

"Sweet gods," Gorabor said, coming up to stand beside him. "Look at the size of that thing."

"Archers," Thegdol barked from behind Tovak, startling him. The sergeant had come up and stood just a few feet away. Thegdol was looking back at the squads. "Take up a position by those boulders, there and there. Yes, I know it will require some climbing, but I want you to have some elevation. Get to it. Jodin," Thegdol continued, "take your squad a short ways ahead. Tell me what you find."

"Thegdol," Jodin said, a strange note to his voice.

The sergeant turned, as did Tovak and Gorabor, to look at the corporal. Jodin held a long arrow in his hand, the tip broken off. The arrow had black fletching on the end. Thegdol walked over and took the arrow. He studied it for a moment, then dropped it. The sergeant rubbed his bearded jaw and glanced around. Having apparently spotted something, he stepped over to a small tree that had been knocked down in the struggle. He pulled a broken spear with a wicked-looking iron point from under its leafy branches.

"Orcs," Thegdol said.

Tovak gave a start at the news. He began studying the ground around the carcass, his eyes searching. Amongst the signs of a fight, there were tracks all around, large boot prints.

"They got here first," Thegdol said, his eyes running over the remains of the monster. He dropped the spear. It landed with a solid thud in the dirt.

"Sergeant," Jodin said, having come forward with his squad. Logath was with him as well. "Do you still want me to move up the canyon?"

"No," Thegdol said and pointed towards where the canyon bent out of view fifty yards away. "Send Staggen up around that bend to eyeball what's there. I need to know if there is anything worth seeing."

"Thegdol," Logath said, his eyes flicking to the remains of the creature, "we need to get out of here, before we're discovered."

Thegdol turned an unhappy look on Logath, but he did not immediately reply.

Jodin stepped away, and within moments, Staggen was moving up the canyon at a jog.

"Seeing the size of this thing," Logath continued, "we would not have been able to take it ourselves, and if we'd tried, we would have surely lost good boys, but they took it down."

And suddenly, Tovak understood where Logath was going with his line of thought.

"Logath is right," Tovak said. "We need to go."

Logath's eyes snapped to Tovak. So too did Jodin and Thegdol.

"If I had to guess," Logath said, "they would have needed at least fifty, possibly more, to take such a monster down. And the gods only know how many casualties they took in the doing of it." Logath turned his gaze back to Thegdol. "Our duty now is clear. We must report what we've learned."

"He's right," Jodin said, "we need to report this to Benthok."

Thegdol turned his gaze back to Tovak.

"On the way here, did you see any other tracks?" Thegdol asked. "Orc tracks?"

Tovak shook his head. "No, Sergeant, I did not."

"Anyone?" Thegdol asked, looking around. "On the hike up here, did anyone see orc tracks? Or anything that could have been a footprint?"

No one said anything.

Staggen came jogging back. He was sweating and breathing heavily.

"Around the bend," Staggen said. "There are wagon tracks and the remains of what looks like a funeral pyre."

"A funeral pyre?" the sergeant asked. "Any idea on how many were lost?"

"No, Sergeant," Staggen said, "but it was a big pyre. They must have lost a good number against the murinok. Oh, and there were priestly marks in the dirt around the pyre, arcane runes and such."

"They have a priest," Logath said with sudden alarm. "Thegdol, we really need to leg it."

Tovak felt a revulsion rise within him at the thought of such a dark priest.

"How far does the canyon go?" Thegdol asked.

"I could not tell," Staggen said. "At least another three hundred yards before it turns again. After that...." Staggen held up his arms.

"We're leaving," Thegdol said. "We melt back into the forest, as quietly as we came, and pray we've not been seen. Let's get moving."

CHAPTER TWENTY

Tovak found himself once again on point, working his way steadily through the forest. As he moved, he scanned about, searching for any hint of movement or tracks. The forest was still. Not even a breeze rustled the trees.

About a mile from the canyon, Tovak spotted something out of the corner of his eye. Off to his right, in a small clearing that had been created where a tree had fallen, he thought he saw some marks on the ground. He paused and looked closer. The carpet of pine needles had been disturbed. He stopped and held up a hand. Both squads took a knee. The archers brought up their bows, arrows held at the ready.

Tovak moved over to the edge of the clearing. He scanned the ground and felt a stab of alarm by what he saw. He turned and motioned to Thegdol. Jodin came forward with the sergeant.

"What is it?" Jodin asked in a hushed tone.

Tovak pointed. "Tracks."

"Ours?" Logath asked, joining them. "On the way out?"

"No," Tovak said and then pointed to their left. "Our tracks are over that way about thirty yards."

"Are you sure?" Thegdol asked.

"Very," Tovak said. "Our boots are smaller and shaped differently than these."

Tovak reached down and examined one of the prints. It appeared identical to the tracks he'd seen in the canyon.

"It looks like at least six sets of tracks," Thegdol said.

"Boots and," Logath said, "are those claw marks?"

"Goblins," Jodin said. "The boots must belong to orcs."

"Or humans," Logath said. "We know some humans work with the enemy."

Tovak pointed the way they'd just come. "From the direction of the heel and toe impressions... they were headed that way, roughly towards the canyon we just came from."

Thegdol glanced in that direction and ran his fingers through the braids of his beard.

"How old are these tracks?" Logath asked.

"I think they are at least two days old," Tovak said. "They don't seem fresher than that. Could be longer, but not by much."

"Are you certain?" Thegdol asked.

"Certain?" Tovak asked. "No, but I'm pretty sure I'm right."

"Well, you're Academy-trained," Thegdol said. "I will take your word on it."

"Could they be part of the group that tackled the murinok?" Logath asked.

Tovak gave it thought, then shook his head. "I don't think so. I didn't see any evidence of orcs leaving the canyon from the side we came in at."

"Those wagon tracks back in the canyon," Jodin said, "were headed in the opposite direction, moving farther down the canyon. I didn't see any going the way we came in."

"Could we have missed tracks?" Logath asked.

"We could have," Tovak admitted, "but not a large group like the one that took down the murinok. There would have been prints all over."

"How far away is our camp?" Logath asked, looking in the direction the tracks were going. The corporal seemed unsettled, almost itching to be away.

"I think a little over a mile," Thegdol said.

"That way," Tovak said and pointed.

"These tracks," Jodin said, "don't seem to be coming directly from where the section is camped. Is it possible they went by us, without knowing we were there?"

"It is," Thegdol said. "They could also have passed by before we arrived, or...."

"They might know we're here," Logath finished unhappily. "If they do, it could spell trouble for us."

"We should follow the tracks," Jodin suggested, "see where they go and also where they've been."

"We should," Logath said, stressing the word should, "report and let the lieutenant decide what to do. There's only a couple of hours of light left."

"Bah, you are too cautious. We need to know what we are facing." Jodin turned to the sergeant. "Thegdol, we could do both. Let me take Tovak and my squad. You and the rest can go back to camp and report."

Tovak felt a sudden thrill of excitement at the prospect of following the orc and goblin tracks.

"That's foolish. There's no telling if you will find anything," Logath said, "and even if you do, you will be coming back in the dark. I imagine at night it's quite easy to get turned around in this forest. You might even blunder into the enemy and with no ready help at hand."

"Not with an Academy-trained scout," Jodin countered.

"He's just fresh off the yuggernok," Logath hissed. "You're putting too much faith in him."

"I don't like the idea of splitting up," Thegdol said. "Orcs and goblins can see a lot better at night than we can."

"Thegdol," Jodin protested, clearly prepared to continue his case for scouting.

The sergeant held up a hand and Jodin fell silent.

"Normally," Thegdol said, "I would be in favor of doing what you are suggesting. As much as I would like to track this bunch down, our orders are clear. We're not far from camp. We will report what we've found. The lieutenant will make the decision on what to do next. Is that understood?"

"Yes, Sergeant," Jodin said.

"All right," Thegdol said. "We go slow and keep our eyes open."

"Do you still want me on point, Sergeant?" Tovak asked.

"Yes," Thegdol said, then turned back to both corporals and gestured at the tracks. "Spread the word about potential company being in these woods."

Logath and Jodin moved off. Thegdol remained a moment.

"You're doing good work," Thegdol said.

"Thank you, Sergeant."

Thegdol glanced over at the two squads and was apparently satisfied that they were ready. "Now, get going."

Pleased with the compliment, Tovak nodded once and started forward again, heading in the direction of camp. After he'd gone a few yards, he glanced back to make sure both squads were following. Satisfied, he continued onward. The rest of their hike back proceeded without incident. As Tovak cleared the forest, he came to a stop at the edge of the field and breathed out a breath of relief.

Thegdol clapped him on the shoulder and strode by, leading them across the field to the camp. The bodies were gone and so too was the other cart. Only Shrike's cart remained, and it was full of heratta. Tovak could smell the cooking fire and, with it, his stomach grumbled. The sergeant stopped at the bridge, then turned back to both squads.

"Fall out," Thegdol said. "Corporals with me. You too, Tovak, should the lieutenant have questions for you."

Tovak suddenly felt uncomfortable, but followed as Thegdol made his way into camp and up to the lieutenant. Benthok had been speaking with Corporal Karn, from Third Section. Thegdol offered the lieutenant a salute as both turned to face the sergeant.

"What's wrong?" Benthok asked. "What happened?"

"Sir," Thegdol said, "orcs beat us to it. They took down the murinok about two miles from here, sometime within the last couple days. We're thinking there were more than fifty of them, as, judging from the shell, it was one big beast. We also observed wagon tracks and found the remains of a funeral pyre, complete with priestly offerings."

"A dark priest?" Karn said quietly. "Just what we need."

Benthok scowled slightly at the corporal's words.

"We came back straightaway," Thegdol said. "I don't think we were discovered, sir."

"There's more," Benthok said, "isn't there?"

"Yes, sir. On the way back to camp, Tovak found tracks about a mile from here. We believe them to be made by goblins and orcs, possibly humans too."

Benthok's expression went grim.

"Not good news," the lieutenant said.

"No, sir," Thegdol said. "Not good news at bloody all."

Benthok's gaze drifted up towards the mountains, a calculating look upon his face.

"How old were the tracks?" Benthok asked. "Were you able to tell?"

"Tovak felt they were fairly recent," Thegdol said.

Benthok turned his gaze to Tovak. "What was your assessment?"

"No more than two days, three at the most, sir," Tovak replied, feeling suddenly incredibly nervous at being the subject of the lieutenant's attention and stating his opinion. "I think, sir."

"It might be a scouting party, sir," Logath said.

"You did not follow the tracks?" the lieutenant asked.

"No, sir," Thegdol said. "With enemy operating in the area, I did not want to split up, especially with the tracks being so close to camp. With sunset only a couple of hours away, I did not want to take the chance of a squad becoming lost in the darkness."

"You made the correct decision," Benthok said.

"Sir, I respectfully request permission to take my squad and follow the tracks back to their source, sir," Jodin said. "I have confidence Tovak could lead us right to them, day or night."

Tovak wasn't sure about Jodin's faith in his nighttime skills, but he felt a return of the excitement.

"Denied," Benthok said curtly, fixing his attention on the corporal. "It's far too late in the day for that. I won't send you out into that forest in the dark. Our purpose here is not to engage the enemy, but forage. That said, I may take a look myself later, but I will not be venturing far from camp."

"Yes, sir," Jodin said, sounding disappointed. Tovak keenly felt the same.

"Shouldn't we march back to the warband, sir?" Logath asked. "Especially considering what happened to Third."

"That is the prudent course of action and I agree we should go," Benthok said. "Unfortunately, we must remain. The captain is due in the morning with Second Section. I do not know where they are at the moment, which means we have no way to reach him." The lieutenant let a hint of frustration show in his expression. It vanished in a heartbeat. "We must stay. If needed, we will hold this position until the captain arrives."

The lieutenant fell silent for a long moment and glanced back up towards the mountains. Tovak felt something was bothering him. Benthok turned abruptly back and looked across the camp.

"Corporal Hilla," Benthok called, "kindly join us."

"Sir." Hilla stepped over to them.

"Who are your best runners?"

"Gulda and myself, sir."

"I am going to send you back to the encampment," Benthok said, "with a report."

"Yes, sir," Hilla said.

"I will send one of my own with you," Benthok said. "I am thinking three is better than two, especially with the enemy operating in the area."

"A third would be most welcome, sir," Hilla said.

"Karr," Benthok called, looking around. "Front and center."

A young, slim warrior from Corporal Gamok's squad stepped over. He looked to be not too much older than Tovak, but he had chiseled features and a hardened countenance.

"Sir?" he said, standing to attention.

"I'm sending Corporal Hilla and Gulda back to the warband with a dispatch. You will accompany them."

"Yes, sir."

"Leave your packs here." Benthok turned his attention back to Gulda. "I figure you'll have a little under two hours to make it down to the plateau before the suns completely set. You will be traveling much of the way in the dark, but it will be open terrain. Do you think you can manage it?"

"Yes, sir," Hilla replied. "I will see that we get there and report. Once we're on the plateau, with all those campfires, there is no missing the warband."

"Excellent," Benthok said. "Now, kindly ready yourselves. I will have a dispatch for you shortly."

She saluted and moved off.

"Shrike," Benthok said.

"Sir?"

"How long 'til your cooking is done?" Benthok said. "I want that fire out."

"If I put it out now, sir," Shrike said, "the meat will be a little underdone, but it should be edible and not make anyone sick. It just won't taste as good."

"Put it out," Benthok ordered, then looked at Thegdol. "We will have no fires tonight, Sergeant. And I want the watch doubled."

"Yes, sir," Thegdol said.

With that, Benthok turned away and moved over to his pack. He sat down and pulled out a dispatch pad, along with a charcoal pencil. He took a moment to sharpen the point with his dagger and then began writing.

"Go take a break," Jodin told Tovak. "You did good today."

"Thank you," Tovak said. He stepped over to his bedroll a few feet away and sat down next to it. He was weary from all the marching. The tension of the day had also taken its toll on him. On top of that, his body still ached and hurt. Life in the army was proving to be more taxing than he'd ever suspected. Yet, not once had he yet reconsidered his decision to join. He had finally begun to build his own Legend and felt satisfaction at that.

As he pulled out his waterskin, Gorabor sat down next to him. With Third Section, the camp was full. Most of the Third were asleep, though one squad was standing sentry duty.

"So, what do you think we're going to do now?" Gorabor asked. "Head back to the warband?"

"The lieutenant decided to stay."

"Why?" Gorabor asked.

"Captain Struugar and Second are due in the morning," Tovak said. "He has no way to reach them. So, we stay."

"Makes sense," Gorabor said. He pulled out a waterskin and took a drink. Tovak took a pull from his waterskin as well.

"Gulda is being sent back to the warband with a dispatch. Corporal Hilla and Karr are going too," Tovak said. "They will be leaving shortly."

"What? Now? Just before dark?" Gorabor appeared suddenly alarmed.

"He's writing out the dispatch," Tovak said and gestured at the lieutenant.

Gorabor's eyes went from the lieutenant to Gulda, who was with Hilla on the other side of the camp. They were getting themselves ready to depart.

"I'll be back," Gorabor said and made his way over to her.

Tovak was tired. He gave a yawn, took a drink, and then stopped the skin closed. He stifled another yawn.

A short while later, the lieutenant stood and stepped over to Corporal Hilla. A few feet away, Gulda was speaking with Gorabor. She detached herself and came to stand with her corporal. Karr joined them. He carried only his spear and a small waterskin tied to his belt. The archers had their bows and a leather-wrapped bundle of arrows tied to their backs. They also carried a waterskin each.

Benthok handed the dispatch to Hilla, then said a few words Tovak could not hear. It looked like he was giving further instruction. She took the dispatch, gave a firm nod, and tucked it into a pocket. The corporal offered a salute before leaving the camp with Gulda and Karr. Gorabor climbed the berm and watched them go.

"Good luck," Tovak said under his breath, "and Thulla keep you safe."

Tovak leaned back on his pack and closed his eyes, prepared to take a nap. A few moments later, he heard footsteps. Opening his eyes, he discovered Benthok standing over him.

"Do you think you've got more in you?" Benthok asked. He turned away, not waiting for an answer. "Come on, we're gonna have a look around. Leave your spear. You won't need it."

Tovak blinked as the lieutenant strode off for the bridge. Fatigue forgotten and feeling a sudden return of the excitement, he pulled himself to his feet and scrambled to catch up.

"Sergeant Thegdol?" Benthok called with one foot on the bridge over the trench as Tovak caught up to him.

"Sir?" Thegdol hurried over.

"Tovak and I are going to have a look around," the lieutenant informed the sergeant.

Thegdol's eyes flicked to Tovak before returning to the lieutenant. "Yes, sir."

"We should be back around sunset, maybe after." Benthok glanced at the suns, which had begun to sink in the sky.

"And when should I begin to worry, sir?" Thegdol asked.

Tovak wondered if the sergeant was joking, but Benthok took the question seriously.

"If we don't return," Benthok said, "then there is trouble out there. Under no circumstances are you to send a search party. Instead, prepare for an attack on the camp. Though I think that possibility unlikely. But, then again, that's why we build defenses when out in the field."

"Yes, sir," the sergeant said.

"Come on," Benthok said to Tovak and led him out of camp. "We will consider this excursion our daily training," he said as they walked out into the field.

"Yes, sir," Tovak said. The previous day had seen the challenge and Circle. Tovak had been in no shape for extra training.

"First," Benthok said, "we'll perform a circuit around the camp at about fifty yards out, looking for orc and goblin tracks. Though that will likely prove a difficult undertaking, what with all of the tracks the section has made in and out of camp. To compensate, we shall do a second circuit around one hundred yards out and a third at five hundred. If the enemy has come to take a look at our camp, we should know."

"Yes, sir."

"Questions?"

"Has anyone been looking for tracks, sir?" Tovak asked. "Before now, that is?"

"I have," Benthok said. "I make it a habit of scouting the perimeter at least twice a day, at every camp we make. The first time, just before dawn, and then again before nightfall. Corporal Gamok, also."

Tovak was surprised by this news. He'd had no idea.

"Any more questions?"

"Not at the moment, sir," Tovak said.

"Good. Let's pick up the pace."

They found nothing on their first and second circuits about the camp. On the third, Benthok stopped to examine a track amongst the pine needles in the forest floor. He motioned Tovak over.

"What do you think?"

Tovak looked at the spot where the lieutenant was pointing. It appeared as if someone had dragged a stick about four inches through the needles. There was no telling what had made the mark.

"It could be an animal track, sir," Tovak said, looking around for more tracks. He could not see the needles disturbed in any other places. "A hopper landing here, perhaps. If it was an orc or goblin, wouldn't there be more evidence of passage?"

"That's a good question," Benthok said in a quiet tone of voice. The lieutenant's eyes were intense. "You tell me. Look around. Study your surroundings. Be sure before you next speak."

Tovak tried not to scowl but began scanning the nearest trees. At first, he didn't see anything. Then his gaze settled upon a sapling five feet away. He moved over to it. One of the branches had been partially broken and was dangling at an odd angle.

"There is some hope for you," Benthok said, moving over to him and reaching out to touch the branch. "Most of the rest of the company would have missed this."

"Someone came through here," Tovak said.

"Something anyway," Benthok said. "Which way was it going?"

Tovak thought about it and then examined the branch. "It was pushed this way, so to the north."

"Again, correct," Benthok said, then pointed to the track in the needles. "When you see a track like this, you should stop and carefully study the surroundings. If you can't find anything more, move outward in a circle. There is a strong likelihood whatever came this way left more evidence of their passage."

"I see, sir," Tovak said.

"Let's look around and see what we can find," Benthok said.

They looked for more tracks but found nothing.

"If it wasn't an animal, whoever it was," Benthok said, "knows how to move through the forest." The lieutenant paused to take a drink from his waterskin. "Which way were those tracks you found?"

"To the north, sir," Tovak said, "though it did not look like those who made them were worrying about concealment."

"Interesting," Benthok said. "Show me."

Tovak led the lieutenant back to the small clearing with the tracks. Benthok spent some time studying the tracks and the surrounding area.

"How old do you think the tracks are?" Benthok asked.

"At least two days," Tovak said.

"That is my assessment too," the lieutenant said. "Well, they appear to be traveling towards that canyon with the murinok, and if their path is true, they passed south of our camp by several hundred yards."

"Do you think there is anything to worry about, sir?" Tovak asked.

"There is always something to worry about," Benthok said, rubbing the back of his neck. "Let me do the worrying, okay?"

"Yes, sir."

"If I had my way," Benthok said, "we would head back to the warband tonight. But as you know, we can't leave the captain and Second Section alone out here." The lieutenant blew out a breath. "Besides, if I started us back, we'd be marching back down to the plateau in darkness. We might walk into an ambush. I don't think we want that, do we?"

"No, sir," Tovak said.

The lieutenant suddenly squatted down next to a tree at the edge of the clearing. He pulled something off the bark.

"What have you found?" Tovak asked, moving over.

"Fur," Benthok said and showed Tovak. "Dain fur if I am not mistaken. There is also some blood here, on the ground."

The lieutenant pointed to a small dark spot that Tovak had missed. Benthok reached down and touched it. "Definitely dried blood."

"A hunting party." Tovak glanced around at the clearing with fresh eyes. He moved over to the fallen tree and saw prints right next to it. They were facing away from the snag. "They stopped here for a break and sat down on the tree." Tovak pointed in excitement, then wheeled around to face the lieutenant. "The kill was leaned against the tree there where you found the fur."

"Yes," Benthok said with a slight grin at Tovak's sudden comprehension. "I fear we will make a scout out of you yet, soldier."

Tovak glanced once more around the clearing. He could almost picture the orcs and goblins resting here. Why had he not seen it before?

Benthok stood and placed his hands on his hips. The lieutenant glanced around at the forest outside the clearing.

"I wish there was time to follow these tracks," Benthok said. "But the light is beginning to fail. I believe it's time to head back and stop Sergeant Thegdol from worrying."

"Yes, sir," Tovak said, keenly feeling disappointment at not following the tracks farther.

"Come on," Benthok said, starting back for camp, "let's get moving."

CHAPTER TWENTY-ONE

"**W**e're under attack!"

The shout shattered Tovak's dreamless sleep.

A chorus of bestial roars mixed with horrific, guttural shrieks filled the night in response. The sound of it was terrifying.

"To arms," another voice shouted. "To arms."

"They're bridging the trench. To the walls."

Disoriented, Tovak sat upright, blinking. Without the light of the campfires, it was dark. The moon was overhead and occluded by a cloud, but it was just enough to see a few feet. He looked wildly around in the darkness. Something hissed by his head, awfully close. The harsh clash of steel on steel snapped him fully awake. There was a horrible, almost horrific scream that spoke of intense suffering and agony. It was cut abruptly off.

"Get to the walls," Benthok shouted. "To the walls."

"Hold the wall." Thegdol's voice came from somewhere in the darkness. "They are bridging the trench. Hold the wall, boys."

A bow twanged from somewhere off to Tovak's right.

"They're coming over the west side." Benthok's voice was thunder, and it carried with it the steel of command. "To the wall."

Barefoot and dressed only in his tunic, Tovak climbed to his feet, his hand going for his sword, which he'd laid by his side before sleep. He pulled it from his scabbard and moved for the wall. Two archers were atop the wall to his right, loosing arrows out into the darkness. One of the archers abruptly screamed and tumbled down the berm, her bow falling from her hands. A spear had gone clean through her midsection.

"Get to the walls," Benthok shouted, and with that command, any thoughts Tovak had of stopping to help ceased. He moved on. The archer on the wall remained in her position, continuing to loose missile after missile out into the darkness, as if her comrade had not been injured.

"More coming from the north," Logath shouted.

"First Section to the west, Third Section to the north," Benthok shouted as Tovak made his way to the west side of the camp, which was closest.

"How are the east and south walls?" Benthok hollered.

"East is clear, sir."

"No enemy to the south, sir."

"Thegdol," Benthok hollered, pointing to the sergeant. "Take the north wall. Lead the defense there."

"I've got it, sir," Thegdol said and moved off in that direction.

As Tovak approached the wall, he saw a pair of orcs pull themselves over the berm. A spear thudded into the ground, just next to him. Tovak stumbled to a startled halt and stared at the quivering weapon, transfixed. A few inches over and it would have hit and most likely killed him.

The clash of arms close at hand tore him from his shock at having almost died. Where before there had been two, now there were three orcs over the wall. Two sentries were desperately battling them. Bodies lay at their feet, which in the moonlight looked like unformed lumps. Whether they were the enemy or not, Tovak had no idea.

Standing on the crest of the wall, the orcs were huge, almost hulking figures. Tovak had never seen an orc before, and now that he had, he felt a bolt of fear course through him. They wore armor covering their chests, with solid-looking helms. In the moonlight, their tusks gleamed in an almost ethereal way. They carried an assortment of weapons: blades, war hammers, axes, and even spears. With every passing moment, more pulled themselves over the wall. These quickly climbed down into the camp, past those that were fighting with the sentries. A half-dozen warriors, screaming war cries and wearing nothing but their tunics, slammed into them. A tremendous clash of weapons filled the air, mixed with the roars from the orcs and shouts and oaths from the warriors.

"Push them back over the wall," Benthok roared at the top of his lungs as he stepped forward and attacked an orc who had just crested the wall. The orc swung at the lieutenant, who ducked, allowing the weapon to slide harmlessly over his head. The lieutenant jabbed forward with his sword, plunging it into the creature's leg. The orc roared in pain and stumbled to a knee. Benthok stabbed again, this time aiming for the chest armor. The blow was so powerfully delivered, it pushed the orc backward. The creature fell back down the other side of the wall and into the trench.

Another orc clambered up and over the wall. It swung its sword wildly at Benthok. The lieutenant dodged back. Something snapped within Tovak and he rushed forward. Screaming, he swung his sword for the orc. The creature blocked and their two swords met with a strong clang that seemed to ring on the air. Tovak brought his sword back to strike again. The lieutenant's sword appeared, as if out of nowhere, and stabbed into the orc's neck. The point emerged from the other side. The creature seemed to sag and toppled forward, knocking Tovak to the ground and landing on top of him.

It was frightfully heavy, and Tovak struggled to lift the body off him. He felt its warm blood coursing over his chest. Then the creature was rolled off and the lieutenant was helping him to his feet. All around them, the fighting raged with a savage intensity that was almost deafening.

More orcs were pulling themselves over the wall. Warriors battered against orcish shields with their spears and blades or whatever weapon they had at hand. One used his trencher and another a poker from the fire. Yet another used nothing but his bare hands to choke the life from an orc as the two of them thrashed on the ground.

A skirmisher screamed in pain, dropping where he stood. Tovak could not see what had injured him. A second cried out in agony, staggering backward as he clutched at his left arm. A third skirmisher lunged with his blade, driving it into an orc's groin. The creature roared.

"Come on, lad," Benthok encouraged as he stepped forward, rejoining the fight. "We need to do our bit. Keep it up, lads. Stick it to 'em. Stick them good."

Tovak went with him. They fought, almost shoulder to shoulder. The fight raging around them, in the darkness, was nothing but chaos. There was no way to follow it. Though he could hear Thegdol and others shouting what sounded like desperate orders, Tovak had no idea what was happening on the other side of camp. All he could focus on was what was before him, and so, that's what he did.

Roars, screams, and battle cries assailed his ears. He did not have time for thought or fear. He stood his ground, trading blows with an orc who had climbed over the top of the berm and was trying to force his way down into the camp. Benthok, to his right, faced what Tovak decided could only be a goblin. The creature was smaller than the orcs and wore a patchwork of armor. It fought with claws instead of a weapon.

The orc swung for Tovak's head. He blocked with his sword and the blow set his fingers to tingling. Tovak reversed his sword and aimed a downward slashing strike at the orc's right leg. The orc reacted too late and Tovak's sword sliced easily through muscle as if it were warm butter. Enraged with pain, the orc bared its tusks at him and staggered back a step on the edge of the berm. It suddenly lost its balance and, arms flailing, toppled backward into space and then was gone.

Tovak looked for his next opponent and saw the goblin was at Benthok's feet, throat neatly sliced open and legs twitching feebly. The lieutenant slashed at an orc wielding a mace, forcing it to raise the weapon and parry. The edge of the lieutenant's blade bit into the wood of the shaft, sending flecks of wood flying into the air. With a savage roar, the orc dropped the mace and jumped forward onto the lieutenant, knocking him bodily to the ground. Before he knew what he was doing, Tovak stepped forward and thrust with his sword, driving the point of his weapon down into the back of the orc's neck. There was a moment's resistance, then the sword drove deep. Tovak felt the blade grate against the spine. He gave the sword a savage twist and felt a crunching. The creature immediately went limp.

Tovak saw motion out of the corner of his eye. He whirled, but it was too late. An orc was swinging a savage-looking sword and aiming straight for his head. He knew it was a killing blow and there was no way he could block it.

A blade snapped in front of Tovak's face, moving forward in a blur that caught the orc's blade, stopping it only inches from the side of Tovak's head. Astonished, Tovak turned to see Jodin standing there, grimacing with the impact of the blow and then struggling to force it aside as he raised the blade away from Tovak's head. Their eyes met for a moment, and without thinking, Tovak grabbed at the orc's wrist near the sword hilt and pulled, hoping to yank him to the side and off balance. The orc tried to jerk free, but Tovak's grip was firm.

Jodin took advantage of the move, stepped closer, and stabbed upwards, thrusting and catching the orc beneath the chin and driving his blade up into its brain. The orc released its grip on the weapon and dropped where it stood. As the creature collapsed, it pulled Jodin forward and off balance. Jodin yanked his blade free to turn and confront an orc that had just made it over the wall. He was too late. The orc lunged and stabbed. The blade took Jodin deeply in the side.

Tovak's corporal screamed, dropping his weapon and drawing back.

Tovak stared, shocked to immobility, as Jodin's legs gave out and he toppled backward, slamming onto the ground.

"Tovak," Benthok shouted as he pulled himself to his feet and struck at the orc that had just taken down Jodin. Tovak came to his senses and turned to see that several more orcs had come over the wall. One was a giant, with bulging muscles and standing at least eight feet tall. It carried a massive iron hammer.

Tovak lunged at the orc, who was now fighting the lieutenant, stabbing it in the hip. The blade point hammered against bone. The creature bellowed and turned towards Tovak but was cut down a moment later as the lieutenant stabbed it in the face, blade going in through the mouth. Blood sprayed into Tovak's face. He could taste the copper tang in his mouth and felt nauseated. For a moment, it blinded him. He wiped it out of his eyes with the back of his arm.

Without missing a beat, Benthok had pulled back, sidestepped, and parried a strike from the giant orc with the hammer. He caught the hammer on the shaft, just missing the orc's fingers by a hair. The lieutenant grunted and stepped back a pace, in a defensive posture. The orc advanced, shouting in a guttural language that Tovak did not understand. It sounded like an order or an encouragement to the other orcs. Was this their leader?

Tovak attacked the orc from the side. It reacted instantly and with lightning quickness. The creature parried with an ear-splitting clang of metal on metal as Tovak's steel met the iron of the hammer. Sparks flew into the air. The strength of Tovak's swing knocked the hammer back and carried through into the side of the orc's temple, slamming against the helm.

Stunned slightly, the creature took a step back. Benthok lunged forward and slashed at the giant. He caught its forearm, opening the arm up to the bone. The orc stepped back, raising the war hammer in a one-handed defensive position. Benthok attacked again, driving the big orc backward towards the wall.

Tovak thrust with his sword and aimed for the exposed neck. The creature twisted and the tip of his sword grated against the chest armor. The orc swung the hammer left and right, in a desperate bid to hold both the lieutenant and Tovak back. Benthok stumbled over a body and almost fell. The orc, shockingly fast, leaned forward and swung the hammer with a slash at Tovak's head. Tovak raised his blade and just barely caught the attack. The force of the blow made his fingers go numb and he cried out from the pain. Gritting his teeth, Tovak tightened his grip, and for a long moment, they strained against one another. The orc roared its defiance at Tovak, who screamed inarticulately back at it.

Benthok, having recovered, stepped in and brought his blade down viciously at an angle. The blade connected between the orc's head and shoulder. It sank deep, cleaving through the muscle and tendon of the neck. The orc roared in agony as it was driven to its knees. A second chop finished it.

"Nice work," the lieutenant said to Tovak. "He was a big one."

The lieutenant was about to turn away towards the fight when a fist came smashing into the side of his head. Benthok's head spun sideways as he crumpled down into the dirt and lay unmoving at Tovak's feet. An unarmed orc stood over the lieutenant. The orc spotted Tovak and bellowed, displaying its tusks. Tovak stepped forward, and as he did, the orc took several steps back. It growled at Tovak as he stood over the lieutenant's body, prepared to defend Benthok, when four skirmishers came charging forward, cutting the orc down in a flurry of strikes.

A horn blew from out in the darkness beyond the wall, three short blasts. It blew a second time. Orcs began shouting amongst each other, and with it, the sound of battle around the camp began to fade, almost completely dying off.

"Don't let them escape," Thegdol shouted from the darkness. "They're withdrawing. Kill as many as you can, boys. Less to fight later."

The last of the orcs before Tovak were already on the berm. They climbed down into the trench or jumped, leaping out into the darkness and disappearing from view. On the other side of the camp, the sound of fighting intensified for several heartbeats, then died away.

Tovak was left breathing heavily. He blinked, not quite believing what had just occurred, nor the fact that he was still alive. Battle was not as he had expected or dreamed it would be. It was ugly and harsh, cruel even. Now that he'd experienced it, he knew he would never be the same. He stabbed the point of his weapon into the dirt.

He turned around. And as he did, he realized that Benthok had fallen almost right next to Jodin. Remembering his wounded corporal, he rushed over and knelt between them both. A single glance told him that Jodin lived, but he'd been badly injured. The corporal had saved his life, possibly at the cost of his own.

A lancing bolt of remorse shot through him. He suddenly felt irrationally guilty about the Adjudication Circle and accepting the challenge. Tovak looked over at the lieutenant. He checked for a pulse and found one. The lieutenant had just been knocked out, at least he thought so.

"I need help here," Tovak shouted, turning back to Jodin. He did not know what to do. Blood was flowing liberally from the wound in the corporal's side. In the darkness, he could not see how bad it was but suspected the worst. "I need help with Corporal Jodin. He's injured."

Tovak felt immense relief as Corporal Karn knelt beside Jodin and rapidly examined the wound, probing it with his fingers.

"Put your palm on it. Use both hands and press hard," Karn said. "If you don't, he will bleed to death. Understand?"

"Yes." Tovak did as instructed and felt the hot, sticky wetness of Jodin's blood on his hands. No matter how hard he pressed, some of the blood seeped through his fingers.

"Good, just like that. I will be right back with a bandage," Karn said and rushed away.

All about was the sound of the moaning of the wounded, the shouting of orders or calling for help. No one was celebrating their victory, if that was what you could call it. From the wall behind him, a bow twanged as one of the archers fired out into the darkness. She was rewarded with a cry of agony.

Karn returned with a large bandage and two lengths of cord. He cut away Jodin's tunic with his dagger, then removed Tovak's hands from the wound. Jodin moaned softly. Karn placed the bandage against the wound, which, without pressure, had begun to bleed heavily again. He quickly tied the cords tight around the corporal's torso and the bandage.

"That should do him for the moment," Karn said.

"Will he live?" Tovak asked. "Please, tell me he will live."

"That's up to the gods," Karn said, wiping his hands clean on the remains of Jodin's tunic, "and ultimately the warband's surgeons. That's if he makes it that far." Karn shook his head sadly. "He took a bad wound."

Tovak looked down on Jodin, feeling intense sorrow.

"Thulla," Tovak said, bowing his head, "grant Jodin a recovery from this wound, for I owe him my life and I do not want him to die. He does not deserve to go this way."

When Tovak opened his eyes, he discovered Karn gazing at him oddly. He realized he'd just revealed his faith to the corporal. He no longer cared. He was done hiding who he was.

"Deserves got nothing to do with it," Karn said softly. "Still, I think he'd welcome your prayers. I know I would."

With that, the corporal stood and stepped away.

"Where's the lieutenant?" Thegdol called.

"He's over here," Tovak said, raising his hand. "The lieutenant is down."

Thegdol hurried over.

"He's only knocked out," Tovak explained. "An orc sucker punched him when he wasn't looking."

Thegdol appeared relieved, but he still bent down and looked the lieutenant over. He checked for a pulse and then opened one of the lieutenant's eyes, staring into it. Satisfied, the sergeant stood and then saw Jodin. A look of profound sadness came over him.

"It's bad," Tovak said. "He saved my life. I'd be dead without him."

"Aye," Thegdol said, "that's what comrades do."

Tovak felt tears brimming in his eyes. He wiped them angrily away and cleared his throat.

Thegdol said nothing more for a long moment. Then, the sergeant glanced around the darkened camp.

"Corporals," Thegdol called, "see to the wounded. I want a head count as soon as possible."

"Yes, Sergeant," came a response.

"On it, Sarge," Karn said from across the camp.

"Shrike?" Thegdol called.

"What do you need?" came Shrike's voice from the far side of the camp.

"You survived, you old bastard," Thegdol said.

"It's becoming a habit, Sergeant."

"Get the fire going, will you?" Thegdol asked. "We'll be needing hot iron to cauterize wounds."

"On it, Sergeant."

"Are they going to attack again?" Tovak asked the sergeant.

"I doubt it," Thegdol said. "The last I saw of them buggars, they were legging it across the field and into the forest.

We gave them a real drubbing tonight, a real drubbing. They should have known better than to tangle with us."

Tovak looked about the camp. Besides a good number of skirmishers that were down, there were even more orc and goblin bodies. Some were still moving. Lok walked up to one that was trying to crawl its way back to the wall. Sword raised, he stood over the creature a moment, with a look of loathing and disgust. Then he stabbed downward into the back of the neck. The creature stiffened and then fell still.

Tovak suddenly found his hands shaking uncontrollably. He gazed at them, wondering why they would not stop trembling. The sergeant noticed.

"That's normal," Thegdol said. "It's just your nerves. Give it time, son. The shaking will pass."

"Sergeant," a voice called. "You are needed over here."

Thegdol reached down and patted Tovak on the shoulder. With that, the sergeant straightened and walked away, leaving Tovak with Jodin and the lieutenant.

CHAPTER TWENTY-TWO

"We've double-checked," Logath said to Thegdol. The sergeant was standing by the fire, just a few feet away from Tovak. He was speaking with Logath, Karn, and Gamok. They had been taking stock after the fight. "We can't find Dagmar, Gorabor, or Staggen."

Tovak's head came up and around. He'd just donned his armor. The enemy attack had finished less than a half hour before. His hands had stopped shaking but his nerves were still on edge. All around, those who hadn't been injured were readying themselves in the event there was another attack. Even the walking wounded, those who could, were preparing themselves.

"To be certain, we checked the dead again. We even searched through the bodies in the trench." Logath gave a tiny shake of his head. "No luck. We think they may have been taken."

"Gorabor?" Tovak breathed in horror, glancing around, searching. He hadn't seen Gorabor since before bedding down for the night. The camp was well-lit, as several fires had been set. His eyes passed over Shrike, who was busy stitching up a skirmisher from Third Section. Tovak did not know him, but he'd taken a nasty cut to the leg. He was grunting as the teamster threaded the needle, but he did not cry out.

Tovak's eyes went to the wounded, who had been lined up in order of need and severity. One of the archers, Tovak believed her name to be Aggatha, was working on an arm wound of an unconscious skirmisher from Third Section, scrubbing it clean with a blood-soaked rag. Behind her, in the fire, rested the tips of several swords and spear points. The metal wasn't hot enough yet, so the cauterizing of any wounds that needed it had not begun. Jodin likely would be one of the first candidates.

Tovak's eyes moved from the wounded and scanned the camp. He saw neither Staggen nor Gorabor. His heart twisted in fear for his friend. Why had he not thought to search for him until now? Why? Tovak cursed himself and glanced once more around the camp, hoping beyond hope it was all a mistake. How could he have let his only friend in this world be taken? He knew such thinking was irrational, but the sense of loss tugged hard on his heart and so too did the guilt.

"Staggen and Gorabor had sentry duty," Gamok said. "They were probably the first overcome."

"Dagmar did not have sentry duty," Logath said. "However, his bedroll was near where Staggen had been posted."

"The enemy came to grab prisoners," Thegdol said, and spat on the ground. "There was never any real intention of overrunning our camp. The bastards only wanted intelligence. Bloody gods."

"Which means," Logath said, "this group that attacked us is part of an organized force. I don't, for one moment, believe we're dealing with a lone tribe. The attack on Third may have been an attempt to gather information as well. Sergeant Kelloth's timely counterattack likely foiled any attempt at taking prisoners."

Thegdol rubbed his jaw as he considered Logath's words.

"If I am correct," Logath continued, "Karach needs to be warned. There could be an enemy army shadowing the warband in these very hills."

Thegdol remained silent, running his hand through his beard, which was spattered with green blood.

"What we need to do is go after them," Karn said to Thegdol, "before it is too late. You know what they will do to our boys."

"We're in no condition to go anywhere," Logath said, aghast. "What would you have us do? Leave the wounded unprotected?"

"We don't need to take everyone," Karn snapped, then looked back at Thegdol. "All I need are a handful of our best. We follow them back to their camp, sneak in, free our people, and then leg it back here."

"You make it sound so easy," Logath said and then pointed out into the darkness beyond the camp. "It won't be a stroll across the meadow."

"I am inclined to agree with Karn," Gamok said. "Leaving our people in their hands doesn't sit well with me. We should go get them. In the doing of it, we may learn the size and composition of this enemy force that Logath thinks is out there. Headquarters would find such information invaluable."

"You both are out of your mind," Logath said. "Thegdol, talk some sense into them."

"Logath," Karn said, "you are too cautious. It's time for you to grow a pair."

Logath stiffened and went red in the face. He balled his fists and opened his mouth to respond.

"Cease this bickering," Thegdol said. "I will not have us fighting amongst ourselves. Everyone is upset. I get that. Let's not take it out on each other."

The sergeant looked meaningfully at Karn, who gave a nod of agreement, and after a moment, so too did Logath. Thegdol turned away towards the nearest fire, staring into its depths for several heartbeats, clearly considering their words.

"Curse all orcs," Thegdol said to the fire.

The corporals waited. Then, the sergeant turned back.

"There's nothing we can do for them now...not in the shape we're in. Half our boys are down or injured in some way."

"Thegdol, please," Karn said. "I've done this before. Let me—"

"Hear me out." Thegdol held up a hand. The sergeant sounded suddenly very weary. "When the captain arrives with Second Section, I am confident he will go after them. I want to go after them too, but I cannot. I have a greater responsibility. We simply have too many wounded who are unable to care for themselves. Though I doubt it, the enemy could come back and hit us a second time." Thegdol paused a heartbeat. "Karn, I don't feel comfortable stripping what little strength we have left, even if it's a small team. No. Any rescue attempt will have to wait until morning and the captain's arrival."

"Thegdol," Karn said, becoming heated, "they may not live 'til morning. You very well know that. If you were in their hands and I in your boots, I wouldn't leave you. I would come for you. We don't leave anyone behind, ever."

"You're not me," Thegdol said, a hard edge creeping into his tone. "With the lieutenant down, I am in command.

No matter how distasteful, this is my decision to make. My mind on the matter is made up. There will be no rescue attempt tonight. We will wait for the captain or the lieutenant to regain his senses. Until then, this discussion is over. Is that understood?"

"Yes, Sergeant," Karn said.

"It is," Gamok said.

"Now," Thegdol said, "half our able-bodied strength is to be on the wall. The rest are to stand down. Logath, you have command of the wall. Gamok, since you're good with the needle, go help Shrike with the wounded. Karn, after we get our armor on, you and I will make the rounds."

Tovak could not believe what he was hearing. His friend was out there, in the hands of the enemy, and Thegdol was just going to abandon him. He glanced towards the forest at the edge of the field. In the darkness, it looked like nothing more than a black, ominous wall.

The enemy had gone in that direction and he wanted to as well. He felt an urge tugging him onward, encouraging him to go after them. The feeling intensified, until it was almost a physical need tugging him forward. Tovak took an involuntary step towards the forest, then stopped, restraining himself. He glanced back at Thegdol, who had moved over to his bedroll and was putting his armor on. The corporals had gone their separate ways.

Tovak's gaze swept the camp again, settling on Jodin. Tovak felt an intense pang of guilt course through him. First Jodin, and now Dagmar, Staggen, and Gorabor. He looked back out into the darkness. Corporal Karn had had the right idea. They needed to rescue the prisoners and now, before it was too late. He understood it was the correct decision. Thegdol was being too cautious, too wary. The enemy were not coming back.

"That's what comrades do," Tovak said, looking once more over at Jodin again.

"What?" Morda asked, a few feet away. He had just tied off the straps on his armor and was putting on his helmet. "What did you say?"

"Nothing," Tovak said and knelt by his pack, which he'd left open. He eyed the spirit deck. Secured in its case, it was sitting on top of his spare tunic. Without a doubt, he knew what it would tell him. There was simply no need to consult it. He understood what he must do. He hesitated a moment, then reached inside the pack, unwrapped *Thulla's Blessed Word*, and placed his hand squarely on it.

"Grant me strength to do what's needed," Tovak prayed in a whisper, for he wanted no one to guess what he was about to attempt. He almost jumped, snatching away his hand, for the book had become warm, scalding hot even. Astonished, he looked at his hand. He wasn't burned.

What was going on here?

Tovak reached down and tentatively felt the book again. The leather binding was cool to the touch. Had it been a sign? Or had he just imagined it?

He felt the intense urge tug at him again, pulling him to go after the orcs. He stared down at the book. No, he decided. It had been a sign from his god. He was about to risk everything, even his own life, and Thulla had given his blessing. The thought of what he was about to attempt terrified him to his core. Tovak took a breath, and as he let it out, a sense of calm determination stole over him, cementing his resolve.

So be it.

Tovak tightened his helmet straps and then secured his waterskin to his belt. He checked his sword, which was nestled into the scabbard and the dagger in its sheath. He tied his sling and half-full pouch of lead shot to his belt.

Satisfied all was ready, he looked around to make sure no one was watching, particularly Morda, who was nearest to him. While bending down to retrieve his spear, Morda had turned his back on him. There was no one between him and the wall, no one to stop him at any rate.

It was time.

Tovak stood and broke into a run for the wall, sprinting for all he was worth.

"Hey," Morda called after him as he straightened. "Where are you going?"

Tovak ignored him, charging as fast as he could run, towards and then up the smooth slope of the berm. At the precipice, he leapt out into the darkness, praying he would clear the trench. He landed hard, just beyond, stumbled, and almost fell. He managed to keep his feet and felt a momentary thrill of exhilaration, like nothing he'd ever experienced. The die had been cast. He was going after his friend.

He glanced back at the trench and saw that it had been filled in at the spot where he'd jumped. The orcs had used bundles of tightly tied sticks to fill and bridge the trench. He could have just walked across it. It almost made him want to laugh. Shaking his head, he started for the forest at a jog. Behind him, the camp was a riot of shouting and commotion.

"Quiet," Thegdol roared and the camp fell still. "Tovak," Thegdol called after him. "I can't bloody see him. Can you?" There was a slight pause. "Tovak, answer me, son."

Already halfway across the field and by the ruins of the old farmhouse, Tovak stopped. He turned back. Silhouetted by the firelight, Thegdol was standing on the wall, along with most everyone else who was able to move under their own power.

"Sergeant," Tovak called back.

"What do you think you are doing, son?"

"I am going to get our people," Tovak called back.

"No," Thegdol said, a firm note entering his voice, "you're not."

"Yes, Sergeant," Tovak said, turning away, "I am."

"Of all the stupid things to do," Thegdol exploded. "You Academy-trained are all the same. You think you bloody well know everything. Going alone is suicide. I am ordering you to stay."

Tovak stopped. He'd just been given an order and it gave him pause for thought. There was no doubt in his mind violating it would have consequences. All he had achieved was about to be cast aside. That was, if he survived.

Thegdol was likely right. Going could see his death. Then again, Tovak knew he could not live with himself if he turned back. Gorabor, Staggen, and Dagmar were out there. The urge to continue tugged at him strongly. There had only ever been one choice.

"I've already made my decision." Tovak started to turn away again.

Thegdol softened his tone a tad. "Son, I know you and Gorabor are friends. Once the captain gets here, we will go and get them. I promise you that."

"I'm going, Sergeant," Tovak said, resolve having firmly settled back over him. "I'd prefer your blessing, but if I don't get it, I am going after them anyway. It needs to be done."

"Karn," Thegdol snapped, steel in his voice. Tovak could see the sergeant turn and point at the corporal a few feet away. Karn had begun to climb down off the wall and into the trench. "You bloody stay still. You're not going and that's final." The sergeant looked around at those gathered on the wall. "Anyone who gets any half-brained ideas to go with him, know that I will order the archers to shoot you down before you can go ten feet. Don't bloody try me."

Silence greeted the sergeant's words. Tovak knew he was almost out of the range of the archers. Even if they could see him, he truly doubted Thegdol would give the order to fire.

"You're a fool," Thegdol said. Tovak could hear the anger and frustration warring in the sergeant's tone.

"Aye," Tovak said, "probably. But I'm still going. I ... I need to do this."

"Fine," Thegdol said. "Go, you damn fool. In fact, I give you my blessing. Risk your miserable Pariah ass, but don't you come crying back to me if you end up dead, boy. Bloody damn fool. I am surrounded by bloody fools."

"Thank you, Sergeant," Tovak said. "I will mark my trail. Look for Thulla's sign."

In apparent disgust, Thegdol waved his hand vaguely in Tovak's direction, then turned and climbed down the wall.

"Go get 'em," Karn called. From those gathered at the wall, a cheer rose up.

Heartened by that, Tovak started jogging for the trees, following the swath of trampled grass left by the enemy. He had some catching up to do.

Tovak finished carving Thulla's symbol, a hand with two fingers up, into the tree trunk. He'd left a trail of blazes, every fifty yards, going back to the camp. When the company marched, they would be able to follow in his tracks to where he now kneeled behind a pine tree in front of the enemy camp. At least, he hoped they would.

From behind the tree Tovak looked over at the ruins of what appeared to be an old town on a hill to the north, about a quarter of a mile away. Between him and the town was a sloping field of grass, scattered over with trees.

Only the walls of the town remained, which told him that it had been abandoned some time ago. Trees had even grown up throughout the ruins. He could smell smoke drifting on the air, though he could not see any fires. This, he knew without a doubt, was the enemy camp.

Tovak counted fifteen tents within the old town. They were of varying sizes, with no sense of uniformity or organization. At least six of the tents were large, and that likely meant their purpose was communal. Tovak could see no defensive trench or wall. There were no sentries in view either. Were they sleeping off the raid? Or were they just arrogant and confident? Or had he simply, in the early morning gloom, missed them?

Tracking the enemy through a dark forest had not proven easy. Several times, he'd lost the trail and been forced to backtrack until locating it again. Worse, it had taken a lot longer than he'd expected to find the enemy camp.

He knew everything depended upon how soon the captain arrived with Second Section. When would the captain march? Would he even march? Or would he cut his losses and return to the warband? As Tovak had followed the enemy's trail, these questions and more had dogged him. No matter what Thegdol had said about going after the prisoners, Tovak simply had no idea if Struugar would. In the end, he'd decided he couldn't count on help. If he ran into trouble, he was effectively on his own.

He glanced up at the sky. It had begun to lighten considerably. At best, sunrise was perhaps an hour away.

He took a sip of water, then returned the skin to his belt. He'd followed the tracks of the raiding party all the way to the canyon, past the monster murinok shell. The tracks had led him farther up the canyon, about a mile, to what looked like an ancient roadbed. This crumbling, rutted, and badly weathered road cut its way upward in a series of switchbacks along the canyon wall. Tovak had climbed the road to the top.

Looking upon the enemy camp, Tovak felt a coil of fear run through him. With the grassland, there was a lot of open ground between him and the first cover, another tree. He glanced to the lightening horizon. He had to get moving. Tovak took a deep breath and started forward at a sprint for the nearest tree, an old gnarled oak.

Reaching it, he stopped and crouched down, peeking out from behind. He could see no movement in the enemy camp. There was no call to arms. He waited, counting to sixty, then sprinted for the next tree and then the one after that. Tovak paused at each, watching and listening for several heartbeats before moving on. As he drew closer to the camp, he began to wonder once again, where were the sentries? Surely an enemy camp this size would have lookouts.

The nearer he drew to the town wall, the less the pull tugged him forward and the more unease he began to experience. He still felt like he was moving in the right direction, but the urgency and intensity of the pull had faded.

Tovak continued until he came to a low wall out in the field. It was a simple stone wall, the kind farmers made to mark boundaries when clearing fields. He wrinkled his nose. The smell of the enemy camp drifted down to him. The stench was plain awful. It spoke of a lack of cleanliness and basic sanitation. The smell was almost strong enough to make him gag.

He moved to the next wall, twenty-five yards away from the first. Every footstep brought him nearer. With each dash, Tovak kept expecting to hear shouts of alarm or for the enemy to emerge from hiding and attack. Incredibly, nothing happened.

Pushing back his fear but remaining cautious, he plunged onward. Tovak made his way up the incline of the hill, to nearly the ruined town's edge. Still nothing, no alarm sounded. The town had once had a defensive wall, which was likely why the enemy had chosen this spot to camp in the first place. The problem was that, over the long years, large portions of the wall had crumbled and collapsed, parts of which one could simply walk through. The enemy had done nothing to rectify this deficiency in their defenses, for which Tovak was immensely grateful.

He moved up to one of the many gaps in the town wall and peeked through, looking left and right. Again, nothing moved. Vines had grown up thickly around and against the walls. Tovak suspected that the stone structures inside the town were centuries old, for the stone had been worn down by the weather. The remains of the structures reminded him of his people's work, but in the dim early morning light, he could not be certain.

Tovak scanned once more, searching for any hint of a sentry or lookout. There were none. Another dose of fear ran though him as the full realization of what he was about to do sank home. Calming his nerves as best as he could, he slipped silently around the wall and up to the nearest tent, just yards away. From within, he could hear what sounded like snoring. He moved around the side and saw a row of tents. He crept from one to the next, carefully avoiding the guide ropes and pausing at each one to listen. Incredibly, all he heard was snoring from within, and still there were no sentries about.

Tovak paused, scanning the area around him. Where were they keeping the prisoners? Perhaps at the center of the camp? He crept forward and came to a wagon park. There were five large wagons. Next to the wagons were stacks of sacks and barrels. The teska that pulled the wagons were picketed a short distance away. None of the creatures paid him any mind.

He slipped around the wagons and came to what had once been a large building. Now it was only a shell. Most of the walls had collapsed and in the center of the ruin grew a large pine tree. Crouching, he worked his way around the building towards what he thought was the center of town. On the other side, he came to another ruin, the walls of which were badly overgrown with thorny weeds and vines.

He knelt and once again looked about, searching. He glanced up at the sky, which had turned an almost scarlet color. He had to hurry things up. Tovak started forward again, creeping from ruin to ruin, pausing to listen and glance around.

He finally came to the center of the camp and froze at the corner of a building as a monotone chant began to his front. He peeked around the corner. A corpulent, bald figure in black and red robes, clearly a priest, stood before a wooden altar, leading the chant. Tovak realized he was a human. Off to his right were six orcs with red paint covering their bodies. They were wearing skull-like masks and were abased before the altar. The orcs were the ones chanting. Off to the priest's left stood a slim figure in black leather armor, a human.

Tovak froze in horror, his eyes snapping back to the altar. The bound body of a Dvergr lay on the altar, chest ripped open, blood dripping down the sides to the ground. Tovak looked at the face. It was Staggen.

The priest was covered from head to toe in Staggen's blood, almost as if he'd bathed in it. The chanting continued unabated as the priest reached inside Staggen's chest cavity and took out the heart and held it up. The chanting increased in volume.

Tovak felt like he might retch.

The sound of footsteps off to his right snapped his head around. Someone was coming. He hastily backtracked and ducked around the other side of the building, making doubly certain not to make any sound. He moved around the trunk of a large pine that had grown up next to a low-lying wall. Peeking around the side, he was able to make out two spindly goblins. They were terribly hideous creatures and half the size of orcs. They wore armor and looked to be some sort of a patrol. Were these the only sentries?

The two goblins came to a stop and gave the group before the altar what Tovak could only describe as a wary look. They turned around and quite hastily went back the way they had come.

Tovak's heart was hammering in his chest. He feared that, had it not been for the chant, they might have heard the thuds. He closed his eyes, mourning the passage of Staggen. He hadn't exactly been a friend, but he was a comrade. Tovak had been too late to save him. Had Gorabor and Dagmar suffered the same fate? He prayed it was not so.

From his new position, he could still see the ritual unfolding. His eyes slipped from the priest to the other human, the slim one. Without warning, rage blossomed in Tovak's heart, and his hand fell to his sword hilt. He felt a disgust for this human, even more so than the priest. It was mixed with a deep-seated sense of unease. The human looked his way. Tovak quickly ducked back under cover.

He waited several heartbeats, then slowly backed away. Once he was safely out of view, he moved back from the center of camp. A row of tents spread out before him. He went to the end of the row and found nothing, other than orcs sleeping away in their tents. It was getting lighter out and he was beginning to feel desperate. Tovak worked his way around to the other side of the camp.

There, he found a tent that was made of finer material. The entire side of the tent facing him had been rolled up. A foreign-looking lamp hung from one of the supports, casting the interior in a soft, almost warm glow.

A rug covered the ground. There was a raised platform off to one side, surrounded by a slightly parted black curtain, exposing a pile of cushions stacked into an obvious bed. A clay plate sat on the edge of the platform, laden with a haunch of meat and some vegetables. A wooden mug stood beside the food, along with a jar. On the opposite side of the tent was an open wooden chest, with a black cloth covering a lumpy assortment of what he supposed to be personal effects. Beside that stood a rough-hewn camp table with a stool.

This must be the commander's tent.

He stepped over and into the tent, looking everything over. He saw a large map on the table that seemed to be of the region. Underneath that there were other maps. Locations had been circled on the map on top. Someone had written on it in a scrawl he could not decipher. He wondered what it all meant, but felt it was important.

A deep, rumbling orcish voice barked something out from the other side of the tent. Tovak froze. This was followed by a reply in a lower-toned voice that was most definitely not from an orc. The orc gave a grunt, then moved off. Tovak almost breathed a sigh of relief, but then he heard footsteps coming nearer. He immediately fled, moving out of the tent as quietly as he could. He got down behind a crumbling stone wall, no more than five feet away, and held his breath. He heard the footfalls cross onto the carpet.

The disgust and loathing returned. Without having to look, he knew it was the man in black, and the sensation was stronger now, much more powerful than before. He'd never felt anything like it. It was almost as if he was standing in the presence of something disgusting and … evil. Yes, that was the correct word. The man was evil, pure and simple. He knew deep in his heart that something had to be done to cleanse this wickedness from the world and he was the one to do it.

There was the sound of liquid pouring, then footsteps, followed by the mug clunking on what he thought might be the table. Tovak raised himself, peered over the wall, and saw the human. The man's back was to him. He was bent over, studying the map. The revulsion inside Tovak intensified tenfold.

Tovak thought he saw a strange pattern of black, smoky tendrils licking at the man's body, as if here and there nearly invisible black flames burned at the extremities. Tovak paused for a moment, blinking to clear his vision, but the tendrils remained, flowing in strange patterns along the arms, legs, and even across the head.

What magic was this?

Tovak was certain he was seeing things, but the sight of the flames only seemed to fuel his disgust and revulsion to new levels. This man had a hand in Staggen's death. There was no doubt in Tovak's mind, he was a servant of evil. This was why Tovak was here, in the enemy camp. The urge had been pulling and tugging him, to this very meeting, not to rescue comrades but to murder. The realization stunned him to his core.

Tovak's anger surged. Not only would the man's death serve as a gift to Thulla, but it would be a reckoning for Staggen's passing. Almost without realizing it, Tovak rose and drew his dagger. He slowly approached, the blade held ready, his knuckles white around the grip. Tovak's heart pounded in his chest. The nearer he got, the greater the revulsion.

Sensing something, the man abruptly whirled round. Their eyes met. Tovak froze in mid-step. The man hesitated also, clearly surprised by Tovak's presence. Then the human snarled and drew an obsidian dagger. The moment of hesitation was shattered. Tovak threw himself forward and, with his free hand, knocked the man's dagger aside. He punched his own blade into the stomach and up as hard as he could. The man gagged, dropping the dagger.

Their eyes locked. The man grimaced in pain and breathed out an agonized breath. Tovak smelled wine on his breath. The man abruptly stilled, as if the pain from Tovak's strike had faded. He smiled at Tovak. It wasn't a happy smile, but one born of cruelty and malevolence. Blood flecked his lip.

"My mistress…." The man was struggling to speak—and in Tovak's own language. Tovak was frozen. "Long ago, she…showed me…my fate at the hands of her enemy. I did not believe…until now…." He coughed and spat up a bubble of blood. "Thank you, follower of Thulla…thank you for delivering me to my mistress. You performed great…service…today."

Tovak was speechless.

The priest's eyes flicked to the back of the tent and the smile grew wider. He started to cry out to sound the alarm. Tovak slammed him to the ground and covered his mouth with his hand. The man shuddered in pain. He struggled to free himself to no avail. Tovak pulled the blade back and, with a quick motion, drew it across the man's throat, sawing hard. Warm blood fountained over his hand and chest. The priest kicked violently for several heartbeats as he choked, and after what seemed like an eternity, he went still.

Tovak breathed out a heavy breath and pulled himself to his feet. He looked down upon the man. Blood had stained the rug, darkening the red patterns. Tovak unceremoniously wiped his hand and the dagger on a small hand towel that had been on the table.

He looked over at the dead man.

What had he meant? More importantly, who was his mistress?

Though he had avenged Staggen's death in some measure, Tovak was seriously disturbed by what had happened. He knew he should feel satisfaction at ending such evil, but there was only regret and sadness, where before there had been anger, disgust, and revulsion.

He let out a ragged breath and re-sheathed his dagger. As he stared down into those lifeless eyes, fixed in death, he realized that whatever black tendrils he'd seen running across the man's body were now gone, vanished, along with the spark of life.

He glanced at the maps that lay on the table. The one on top seemed to be of the Grimbar Mountain Range. The maps were old, ancient, and threadbare. He understood he had to take them. They might contain valuable intelligence for the warband. He folded them carefully up and tucked them behind his chest plate. He prepared to leave, but something made him pause again. He stared down at the dead man.

He noticed something he'd not seen before. The man had been wearing a pendant. It was a black spider, with ruby gems in place of its eyes. The sight of it filled Tovak with utter revulsion, almost making him sick to his stomach. Then he remembered Gorabor. He tore his gaze from the pendant. He realized he had not much time. Eventually, someone was bound to find the body, and when that happened, they would come looking for him.

He eyed the pendant for a long moment. Somehow, in some way, he knew it was dangerous. Careful not to touch it, he dragged the body onto the bed to make it look like the man was sleeping and closed the black curtains, then carefully looked to see if anyone was about and stepped back outside.

The first of the two suns was just peeking above the horizon and had begun to bathe the land in the first rays of daylight. Tovak sidestepped along the back of the tent and glanced around the corner. He did not see anyone.

As quickly and quietly as he could, he made his way towards the side of the camp he'd not explored yet. He passed several more tents and then saw what looked like a large wooden cage ahead. He snuck up to it, careful not to betray any noise.

Inside, Gorabor and Dagmar lay on the wood floor of the cage. Their hands and feet had been bound in rope. They'd also been gagged. Both were bloody and looked as if they'd been beaten. He made his way up to the cage. Dagmar was lying on his side, facing him. His eyes snapped open and for a moment there was terror. That faded as they widened in recognition.

Tovak held his finger up to his mouth. Dagmar gave a slow nod. Tovak found the cage was not locked. He thanked Thulla for that little blessing and swung the gate open, wincing as the metal hinges creaked with age and lack of oiling. Not waiting for any kind of a response, he stepped inside and drew his dagger.

Gorabor turned his head. One eye was swollen shut and it looked like his nose had been broken, since it was swollen almost twice its normal size. Gorabor's good eye blinked furiously and he tried to speak through the gag. Tovak put his finger to his lips and shot his friend a wink. Gorabor relaxed a fraction. Tovak quickly cut Dagmar's bonds. He started in on Gorabor's bonds as Dagmar removed his own gag and began rubbing his wrists. Gorabor was free a moment later.

"Can you walk?" Tovak whispered.

"I can and will," Dagmar insisted.

Gorabor gave a nod as well, then looked towards the center of camp. "We have to get Staggen. They took him away a short while ago. We can't leave him."

"He's dead," Tovak said. "I saw his body. We have to get out of here now, before they discover I've freed you."

"No," Gorabor whispered in dismay, shoulders slumping, "not Staggen."

"Where's the rest of the company?" Dagmar asked.

"Not here," Tovak said.

"It's just you?" Dagmar seemed appalled. "You're joking, right?"

"I'm it," Tovak whispered back as he stepped out of the cage and scanned their surroundings. He motioned for the other two to follow. At first, for some reason, they did not move. "You can stay, if you want. Or you can come with me."

"I'm coming," Dagmar said firmly and stepped outside. He limped and it was clear his ankle was giving him some trouble. "I don't think it's broken, but I twisted it something good when they were dragging us back here. It caught on a tree root."

"Help him," Tovak told Gorabor.

Gorabor stepped up and Dagmar threw an arm around his shoulders. Tovak heard someone shifting around in the nearest tent. The others did as well. They froze.

This way, Tovak signed to them and pointed. He started off, leading the way. They moved silently, but with Dagmar's ankle, it was slow going. Tovak led them out of the camp and around it, working their way along the town's outer wall, back to the path he'd taken in. The first of the two suns had fully crested the horizon by the time they reached the point where he'd entered the camp. He knew that all it would take was for someone to look outside and spot them as they made their way across the open field. This time, there would be no dashing from tree to tree. Dagmar was just barely able to hobble along with Gorabor's help.

"This is the only way?" Dagmar asked and pointed out into the field.

"It's the way I know," Tovak said. "We could try a different direction and try to make it back to camp the long way, but I have no idea what the terrain will be like. It could end up being very rugged and we might get turned around."

"Right," Dagmar said, "this way it is. Let's go."

Almost impossibly, they made it to the road that led down into the canyon without being spotted. Tovak could hardly believe their good fortune as they started down. He was beginning to think they might get away.

"Can I have some water?" Dagmar asked, looking at Tovak's waterskin as they reached the canyon floor. "My throat's as dry as a desert."

Tovak handed over the skin, which was about half-full. Dagmar drank deeply, then passed it over to Gorabor, who drained it before handing it back.

"We need to pick up the pace," Tovak said, "and put some distance between us and that camp. It's half a mile to the murinok kill."

"Let's get going then," Dagmar said.

They started moving again, working their way back through the canyon. With Dagmar's injury, the pace was painfully slow. Tovak found himself glancing back repeatedly, searching for signs of pursuit. In his heart, he knew it was only a matter of time 'til the enemy discovered the man's death and their prisoners' escape.

"Where's the rest of the company?" Dagmar asked, wincing in pain as he did his best to hobble along with Gorabor's help. "Gods, it hurts."

"Yeah," Gorabor said, "don't get me wrong, Tovak, I am really happy to see you, but where is the company?"

"Thegdol wanted to wait until morning and the captain's arrival," Tovak said, glancing nervously back once more. "So I thought I'd come instead."

"The sergeant's gonna be irate when he gets his hands on you," Dagmar said with a nervous laugh. "Though he will have to go through me to get a piece of you."

The sentiment warmed Tovak's heart and he found himself grinning at the veteran.

"I doubt you could fight off a gnome in your current condition," Gorabor said.

Dagmar gave another laugh, which degenerated into a coughing fit that wracked his body terribly. He stopped hobbling as he coughed. Tovak wondered if his injuries were graver than they appeared. There was nothing to do about it now. Their sole focus needed to be escape.

"Probably right," Dagmar said, when he'd recovered. They began moving again. "Those gray bastards are tough. Don't ever turn your back on one."

A horn sounded, seemingly from a great distance behind them. All three glanced back up the canyon.

"Oh, shit," Dagmar said, and they picked up their pace. "They must have discovered we escaped."

"We have to move," Tovak said. "Like the sergeant, they're gonna be pissed too. I killed their leader."

"You what?" Gorabor asked, looking over. "The tall human?"

"They were all frightened of him," Dagmar said.

"He scared me too," Gorabor admitted.

"Come on," Tovak said. "Save your breath. We have to make it out of the canyon and to the forest. If we can do that, we stand a chance."

"You know," Dagmar said as he hobbled along, wincing with each step while leaning heavily on Gorabor. He was sweating profusely from both the exertion and the pain. "I think I would have preferred it better had you convinced Thegdol to bring the company."

"I'll try to remember that the next time you up and get captured by the enemy," Tovak said.

"There won't be a next time," Gorabor said, "if we don't pick up the pace."

"So," Dagmar said, looking between the two of them, "you both think I will get captured again, do ya? Once is enough, thank you very much. How about some help here, Tovak?"

Tovak stepped over and took Dagmar's other arm over his shoulder and, half carrying him, they managed to move a little faster.

CHAPTER TWENTY-THREE

A horn sounded from behind them. Tovak turned his head and looked back. So too did Dagmar and Gorabor. He could see four figures, the closest of which was at least three hundred yards back. They were staggered out and running towards them at a steady, almost measured pace. A fifth had stopped and was blowing a horn repeatedly. Tovak felt ill at the sight of pursuit so close.

"Goblins," Dagmar said. "They are the scouts, the dogs to run us down. Orc infantry won't be far behind."

Tovak knew without a doubt the goblin with the horn was signaling the orcs. He detached himself from supporting Dagmar and pulled out his dagger. He handed it over to Gorabor.

"So you have a weapon," he said as Gorabor took it.

"What are you going to do?" Dagmar asked suspiciously.

"Slow them down," Tovak said and then pointed just ahead of them about twenty yards. "Around that bend is the murinok corpse, and just beyond that the forest. Make for the trees as fast as you can."

"I'm not leaving you behind to die," Gorabor said. "How can you ask that of me?"

"We're staying," Dagmar said.

"Neither of you is in a condition to put up much of a fight. Listen, there's no time to argue," Tovak said. "I'm only going to slow them down. I will be right behind you. Now... move. Before it's too late."

"You better be right behind us," Gorabor said.

"I will be," Tovak said.

"Don't make me regret beginning to like you," Dagmar said as he once again leaned on Gorabor's shoulder. "We will meet you in the trees."

"Count on it," Tovak said, putting as much conviction into his tone as he could muster. He pointed. "Now go."

With that, Gorabor and Dagmar began moving. Tovak watched them for several moments, then turned to face the oncoming goblins. The first had closed the distance to two hundred fifty yards. The lead goblin slowed to a jog as it saw him turn to face it.

Tovak began slowly backing up towards the bend, thinking how he wanted to handle what was coming. He pulled his sling out and opened his bag with the lead shot inside. He drew out a bullet, glanced up, and saw that the first of the goblins had picked up the pace and was now less than two hundred yards away. Nerves overcame him, so much so that as he put the shot in the sling pouch, he fumbled slightly and dropped the bullet. Tovak cursed himself.

"Stay calm," he said. "Just stay calm."

Instead of picking the shot up... he reached for another and fell back several more paces. He made sure not to drop this one, for he knew his life counted on what was coming next.

Tovak took a calming breath. He let the range close, slowly backing up towards the bend in the canyon. When the lead goblin was seventy yards, he stopped, focused on his target. For a short sling, it was a long shot. He cast, throwing hard to make sure the bullet had the velocity to injure. The sling cracked loudly, echoing off the walls of the canyon.

The shot missed, landing a foot to the left and behind the creature. The lead ball kicked up a spray of dirt into the air. The goblin, seeing him reaching for another shot, began to sprint. It also began to weave and dodge as it came on, making the next cast that much more difficult.

Tovak put the bullet into the sling pouch. The distance closed to fifty yards. He took another calming breath, focused his mind on his target, and cast, this time with less force, for the goblin was much closer. The shot flew true, impacting the goblin in the upper left leg with a meaty *thwack*. Screaming like a wounded beast, the creature went down in a tumble of arms and legs. The goblin just behind it slowed, as if it were suddenly having second thoughts. That gave Tovak time for another shot.

He cast, and as he did, the goblin threw itself to the side and rolled. The shot missed. He considered taking another throw, but the next goblin was at least one hundred yards behind the one he'd just tried to hit.

Instead, Tovak took advantage of the situation. He turned and ran. Ahead, he saw Dagmar and Gorabor round the bend in the canyon, hobbling out of view. He glanced back and saw the goblin was back on its feet and racing after him. Tovak sprinted harder. As he neared the bend, he decided that once he was safely around the corner, he would turn and engage the goblin in single combat. He tucked the sling into his belt and pushed for all he was worth.

Rounding the corner, he saw Gorabor and Dagmar fifteen yards ahead. They were glancing back at him.

"Run," he shouted and slid to a stop, just around the bend and so close to the rock face he could have touched it. Turning, he yanked his sword out and prepared to strike. A heartbeat later, the goblin rounded the corner at a breakneck pace. As it saw him and the poised sword, it screamed madly and tried to stop. But it was too late. Tovak swung with all his might. The blade slammed home against the goblin's neck, cutting the scream short. The swing, combined with the goblin's momentum, took the creature's head clean off. Green blood fountained up into the air as the head went flying and the body slammed into the ground.

Breathing heavily from his run, Tovak spared a glance behind him and saw Dagmar and Gorabor had reached the murinok. The third goblin came around the bend a few yards away. Tovak's head snapped back around. The creature immediately charged him, claws like daggers extended for the kill. Tovak dodged to the side, ducking and swinging his sword low in a desperate bid to strike it. The edge of the weapon bit into the goblin's thigh. Squealing and crippled, the creature went down to one knee before collapsing onto its back. The goblin cradled its bleeding leg with both hands.

Knowing there were still two more of the creatures, Tovak left it writhing on the ground. He ran after Dagmar and Gorabor. Something thwished past his head. He glanced back and saw one of the goblins had a bow and was nocking an arrow. Putting his head down, he sprinted as fast as he could for the murinok shell and dove behind it, landing hard. A heartbeat later, an arrow smacked down into the dirt, just where he'd been.

Tovak dropped his sword, took up his sling and a lead shot. He jumped back up, spotted the two goblins advancing. They were less than twenty feet away. He threw, aiming for the one with the bow.

It was an easy shot and the bullet smacked the goblin square in the forehead with a solid-sounding *crack*. The force of the blow knocked it backward and to the ground, where it lay twitching. The last goblin charged. Knowing he would not have time for another throw, Tovak dropped back down behind the murinok shell and picked up his sword. As he did, he stole a look to his right and saw that Dagmar and Gorabor had almost made it to the trees.

"Run," he shouted again, then dashed after them. He heard the goblin's pounding feet. A look told him it was overtaking him. He stopped, whirling about, sword held at the ready.

"All right," Tovak shouted at it, dropping into a combat stance, "it's just you and me, you bastard."

The creature came to a stop about five feet from him. It appeared wary, cautious.

"You have good cause for concern," Tovak shouted at it. "I took down your buddies and you're next."

It stood there, simply eyeing him. This was the first time he'd gotten a close-up look at a live goblin. The creature wore leather chest armor and baggy pants. Its skin was green and smooth. Strange runes and tattoos ran up and down its arms. The hands and feet had black claws that appeared retractable. They also looked razor-sharp and were at least four inches long.

The face was hideous and alien, with a small nose that had been pierced with a ring and beady red-pupiled eyes. An ugly scar ran from the creature's left cheek back to its pointed ear. Tovak could read the intelligence in its gaze as it considered how best to get to him.

Tovak wondered how Dagmar and Gorabor were faring. He wanted to look back to see they'd made it to the trees, but he dared not take his eyes off the goblin, for he knew the moment his attention wavered, it would attack.

Instead, it was the goblin that glanced back, behind it and up the canyon.

"Oh no," Tovak breathed as he followed the creature's gaze.

Coming around the bend was a group of orcs. There would be no running now. The goblin turned back and opened its mouth in a wicked grin, filled with long yellowed teeth. Knowing his fate was sealed, Tovak charged, lunging forward with his sword and catching the creature off guard. He stabbed it in the belly, just under its chest armor. The goblin fell back and to the ground, clutching at its stomach.

Tovak took several steps back. The orcs were less than thirty yards away. There were at least a hundred of them. More were coming around the bend. Seeing him, they slowed from a jog to a walk and began spreading out.

Tovak's breathing was labored from his run. He wiped sweat from his eyes. He had pushed his body almost beyond endurance. His legs shook from the strain and his arm trembled as it held the sword. It was over. He knew that. He had freed his two companions, who he hoped would make it to safety.

Tovak understood he wouldn't. Today, this morning, his life would end and so too would his quest to reclaim honor for himself and his family. The only question now was how dearly the enemy would pay in blood for his life. And Tovak fully intended to make them pay.

"Come on," Tovak shouted at them. "Come and get me, you filthy bastards."

The orcs came to an abrupt halt. They suddenly seemed less eager than they had moments before. In fact, several began taking steps backward.

"Can't bear to face me, huh?" Tovak shouted at them, his voice trembling slightly with exhaustion. "I killed your leader. And I'm ready to kill you too. Bring it on."

"I think you've done enough for today, lad," a firm voice said from behind.

Tovak blinked and looked back around to find an officer in heavy armor with a green patterned cloak and sword drawn, striding confidently up to him. Behind him and emerging from the trees was a line of heavy infantry, all with matching green cloaks, carrying shields and spears. Behind them was yet another line of heavy infantry. A standard-bearer walked between the two lines. The standard fluttered in the breeze. It was green and featured a silver war hammer. A full company of strikers was emerging from the trees. They began beating their spears against their shields in a rhythm that seemed to shake the very air.

Tovak blinked, wondering if he was seeing things. They weren't Second Section's skirmishers. This was a line unit. Where had they come from? Tovak's exhausted brain was having difficulty comprehending what was happening.

The officer stopped at Tovak's side, his eyes on the orcs, and patted him on the shoulder. "I believe we can handle it from here. Time to take a break, eh?"

"Yes, sir," Tovak said as the first line of infantry moved around and past them and then the second line also.

"Fifth Company, halt," the officer shouted as he left Tovak and stepped up behind the two lines of strikers. "Dress your lines, boys. Tighten it up. Let's look smart for the big bastards before we begin murdering them."

Tovak saw a second company of strikers, wearing blue cloaks, emerging from the trees. The orcs gave a roar of defiance as Fifth Company continued to beat the inside of their shields with their swords.

"Captain Greng," a second officer said to the first as he approached Tovak and pointed towards the orcs, "it looks like we might have a fight after all. They seem to be up for one."

This new officer wore elaborately etched armor and a red cloak. His helm sported a red crest. He had a rugged look about him and a confidence that spoke of a familiarity with command.

"It seems that way, sir," Greng said and then gestured towards his front. "More of the enemy are arriving."

Tovak turned and saw another hundred orcs joining the first group.

"Thank you for bringing them right to us," the officer in the red cloak said to Tovak. "That was good thinking."

"Yes, sir," Tovak said, not quite knowing what to say. It seemed better to just agree with him.

"Captain Haenth." The officer turned, looking back on the other company of strikers that had emerged from the trees. He was addressing their officer, who marched before his company and next to his standard-bearer. The second company's standard was blue with a large black dragon skull.

"Sir?"

"Would you kindly align your company next to the Fifth, on the right?"

"Yes, sir," Haenth replied and then snapped a series of orders to his company, altering their advance to shift over to the right.

The officer in the red cloak turned back to Tovak.

"That"—the officer hesitated a moment before continuing—"was one of the bravest things I've ever seen, son. Your stand gave us time to form a line of battle. Captain Struugar is lucky to have you in his company. I wish I had ten of you."

"Thank you, sir," Tovak said and was abruptly overcome with emotion. He had succeeded and survived. It scarcely seemed possible that he'd been delivered from certain death. He would live and so too would Dagmar and Gorabor. Tears sprang from his eyes and he gave an involuntary sob as he reached the end of his emotional rope.

The officer laid a hand on his shoulder. "Move to the rear and rest easy, lad. Your part in this business is done."

Tovak cleared his throat but could not speak. He suddenly felt foolish and embarrassed for losing control in front of this officer. He wiped at the tears with the back of his forearm.

"Yes, sir," he finally managed.

"There's no shame in tears," the officer said, seeming to understand Tovak's thoughts. "Even the bravest cry now and again. Chin up, for you earned Legend this day. I am sure by nightfall you will be the talk of the warband."

The orcs gave a massed roar. The officer turned his head in that direction and looked for a long moment. The enemy were forming a battle line with three ranks.

"Now," the officer said, "if you will excuse me, I do believe I have a battle to fight."

The officer stepped away, leaving Tovak alone. Exhausted, he realized he was still holding his bloodied sword. He stuck it point-first into the ground. He wiped at his tears again, this time with both hands.

"You did it, you damn fool."

Tovak turned to find Thegdol striding up. Behind him, at the tree line, were a handful of skirmishers from Third Section, along with Corporal Karn. With them was Dagmar sitting on a rock, next to Gorabor. Dagmar shot him a huge grin.

"Not completely," Tovak said, feeling a stab of guilt. "I couldn't save Staggen. They killed him before I got there."

"I heard," Thegdol said.

"If I'd have been quicker," Tovak said, "I might have saved him."

"I'll hear none of that talk," Thegdol said. "You did all that could be done, and against the odds you managed to save two comrades. No one could have done better, son. Take comfort in that."

Tovak gave a weary nod.

"I should still put you on charge," Thegdol said, "for what you did. It was reckless."

"You won't," Tovak said wearily.

"Oh?" Thegdol asked.

"Don't you recall? You gave me permission to go, Sergeant. I think most of the section heard that."

"You cheeky bastard," Thegdol growled but looked amused. He sobered and became deadly serious. "Do it again, boy, and I will skin you alive, understand?"

"Yes, Sergeant," Tovak said.

"Prepare to advance," the officer in the red cloak called.

"Who is that?" Tovak asked.

Thegdol turned a surprised look on him. "You mean you don't know?"

Tovak shook his head.

"That's Karach, our boss," Thegdol said.

Tovak turned a stunned look on Karach, the warband's commander.

"He is the finest combat leader amongst the clans," Thegdol continued with evident pride. "We are lucky to have him."

"How?" Tovak asked. "How is he here?" He pointed at the two companies of strikers. "How are they here?"

"The lieutenant sent Corporal Hilla back to the warband with a report and a request for reinforcement," Thegdol said. "About an hour after you left, Karach arrived with two full companies. We set out shortly after."

"You found my blazes," Tovak surmised. "That's how you got here so quickly."

"Aye, we did," Thegdol said. "It helped us find our way." The sergeant paused and then gestured at the warchief. "I told Karach you went on my orders to track them down and mark the way. If he knew the truth... well, let's just say no matter what brave deeds you accomplished, he'd likely have given you the boot from the warband. Tovak, we do things as a team and follow orders. There is no place for those who think they don't have to play by the rules. Best you learn that now."

"Yes, Sergeant," Tovak said, feeling a terrible weariness steal over him.

The heavy infantry, a few yards from them, gave a massed shout. The orcs replied in kind.

"Where is the captain?" Tovak asked, realizing he was nowhere to be seen. "The lieutenant?"

"Captain Struugar and Second Section had not yet arrived by the time we left," Thegdol said, a concerned note in his tone. "The lieutenant was a little dazed by the blow he took. Still, he wanted to come. Karach ordered him to remain at camp."

Tovak gave a weary nod.

"Oh." Tovak drew the folded maps from under his armor. He handed them over to Thegdol. "I found these in the enemy camp, after I killed their leader. I thought they might be of some use."

Thegdol raised an eyebrow at that. He unfolded the large map. The sergeant studied it for a moment, then sucked in a breath. "Son, I think Karach is going to be very interested in this."

"What is it?" Tovak asked. "I couldn't read it."

"Common tongue," Thegdol said and tapped the map with a finger. "This map seems to indicate enemy positions in this region, garrisons, camps, towns. It should come in very handy. This map will likely save lives in the days to come."

There was a sudden massed roar. Both Tovak and Thegdol turned. The orcs had formed up into a boxlike formation. The enemy had begun advancing on the two companies.

"First and second ranks," Karach shouted, "ready spears to throw." There was a pause as the front rank took a step forward and raised their spears. The second rank took a step back and did the same. "First rank, release."

A wave of spears arced up into the air. It fell into and around the formation of orcs with a clatter. Several orcs collapsed or fell out, a spear having struck home. The orc formation continued to close the distance.

"Second rank," Karach called, having waited a full ten count to allow the enemy to draw nearer. "Release."

Another wave of spears arced up into the air, crashing down on the orc formation. This toss was more accurate. There were screams, cries, and roars of rage.

"Draw swords and prepare to advance," Karach roared. "Tighten up the line. Ready shields." The front rank's shields were brought up, swords held at the ready. "Let's meet them with Dvergr steel, boys. Advance."

The heavy infantry gave a cheer and began moving forward, one measured step at a time. The orc formation, after the two spear tosses, had lost much of its cohesion, but they were still advancing and seemed eager for a fight. An officer followed to their side and seemed to be encouraging them onward.

The distance closed to twenty yards, then ten. At that point, the officer shouted out an order and the orc formation dissolved as they charged forward, crashing into the Dvergr shield line. It was almost as if the orcs had run into a stone wall, for the strikers held firm.

This was the first time Tovak had seen a real battle. It was loud, much louder than the raid on the camp, and it beat down on the senses. The strikers fought from behind the protection of their heavy shields, stabbing and slashing outward with their swords at the enemy.

Karach was moving slowly back and forth behind the line, giving direction where it was needed. The fight seemed rather one-sided to Tovak, for the infantry was heavily armored and they outnumbered the enemy at least two to one.

"Push them," Karach shouted. "Throw your shoulders into it. Push them."

The shield wall began to move forward, one foot at a time. With a great effort, they forced the enemy back.

"This won't last long," Thegdol said. "The enemy don't have shields and are lightly armored. They don't stand a chance. They are likely from a skirmishing unit, like ours. Pride and fear of losing face is what brought them to battle, and they will suffer for it."

Sure enough, the enemy broke less than thirty heartbeats later, fleeing back the way they'd come. The strikers broke ranks and pounded after them, killing all they could catch. Many were able to escape, for the strikers were heavily encumbered and the orcs were not. Still, the orcs had left a considerable number of dead and wounded behind. They had paid a steep price for their stand against two line companies.

As they watched the strikers pursue the fleeing enemy back up the canyon, Tovak suddenly felt the incredible weariness return. His legs unexpectedly gave out. Thegdol caught him before he could fall and helped him over to where Gorabor and Dagmar were resting.

Corporal Karn hustled over and assisted, helping Thegdol gently lower Tovak to the ground a few feet from Dagmar and Gorabor.

"Thank you," Tovak said and felt a wave of dizziness pass over him. He closed his eyes tight, then opened them. The dizziness passed.

"Thegdol," Karn said, looking at his sergeant, "with Jodin down and likely out of action for the foreseeable future, I'd be honored to have Tovak in my squad. Would you mind if I take him?"

Tovak looked at Karn, astonished and at a loss for words. He was a Pariah and Karn wanted him in his squad?

"I'll take you in, boy," Karn said, "that is, if you don't mind joining Third Section and the sergeant agrees."

"Can Gorabor come too?" Tovak asked hastily, with a look to his friend.

"You can have both of them," Thegdol said. "Try to keep them out of trouble, will you, Karn? Because I can't seem to do that."

"Me too," Dagmar said and jabbed a thumb at Tovak. "I want to stick with him. I'll keep him out of trouble for you, Karn."

"Are you gonna teach him how to properly shirk duty?" Karn asked.

"I've never shirked a day in my life," Dagmar said, appearing scandalized.

"Right," Karn said. "In my squad, I won't tolerate your nonsense. Still want in?"

"Logath won't be happy losing you," Thegdol said.

"Bugger Logath," Dagmar said. "Tovak came for me and saved my sorry ass. I bet Logath argued against going."

"Right then," Thegdol said and let out a heavy breath, "you can have all three of these knuckleheads."

"Thank you, Sergeant," Karn said.

"They're your headache now." Thegdol stepped away towards the officers, one of whom was beckoning him over.

"Welcome to Third Section," Karn said, looking over at the three of them.

Pleased, relieved, and thoroughly worn out, Tovak laid back on the ground and stared up at the blue sky. Small puffy white clouds floated high above. It was beautiful.

"Thank you for the blessing of life, Thulla," Tovak said to himself. He would add a prayer knot of thanks to his beard later. He reached up and drew his Age of Iron ring out from where he wore it about his neck. With a tug, he ripped it free and held the simple band made of rough iron between two fingers. He had been embarrassed of its poor quality. No more. He was done hiding things about himself. He was who he was and that was the end of it. He slipped the ring on his right pinky finger.

"It turned out to be one fine day," Dagmar said to Tovak, "didn't it?"

"A very fine day," Tovak agreed.

EPILOGUE

General Kenteg gazed down upon the orc messenger, who knelt before him, head pressed to the carpet that covered the grass. The messenger was a young bull, clearly just past the rut. He was dirty from his travels and filled Kenteg's personal tent with the stale smell of sweat and fear. He was trembling slightly. Kenteg knew the messenger had traveled far and, from the date of the dispatch, had made good time too. Kenteg's gaze moved to the dispatch in his hand and then back to the messenger.

"You know the contents?" Kenteg asked, doing his best to control his anger. He handed the message over to his aide, Barick, who immediately began reading. Barick furrowed his heavy brow in clear disbelief before baring his tusks in a grimace of irritation. Kenteg felt like doing the same, but restrained himself.

"I do, General." The messenger straightened. He sounded weary, near exhaustion. "I was there when it all happened, sir. It was I who discovered Captain Jarenth's body."

"How many survived the battle that followed?" Kenteg asked.

"Barely sixty, General," the messenger said, anger and disdain creeping into his tone. "Lieutenant Mesog ordered us forward. It was a mistake to attack the dwarves. We were outnumbered. They were heavy infantry and chewed us up something quick. There was only one outcome from the moment they emerged from the forest: our defeat."

Kenteg flexed a fist in frustration. Mesog had been a fool to attack such strength. Scouts against warriors of the line was an unequal contest. He should have fallen back, but passions amongst his people ran high. Mesog likely feared a losing of face in front of the enemy and so the fool had wasted good warriors and even better scouts.

The messenger was right. It had all been a mistake, one that had serious potential repercussions for Kenteg personally. The thought drove his anger white-hot. That there was a warband out on the plateau, when there shouldn't be, was cause for concern and a serious headache. Worse, if the dwarves discovered what he was after, there would be trouble. With effort, he forced his normal studied control to return. Façade back in place, Kenteg ran a finger down his right tusk as he thought the matter over. The silence in the tent dragged out.

"Lieutenant Mesog died as well?" Kenteg asked, for Mesog had not written the dispatch. Some lowly priest had.

"No, sir," the messenger said. "He was badly injured. The priest feels, given time, he will recover."

"What is your name?" Kenteg asked, deciding that Mesog's life would be numbered in days.

"Legick," the messenger replied.

"Legick," Kenteg said, "you did good bringing me this news."

"Thank you, sir," Legick said. "It was a difficult journey."

"I understand," Kenteg said, softening his tone. "See the camp cooks. Get yourself fed. After you've rested, you will be heading back, along with new orders for your company. You may go."

"Yes, sir." The messenger breathed out a barely audible, yet clearly relieved, breath. He stood and saluted, then turned away. Kenteg stepped forward, drawing his dagger. Coming up behind the messenger, he grabbed Legick firmly around the mouth and plunged the blade into the side of the neck, severing the jugular. It was over almost before it began, as Kenteg flexed his powerful muscles and snapped the neck to ensure the death was quick and clean. Legick, as an honorable warrior, deserved nothing less. He went limp in Kenteg's arms.

Regretting the necessity of the killing, Kenteg gently, almost reverently, lowered the body to the ground. He straightened, gazed down on the body for a moment, then stepped over to his camp table. His breakfast lay untouched, where he'd left it. The porridge had gone cold. He retrieved a small hand towel.

Barick was staring at him. There was no reproach or disapproval in his aide's gaze. He too understood that necessity had required the killing of the messenger. There had been no choice. Legick's fate had been sealed the moment he entered the tent.

Kenteg carefully began wiping his blade clean on the towel, a feeling of intense distaste washing over him. Blood had soaked into his rug, ruining it. He eyed it sourly, knowing it would have to be replaced.

"This is a mess," Barick said, breaking the silence in the tent.

"If you are referring to the rug, I can always get another," Kenteg said. "If by mess you are meaning the matter with Jarenth's company, then yes, it is a problem for us."

"The latter," Barick said. "I don't care about your rugs. Your taste in rugs is terrible."

"You think so?" Kenteg asked, almost amused. Then the anger returned. "Jarenth and that other fool,

Ghitago...between them, they attacked not one, but two dwarven camps within miles of one another. Is it too much to ask that my company commanders follow orders?"

"It is a pity neither survived," Barick said.

"Do you think my orders were clear enough?" Kenteg asked.

"They were very clear, General," Barick said and set the dispatch down on the table. "Shadow the enemy and avoid all contact. I drafted those orders myself." Barick paused, looking upon Legick's body. "Perhaps a few examples need to be made?"

"That would draw too much attention," Kenteg said. "This must be kept quiet."

"At least we know who we face." Barick gestured towards the dispatch.

"The Blood Badgers," Kenteg said, "not my first choice."

"With any luck, the dwarves will think they are facing advance units only and not an entire army."

"We have to assume the opposite," Kenteg said, "but...I pray you are correct."

Barick said nothing to that, which told Kenteg that he too understood the truth in the matter. The dwarves had been put on notice and now knew there was an army operating nearby. They would take steps to protect and guard themselves against attack.

Kenteg returned his gaze to the dead messenger, who had ruined his rug.

"You will take trusted warriors," Kenteg said, after a brief hesitation, "and find the remains of Jarenth's company. None are to live to tell their tale. Krix can never know about this debacle. If he discovers the truth, our heads will end up on a pike...or worse, he will see us stretched over a priest's altar."

"I understand," Barick said quietly. "What of the remains of Ghitago's company?"

"Those goblins are likely still running for the hills," Kenteg said. "We will never see them again. With luck, the wild gnomes that inhabit these mountains will get them. With their continual raids, they've certainly caused us enough of a hassle."

"We are trespassing and the gnomes rightly don't like it," Barick said. "By treaty, this is their land." Barick blew out a breath. "To be certain, I think it would be wise to mount an expedition to hunt down the survivors from Ghitago's company."

Kenteg thought about the suggestion. Knowing the gnomes, it would likely prove to be a costly venture, weakening his strength further. "Do it. Spread the word they are deserters who murdered Ghitago."

"If you throw in a little gold," Barick suggested, "I would think that should provide incentive enough to overlook any potentially embarrassing questions."

"A gold crown for each head, then," Kenteg said. "That should also serve to scare the rest of our goblins in line. I wish I'd never been burdened with them. At least the humans are useful in a battle."

"Agreed," Barick said.

Outside, the sound of beating wings turned both their heads towards the entrance flap of the tent. Kenteg felt a tickle of fear. A wyrm screeched its deafening cry. It was followed by a hard thud as the massive beast landed not too far off. Kenteg knew, without a doubt, who had come to see him.

"General," a guard said, holding the tent flap aside. The guard hesitated a moment as he took in the body on the rug. "Lord Krix has arrived."

"I will be there shortly," Kenteg said. He knew it would take time for Krix to unstrap himself from the saddle and dismount.

"Yes, sir," the guard said and allowed the tent flap to fall back in place.

"You will leave immediately," Kenteg said to Barick as he placed the now-clean dagger on the table. He took up the dispatch and crumpled it up before tossing it into a small brazier in the corner. The message flared into brilliant flame then rapidly darkened as the parchment curled in upon itself. "Do not come back until the job is done."

"Yes, General," Barick said, "as you command."

Kenteg gave a nod, tightened the belt on his tunic, then strode for the tent entrance and stepped outside. Though the sky had begun to lighten, the first of the two suns had yet to rise. The air was cool, almost crisp.

His army encampment spread out in all directions, thousands upon thousands of tents. Fires, almost too numerous to count, pushed back against the early morning gloom. Soon those tents would come down and the fires would be extinguished as the army prepared to march.

With the arrival of the wyrm, the usual cacophony of the early morning camp had gone silent. The massive beast was jet-black, and fearsome-looking. Its head, scarred from battle, swung around to face him. The jaws parted and a tongue of flame licked outward. A massive claw dug into the ground. The dragon should have sent a ripple of fear and apprehension through him, but it did not. What did was the man climbing off the dragon's back and down from the saddle.

He was Krix, Lord Commander of the Horde. It galled Kenteg that he had to bend his knee to this human, and yet at the same time, he feared what would happen if he didn't. Krix was favored by the gods of the alignment and their chosen commander. The council had placed their faith in him and Krix had delivered. Under his command, the Horde had conquered nearly two thirds of this world and soon would take the rest.

Krix was tall for a human. He wore no armor, nor did he carry a weapon. All he had on was a plain black tunic with a thick gray belt, a black traveling cloak, and muddy boots. His face was as hard as ice and his gaze had been known to make others tremble in fear. Kenteg had always sensed a clear menace about the human that spoke of great danger best not stirred.

Kenteg had never witnessed Krix use the powers the gods had gifted him. He hoped it remained that way. The Lord Commander was a monster in disguise and one of the few humans to be truly and utterly feared.

Krix jumped the last few feet to the ground. He stretched out his back before spotting Kenteg. He started over, slowly pulling off his black leather gloves, one finger at a time. He tucked them into his belt. Behind him, the dragon gave a screeching roar before settling down upon the ground and curling up as if to go to sleep.

"General Kenteg," Krix said, speaking fluent orcish. He rubbed both hands together for warmth. "It is good to see you."

No warmth reached the Lord Commander's tone.

"You as well, my lord," Kenteg said as he knelt and bent his head. Though in truth, he wished Krix would stay away and leave him to do his job. These visits of the Lord Commander had, of late, become more frequent. He was very much aware they could one day prove unhealthy for him, should he catch the Lord Commander in the wrong mood. Weakness, or even the perception of it, was something Krix did not tolerate.

"Rise," Krix said in a weary tone. "It has been a long flight and I have more traveling that needs to be done before the day is out. I would dispense with our business as rapidly as possible."

Kenteg stood. "How can I help you, my lord?"

"I have come," Krix said, "for a personal report on your progress."

"I see, my lord," Kenteg said, having expected nothing different.

Krix's gaze traveled over his shoulder. Kenteg turned to look. His guards were removing the body of the messenger, dragging him upon the ground by the legs and away from his tent.

"Having problems?" Krix asked, raising an eyebrow.

"I needed to administer some discipline," Kenteg said. "I decided a personal touch was required."

"And that, my general, is why I have placed my faith in you. You are not afraid to get your hands dirty."

"As always, my lord, I am honored by your trust," Kenteg said, then decided to return to the matter at hand. He wanted Krix on his way as rapidly as possible. "We are close to locating Grata'Dagoth. I assure you, my lord, it is only a matter of time until the fortress, or what is left of it, is found ... days at best."

Krix did not reply. His gaze returned to the messenger being dragged away. The Lord Commander's eyes narrowed.

Did he know? How could he?

"In the searching of the ruins of this land, we uncovered a prophecy," Kenteg said, more to distract Krix than anything else. "I was about to send a dispatch on its find."

"A prophecy?" Krix turned back to face him with an intense look. "What prophecy?"

"A dwarven prophecy," Kenteg said, abruptly on guard, for Krix's dark-eyed gaze was focused squarely upon him, as if Kenteg were suddenly the most important person in the world. "It was etched into the stone walls of a tomb. My scribes copied it down. The wording is cryptic, written in ancient dwarven, but we have much of it already transcribed. The wizard is helping, which has sped things along."

"And?" Krix asked impatiently.

"The prophecy speaks of a gathering of dwarven nations," Kenteg said, nervously, "and the rise of new or, really, old powers upon this world. It gets a little confusing at that point, my lord."

"Does it now?" Krix stroked his shaven chin for several heartbeats. "If it is genuine prophecy, you have once again reinforced my faith in you, General."

"I believe it to be genuine," Kenteg said. "So too does the wizard."

"Well then," Krix said, "I would very much like to see this prophecy."

"It is in my headquarters tent," Kenteg said and gestured towards the next tent over. The sides had been rolled up and numerous clerks could be seen working underneath lamp-light. A wizard of the black was in there too, somewhere. Kenteg disliked the wizard, who cared not for authority or the chain of command. The wizard went where he wanted and did what he desired, no matter the consequences. He had caused more than a little difficulty for Kenteg.

"Let's go see this prophecy you've found," Krix said, "for I have seen one similar to what you have described."

"Yes, my lord," Kenteg said, but he was only speaking to the Lord Commander's back, for Krix had already started for the tent at a brisk pace. Kenteg hurried to catch up.

The End

Enjoy this short preview of Marc's First book:

STIGER'S TIGERS

Chronicles of an Imperial Legionary Officer

ONE

Two road-weary riders, both legionary officers, crested the bald hill and pulled to a halt. A vast military encampment surrounded by entrenchments and fortifications took up much of the valley below them in a shocking display. Smoke from thousands of campfires drifted upward and hung over the valley like a veil. After months of travel, the two riders were now finally able to set their eyes upon their destination—the main encampment of General Kromen's Imperial Army, comprising the Fifteenth, Eighteenth, Twenty-Ninth, and Thirtieth Legions. These four legions had been dispatched by the emperor to put down the rebellion burning through what the empire considered her southern provinces.

The awful stench of the encampment had been on the wind for hours. This close, the smell of decay mixed with human waste and a thousand other smells was nearly overpowering. What should have been relief at finally reaching their destination had turned to incredulous horror. Neither of them had ever seen anything like it. Imperial encampments were typically highly organized, with priority placed on sanitation to reduce the chance of sickness and disease. The jumble of tents and ramshackle buildings laid out before them, surrounded by the fortifications, spoke of something much different. It told of an almost wanton criminal neglect for the men who served the empire, or perhaps even incompetence in command.

An empty wagon, the first of a sad-looking supply train, rumbled around past the two riders, who refused to give way. The driver, a hired teamster, cursed at them for hogging the road. He took his frustration out on a group of dirty and ragged slaves sitting along the edge of the road. The slaves, part of a work gang to maintain the imperial highway, were forced to scramble out of the way, lest the wagon roll over them as it rumbled around the two travelers.

An overseer resting on a large fieldstone several feet away barked out a harsh laugh before shouting at the slaves to be more careful. One of the slaves collapsed, and yet both riders hardly spared him a glance. Slaves were simply beneath notice.

The supply train's nominal escort, a small troop of cavalry riding in a line alongside the wagons, was working its way slowly up the hill toward the two officers and away from the encampment. Much like every other legionary the two travelers had come upon for the last hundred miles, the cavalry troop was less than impressive, though somewhat better looking in appearance. Their armor wasn't as rusted and had been recently maintained.

Several empty wagons rumbled by the two, which saw additional invectives hurled their way. They ignored the cursing, just as they had disregarded the wagons and the plight of the slaves. Where they had come from, it would have been unthinkable for someone to hurl invectives at an officer, who was almost assuredly a nobleman. At the very least, a commoner would invite a severe beating with such behavior. Here in the South, such lack of basic respect seemed commonplace.

One of the travelers had the hood of his red imperial cloak pulled up as far as it would go and tilted his head forward to protect against a light drizzling rain, which had been falling for some time.

The other had the hood of his cloak pulled back, revealing close-cropped brown hair and a fair but weather-hardened face, marred only by a slight scar running down the left cheek. The scar pulled the man's mouth up into a slight sneer. He looked no older than twenty-five, but his eyes, which seemed to miss nothing, made him look wise beyond his years. The slaves, having settled down in a new spot, watched the two warily.

As the first of the cavalry troop crested the hill, which was much steeper on the encampment's side, the lieutenant in command pulled his mount up.

"Well met, Captain," the lieutenant said. The lieutenant's lead sergeant also stopped his horse.

The cavalry troop continued to ride by, the men wearing their helmets to avoid the drizzling rain but miserably wet just the same. The lieutenant offered a salute, to which the captain simply nodded in reply, saying nothing. The captain's gaze—along with that of his companion, whose face was concealed by the hood of his cloak—remained focused on the encampment below.

After several uncomfortable moments, the lieutenant once again attempted to strike up a conversation. "I assume you came by way of Aeda? A miserable city, if you ask me. Can you tell me the condition of the road? Did you encounter any rebels?"

The lieutenant shivered slightly as the captain turned a cold gray-eyed gaze upon him.

"We saw no evidence of rebels," the captain replied in a low, gravelly voice filled with steel and confidence. "The road passed peacefully."

"That is good to hear," the cavalry officer replied. "I am Lieutenant Lan of the One Hundred Eighty-Seventh Imperial Horse Regiment. May…may I have your name, Captain?"

"Stiger," the captain growled, kicking his horse into motion and rapidly moving off the crest of the hill, down toward the encampment.

The lieutenant's eyes widened. Stiger's companion, without a word or a sideways glance, followed at a touch to his horse, leaving the lieutenant behind.

The door to the guardhouse opened and after a moment banged closed like it had undoubtedly done countless times before. Stiger and his companion stepped forward, their heavy bootfalls thunking across the coarse wooden floorboards that were covered in a layer of dirt made slick from the rain. The floor had not been swept in a good long time.

"Name and purpose?" a bored ensign demanded, his back to the door. A counter separated the ensign from any newcomers. He was sitting at a table, attempting to look busy and important by writing in a logbook. After a few moments, when the ensign heard nothing in reply, he stood and turned with obvious irritation, prepared to give the new arrivals a piece of his mind. He was confronted with two wet officers, one a captain and the other a lieutenant.

Stiger locked the ensign with a piercing gaze. The ensign was old for his rank, which was generally a sign that he was unfit for further promotion. Instead of forcing such a useless man out of service, he was put in a position where he could do little harm and perhaps accomplish something useful. It had been Stiger's experience that such men became bitter and would not hesitate to abuse what little power was available to them.

Flustered, the ensign tried again. "Name and purp—"

"Captain Stiger and companion," Stiger interrupted, with something akin to an irritated growl. The captain slowly placed his hands on the dirty counter and leaned forward toward the man. The ensign—most likely accustomed to dealing with lowly teamsters, drovers, corporals, and sergeants—blinked. His jaw dropped. He stood there for a moment, dumbfounded, before remembering to salute a superior officer, fist to chest. Stiger said nothing in reply, but gestured impatiently for the ensign to move things along.

"Forgive me, sir," the ensign stammered. It was then, as the lieutenant who accompanied the captain pushed back the hood of his cloak, that he noticed Captain Stiger's companion was not human. The ensign's mouth dropped open even further, if that was possible.

"Lieutenant Eli'Far," the elf introduced himself in a pleasantly soft, singsong kind of voice that sounded human, but was tinged with something alien at the same time. Eli was tall, whipcord thin, and very fair. His perpetually youthful face, complete with blue almond-shaped eyes and sharply pointed ears, was perfect. Framed by sand-colored hair, perhaps it was even *too* perfect.

"I have orders to report to General Kromen," Stiger stated simply, impatient to be done with the fool before him.

"Of course, sir," the ensign stammered, remembering himself. He slid a book across the counter. "If you will sign in, I will have you escorted directly to General Kromen's headquarters."

Stiger grabbed a quill, dipped it in the inkbottle sitting on the counter, and signed for both himself and Eli. He put down the quill and pushed the book back toward the ensign.

"Corporal!" the ensign called in a near-panicked shout.

The guard corporal poked his head into the guardhouse.

"Captain Stiger requires an escort to the commanding general's headquarters."

The corporal blinked as if he had not heard correctly. "Yes, sir," he said, fully stepping into the guardhouse, eyes wide. "This way, gentlemen," the corporal said in a respectful tone. It was never wise to upset an officer, and even more irresponsible to offend one from an important family, no matter how infamous. "I will escort you myself. It is a bit of a ride, sirs."

The two traveling companions followed the corporal out of the guardhouse. They stepped back into the rain, which had changed from a drizzle to a steady downpour. Eli pulled his hood back up, once again obscuring his features. Stiger left his down. They retrieved their horses from where they had secured them and mounted up. The corporal also mounted a horse that was waiting for such a purpose and led them through the massive wooden gate that served as the encampment's main entrance. Stiger was disgusted to see the sentries huddled for cover under the gate's overhang. Those men should have been on post despite the weather.

Stiger had thought it impossible for the stench of the encampment to get any worse, yet it became much more awful and unpleasant once they were clear of the gate. It made his eyes burn. He had only ever once encountered a worse smell. That had been years before on a distant battlefield, with the dead numbering in the many thousands under a brutally hot sun, rotting quicker than they could be buried or burned.

Massive numbers of tents and temporary ramshackle wooden buildings spread out before them, amongst a sea of mud flowing with animal and human excrement. The three worked their way slowly through the muddy streets with rows of tents on each side. They came upon a small stream, muddy brown and swollen from the day's rain, running through the center of the encampment. The stream was threatening to flood nearby tents.

A rickety wooden bridge, which looked as though it had been hastily constructed to ford the small stream, appeared at risk of being washed away by the growing rush of water. Unconcerned, the corporal guided them over the bridge and to a large rough-looking building directly in the center of the encampment. An overhang and porch had been constructed onto the building, almost as an afterthought, but probably in response to the rain and mud.

Several staff officers on the porch loitered about in chairs, idly chatting and smoking pipes or playing cards, as the three horsemen approached. It was clear this was the main headquarters. A rough planked boardwalk that looked like it might sink into the mud at any moment connected the building to a row of larger tents and other nearby buildings. The porch and boardwalk served the purpose of saving the officers from having to get their perfectly polished boots muddy.

A dirty and ragged slave, ankles disappearing in the muck, stepped forward to take the reins of their horses as the two officers dismounted. Stiger tried to avoid thinking about what was in the mud as his boots sank into it.

"Good day, sirs." The corporal saluted and swung his horse around, riding away before anything more could be required of him. Stiger understood that the man was relieved to be on his way. It was said that bad things tended to happen around Stigers.

"This camp is an embarrassment," Eli said quietly to Stiger. "It is very unfit."

"I hazard half the camp is down sick," Stiger responded in sour agreement. He had never seen a legionary encampment in such a state. "Let us hope we are not detained here for months on end."

The two walked through the mud and up the steps to the front porch of the headquarters building, where they hastily kicked and scraped the muck from their boots. The headquarters building was not at all what one would expect for the commanding general of the South. The finely attired officers on the porch purposefully ignored the new arrivals. Stiger hesitated a moment and then stepped toward the building's entrance, reaching for the door.

"Where exactly do you think you're going?" a young staff captain sitting in a chair demanded disdainfully without looking up from his card game. The man was casually smoking and took a rather slow pull from his pipe, as if to show he was in charge.

Stiger turned to look at the staff captain, who wore expensively crafted legionary officer armor over a well-cut tunic and rich black boots. The armor was highly polished and the fine red cloak appeared to be freshly cleaned and brushed. There was not a hint of mud or dirt anywhere on the officer. He almost looked like the perfect toy soldier. Stiger took him to be of the soft type, a spoiled and pampered nobleman, likely from a minor yet wealthy house. At least wealthy or influential enough to secure his current position. Much like the ensign in the guardhouse, Stiger had also unfortunately encountered this kind of officer before—a bootlicking fool. Stiger's lip curled ever so slightly in derision. The bootlicker, more concerned with his fawning entourage of fellow officers, did not seem to notice. Eli, however, did. He placed a cautioning hand on Stiger's arm, which had come to rest upon the pommel of his sword.

"I am ordered to report to General Kromen and that is what I intend to do," Stiger responded neutrally, casually pulling his arm away from Eli's restraining hand. The elf sighed softly. "Unless, of course, the general is not present. In that event I shall simply wait for his return."

"Oh, I believe the general is in," the captain said with a sneer. "However, you do not get to see him without my personal permission."

Several of the other officers snickered.

"Perhaps you should say... please?" one of the other officers suggested with a high-pitched voice. The others openly laughed at this.

Stiger's anger flared, though he kept the irritation from his face. The captain was likely an aide to the general, a player of camp politics, working to control access and thereby strengthening his powerbase. He was the kind of man who was rarely challenged openly. He was also someone who would most definitely hold a grudge if he was ever slighted or offended. In short, he was another arrogant fool, and Stiger loathed such men.

Suffer the fool's game or not? Stiger was new to the camp and the last thing he wanted was to get off on the wrong foot. Still, the captain's manner irritated him deeply. The man should have behaved as a gentleman, and yet he had blatantly offended Stiger. Should he continue, Stiger would be justified in issuing a challenge to satisfy honor. Somehow, Stiger doubted General Kromen would approve of him killing, or at best maiming, one of his staff officers on his first day in camp.

"Stop me," Stiger growled. He opened the door and stepped through. The staff captain scrambled out of his chair and gave chase, protesting loudly.

Inside, Stiger was greeted by a nearly bare room. The interior was intentionally darkened, the windows shuttered. Several lanterns provided moderately adequate lighting. A fireplace, set along the back wall, crackled. The chimney, poorly constructed, leaked too much smoke into the building. A table with a large map spread out on it dominated the center of the room. Three men stood around the table, while another, a grossly obese man, sat in a chair with his elbows resting heavily on the tabletop. He had the look of someone who was seriously ill. His face was pale and covered in a sheet of fever sweat. They all looked up at the sudden intrusion, clearly irritated. Two were generals, including the one who was seated, and the two others held the rank of colonel.

"What is the meaning of this intrusion?" the general who was standing demanded. He had a tough, no-nonsense look about him.

"I am sorry, sir," the bootlicking staff captain apologized, pushing roughly past Stiger and Eli. "I tried to stop them."

"Well?" the general demanded again of Stiger.

Unfazed by the rank of the men in the room, Stiger pulled his orders from a side pocket in his cloak and stepped forward. "I am ordered to report to General Kromen for duty."

"I am General Kromen," the large, seated man wheezed before being consumed by a wracking cough. After a few moments he recovered. "Who in the seven levels might you be?"

"Captain Stiger reporting for duty, sir." Stiger assumed a position of attention and saluted.

"A Stiger?" the staff captain whispered, taking a step back in shock.

The other general barked out a sudden laugh, while General Kromen went into another coughing fit that wracked his fat body terribly.

"Captain Handi," General Kromen wheezed upon recovering, waving a hand dismissively. His other hand held a handkerchief to his mouth. "It would seem," he coughed, "we have important matters to discuss. You may go."

The captain hesitated a moment, looking between the standing no-nonsense general and the seated one before saluting smartly. He left the room without saying another word, though he managed to shoot a hate-filled look at Stiger as he passed.

"A Stiger!" Kromen exclaimed in irritation once the door was closed. "Who is your companion?"

Eli reached up and pulled back his hood, showing his face for the first time.

"Hah!" Kromen huffed tiredly. "An elf. I swear, I never thought I'd see one of your kind again, at least in this life."

"Sadly, we are few in these lands, General," Eli responded neutrally, with a slight bow.

"An elf, as well as imperial officer? I thought you fellows had given up on the empire," the other general stated.

"The emperor granted a special dispensation to serve the one known here as Ben Stiger," Eli answered, nodding in the direction of the captain. The nod had an odd tilt to it that reminded everyone present he was not quite human. Human necks just did not bend like that. "The rank conferred was to help me better serve."

"You serve a human?" the standing general asked with some surprise before turning back to Stiger. "What did you do to earn that dubious honor, Stiger?"

"I, ah…" Stiger began after a slight hesitation, "would prefer not to discuss it, sir."

"The emperor," Kromen breathed with a heavy sigh, steering the conversation away from a direction that Stiger was clearly uncomfortable speaking on. "The emperor and the gods have forsaken us in this wicked and vile land."

Kromen was an old and wily politician. Stiger suspected that the general would not press him, but would instead write back to his family in the capital to get an answer. Information was often more important than the might of an entire legion. More importantly, Stiger knew that Kromen wanted to know why a Stiger, a member of one of the most powerful families in the empire, was here in the South, and that required moving the conversation along.

"Perhaps not…You asked for combat-experienced officers and men of quality. Well…here stands a Stiger," the other general said after a moment's reflection, taking General Kromen's subtle nudge to change the subject. Stepping over, he took Stiger's orders. "Were you in the North?"

"Emperor's Third Legion," Stiger replied.

"The Third gets all of the shit assignments." The general handed the orders over to General Kromen, who opened them and began reviewing the contents. Silence filled the room, and all that could be heard was the pop of the logs in the fireplace and the rustle of parchment as General Kromen read.

"An introduction letter from my good friend General Treim," Kromen breathed hoarsely as he read.

Stiger was familiar with the contents of the letter. According to the letter, the emperor had directed Treim to send a few of his best and most promising officers to the South. Stiger could imagine Kromen's thoughts as the general looked up briefly with a skeptical look. The general was finding it hard to imagine that Treim would release one of his truly outstanding officers. The politician in Kromen would scream that there was more here than met the eye. Perhaps even the general might consider this whelp of a Stiger was actually a spy for his enemies in the senate looking to gain some advantage. Though the Kromen and Stiger families were not actually enemies, they were not allies either.

"Interesting," Kromen said after a few silent minutes, and then turned to the other general. "General Mammot, it seems that our good friend General Treim has dispatched this officer at *our* request. The letter indicates more such officers of quality are on the way. Interesting, don't you think?"

"Very," General Mammot replied dryly. "How long did it take you to travel down here, Stiger?"

"Three and a half months, sir."

General Kromen was consumed by another fit of coughing. He held a handkerchief to his mouth, hacking into it.

"Impressive time," General Mammot admitted with a raised eyebrow and turned to Kromen. "Do you think he can fight?"

"General Treim," cough, "seems to think so." Kromen handed over the letter of introduction, which General Mammot began reading. After a moment, he stopped and looked up, a strange expression crossing his face.

"You volunteered and led not one, but two forlorn hopes?" Mammot asked in an incredulous tone. "Do you have a death wish, son?"

Stiger elected not to respond and remained silent. Mammot continued to read.

"Seems General Treim sent us a fighter, and the elf comes as a bonus." Kromen took a deep and labored breath, having somewhat recovered from his latest coughing fit. He seemed to make a decision. He looked over meaningfully at General Mammot, who paused in his reading and caught his look. "We were discussing a pressing issue …"

"We were," Mammot agreed.

"Well then … since we are now saddled with a … Stiger, perhaps he might prove of some assistance in resolving this irritating matter with Vrell? Don't you agree?"

General Mammot frowned slightly and considered Stiger for a moment before nodding in agreement. He waved both Stiger and Eli over to the table with the map.

"Stiger," Mammot said, "allow me to introduce Colonels Karol and Edin. They are brigade commanders from the Twenty-Ninth."

"Pleased to meet you, Stiger," Colonel Karol said, warmly offering his hand. "I fought with your father when I was a junior officer. How is the old boy?"

"Well, sir," Stiger replied. His father was a touchy subject with most other officers. He found it was best to be vague in his answers to their questions. "His forced retirement wears on him."

"I can understand that," Colonel Karol said. "Perhaps one day he may be permitted to once again take the field."

"I am not sure he ever will," Stiger replied carefully. Many would feel threatened by such sentiments.

Colonel Edin simply shook hands and refrained from saying anything. Stiger could read the disapproval in the man's eyes. It was something the captain had grown accustomed to from his fellow officers.

"Now that we are all acquainted," General Mammot began, directing everyone's attention to the map on the table, "we have an outpost four weeks' march from here, located at Vrell, an isolated valley to the east with a substantial population." Mammot traced a line along a road from the encampment to the outpost for Stiger to follow. "Specifically, the outpost garrisons one of the few castles in the South. We call it Castle Vrell. The locals call it something different."

"We have not heard from them for several weeks," Kromen rasped. "We have dispatched messengers, but none have returned. It is all very irritating."

"The castle is a highly fortified position," Mammot continued. "There are over nine hundred legionaries defending it and the valley. Vrell is an out-of-the-way place, surrounded by mountains and a nearly impenetrable forest. We think the castle unlikely to have fallen to enemy forces." With his hand, Mammot traced a new line on the map, well south of Vrell. "The rebels control everything south of this line here… There are no roads traveling to rebel territory from Vrell. Beyond the mountains, it is all thick forest for about one hundred miles to rebel territory. The only road to Vrell moves from the encampment here, eastward, through the Sentinel Forest and terminates at the valley. It is our opinion the enemy has simply cut our communications with a handful of irregulars."

"The garrison commandant, Captain Aveeno, has been complaining for months of rebels harassing his patrols and stirring up trouble," Colonel Karol spoke up. "Then suddenly, nothing… no word."

"The garrison is due for resupply," Kromen added, taking another labored breath. "Normally we would send a simple cavalry escort. However, with the road apparently infested with rebel irregulars, a foot company appears to be the more sensible approach."

"The Third has been heavily involved up north in the forests of Abath," General Mammot said. "We would appreciate your expertise on the matter."

"Sounds like a difficult assignment," Stiger said, noncommittally. "How are the rebels equipped in this area?"

"Poorly." Colonel Edin spoke for the first time. "This terrain presents a very difficult obstacle for the rebels to overcome. We have only ever encountered light units, mostly conscripted farmers... the equivalent of bandits."

"What is the condition of the road?" Stiger leaned forward to study the map more closely. Eli stepped closer as well. The map was a simple camp scribe copy.

"Poor, but passable for wagons," Karol admitted. "Imperial maintenance crews repaired it just three years ago, so there should be no significant problems for the supply train."

"I don't see any towns and villages." Stiger found that odd for such a long road.

"There are—or were—a handful of what you might call farming communities," Edin admitted. "Really the remnants. I personally would be surprised if you discovered anyone left."

"Reprisals?" Stiger asked, looking up at Edin. He already knew the answer.

"That was my predecessor's work," General Kromen answered carefully. "A nasty business, though he did a good job in clearing the bastards out. There should be no one left to support the rebels, at least we think, until you get to Vrell. The valley's population is not with the rebels. For some strange reason, they seem to think of themselves as imperials, or at least descended from imperial stock. That said, they are not exactly friendly, at least according to Captain Aveeno's last reports."

"Captain Aveeno could have sent a force to break through, could he not?" Stiger asked.

"Not very likely," Mammot answered with a heavy breath. "Captain Aveeno, the garrison commandant, is a bit cautious. He likely would have put everyone on short rations and kept them in defense of the castle and valley, rather than take the risk of losing additional men."

"Aveeno comes from a good family," General Kromen wheezed, speaking up in defense of the man. "However, he is a timid sort, which is why he is commanding a garrison instead of leading a line company."

Stiger nodded, understanding what had not been said. General Kromen was likely Aveeno's patron, hence his defense. "A good company should be able to get through, then," Stiger said, looking down at the map once again. "Should the rebel forces operating in the area prove superior, a company will likely be able to get word out or at least fight its way back."

"Excellent," Kromen said, looking from Eli to Stiger. "How would you like the job? I have an absolutely terrible company that just became available. With your experience, you are perfect for working it into shape!"

Stiger was surprised he was being given a mission that would take him away so soon after arriving. Though marching with unfamiliar men into territory overrun by rebels was not a terribly appealing idea to the captain, his initial impressions of the legionary encampment led him to believe that such a march would be preferable to risking an untimely death by lingering sickness. He knew that the command he was being offered was most probably, as the general said, a truly terrible assignment. If the men had been idle for months, as he suspected they had, they would be sick, poorly equipped, and out of shape, and discipline would be lacking. So it all came down to risking potential death from slow, lingering sickness and disease or possible death by sword... Stiger intentionally drew out the silence, as if he were mulling it over. Surely there were other, more effective companies that could be more readily chosen. The two generals, he knew, were also making light of the assignment so that it seemed too easy... too good. That bothered Stiger, and he wanted to know why, but could not come right out and ask.

"I would need to outfit the company for a hard march into the wilderness," Stiger said.

"You can draw anything you might require from supply," Kromen responded, almost a little too quickly, which surprised Stiger.

What wasn't he being told?

Stiger had known that his arrival might be a headache for General Kromen. Stiger's family had influence. His presence here might be viewed as the attempt to place a spy within the Southern legions, a spy who was possibly reporting directly to the emperor or Kromen's enemies in the senate.

"We need to open communications with Vrell," Mammot added. "We can issue your company fresh arms and equipment. I will also assign some of our most experienced sergeants to help you work them into fighting trim."

"Could I meet and approve the sergeants first?" Stiger asked. He had known some pretty terrible sergeants, from ass-kissers to sadistic bastards. Instead of being dismissed from the service, such men were frequently transferred from one unit to another.

"Of course," Kromen said.

"How long until the supply train is ready?" Stiger asked, thinking about the training of his men. He needed time to become acquainted with them and to work them into shape. All legionaries received the same basic training. It was a matter of restoring discipline and finding out how rusty they had become.

"Two weeks," Mammot said. "At least, we hope the train will arrive within two weeks, but certainly no more than four. It is due to leave from Aeda any day."

"Good, that would give me some time," Stiger said. He looked at General Kromen, thinking hard. "I would want to train the men my way, with no outside interference."

"Acceptable," General Kromen said with a deep frown. No general enjoyed being dictated to, especially by a young, impudent captain, even if he was a Stiger. Still...Kromen seemed to put up with it, and Stiger decided to push for more.

"That would involve training outside the encampment and living beyond the walls," Stiger added. "I would need space to prepare the men...construction of a marching camp, route marches, arms training..."

"If you are willing to brave a rebel attack outside the protection of the walls, you can do whatever you flaming wish," Kromen said, his dangerous tone betraying a mounting anger. "Anything else you require, captain?"

"No, sir," Stiger said, pleased at having escaped the confines of the encampment so easily. In all likelihood, whatever he had been set up for would prove to be a real challenge. "I will take the job."

"Very good." General Kromen flashed an insincere smile. "Colonel Karol will arrange to have you introduced to your men. He will also see to outfitting your needs." Kromen waved dismissively, indicating the audience was over.

Stiger saluted along with Colonel Karol. They turned and left, emerging onto the porch with Eli in tow. Stiger found Captain Handi resting in the same chair. The captain shot Stiger a look that spoke volumes. Doubtless Handi would be looking for ways to get his petty revenge. Stiger simply ignored him.

"You have a tough job ahead of you," Karol admitted. "The men I am giving you are in truly terrible shape and have been poorly led. Their previous commander was executed for gross incompetence. His real crime, however, was excessive graft and insufficient… shall we say, *sharing*."

"I have always enjoyed a challenge," Stiger replied softly.

"Let us both hope this particular challenge does not kill you," Karol responded. The colonel glanced to the side at the lounging officers toward Handi, who was aiming a smoldering glare at Stiger. "Captain Handi, be so good as to personally fetch Sergeants Blake and Ranl. They should be working over at my headquarters."

"But, sir, it's raining," Handi protested, gesturing at the steady rainfall beyond the cover of the porch.

"I rather imagine that the emperor expects his legions to operate in all types of weather," the colonel responded rather blandly. "Have them report on the double to the officers' mess."

Colonel Karol turned away and stepped out into the rain. He led them along the improvised boardwalk system toward another smaller ramshackle wooden building with a chimney billowing with soft blue-gray smoke.

"Wouldn't want that spoiled bastard to get his fine boots muddy now, would we?" Karol asked once they were out of earshot. Stiger found himself beginning to like the colonel.

A NOTE FROM THE MARC

I want to thank you for reading *Reclaiming Honor*. I sincerely hope you enjoyed it. Tovak and Gorabor's journey will continue in 2020! Writing a book like this takes a tremendous amount of time, effort, and energy. A review would be awesome and greatly appreciated.

Important: If you have not yet given my other series—Tales of the Seventh or Chronicles of an Imperial Legionary officer, or The Karus Saga a shot, I strongly recommend you do. All three series are linked and set in the same universe. There are hints, clues, and Easter eggs sprinkled throughout the series.

The Series:

There are three series to consider. I began telling Stiger and Eli's story in the middle years...starting with Stiger's Tigers, published in 2015. *Stiger's Tigers* is a great place to start reading. It was the first work I published and is a grand fantasy epic.

Stiger, Tales of the Seventh, covers Stiger's early years. It begins with Stiger's first military appointment as a wet-behind-the-ears lieutenant serving in Seventh Company during the very beginning of the war against the Rivan on the frontier. This series sees Stiger cut his teeth and develop into the hard charging leader that fans have grown to love. It also introduces Eli and covers many of their early adventures. These tales should in no way spoil your experience with *Stiger's Tigers*. In fact, I believe they will only enhance it.

The Karus Saga is an adventure set in the same universe … and on the same planet as Reclaiming Honor. This series tells how Roman legionaries made their way to the world of Istros and founded Stiger's empire. It is set amidst a war of the gods and is full of action, intrigue, adventure, and mystery.

Give them a shot and hit me up on Facebook to let me know what you think!

Best regards and again thank you for reading!

Marc

Care to be notified when the next book is released and receive updates from the author?

Join the newsletter mailing list at Marc's website:

http://www.MAEnovels.com
(Check out the forum)
Facebook: Marc Edelheit Author
Twitter: @MarcEdelheit

You can also see what's up with Quincy at:
http://www.quincyallen.com
or register for his newsletter at:
http://www.quincyallen.com/join-up/